BETRAYAL
AT THE
BORDER

Mark M. Bello

A Zachary Blake Legal Thriller

Published by 8Grand Publications

Printed in the United States of America

ISBN: 978-1956595031

"Give me your tired, your poor,
Your huddled masses yearning to breathe free,
The wretched refuse of your teeming shore.
Send these, the homeless, tempest-tossed to me,
I lift my lamp beside the golden door!"

Emma Lazurus

Chapter One

"Freeze!" Emilio Gonzalez shouted with glee. He and his big sister, Emma, were playing outside in the small backyard of their Lincoln Park, Michigan home. The game was a version of tag, a game they played together since Emilio could walk. This version was inspired by *Frozen*, their all-time favorite movie.

Emma was nine; Emilio was seven. While both were quite athletic, Emma was a much faster runner and on the school soccer team. Emilio looked up to her, so these rare moments of triumph were quite satisfying to the little boy.

It was an unusually hot late summer in the Detroit metropolitan area. The kids spent most of the day in the house, watching videos—primarily *Frozen*, which they watched repeatedly. Since daylight savings time extended summer days, the kids were permitted to go outside after supper. On this particular evening, they played as if they were released from 'time out,' filled with joy and excitement, as well as the pleasure of each other's company.

Emma loved the game and wanted to play it all the time; Emilio was less enthusiastic. After all, *Freeze* not only demonstrated Emma's physical superiority, it also required Emilio to play a girl, whether Elsa who froze her big sister, or Anna who got frozen. Emilio played because he loved playing *any* game with his big sister. As a condition of the game, Emma had to promise not to tell any of their friends—it had to be their secret. If his school friends found out, they would never stop teasing him.

The game was the siblings' favorite movie version of *Tocaito*, an old Venezuelan game their mother taught them. In *Tocaito*, one player touches the other, who immediately becomes a statue. After seeing *Frozen*, Emma and Emilio recognized the movie's parallels to the themes of *Tocaito*. They changed the traditional game to *Freeze* to honor the movie. If, for instance, Emilio touched Emma, instead of becoming a statue, she became frozen. Emma would have to stay that way until Emilio chose to unfreeze her.

This activity resulted in some tense moments between the siblings because Emma was bigger and faster than her younger brother. Consequently, Emilio was frozen almost all the time and would quickly tire of the game. Loving the game and being a good big sister, Emma often let Emilio freeze her, just to watch the joy and excitement the little boy would exhibit every time he caught her. She *loved* her little brother. He was her best friend, and she was fiercely protective of him. However, sometimes she could not help being competitive.

"Freeze!" She tagged him right back and began backpedaling away.

"You can't do that!" Emilio cried. "You were frozen! How can you tag someone when you're frozen?" The boy had a point.

"Because you can. We are playing by Mama's rules, remember?" Emma was conveniently applying the rules of *Tocaito* her mother taught them so many years ago. Or, perhaps, she was making up her own new rules, an annoying habit Emilio began to notice as he got older.

"That's cheating!" Emilio pouted, folding his arms across his chest and furrowing his brow. "That's a different game. That's *Tocaito*!"

"No, it's not. I can freeze you back. We didn't say what the rules were, so I can make them up as we go along," Emma rationalized her behavior, out of breath from backpedaling.

"I quit!" Emilio snarled, tears forming in his eyes. "You're a cheater!" He stomped his feet, turned, and headed toward the house.

"Wait, Emilio, wait! We'll play your way," Emma conceded.

Emilio turned—his angry demeanor instantly joyful.

Emma liked bending the rules. Rules were boring to her. She wanted to play games 'Emma style,' making up rules as she went along. Even when someone else taught Emma a game, she liked challenging and changing rules. She thought games were much more fun played *her* way. Her brother was willing to tolerate this occasionally, but her friends were not, evident by how little they asked her to play.

Emma once held the unofficial monkey bar record at school. One day, she noticed her friend, Amanda, going back and forth on the bars as her friends counted out loud. Amanda was getting close to Emma's record.

Emma ran to the monkey bar on the opposite end of Amanda, jumped up, grabbed hold of the bar with both hands, and headed in Amanda's direction. The two girls met in the middle.

"Get out of the way!" Amanda shouted in a panic. "I was here first!"

"You get out of the way," Emma countered. "I was here second."

Amanda lifted one of her hands off the bar and tried to reach behind Emma to pass her. Emma arched her backside forward, forcing Amanda to lose her grip and fall off the bars.

"That's cheating," Amanda cried. "I was going to beat your record!"

"But you didn't," Emma teased. "If at first you don't succeed . . ."

"I'm telling Miss Brooks," Amanda interrupted. Miss Brooks was the playground supervisor. When Miss Brooks heard and confirmed the story, she took away Emma's record and gave it to Amanda. Emma was not happy.

"She has to beat me! Everyone knows she didn't beat me," Emma argued.

"You have to follow the rules, Emma. And you need to be a good sport. If Amanda can't beat you fair and square, that's one thing, but you can't cheat to prevent her from beating you," Miss Brooks ruled.

"Rules are for losers," Emma insisted. "To beat me, she has to beat me!"

"But you cheated and *prevented* her from beating you. That's not fair. In America, we play by the rules," Miss Brooks explained.

Emma learned a hard lesson that day, but with Emilio, she could digress once in a while. He might get angry with her from time to time, but she would never lose his love.

Maybe there's a reason for rules. Maybe Miss Brooks was right—Emilio may stop playing with her too if the game isn't fair.

The children continued to play until the sun went down. They were red-faced and sweaty when Mama called them into the house. Mama asked who won the game because the winner got the first bath or shower. Contrary to her nature, Emma declared Emilio the winner, a declaration that caused the little boy to shout with glee. He ran off to the bathroom.

The Gonzalez children were both born in Lincoln Park. The city was a part of the Downriver Community, southwest of Detroit. Their little three-bedroom bungalow was the only home they had ever known. In a city of approximately 37,000, only 20% were of Latino descent, nearly a 50% increase since 2010.

Emma and Emilio's parents, Mary Carmen and Miguel Gonzalez, immigrated to Lincoln Park in 2011 when Mary Carmen was pregnant with Emma. Papa found a job, mixing compounds at an adhesive and filler plant in nearby Riverview. Emma was born soon after her parents moved into the house. Two years later, her little brother was born.

When they were old enough to be placed in daycare, Mama secured a job at the same filler plant as her father. The two siblings depended on each other. They were attached at the hip until Emma was old enough to go to Kindergarten. It was a very traumatic time for Emilio. He started behaving as if his sister died.

Emma promised to play with him after school, but Emilio carried on to the point where Emma pushed back and refused to go to school. Promises of candy and ice cream after Mama got home from work finally persuaded both children to go separate ways. As time went on, they adapted to the new routine.

Two years later, Emilio started Kindergarten, and all was forgotten—the siblings were reunited at Raupp Elementary School. Both children spoke fluent Spanish and English and did well in school. The children were now entering fourth and second grade, respectively, and thriving.

The Gonzalez children made friends easily and were well-liked in the school. Emma and Emilio were *Americans*. Although

Mama taught them Venezuelan games and customs and tried to convey a sense of their Latino heritage, the kids had experienced life in no other country but America. They spoke fluent English, celebrated the Fourth of July and Thanksgiving, and proudly recited the Pledge of Allegiance. Emma collected dolls while Emilio collected baseball cards—he *worshipped* Miguel Cabrera of the Detroit Tigers and treasured his 2012 Cabrera Triple Crown card. Emma and Emilio did everything other American children did.

Their parents were determined to raise them in America, with American values and an American education. They dreamt of a better life, with higher education and, perhaps, affluence for their children. But these dreams were clouded by a secret reality—the Gonzalez family, as 'American' as they appeared, protected an important family secret, far more important than the *Frozen* game. This one could derail all of their dreams.

Emma and Emilio were taught to be careful and quiet, even though they didn't understand why this was a big deal. But they knew Mama and Papa feared their secret would one day be discovered. Their parents' fear was so intense; Emma and Emilio were frightened too.

Emma was conflicted. Mama once taught her that telling and keeping secrets was bad. She shouldn't tease her little brother by telling him she knew something he didn't know. She shouldn't keep things from her friends, and, most of all, she shouldn't keep any secrets from Mama and Papa. So, why was this secret okay?

Mama carefully explained the delicate situation to her children: She and Miguel came into the country legally but stayed longer than they were welcome. As a result, Mama and Papa were not citizens and did not have the protection some of their friends' parents had. They could be picked up by the police at any time, put in jail, and even sent back to Venezuela, where conditions were terrible, especially for people who ran away and were later returned by government mandate. It didn't matter if their minor children were citizens. If the family secret were discovered, her mother decried, it could mean *hasta la vista*, forever.

The threat of permanent separation from her parents terrified Emma. A secret preventing her from losing them, perhaps forever, was one worth keeping. Emilio was too young to understand, but Emma made him pinky swear to silence.

After their initial, ominous disclosure, Miguel and Mary Carmen consistently reminded their children of the importance of secrecy. Emma and Emilio were expected to keep it, no ifs, ands, or buts. Miss Brooks taught Emma that breaking the rules was unacceptable and had consequences. Emma was punished for preventing Amanda from breaking her record. But was it okay for Mama and Papa to break the rules? *Of course, it's okay! We want to stay here in America!*

Emma didn't appreciate this at the time, but her family's furtiveness about their immigration status explained her negative feelings about rules. She decided at a very young age that rules were made to be broken. What sense did it make to send people back to a country that didn't want them and would harm them if they returned? *If those are the rules, they need to be changed.*

As Emma got older, she noticed things that provided a better understanding of her parents' fear. After dinner, her parents often watched the evening news. Emma witnessed people protesting at the southern border to Mexico and heard phrases like 'send them back' and 'build the wall.' Video footage of arrests, family separations, and kids in cages was heartbreaking. Emma was a free American like her friends and neighbors, but she would never be free of worry that her parents might be captured. Mainstream media considered families like hers 'undocumented.' Over time, Emma understood the reason why her parents broke the rules and kept the family secret. Because Miguel and Mary Carmen were undocumented, they couldn't travel, not even across the northern border into Canada from Detroit, so they never took vacations. Emma and her family never went *anywhere*.

While Emma understood, she was still slightly conflicted. She learned about crime in school. People who did bad things went to jail. It was 'illegal' to steal, to hurt someone, and to drink and drive. Mama and Papa didn't do any of those things. They obeyed every American rule. They were decent people, good neighbors, and solid citizens. How could they be criminals?

Mama and Papa's citizenship status was not a subject of conversation in the community. Few people knew they were undocumented because while some people embraced immigrants, others tried to make their lives difficult. Landlords were encouraged not to rent to 'foreigners,' and employers were encouraged not to hire them. Some communities attempted to block immigrant access to jobs, housing, education, and healthcare, a coordinated strategy to prevent large numbers from moving into those communities or neighborhoods. Citizens didn't want 'brown people' swooping in and taking their jobs. Other communities embraced immigration and thrived because hard-working immigrants started businesses, worked for other citizens or independently, provided childcare service, housekeeping, or odd repair jobs.

One evening, after dinner, the newsman said President Golding was considering a series of raids on immigrants in targeted areas around the country. One of the areas mentioned was Detroit. Golding said it was time to 'deport the undocumented in fairness to those who enter our country legally and obey our laws.' *Did those people complain or something?* Emma pondered.

"Mama, what does 'deport' mean?" Emma asked inquisitively after the newscast ended.

"It means people who are here without proper papers might get sent back to the country they came from, *hija*," Mary Carmen advised.

"What does ice have to do with it?" Emma glanced at the refrigerator.

"Pardon me?"

"They talked about ice on television."

Mary Carmen looked at the refrigerator and smiled. "They weren't talking about ice from the fridge, *hija*; they were talking about immigration policemen. *ICE* stands for Immigration and Customs Enforcement, I—C—E. Get it?"

"What does this *ICE* do?"

"They find people who are here without proper papers. If people can't prove they are citizens or have a right to be citizens, they get sent back to the country they came from."

"Can that happen to you and Papa? Do you have these proper papers? Are you and Papa criminals, Mama?"

"That's a difficult question to answer. Papa and I came to this country a long time ago. We arrived legally and followed all of the rules, but our papers expired before we could become citizens. We were supposed to go back to Venezuela, but you were just a baby, and it was *dangerous* back home. Here in America, Papa had a good job; we had a nice home, and lots of friends and relatives in the area. We couldn't possibly go back to the old country.

"We decided to stay and try to work out our paper problem later. As the years went by, the government made it more difficult for us to become citizens. We were caught in a trap. We weren't supposed to stay, but we couldn't go back, either."

"What are you going to do? The newsman on television says *ICE* is coming to Detroit."

"I don't know, sweetheart. Papa says everything will be okay. Maybe they won't come to Lincoln Park. Maybe they will only come to Detroit. All we can do is hope and pray."

"From now on, I'll say a special prayer at bedtime, Mama."

"Oh, Emma, thank you! That makes me feel so much better. I'm positive God will listen to *you*. You are my special little girl!"

Emma almost burst with pride. She would pray extra hard tonight. Mama and Papa were counting on her.

***

The Gonzalez family continued to live their lives as if there was no threat to their safety or freedom. What choice did they have? President Golding and *ICE* made good on their threats to communities in Texas, Mississippi, Arizona, California, and Florida, but raids had not yet happened in Detroit. However, everything changed in mid-September, the second week of school.

Reporters interrupted evening programming to announce *ICE* raids on businesses and manufacturing plants in Detroit and surrounding communities. Emma was horrified. She was convinced *ICE* would walk into Mama and Papa's plant or, worse, break into their home and take her parents away, right before her eyes. She implored Mary Carmen and Miguel to stay home from work and hide or get in the car and drive away. She didn't care where they went, provided they went somewhere where *ICE* was not grabbing people off the streets and taking them away.

Miguel tried to soothe his daughter. He told her everything was under control at the plant. The people he worked for would take care of them. They were ready if *ICE* agents came. People called lawyers were waiting by the telephone. They knew immigration law better than anyone and would protect Miguel and Mary Carmen.

"We are good citizens. We work hard, contribute to the economy, and pay our taxes," Miguel explained. Emma understood only the 'work hard' and 'good citizen' parts of his explanation. *He's not a citizen, though*, she reasoned, with maturity beyond her years. *That's the problem!*

Of course, none of Miguel's assurances were true. Miguel and Mary Carmen were undocumented. They had a small savings account and too little money to hire expensive lawyers to fight deportation. If *ICE* raided the plant, there was little the Gonzalez family or any other similarly situated family could do to prevent the consequences. They couldn't run, and they had no place else to go. If they did decide to run, without their jobs, they would soon run out of money. They knew the day would come when their freedom would be threatened, but they hoped it would be later than sooner, perhaps after some type of amnesty program was introduced for people in their situation.

The following day, Miguel and Mary Carmen kissed their children goodbye and put them on the school bus. They pre-arranged with their pastor and members of their church to monitor the situation and make sure the kids were picked up and housed if anything happened at the plant. The church rallied to their side, offering the children room and board, if necessary.

The couple watched and waved as the bus disappeared down the street. Emma and Emilio sat at the back window, waving, watching their parents disappear.

Will we see each other again? Miguel wondered, his eyes tearing as the bus drove away.

"Mis hijos!" Mary Carmen cried, clutching her husband, burying her face in his chest. "What will become of them?"

The couple embraced for a few precious moments. Finally, they separated and walked to the car.

Chapter Two

Canan and Karim Izady were naturalized citizens of the United States. They were from Kurdistan and citizens of Syria. The Izadys fled their home country in 2014 when *ISIS* launched an offensive on the Kurdish city of Kobani. While their parents and religious elders arranged their marriage, Canan and Karim had already been a couple for years and were deeply in love.

Leaving their home was not easy, despite constant conflict and human suffering. Immigrating and obtaining citizenship was a grueling process. Still, the couple was determined to have children in a free country, one without the daily fear of conflict everywhere. Shortly after they left Kurdistan and arrived in Detroit, the President of the United States implemented a travel ban of Muslims from Syria. The couple's relatives were now trapped in Syria.

Canan and Karim were alone in America. They settled in Dearborn, west of Detroit, home to the largest concentration of Muslim American citizens in the United States. The couple persevered, made new friends, and, against all odds, applied for citizenship. Karim was an engineer of some renown—his influence and affluence paid off. The couple was fast-tracked to an EB-1 First Preference Visa, permanent residence status, and, finally, citizenship, thanks to Marshall Mann, immigration lawyer extraordinaire and partner at the prestigious Bloomfield Hills Law Offices of Zachary Blake. Blake's firm was referred by Imam Ghaffari of the Mosque of America.

The couple celebrated their good fortune at a fancy downtown Detroit hotel. Exactly nine months later, their daughter, Hana, was born, a happy consequence of that celebration. Hana was a United States citizen, a birthright granted by the 14th Amendment to the Constitution.

Kurdistan is not a country; it is a cultural community that spans several countries. After the fall of the Ottoman Empire and post-World War I, the Sykes-Picot Agreement and, eventually, the Treaty of Lausanne, split the region and drew borders between Turkey, Syria, Iraq, and Iran. Since the original agreement and subsequent treaty did not establish a Kurdish homeland, this left Kurdish people straddled at the borders of each country, essentially, a people without a country. Today, there are approximately forty million Kurds scattered between the four countries. Primarily because they are a people without a country, Kurds have often suffered attacks, genocide, and massacres at the hands of oppressive regimes in each of the countries they call home. Throughout the years, Kurds have attempted to form their own regional governments, with their own army and rulers. In twenty-first century Kobani, Syria, the Kurds lived in relative peace. In 2003, they formed the Democratic Union Party, which took hold and spread rapidly among the Syrian Kurdish population. In 2011, the so-called Arab Spring reached Kobani, which resulted in the withdrawal of Syrian military forces in the region. Ironically, that is when the trouble began.

The Kurdish government was a bit more progressive than its neighbors. Political groups supported women's rights, environmental common sense, education, health care for its citizens, and diplomatic relationships with other countries. They forged a "Social Contract" which separated 'state' from 'religion,' banned underage marriages, recognized human rights for women and children, banned female circumcision and polygamy, prohibited discrimination, and declared men and women equal under the law. These were all positive developments for Canan and Karim Izady.

But when Syria withdrew its troops and civil war broke out in the country, President Assad of Syria left the border open to terrorist organizations. He did this, in part, to quell the uprising of citizens protesting oppression and the lack of social justice in Syria. Low income, a high cost of living, rampant unemployment, and even homelessness plagued the Syrian people.

While internal conflicts and petty political disputes contributed to the demise of peace, *ISIS* forces attacked Kobani in the fall of 2014. Kobani was strategically located near pipelines and provided supply routes to the Turkish border. As such, it was a prime target for *ISIS*. It was also a vital city to defend, and the Kurds and multiple allies endeavored to do just that. As a result, a brutal war broke out. In the beginning, it appeared the city would fall under *ISIS* control, but United States air strikes slowed the siege.

In the meantime, close to 200,000 people fled Kobani and surrounding areas. Most found their way to shelters and refugee camps. Like Canan and Karim, the more affluent found their way to America and a new life in the land of the free. Over time, Kurdish forces and its allies managed to retake control of most of the region. By 2015, the city, although severely damaged, was free of *ISIS* control.

Recently, the United States government considered a full withdrawal of troops in the region. This terrified Canan and Karim because they still had loved ones in the region. They wanted to travel to Kobani with Hana so the child could meet her extended family and, perhaps, to arrange for relatives to travel back with them to America. All reports indicated it was currently safe to travel to the region.

The trip was arranged, but, at the last minute, a crisis at work prevented Karim from traveling abroad. He decided to cancel the trip, which devastated Canan. She had spoken to her mother and grandmother, and all were excited about the reunion. This was to be her grandmother and great-grandmother's first time meeting their precious Hana. She insisted on taking the trip. Perhaps Karim could join them later. Karim protested vehemently, but his wife was an American woman and would not be dissuaded. They reached a compromise. Karim reluctantly consented to the trip, provided his family traveled through Syria accompanied by Karim's long-time friend and a former soldier, who would act as a guide and a bodyguard, protecting Canan and Hana from harm.

As Karim Izady drove his family to Detroit Metropolitan Airport in Romulus, he could not shake the feeling of dread he felt from the moment he agreed to the trip. Even with his long-time friend, Avi Baran, meeting them in Syria and guarding them throughout their visit, he could not shake the feeling. He knew it was useless to protest. He enjoyed life in America and appreciated American-style freedom. That style included a strong, independent, and free-thinking wife. A part of him wished, for these moments only, they were a more traditional male-dominated Muslim couple.

They reached the international terminal. As usual, airport traffic was heavy, and Karim had to double-park to the left of a Metro Car parked at the curb. He exited the *SUV*, walked to the back of the vehicle, and opened the large tailgate. As he unloaded the luggage, Canan unbuckled Hana from her car seat in the back and carried her to Karim. Karim took one look at his beautiful wife and daughter and began to cry.

"I love you. Please don't go," he cried. Immediately, he retracted. "I'm sorry. I'm so sorry—of *course,* you should go. Your mother and grandmother deserve to meet this beautiful child. I am just so worried, my love."

"Everything will be fine, my sweet. Avi will take care of us. If conditions on the ground were too dangerous, Avi would have warned us not to come. You know how capable he is. Besides, you've heard the same reports I have. The city is much safer than it was. *ISIS* has been defeated, and America is pulling out of the region. That should give you comfort."

"On the contrary, I would feel much better if America was *not* abandoning the region. *ISIS*, the Syrian government, even the Turks may become emboldened when America leaves. None of them have much love for the Kurds."

"We Kurds are a tough bunch. America could not have freed Kobani without us," she smiled. "Everything will be okay."

"By the grace of *Allah*," he looked to the sky in prayer.

"Come here, my love. Give me and your beautiful daughter a hug and help me get these bags to the counter."

Karim did as his wife instructed, then waited while the attendant handled their luggage and checked in Canan and Hana. Karim bobbed his head back and forth to his double-parked vehicle; airport police might object to the unattended vehicle. The attendant completed his work, and Karim handed him a five-dollar bill. His eyes watered again as he gathered his wife and daughter in a fierce hug, one to last two weeks.

"Be safe . . . I love you," he cried as they walked into the terminal. "Don't go anywhere in Syria without Avi," he called out. Canan turned to him, one last time, took Hana's hand, and waved 'bye-bye.' She blew her husband a kiss, turned, and disappeared into the terminal.

Karim turned and walked to the car. "They will be fine . . . they will be fine . . . they will be fine . . . *Allah* will guide and protect them," he muttered aloud. But an ominous voice in his head told him otherwise.

Chapter Three

Zachary Blake and Marshall Mann were having breakfast at Little Daddy's restaurant—a diner located a short distance from their Bloomfield Hills office on Woodward Avenue. The two lawyers were friends as well as partners. They became fast friends a few years ago, when Zack needed an immigration lawyer to handle a threatened deportation of a couple of naturalized citizen-clients.

Zack represented the couple's daughter, who was falsely accused of murder. The newly elected President of the United States, an anti-Muslim zealot who tried to implement a Muslim ban on travel to certain Muslim countries, sought to make an example of the young woman's parents by deporting them. Instead, Mann went to federal court and made a fool out of the president and his attorney general.

Zack was so impressed with Marshall's work on the case; he offered Marshall a partnership and the opportunity to create an immigration division at the prestigious Law Offices of Zachary Blake. This new division became an immediate success. Marshall now supervised a team of four lawyers and the immigration division was now a vital part of Blake's legal service center.

Marshall and his team continued to represent members of the Muslim population who were unfairly targeted by the government for deportation or other penalties because of their religion or national origin. Although the evil president, Ronald John, had recently resigned in disgrace over unrelated criminal behavior, his successor continued some of his most draconian policies. As a result, a new immigration frontier developed. People trying to enter the country on the southern border were being herded into cages or sent back to their countries of origin. In addition, a crackdown was implemented on Latinos already in the country. Marshall was filling Zack in on the many clients who contacted him with concerns about possible deportation and how to avoid it.

"It's unbelievable, Zack! Nothing has changed—it's as though RonJohn is still *POTUS*," Marshall sighed.

"Golding is a John protégé. Too much to expect he'd be different, wouldn't you say?" Zack reasoned.

"But it started out that way. I thought he'd at least be a decent *human being*, even if I disagreed with his politics," Marshall grumbled.

"Come on, Marsh. He's a hell of a lot better than John, and besides, he won't be there much longer."

"He can do a lot of damage while he's here."

"What kind of issues are we talking about?" Zack probed.

"I'm sure you've heard some of this stuff on the news. There is a real humanitarian crisis going on at the southern border, and the government is making it worse."

"I watch the news, Marshall."

"No offense intended, Zack. I know you care. How do we get the government to care? How do we stop this disgraceful behavior?"

"Is it really that bad?"

"Worse! People are walking hundreds of miles in caravans. A surge of migrants arrives at the Texas-Mexico border, and the system is not equipped to handle all of them. Border control is at a breaking point, and along comes Stephen Golding with his new policies, aimed not only at the undocumented but at asylum seekers, too."

"I'm not sure I understand the difference."

"It is not considered illegal to seek asylum, Zack. These people have never been incarcerated at the border the way they are today. The situation is reaching crisis level."

"How so?"

"There are too many of them. People can't shower or brush their teeth. Sick kids go without medical care, coughing and crying all night long. Toilets don't work—the stench is unbelievably foul. It's so bad that people are throwing up, and you've got the smell of vomit *on top of* the piss and shit smells."

"Oh my God, Marshall, where are you getting this from?" Zack was appalled.

"Clients are asking me if I can represent their relatives down there. They're reporting what they hear from their loved ones. I've also talked with some non-profits I do pro bono work for— they describe the same types of conditions near El Paso and the Rio Grande Valley."

"What else have you heard?"

"People being thrown in cages, hundreds jammed into a single cage, seated on the floor, standing, however they can fit them in. People aren't permitted to shower or bathe for days. They're wearing the same filthy clothes they wore when they came into the country. Sanitation is non-existent, and conditions are deplorable. I've talked to some lawyers down there, and they describe horrid conditions, unsafe, unsanitary, and overcrowded. It's a real mess."

"What about *Flores*?"

Flores was the 1997 federal court settlement of a nine-year-old case, *Jenny Lisette Flores, et al. v Janet Reno, Attorney General of the United States*. What is now known in legal and political circles as the *Flores Agreement*, it established a nationwide policy for the detention, release, and treatment of minors in the custody of the Immigration and Naturalization Services (*INS*). It also superseded all previous *INS* policies inconsistent with its terms. In short, the agreement mandated 'safe and sanitary' conditions.

"Conditions are a clear violation of the *Flores* standard."

"So, start there."

"I'm not sure what good I can do. There are too many people in too many overcrowded and unsanitary facilities. They can't release them all, and, besides, the migrants have nowhere else to go. Conditions are prison-like. I was about to go down there to handle the incarceration of a client's Angolan relatives. These guys were placed in a facility in Del Rio and weren't being permitted to bathe or brush their teeth. Before I could get down there, they were released. They ended up in a migrant shelter in San Antonio, where conditions were substantially better. They are placated. With all of the people who need legal help, it made no sense to go down there for people who were reasonably satisfied with their current placement. Federal authorities are overwhelmed down there."

"What can I do to help, Marsh?"

"Nothing yet, Zack, but I appreciate the thought. If we get involved, we will not only have to provide free legal services, but we're going to have to spend a lot of money in travel and logistics for people we try to help. I don't have that kind of coin."

"But I *do*. If and when you decide to get involved, the firm will cover whatever you deem necessary. Fair enough?"

"I knew I liked you. I'm so glad I took you up on your offer to join your firm and create the immigration division. I can do so much more for people with the kind of resources your firm can provide. I can't tell you how much I appreciate your support."

"My pleasure, Marsh. *Our* firm, by the way."

"Huh?"

"You said *your* firm. Last I checked, you were a partner in the firm."

"You're right. I'm not used to being someone else's partner."

Zack laughed. "Yeah, I know what you mean. After the break-up with *my* former partners, I kind of liked being a lone wolf, too. But partners, associates, and a large support and research staff come in handy, sometimes—so does having a boatload of money."

"Amen to that," Marshall grinned, holding up his coffee mug in a   mock toast.

"Jennifer and I believe in paying our success forward. It's important to us, especially to Jennifer." Jennifer was Zack's wife. She was once his client. Back in the day, Jennifer and her two boys retained Zack to handle their clergy-child abuse case. Zack's life was in the toilet, at an all-time low at the time. Jennifer, the boys, and the case brought him back from the brink. His success in the case was legendary in Detroit's legal community. When the case was resolved, Zack and Jennifer dated, fell in love, and eventually married. Zack adopted the two boys, now in college, and loved them as if they were his own sons.

"How is the lovely lady?"

"Jenny's great. She and those boys are the best things that

ever happened to me."

"The case wasn't too bad, either."

"The hardest case of my life—the great financial result and subsequent fame brought more quality cases to the firm. The windfall provides the means to do the pro bono work we're talking about. So, let's get back to it, Marsh. Do you or Amy have a suggested strategy for the southern border?" Amy Fletcher was Marshall's chief associate in the immigration division. She was relatively new to the firm, but Marshall could not imagine practicing law without her by his side.

"As I said before, we're not sure yet—I've discussed it with Amy, but I wanted to have a preliminary conversation with you to determine whether assistance was feasible. Rumor has it that *ICE* plans to target undocumented workers right here in Detroit. We may have our hands full with the local stuff."

"Let me know if you guys need more support staff. Are you and Amy good with current resource levels?"

"For now."

"Remember, you have carte blanche to create the necessary infrastructure. Immigration is your baby and your department."

"Thanks, man. You've certainly proven that with Amy. And we appreciate the support."

"This whole situation sounds horrible. You can count on the firm's resources, whatever you decide to do."

"Thanks again, Zack. We're still trying to sort it all out. Migrants are arriving in busloads. *CBP* says they are taking civil rights abuses seriously and pledge to investigate every allegation to the fullest extent possible. Maybe they are looking for volunteers. We'll see."

"I'll bet there's a funding shortage, too. Do those pricks in Congress or President Golding care about a bunch of people who they consider undocumented? I don't think so." Zack groused.

"Jesus, Zack—how do you really feel?"

"You know what I'm talking about, Marshall. We've been waging class warfare in this country for centuries. The racial and socio-economic divide is worse than ever. Dr. King is rolling over in his grave. These non-citizens at the border can't even vote. How can we trust the same public officials, those who won't take care of the weakest members of our *voting* population, to take care of even weaker *non-voters*?"

"I see your point, Zack," Marshall conceded. "Maybe I'll go down there with your checkbook and make sure people are fed and clothed properly," Marshall suggested with a smile.

"Like I said, Marsh, carte blanche."

"I'll keep you posted."

"Please do—got to run. I've got a meeting."

"I'm going to finish my coffee. I really need something stronger." Marshall grimaced.

"Hang in there, Marsh." Zack rose from the table and looked at his watch and down at the check. "Shit! I'm late! Get that, would you?" Zack requested as he ran out the door.

Marshall smirked as he watched Zachary Blake enter his BMW convertible and drive away. He gulped a large swig of coffee and studied the breakfast bill. "Who's the multi-millionaire, again?" he asked out loud.

Chapter Four

Miguel and Mary Carmen Gonzalez arrived at the Riverview filler plant; conditions seemed normal. The couple was two of twelve undocumented immigrants employed at the plant. All came into the country legally but stayed over the limit because of a great family life and excellent work conditions that could not be duplicated in their countries of origin.

Mary Carmen's job was to clean, set-up, and monitor production line equipment. Occasionally, she operated the equipment, completed all required documentation, and scheduled quality checks. Miguel was an operator, also responsible for filling containers. Both jobs were tedious and difficult, but Miguel and Mary Carmen loved the work, appreciated their jobs, and were happy to be in the United States of America, the land of the free, until that day.

That day, as the Gonzalez family feared, *ICE* agents raided the Riverview-based filler plant. The first notice of a problem came when workers heard the loud whir of helicopter blades. Shortly afterwards, a helicopter landed on the street outside the small plant. A caravan of vehicles, detention vans, an *EMS* unit, and some unmarked black sedans surrounded the plant. Agents stormed in, scaring the hell out of everyone. Two women fainted on the spot and were rushed to a nearby hospital.

The affected workers were herded together in the break room, told to place hands behind heads, and not resist. Women were taken first, in groups, to the ladies' room, where a male officer subjected them to invasive body scans. These so-called 'scans' included the officer feeling around inside their underwear and bras. The men were subjected to similar scans in the men's room, but the exams were far less invasive or prurient than those performed on the women.

Mary Carmen shouted at her captors in broken English. "My children are in school! I must go to them, *por favor*!" She pleaded.

Her cries were ignored. She could only pray that neighbors and teachers would rise to the occasion and care for her kids, as previously arranged. She was devastated, borderline hysterical that her kids would end up in foster care or social services. If she and Miguel were deported, what fate was better for her kids, foster care in America or danger in Venezuela with their parents? *What a horrible choice!*

Miguel was equally distraught. He turned to his captor. "We are law-abiding people! We have a family! We go to work, pay our taxes, go to church on Sunday. We shop in your stores! We are kind to our neighbors and support our neighborhood school. Our kids are there now. Please, I beg you; let us go and care for our kids."

Pandemonium erupted, and all detainees began speaking and pleading with their captors at the same time. Some tried to break free and were rewarded with a whack from a billy club.

In the end, agents arrested thirty people, every Latino in the place. Scary men dressed in riot gear led terrified workers away in handcuffs to face civil charges for being in the country without proper documentation or status. A special agent executing a criminal search warrant has the authority to detain all individuals at the enforcement site, including supervisors, for as long as they deem necessary. Not a single white supervisor was among those arrested or detained.

A couple of workers became ill or had medical conditions that resulted in their release. Later, those released workers confessed to guilt feelings and sleeplessness because they were released while others were subjected to terrible abuse and neglect. Others were released, without apology, when agents determined they were United States citizens with proper papers.

Mary Carmen, Miguel, and others were taken by van to what appeared to be an abandoned warehouse. Handcuffs were removed, and the workers were shoved inside. Bottles of water were given to each detainee as they entered the empty warehouse. There was no furniture. Mary Carmen and Miguel walked to the back and sat down against the wall. Mary Carmen eyed her husband, buried her head into his chest, and sobbed.

***

News of the raid soon reached administrators at Raupp Elementary School in Lincoln Park. The principal and vice-principal had been made aware of the possibility that Miguel and Mary Carmen Gonzalez would be arrested. The couple pre-arranged accommodations and care with the parents of classmates, but school administrators had an obligation first to notify Social Services and persuade them to sign off.

Before notifying Emma and Emilio or their respective teachers, Principal Curley made a telephone call. Less than an hour later, he welcomed Dolores Martinez into his office. A social worker from the Downriver office of Immigration and Naturalization, Dolores was aware of the recent raids. Mr. Curley filled her in on the family situation and the fact that neighbors volunteered to pitch in. He implored her to consider alternatives to foster care.

Dolores was a kind, caring, and understanding woman. Her personality was one of the reasons she chose social work. She would do what she could but had to follow the law.

"We don't know whether Emma's and Emilio's parents will be deported. They must be given due process. Perhaps they'll be released with a tether, pending the outcome. I have more latitude when considering temporary rather than permanent placements. We'll have a different conversation if the parents are deported," she explained.

"Understood," Curley retorted. "You can check out the family and home where the kids will stay. I'm sure you'll find everything in order. Our families are not well off financially, but they live in stable, happy homes. This is a great place to live— the Gonzalez family is an important part of our neighborhood family."

"Look, Mr. Curley, I will be blunt. I'm not a fan of these raids, separating families, or ripping babies out of the arms of parents. I'm not a fan of arresting otherwise law-abiding, hard-working adults. I'd like to see more compassion and pathways to citizenship. Having said that, I have to do my job."

"I wasn't suggesting otherwise, Ms. Martinez."

"Call me Dolores."

"And you can call me George."

"George, these more aggressive enforcement activities by *ICE* are very troubling to those of us in social work. Citizen-children and undocumented parents live in constant fear, an unhealthy situation. The threat of family separation and economic hardship weighs heavily on the family unit, even its youngest members. While a young child may not completely understand the situation, he or she understands there is a serious problem.

"After an arrest like this, many children are forced to miss school. Some have to move away from the community; they may lose academic focus. In addition, separation anxiety often causes depression, self-doubt, and a deficit in love and attention usually present in the child's life. My job is to minimize the potential for these types of problems. I applaud this family and the community's effort to pre-arrange a stable environment for these kids. Let's hope this is all *very* temporary."

"Amen, Dolores. You have certainly made me feel better. Where do we go from here?"

"Do you have a private room and telephone I can use?"

"Right this way." Curley rose and pointed to the door. Dolores exited in front of him, waited for him to lead the way, and followed him to an empty small conference room.

"Phone's over there." He pointed to a telephone on a small table toward the back of the room. "Let me know if you need anything." He walked out, leaving Dolores alone to make her call.

A short time later, Dolores knocked on his open door. "I have some news."

"I'm all ears," Curley smiled and pointed to a seat in front of his desk. Dolores sat down.

"Mr. and Mrs. Gonzalez are being held on a detainer order."

"What's that?"

"Apparently, *ICE* has determined both of them are undocumented . . ." She hesitated.

"Go on . . ."

"Mr. and Mrs. Gonzalez and the others are being held by local law enforcement at a makeshift jail type facility in an abandoned warehouse. *ICE* has forty-eight hours to bring charges. If everyone follows protocol, and agents don't charge them, they will be released."

"What's the likelihood of that?"

"It's been known to happen. Besides, even if they are charged, *ICE* might release them with an ankle monitor after a brief court appearance."

"That sounds good."

"Well, not so fast. If the locals file criminal charges, then the Gonzalez' would have to post a bond or stay locked up."

"How much would they have to post? These are not wealthy people."

"I don't know. Let's cross that bridge when we come to it. Do either of them have a criminal record?"

"No! They are fine people. People in their situation should be granted citizenship, not be locked up like criminals. Their kids are *citizens*, for crying out loud!"

"I understand. But that's not my call." She was defensive.

"I know. I'm sorry. I didn't mean to take it out on you."

"No problem. Anyway, we'll know more after forty-eight hours. For now, I have approval for the children to stay with the neighbors you mentioned."

"That's terrific news—it will make this situation far less traumatic when I tell them about their parents."

"They don't know yet?"

"No. I wanted to resolve the placement situation first."

"I guess that makes sense. Do you want me to break the news to them?"

"Can we do it together?"

"Certainly."

"Do you have a lot of experience with this sort of thing?"

"This sort of thing, as you call it, doesn't happen all that often, although these days, more than I'd like. Yes, I have experience, but not a lot."

"This is going to be quite traumatic for these kids, isn't it?"

"Again, this is all premature, but, yes, if detention or incarceration becomes a long-term situation, it could be quite traumatic. This could take days or months to resolve, in which case we would have to consider a more permanent placement. On the other hand, *ICE* has the authority to release detainees on humanitarian grounds. In fact, in these early stages, these grounds include detainees being sole caregivers for citizen children."

"Wouldn't that be great?"

"That's short-term. Long-term, those considerations go out the window. We need to get this family a *lawyer* stat. If they are not released in that forty-eight-hour window, these folks could be deported. If that happens, they lose custodial rights to their kids. We can't let that happen."

"Can you recommend a lawyer?"

"Yes. He's a terrific immigration lawyer, but he's not cheap."

"Well, I like the 'terrific' part. Maybe the community could chip in. What's this guy's name?"

"Marshall Mann. Are you familiar with Zachary Blake?"

"Sure, everyone's heard of Zachary Blake and his recent string of high-profile courtroom successes."

"Mann is Blake's immigration guy. They work together. I just happen to have his card in here somewhere." She fished around in her purse and came up with the business card.

"Would you mind calling him? Telling him the community will try to raise funds?"

"Sure, George. I'd be happy to. For now, though, let's get this temporary placement situation resolved. We need to talk to the children and give them the bad news."

"I'll call their classrooms. Thanks for your kindness and compassion."

"That's what I'm here for."

Emma and Emilio were called down to the principal's office and given the news they had been dreading for years. They were terribly upset, but Dolores was impressed at their maturity. It seemed their parents prepared them for this moment. The children were pleased to hear they would be staying with classmates' families in the neighborhood. They brightened when told their parents might be released after forty-eight hours. Dolores told the kids she would consult a lawyer on their behalf.

"Do you know what a lawyer is?"

"Someone who represents you in court?" Emma guessed.

"Yes, but it is more than that, sweetheart. A lawyer can help someone with an immigration problem even *before* it gets to court. That's what we're going to try to do here. Understand?"

"I . . . think so," Emma stammered. She glanced at Emilio, who looked confused and terrified at the same time. She took his hand in hers and smiled.

Quite the little lady, Dolores smiled. "I'm going to call the lawyer right now, so you guys can hear the conversation. Would you like that? I'm not sure he's in his office, but we can try, okay?"

"Okay," Emma brightened.

"Here goes." Dolores dialed Mann's number on a speakerphone. The speaker rang three times and clicked. A voice sounded through the speaker box.

"Law Offices of Zachary Blake, Kristin speaking. How may I direct your call?"

"Marshall Mann, please?"

"Who shall I say is calling?"

"This is Dolores Martinez. I may have a new case for him."

"I'll see if he's in. Hold, please." Music on hold came through the speaker until the phone clicked, and the music was interrupted by a man's voice.

"Dolores! It's so nice to hear from you. How the hell are you?" Mann chirped.

Dolores chuckled. "Marshall, sorry to bother you, I'm sitting here with a school principal and two elementary students."

"Oops. Sorry for the salty language. Do I get detention?"

Curley and the kids laughed. "No detention, this time, Mr. Mann. Next time you will have to write 'I will not use salty language' ten times on a piece of paper," Curley joked.

"That guy sounds like a principal. Kids? Is this guy a nice principal or a mean one?"

Emma and Emilio giggled. "He's a nice principal," Emma replied, staring at the speaker box.

"What's your name, young lady?" Marshall's voice wondered.

"Emma. And this is my brother, Emilio." She looked over at her brother as if Mann could see them.

"Nice to meet both of you. How may I help you guys today?"

Dolores took over the conversation and filled Marshall in on everything that transpired. Marshall was happy she called—he'd been itching for a fight with *ICE* and the administration over the crackdown and new protocols. When Dolores finished her story, she paused, and she, Principal Curley, and the Gonzalez children awaited Marshall's response.

"I promised the principal I wouldn't use salty language, so, what a bunch of creeps! There are far better ways to handle these things than raiding plants, separating kids from parents, and arresting otherwise innocent folks. The parents don't have a record of any kind, do they, Dolores?"

"No, Marshall, I'm assured they do not."

"Good. Well, folks, I'm glad we have temporary shelter. The first forty-eight hours are crucial—I'm sure Dolores told you that."

"She did," Curley noted.

"I don't think the kids will understand this, but, at this point, their parents have three options: They can apply for asylum, withholding of removal, or United Nations convention relief from cruelty or inhuman punishment or treatment. Second, they can ask to see a judge and try to get him or her to stop the deportation on humanitarian grounds. Third, they can choose to leave the country voluntarily, without being forced to. If they choose that option, they will be permitted to gather their belongings, reunite with their family, and everyone could go back to their original country."

"But this is our home, Mr. Mann," Emma cried. "Emilio and I have never been to Venezuela."

"These kids are United States citizens, Marshall," Dolores reminded him.

"So, option three is out?"

"Conditions in Venezuela are not good, especially for those who chose to leave. Yes, option three is out."

"Then we'll see what we can do with options one and two."

"Marshall, there is another problem," Dolores warned.

"What's that?"

"These are poor people. They can't pay you . . ." Dolores began.

"We're going to have a fundraiser for your fees, Mr. Mann," Curley interrupted.

"Go ahead and have your fundraiser, Mr. Principal. What's your name, again?"

"Curley, sir. George Curley."

The kids giggled. *George?*

"Go ahead and have your fundraiser for this family. They are going to have financial issues because they won't be working for a while. I'll show up and contribute, and so will my famous partner, Zack Blake. As for the fees, they are pro bono in this situation."

"Pro bono?" Curley inquired.

"Free of charge. I have been looking for a cause celeb to take on *ICE* and this administration's draconian policies. I would pay *you* to handle this case. Look at all the free publicity I'm going to get!"

"That's wonderful, Mr. Mann! What a nice gesture! Did you hear that, kids?" Curley's excitement was contagious, but the kids didn't understand.

"Thank you?" Emma managed, not appreciating what she was thanking the speaker for.

"Why are you thanking me?" Marshall quipped.

"I . . . I'm . . . not sure," Emma stuttered.

"I'm going to take care of this for you. If everything goes the way I hope, you will see your parents soon. How does that sound?"

"Terrific!" Emma cried.

"Cool!" Emilio added with a smile.

"Cool, man," Marshall cooed into the speaker. "High-five!"

"Huh?" Emilio was confused. *How do I high-five a voice?*

"Hit the speaker, young man!" A loud noise came out of the speaker as Marshall Mann high-fived Emilio. Emilio hit the speaker.

"Okay! We have a deal on a high-five handshake," Marshall exclaimed. "It was nice talking to all of you. I need you to take me off speaker so I can talk to Dolores and get the details."

Curley pushed a button, handed the receiver to Dolores, and left the room with the children. He walked them back to class.

"Will Mama and Papa be okay, Mr. Curley?" Emma wondered.

Curley did not want to convey false hope. He believed kids were entitled to the truth with no sugar-coating. "We have a fight on our hands, Emma, but Mr. Mann seems to be a good guy. He sure knows what he's doing, don't you think? Hopefully, everything will be fine."

"I hope so."

"So do I, honey. So do I."

Chapter Five

Canan and Hana Izady exited the plane, exhausted from the long journey. If things went according to plan, Avi would meet them at baggage claim and fast-track them through customs. Afterwards, they would retrieve the luggage and be on their way. A chartered van was arranged to take the three of them to Kobani, about 600 kilometers from the airport. There were closer, smaller, airports, but those did not have sufficient security to please Karim, who insisted on being in charge of trip logistics. As a result of his stubborn over-protectiveness, his family would now have to endure a grueling and treacherous seven-hour drive from Damascus to Kobani. Canan was not happy. *What was Karim thinking?*

Mother and child breezed through the tunnel that connected the plane to the terminal. Canan was pleased to stretch her legs after a long plane ride. She held a sleeping Hana in her arms and gazed down at her peaceful face. *The world should know such salam. I hope everything will be okay.*

She walked through the terminal and followed the signs to baggage and customs. A handsome dark-skinned man held up a sign that read "Canan and Hana Izady." Canan approached him.

"Avi?" Canan inquired. "Is that you? You look different somehow."

"It is me," the man smiled. "How was your flight? You still have a long journey ahead of you. What was Karim thinking?"

"I was just wondering the same thing. Aren't there closer airports? Are they safe?"

"Yes, there are closer airports. Safety is a concern—Karim was, perhaps, correct to be careful. But the drive to Kobani is a long one, and there are areas between here and there that are not so safe. It is . . . how do you say in America . . . a mixed bag."

"The world is dangerous, Avi. We can't stop living our lives. Hana has never met my mother or my grandmother." Canan rationalized.

"We will have to do something about that, then," he grinned. "Do you have much luggage?"

"Considering I'm a woman traveling with an infant, no," she laughed. "A large bag and a carry-on. Since I was checking the large one, it didn't make sense to carry the other one. Checking it was easier."

"I have made all of the arrangements. We should fly through customs without a hitch. You are a citizen, after all."

"I haven't forgotten, although it seems so long ago."

"Only four years and you've forgotten us already?"

"Would I be a terrible person if I said I was happy to leave? Syria's experienced all of this war—all of this death and destruction—and for what? An ideology? And the way everyone in the region treats the Kurds? I admit it, Avi. I was happy to leave. But, no, this is my homeland. I could never forget . . ." She drifted off in thought and suddenly snapped out of it. "How are we getting to Kobani?"

"I have arranged a driver and a van, more like a limousine. He is waiting for us outside baggage claim."

"Has this driver been checked?"

"You mean a background check?"

"Yes."

"As well as possible around here. We have used him before. He's driven government diplomats."

"That is no reassurance. The government doesn't like the Kurds."

"How would he know you're a Kurd?"

"I guess he wouldn't. If he's passed all of your and Karim's tests, I guess he passes mine."

"We'll be fine. Here's baggage."

Avi retrieved their luggage. A wad of cash facilitated a speedy exit through Syrian customs. The agent seemed to know Avi quite well. As they exited the terminal, the first thing Canan noticed was the stifling heat. She'd forgotten how oppressive the heat was in Syria and was happy she wore light clothes.

She immediately became self-conscious. She wasn't wearing a *burqa* or even a *hijab*. *Would this be a problem?* She followed Avi as he approached a large Mercedes van parked at the curb. A man exited the driver's seat as soon as he saw Avi and company approach.

"Hassan? This is Canan, and this beautiful creature is Hana. Canan. Hana, meet Hassan Amadi."

"How do you do?" Canan turned to Hana, who was now awake. Mother instructed daughter to say 'hi.'

"Hi," Hana cooed.

"She loves that word. It's very easy," Canan laughed.

"She pronounces it beautifully. Welcome to Syria. Kobani, eh? These days, I don't get many requests to travel there."

"No? Why? I understand hostilities have ended."

"True, but there is nothing there. The whole town has been leveled. It's a wasteland." Apparently, Hassan had not been told Canan had family in Kobani.

"There are still people there, Hassan, aren't there? My mother and grandmother are there. I have other relatives there. I have an address. We won't have any trouble finding them, will we?"

"I'm so sorry. I didn't realize the purpose of your visit. Did you communicate with your family members before you left for the trip?"

"Yes."

"Then they should be at the address they gave you. Everything should be fine. The city has taken a beating, but a few brave souls are trying to rebuild. I didn't mean to scare you. I was referring to events that have happened in the past. Nothing too terrible has happened recently."

With those glowing words of encouragement, the group climbed into the van. It was quite luxurious by Syrian standards. Each seat was a captain's chair with a lap and shoulder seat belt. A car seat had been acquired for Hana. Hassan strapped her in and tightened the harness. Canan took the seat next to her daughter and directly behind Hassan. Avi climbed into the front passenger seat.

"Everyone ready?" Hassan fiddled with the navigation device, and a map appeared on the screen above the dashboard. He scanned his passengers and received a 'thumbs up' sign from the adults. Hana saw the sign and tried to mimic her mother. She raised her fist instead.

The van zoomed out of the airport and onto a modern highway. Canan and Hana's Syrian adventure had begun. Canan gazed out the window at the passing landscape. She recognized nothing of her former home. She desperately wanted to see her mother and grandmother. She wanted Hana to meet them, see her homeland, and be introduced to her heritage. No matter how hard she tried, however, she could not overcome a feeling of impending doom.

I am an American citizen with an American passport in a country that hates Americans, and we have to drive six hundred kilometers across the country. What was I thinking? Why would I bring a child to such a hostile place? Karim was correct—I'm nuts for doing this. But Mama and Nana deserve to see Hana, don't they? I want my baby to meet my mother. What's wrong with that? Besides, the war is over. What could possibly go wrong?

Chapter Six

The following day, Marshall Mann and Zachary Blake entered Riverview Police headquarters into the car's navigation system and were provided directions to the Civic Park Drive. Following the directions, Zack pulled into the parking lot about forty minutes later. They walked in, flashed business cards, and asked the desk sergeant for the man in charge.

"What's this about, gentlemen?" the sergeant inquired.

"The recent raid at the filler plant," Marshall responded. "We've been retained to represent two of the detainees."

"Got it. Hang on a second." The sergeant spun his chair around, picked up a phone, and pushed a few buttons on the phone. "A couple of lawyers here to see one of the plant detainees," he muttered into the receiver. "Yeah, sure, I'll tell them." He hung up the phone and turned his chair back around.

"Chief says they are not permitting visitors at this time."

Zachary Blake was not a man who easily took 'no' for an answer. "We aren't visitors. We're attorneys. We have a right to see our clients. More importantly, our clients have a right to see us."

The guard glanced at the business cards. "Are you Blake or Mann?"

"Blake."

"I don't make the rules, Mr. Blake. I follow orders."

"Call your boss back and tell him that my next move is to call the press, tell them the Riverview Police and *ICE* are working in concert to deny my clients access to their attorneys. After that, I will visit the courthouse, press in tow, and obtain a court order compelling you to permit us to see our clients, a right granted by the Sixth Amendment to the Constitution. Do you guys want all that negative publicity on *top* of the bad press Riverview and *ICE* got for the raid?"

"Shit!"

"Shit is right," Zack cackled. "What's it going to be?"

"Hang on." He turned his chair again and dialed the phone. He muttered illegible comments into the receiver, hung up the phone, and turned back to the attorneys. "He's coming out," he grumbled.

"Who's coming out?" Zack pressed. "What's his name?" Marshall Mann turned from the desk and chuckled, his back to the sergeant.

"Chief Sanders."

"Wise decision by Chief Sanders," Zack grumbled. The sergeant rolled his eyes. Soon, loud footsteps were heard, and a huge man in uniform approached the desk. He was at least six foot five with thin hair, a bulbous nose, and a protruding belly. *Too many donuts?* Zack wondered.

"What seems to be the trouble?" Sanders grunted, approaching the desk.

"These lawyers are demanding to see two of the detainees, Chief," the sergeant advised, handing Sanders the business cards.

"Zachary Blake? *The* Zachary Blake? It's not too often we get a bona fide celebrity visiting our precinct. Benner, why didn't you tell me that the attorney was Blake, you idiot!" Benner hung his head in shame.

"Hold the phone, Chief," Zack retorted, defending Benner. "What difference does it make whether I'm Zachary Blake or a public defender? These people were pulled from their workplace by force, despite having broken no law at the time of arrest. Aside from their possibly unconstitutional arrest, they were not permitted to see their families or contact their lawyers. They may be undocumented—they may not be. If they are not, you and *ICE* will answer to me. But your callous violation of their civil rights is appalling. What kind of police force are you running here? Is this America or some third world dictatorship?" Benner turned his chair and suppressed a laugh.

"Well . . . uh . . . see here . . . uh . . . Blake, I'm like Benner, here. *ICE* gave us protocol to follow. My job is to follow it. But . . . uh . . . like I said . . . you're here and your clients are here. I'm the chief and I don't see any harm in allowing you or any other lawyer to see a detainee. I have that authority." He lifted his nose in defiance of whoever issued whatever order. All four men paused.

"What are you waiting for, Chief Sanders? We want to see our clients *right now*!"

"I'll call down to the warehouse. Benner, take Mr. Blake and . . . uh . . . Mr. . . ." He snuck a peek at the other business card. "Uh . . . Mann to the warehouse. I'll arrange for a room and have their clients brought to them."

"Yes, sir!" Benner stood and saluted. "Right this way, gentlemen." He pointed toward the rear exit and led Blake and Mann toward it. He stopped and turned to Blake.

"Thanks for defending me, Mr. Blake. I was only doing what I was told," he explained.

"I understand, Benner, but do any of you push back on this stuff? These are *human beings*! This is America, dammit! Are we going to let the feds trample on the Constitution?" Zack was only semi-serious—he was trying to get a rise out of the guy.

Benner dropped his head in shame. "I'm right there with you, Mr. Blake. This shit, excuse my French, is way above my pay grade. I don't have much say in the matter."

"Neither did the storm troopers in Nazi Germany, Benner. They were only following orders too, right?" Zack snarled. Marshall Mann turned away, once again stifling a laugh.

"Nazi Germany, sir?"

Zack decided to lighten up on the guy. "Probably a bad comparison, Benner, but these people deserve better than this. Tell you what—how about we agree you won't deny the next lawyer a visit with his client? I'll get off my soapbox? Deal?"

"Deal, Mr. Blake," he smiled.

They walked across a huge parking lot past a surprisingly large number of out-of-service Riverview Police Ford Explorer *SUV*s. Zack eyed the rows of trucks. *How many cops and cop cars does a small-town police force need?*

At the end of the parking lot sat a large, nondescript warehouse. It looked like a place where the force would keep large equipment, perhaps SWAT vehicles or weapons. Two armed guards patrolled the front of the warehouse, walking back and forth, crisscrossing at the entrance. Benner walked up to one of the guards and whispered something. The guard removed a walkie-talkie from a shoulder harness and spoke into the unit. The door opened immediately, and two more guards stuck their heads out of the opening.

Apparently, Chief Sanders made his phone call because the lawyers were expected and immediately invited inside. Mann and Blake thanked Benner and said goodbye after being introduced to a federal officer named Dirk Weber, the *ICE* officer in charge of the warehouse prison. The men entered the warehouse. The place was stifling hot and reeked of body odor and human waste. Marshall and Zack gagged at the smell. Weber handed them cloths to hold over their noses.

Well over one hundred men and women, arrested at three separate raids in the city, sat on the floor, their backs against the four walls, chatting in Spanish or staring into space. A bridge table sat in the middle of the floor, holding bottles of water, crackers, and cookies. This was the only nourishment made available to these prisoners. Zack and Marshall were appalled at the conditions but said nothing.

Weber led them to a back room, which served as a break room for the guards. The room featured a bridge table and chairs, and two vending machines, containing cold water, a variety of Pepsi products, sandwiches, fruit pies, candy bars, and chips. The only window in the place had a room air conditioning unit installed. *God forbid they offer some of this stuff to these hostages*, thought Marshall.

Weber invited them to sit and asked if they wanted anything. Zack picked out a sandwich, a Pepsi, and an apple pie and motioned for Marshall to do the same. They sat down at the bridge table. Weber retrieved the items from the machine and placed them on the table. The door opened, and another armed officer escorted a man and a woman into the room. They were both small in stature, filthy and brown-skinned. Both had looks of bewilderment and fear on their faces. Zack held out his arm to the table and invited them to sit down. After they were seated, Zack addressed Weber and the other guard.

"We'd like to speak with our clients alone, please, gentlemen. You know, attorney-client privilege and all that? You are familiar with the United States Constitution, are you not?" Zack mocked.

"Funny guy," Weber huffed. "We know the law, counselor."

"All evidence in this warehouse to the contrary," Zack charged. "Please leave."

"We'll be right outside if you need us," the other guard spoke for the first time.

"Need you for what? Protection from these vicious, dangerous criminals?" Zack eyed his diminutive and helpless clients. "Get the hell out of here, please. We'll call for you when we're done," he groused.

The men finally took their leave. Zack and Marshall slid the vending machine goodies toward their new clients.

"Please eat," Zack offered. "Do you speak English?"

"Yes," the man replied, taking a sandwich and handing the other to the woman. "*Gracias* for the food."

"You're welcome. How long has it been since you've eaten?" Mann wondered.

"It has been a while. We've had nothing but a small bottle of water, and some cookies or crackers, since we've been here," the man revealed.

"Did they tell you who we are and why we're here?" Mann queried.

"No, they didn't."

"We are your lawyers. Your community has hired us to represent you."

"Our community?" The woman spoke for the first time, a look of confusion on her face. She shoved the sandwich in her mouth.

"Yes, a social worker with immigration recommended us to your kids' principal."

"That's very nice, but how will we pay you? Have you spoken to our children? What is happening with our children?" The woman worked herself into a panic.

"Your kids are fine. They are being well taken care of by your neighbors, just as you planned. As for attorney fees, let's not worry about that right now. Let's worry about getting you out of here," Zack suggested. "Now, tell us what happened at the plant, how you came into the country, and what the agents said and did after they arrested you. Don't leave anything out."

The man smiled, probably for the first time in days, and told Marshall and Zack the entire story of the raid, their arrest, and brutal treatment by *ICE* officers. Many people were injured, some seriously, during the raid. Four men and three women sustained injuries serious enough to require medical treatment. One woman needed to be airlifted by helicopter to Henry Ford Hospital in Wyandotte. Another was hospitalized with multiple broken bones when she climbed a stack of boxes trying to reach shelter on the roof. She was *that* fearful of the raid, immigration officials, and the chaos of an uncertain future in the American immigration system. An *ICE* officer toppled the boxes, and the helpless woman fell twenty feet to the ground. The officers thought this was hilarious until they realized she was seriously injured.

Mary Carmen and Miguel were not injured during the raid. They followed orders, did what they were told, and quietly acquiesced to their arrest and imprisonment. Their biggest fear, aside from the possibility of disease or death from the horrible conditions of this temporary prison, was the possibility of permanent separation from their children.

"How can they separate children from their parents? What will become of our family, Mr. Blake?"

Zack turned to Marshall. "Marshall?"

Marshall turned and locked eyes, first with Mary Carmen, and then with Miguel. As he glared into Miguel's eyes, he spoke.

"First and foremost, you must remember that you are undocumented. While you came to this country properly, you overstayed your visa. We all know that. So, to answer your question in blunt terms, they can separate you from your children because you have broken the law. I'm not judging you for what you did, and I understand why you had to do it, but those are the harsh realities of your situation. Do you understand?"

"Yes," Miguel conceded, hanging his head.

"Hey, chin up!" Marshall cheered, bending over the tabletop, tilting his head to meet Miguel's glare. "I've represented many people from Venezuela. I know how it is over there. I know it's terribly overcrowded. I know about food and water shortages, lack of hygiene, and economic hardships. I also know there is violence in the streets, terrible living conditions, and limited access to medical supplies. In other words, Miguel, Mary Carmen . . ." Marshall again turned from one to the other. "I understand why you came here and why you decided to stay, even though you were undocumented. Unfortunately, though, you *are* undocumented, understood?"

"Yes, Mr. Mann," whispered Mary Carmen.

"Now, to answer the 'what will become of my family' question you asked me, the honest answer is: I don't know yet. Here is what could happen over the next few days or weeks. *ICE* might try to hold you here indefinitely. I will fight to prevent that with every fiber of my being. The better alternative, especially if I can get a judge or one of his or her assistants to see this place, is to let you go home."

"Is it possible?" Mary Carmen cried.

"Yes, it is possible. *ICE* doesn't always keep everyone it arrests in custody. Sometimes it will release people, especially the parents of young children. You would probably have to wear some type of monitoring device, perhaps an ankle bracelet of some sort, and you will be required to keep regularly scheduled check-ins with *ICE*. Now, *ICE* can still try to deport you while this is happening, but you won't have to spend time in this horrible place or anything like it."

"What are the chances?" Miguel inquired.

"Judging by the looks of this place and the fact that *ICE* probably has more raids planned, I would say they are pretty good. They have already run out of room."

"So, we get to go home. Then what?" Mary Carmen was anxious.

"*Assuming* you get to go home, the next step will be for *ICE* to make an initial determination whether to institute removal proceedings and, if so, to press charges against you. In your case, the charge would be overstaying a nonimmigrant visa. Have either of you ever committed a crime or been in trouble with the law?" Marshall smiled.

"No, never, neither of us," Miguel boasted.

"Good, that will help. Again, assuming I can get you out of here, and, even if I can't, a deportation officer will serve you and the immigration court with a formal *Notice to Appear*. If you are still in detention, *ICE* is required by law to serve you with the *Notice to Appear* within 72 hours. This notice will list the charge or charges filed against you. At that point, you have the right to appear before an immigration judge. We can do three things at that point: We can fight the charges, accept the charges and seek relief from removal on other grounds, or accept the charges and the deportation. You don't want option three, correct?" Marshall smiled.

He has an easy way about him. I like this man. Mary Carmen hesitated before mumbling: "No, Mr. Mann, we do not want option three."

"I didn't think so," Marshall laughed. "Please understand, just because you've overstayed doesn't mean it's a slam-dunk that you'll be deported. There are many defenses to deportation, even for an undocumented person. Would you like to hear what they are?"

"Yes," Miguel chirped, his spirits lifting.

Before Marshall could respond, there was a knock on the door. Zack went to open it. Dirk Weber stood at the threshold.

"About time to wrap this up."

"Why? Under what authority?" Zack snarled.

"Err . . . uh . . . ." Weber was taken aback by Zack's bravado.

"You going somewhere, Weber? Are my clients? Do they have chores or something?"

"Well . . . uh . . . no."

"They were arrested and brought here without advice of rights, without being offered an attorney or a social worker. They've been locked up in this God-awful place for almost forty-eight hours. They aren't going anywhere, except, perhaps, to a judge to discuss the deplorable, cruel, and unusual lock-up where they were held captive. Marshall and I are not going anywhere until we complete our interrogation. And, if you decide to remove us, I will sue *ICE*, you, Homeland Security, Health and Human Services, the United States Citizenship and Immigration

Service, and President fricking Golding. Do you understand me?" Zack roared.

"Well . . . uh . . . um . . . I . . . uh . . . I don't suppose a little more time will harm anyone," Weber stuttered.

"And get us more sandwiches and pop, would you please?" Marshall piled on, grinning at his hungry clients.

"Will do, Mr. Mann. Anything else?"

"That's it for now," Zack dismissed him and literally shut the door in his face, pushing the shell-shocked cop out of the threshold with the door.

"Wow!" Mary Carmen shrieked. "Are you like this in court?"

"Worse," Zack smiled. "Marshall, please continue. Refreshments are on the way."

"Where was I?" Marshall muttered, looking puzzled

"Defenses to deportation." Zack reminded him.

"Right, thanks."

"You're welcome."

"Let's see . . . defenses to deportation . . ." Marshall Mann was an excellent, aggressive advocate and lawyer. But even he had to marvel at the verbal skill, command, and presence of Zachary Blake; how effectively he handled the hostile law enforcement officer. It was easy to understand why Zack was one of the finest trial lawyers in the country.

"Okay, this might get a bit technical, but try to stay with me," Marshall continued.

"I will," Zack kibitzed, rolling his eyes at Mary Carmen and Miguel, who laughed.

"Funny guy, Blake. May I continue?" Marshall sighed.

"You may."

"Where was I?"

"Defenses to deportation," Zack repeated.

"Right."

Before Marshall could open his mouth again, Weber knocked at the door. Zack opened it. Weber hesitated at the threshold, waiting for Zack's permission to enter. Zack had completely knocked the arrogant federal cop off his game.

"Don't just stand there, Weber. Come on in. We're hungry."

"Brought you a few sandwiches, some snacks, and drinks. Will there be anything else, Mr. Blake?"

"You might consider passing some of this stuff around to all those folks who have been living on crackers and water for the last few days," Zack grumbled.

Weber paused as if considering Zack's request.

"We're good, Weber. We shouldn't be too much longer." He again shut the door in Weber's face.

"Defenses to deportation," he turned to Marshall.

"I remembered. The first thing we must do is to argue this whole damn circus is wrong and you guys weren't deportable in the first place. When you appear before the judge, you will be asked to admit or deny the facts that led to your arrest. You must either admit or deny the charges. You will, of course, deny them. Why? Because it is *Homeland Security's* obligation to present evidence and *prove* that you should be removed. Please understand, I'm saying we make them prove it; I'm not saying it isn't true. We all know you overstayed your visa. So, you are undocumented and probably removable. The next argument is that *DHS* seeks to remove you for the wrong reasons. If they can't show you're removable and can't state a valid reason, the judge has to dismiss the case."

"Is this possible?" Miguel wondered.

"It is possible, Miguel, not probable."

"Then, why do this?" Mary Carmen inquired.

"To make them prove their case. If they can't, you go home. Why should we concede this?"

"Makes sense to me," Zack chimed in. "Assuming it doesn't get summarily dismissed, what's next?"

"Even if *DHS* meets its burden and a judge decides you are deportable, you may still contest deportation. Again, the department has to *prove* the case. We don't have to give them any ammunition. I'm not suggesting you lie, but I am suggesting you not volunteer anything that might help them prove their case. Lying, for instance, could cause you to forfeit your right to apply for relief from removal, an asylum claim, for instance. Your credibility is very important in an asylum case."

"We don't lie," Miguel declared.

"Yes, you do, Miguel. You've been lying on the job and home rental applications, but that is not the same as lying to a judge. My best advice is to say nothing and let me do the talking." Miguel's defiant tone was gone in an instant.

"Tell us *everything*, but do not talk to anyone else about your case. Even if the judge asks you a question in court, don't answer. We will do the talking. The judge has no right to ask you anything unless we put you on the witness stand. The bottom line here is that just because you were caught doesn't automatically mean you will be deported. By the way, I know these conditions are deplorable, but you are lucky they decided to keep you close to home. Many people are taken to different states, sometimes cross-country. Has anyone asked you to sign anything?"

"No. Why?" Miguel wondered.

"Because I would not put it past these bastards to stick a document in front of you, without any explanation, and presto, you've signed away your rights."

"They would do that?" Mary Carmen was shocked.

"Who knows? Starting with the John Administration and now the Golding Administration, there is a huge bias against people who enter the country through our southern border, especially those who are undocumented. I wouldn't put anything past these bastards."

"We have signed nothing," Mary Carmen confirmed.

"Good. So, you *will* have your day in court. Have they given you an opportunity to contact your consulate?"

"No. In fact, it never occurred to me." Miguel shook his head, disgusted at himself.

"Don't beat yourself up. Very few think to do it, and even less know they have the right to make a call. Usually, all the consulate does is refer you to an attorney and you already have one."

"And a great one, my friends," Zack interrupted. "Marshall, what can we do to get these nice people out of this place, now?" he was getting impatient.

"I'm going to lean on Weber. He seems to be the federal officer in charge of this place."

"For what purpose?" Zack wondered

"I am reasonably certain Weber has the right to bond our clients out of here. Another of your infamous tirades and threats to involve the press should do the trick."

"I *love* threats and tirades," Zack chirped. "Now?"

"Why not?"

"Excuse me?" Mary Carmen peeped. "What are you talking about?"

"Sorry, don't mind us lawyers. We almost forgot you were here," Zack chortled. "Marshall is going to try to get you out of here, right now. How does that sound?"

"That would be wonderful, Mr. Blake!" Mary Carmen cried. "Mr. Marshall, is this true?"

"Let's not get ahead of ourselves, but yes, it is possible."

"What do we have to do?" Miguel wondered.

"Nothing. I keep telling you. You do nothing. Let me do all the talking and all the work. Okay?"

"Okay."

One hour later, Miguel and Mary Carmen Gonzalez, Zachary Blake, and Marshall Mann followed Officer Weber through the detention center. Mary Carmen carried a bag of sandwiches and other goodies. She began tossing them behind her to starving detainees. As the remaining detainees started to comprehend what was happening, a trickle of applause commenced. By the time the couple reached the exit, the applause and cheers were deafening.

Zachary Blake turned to the crowd and held up his hand for silence. The detainees immediately obliged.

"Ladies and gentlemen. You have rights! Demand to see an attorney! If they don't let you contact one, demand your release. Marshall and I will be back tomorrow to make sure you are being afforded your rights." The crowd cheered.

Zack turned to Weber with an icy glare. Weber tried to meet his glare and then dropped his eyes to the floor. *Shit! He'll be back tomorrow?*

Chapter Seven

As Canan, Hana, Avi, and Hassan headed from Damascus to Kobani, most of the traffic headed the opposite way, coming from nearby villages ahead. In fact, opposing traffic was congested, stop-and-go. Car after car they passed was overcrowded with people, often with 8 or 9 to a vehicle. People hung out windows and waved as they passed by. Belongings were secured on top with flimsy rope—beds, mattresses and frames, furniture, bags, suitcases, and the like adorned each vehicle, large and small.

The van was air-conditioned, but the heat was oppressive, so the air didn't help. Hassan kept the driver's side window cracked and constantly turned off the air conditioning explaining that the van would otherwise overheat. When he turned down the air, he'd crack the window a bit wider. A blast of hot air hit Canan and Hana in the back seat. Hassan and Avi were chatting in the front seat, but wind noise prevented Canan from hearing anything they said. Canan wondered if they were discussing possible danger zones on this lengthy highway to hell.

Traffic began to slow in their direction, first gradually, just a slight change in speed, and then, almost to a crawl. Hassan slammed his fists against the steering wheel and cursed loudly. Hana glanced, fearfully, to Canan. Canan smiled and tried to offer comfort, though she couldn't understand Hassan's sudden burst of anger. As the vehicle slowed, so did the wind. Canan could hear much better, but the vehicle became stifling hot. Sweat began to drip from her forehead and armpits. Hassan turned on the radio to see if he could find out what was going on. The newscaster was discussing a new campaign at the Turkish border and the presence of *ISIS* fighters along the route to Aleppo.

Hassan picked up his phone and keyed in a number. Traffic picked up a little as he waited for the call to connect. By the time the recipient picked up, the wind drowned out the conversation. Canan again was left to wonder what it was all about.

Canan considered the traffic volume headed back toward Damascus, where her entourage had begun their journey. She tried to scan each vehicle as it went by. Were any of them friends or relatives? Traffic now slowed in both directions, and Canan could make out faces, people of all ages, scared, determined, defiant, happy, tearful, adventurous—such a range of emotions. Years of civil war had caused so many to leave a place that so many had called home for centuries.

So many people, all of their belongings packed into vehicles. Their whole lives had been lived in the north—everything they built was probably there. Why were they leaving now? Was something happening? Where are they going, and where will they stay? How dangerous is this trip? Should we turn back?

Whatever caused the slowdown was over, and traffic resumed to previous speeds. Hana fell asleep in the warm breeze, and Canan felt herself beginning to doze off as well. She must have fallen asleep because she was jolted awake when the van began to slow again. The windows were closed; the air conditioning was working better, and the air was considerably cooler in the van. She noticed that dusk was upon them, and headlights were illuminated on all passing vehicles.

"Traffic?" She leaned forward and questioned Avi. She scanned her surroundings and was surprised to see that they were one of few vehicles on the road. Hassan slowed to almost a stop for no apparent reason. Canan sensed the tension in the front seat.

"Actually, I believe it's a roadblock," Avi casually observed. A roadblock in this area was not necessarily something to be concerned about. The Syrian government had random checkpoints all over the country. Checkpoints made sense on the way to the northern border with Turkey, especially considering the conflict. Syrian soldiers would check ID and search vehicles for contraband or weapons.

"We can see the barriers, but we cannot make out the soldiers. That's why we slowed down," explained Hassan.

"I don't understand," Canan was confused.

"These might not be soldiers."

Canan instinctively glanced at Hana. "Terrorists?" She shuddered.

"We can't tell. We will proceed with caution," Avi warned.

The van creeped forward. Canan realized she was holding her breath and shivering, despite the intense heat. *Thanks to Allah, my princess is sleeping!*

Hassan could now make out the soldiers at the checkpoint. They were dressed in black from head to toe, faces covered with black hoods and masks. They carried assault rifles. Jeeps and Hummers blocked traffic on both sides of the highway. A couple of the men carried torches, which illuminated their masks. Hassan looked left, right, and into his rearview. There was nowhere to go.

Canan huddled closer to her sleeping child as the vehicle inched slowly toward the checkpoint. Hassan and Avi were constantly leaning toward each other, mumbling quiet words Canan could not hear. Hassan steered the van off onto the shoulder a couple of times, so Avi could check out what was happening in front of them. The good news was that vehicles were being stopped, conversations were had between drivers and checkpoint guards, and vehicles were then allowed to pass through the checkpoint.

Avi turned to the back seat and whispered, "I'm not sure who they are, but no one is being detained for longer than a few minutes. Hopefully, they will let us pass with no problem."

"May *Allah* will it so." Canan prayed.

Hassan cracked the driver's side window in anticipation of a conversation with the guards. A blast of hot air and tiny sand particles smacked Canan in the face. She glanced at Hana, still asleep, and covered her face with a thin blanket. The wind picked up, and sand was blowing over the highway. Hassan leaned away from the window to avoid it. Canan was immediately uncomfortable, with sweat trickling down her temples.

Avi wrapped his hand wrapped around his pistol in anticipation of a confrontation with the checkpoint guards. He wasn't sure who these men were or how many there were, but he promised Karim that he would protect his family. Wondering whether the gun would protect them or place them in greater danger, Avi decided to put the weapon in the glove compartment. Slowly, the van approached the checkpoint. Avi counted ten heavily armed men.

One of the guards asked Hassan for identification, and he complied. While the two men engaged in conversation, a second heavily armed guard came around the front of the van and approached the front passenger side window. He demanded Avi's identification papers, and Avi complied as well. While looking over the papers, both guards asked questions about the passengers and their destination. Both men told the truth. Hassan was a professional driver hired by Avi to take him and the backseat passengers to Kobani. Avi was a family friend, hired by the woman's husband to escort her and the child to Kobani to visit family.

The guard on the driver's side leaned his head through the window and addressed Canan. "Identification, please?" he demanded. The man's breath was hot and foul. He reeked of body odor. Hassan tried to deflect the exchange.

"We have told you. She is going to Kobani to visit family."

"From where is she visiting? Identity papers, please." The guard persisted. And there it was—these men were checking the countries of origin for all vehicles going through the checkpoint. Avi was uneasy. *These men are not Syrian soldiers.*

Canan presented Hana's and her passports to Avi. Avi, in turn, gave them to the guard. The guard studied the passports, waved others over to the vehicle, and nodded to the guard on the other side.

"Step out of the vehicle," he ordered.

"Why?" Hassen demanded.

"Because if you don't, I will kill your friend here," the guard threatened, pointing an assault rifle at Avi.

"We're not looking for trouble—we just want to get to Kobani. What is the problem?" Avi pleaded.

"The woman and child are American," the passenger side guard muttered. He, too, pointed his assault rifle inside the vehicle. "Step out of the van. I will not ask again."

"What difference does it make that they are from America? Canan is originally from Kobani."

"Kurd?" The guard addressed Canan. Five men now surrounded the van, pointing assault rifles.

"Yes," Canan admitted. "Why? Does that matter?" She wondered.

"Kurdish *and* American? As they say in your country, we have hit the home run!" The guard proclaimed in broken English.

Avi and Hassan were now officially terrified for their passengers. Canan did not comprehend the reason for the guard's excitement.

"For the last time, step out of the van!" He shouted.

Avi and Hassan glanced at each other and shrugged. Avi turned to Canan and motioned her to exit the vehicle. Hana was now awake and softly whimpering. Canan slowly unlatched her seatbelt and then Hana's car seat buckle. She hoisted Hana up and out of the car seat and backed out of the van.

Avi and Hassan carefully exited the front seat with their hands raised.

"Do you have weapons?" A guard demanded.

"Pistol in the glove box," Avi admitted.

The guard reached into the glove box and retrieved the pistol.

"Search them," a guard, apparently the team leader, ordered one of the men. A quick search of the four occupants and the vehicle revealed no additional weapons. Hana began to screech in fear.

"Shut that child up," the head guard shouted. "Or I will do so," he threatened.

Canan began to bounce the child, humming and motioning her to be still. Hana calmed slightly.

The guard turned to the two men. "You have two options: One, we kill all of you right now, or two, you return to your vehicle and continue on your way."

"Obviously, we choose option two," Avi quipped.

"Without the woman and the child," the guard taunted.

"What? Why?" Avi knew the answer.

"Because they are valuable. Someone will pay very good money for them, no?"

"How much do you want?" Hassan demanded. "I'll see what I can arrange."

"No, not here, not now. I want their family to know they are hostages," the guard replied. "More money that way. Here is what we will do." He paused, thinking as he spoke, motioning Avi and Hassan toward the van.

"You men—get back in your van and continue on your way. The woman and child will stay with us. I do not want to see you on the other side of the highway back to Damascus unless it is with family members who seek to pay ransom. Do you understand? Get to Kobani—tell whoever is waiting for these two—we have the woman and child, and we will return them for one million U.S. dollars."

"One million dollars? Are you crazy? My family is poor. They have been caught up in a long war, as you well know! They don't have that kind of money! In fact, they don't have any money at all," Canan retorted.

"You will have to figure it out, then, because we will not release you unless we get paid."

"We cannot leave them alone with you. One of us will stay behind with the woman and child," Avi proposed.

"No. Both of you will go to Kobani and bring me my money," the guard insisted. "Now get in the vehicle—be gone!" He pointed his weapon at the two men and clicked the trigger.

Avi turned to Canan. "We have no choice, Canan. We will be back. I will make the arrangements. I promise."

"I like the sound of that," the guard approved. "On your way. Be gone, now!"

Avi and Hassan entered the van and drove off. Hassan peered into the rearview mirror as one of the guards pointed a rifle at and escorted Canan and Hana to a waiting Hummer. As the doors closed, the all-terrain vehicle immediately set off in a cloud of dust across the highway and into the desert.

"What do you want to do, Avi?" Hassan eyed his companion.

"Follow them."

"Follow them? Are you crazy?"

"Do you have a million dollars?"

"Of course not; you know this!"

"Well, neither do I, and neither does Canan's family. I know this for a fact."

"So what are we going to do?"

"We are going to follow them and kidnap them back."

"Uh . . . okay . . . as long as you have a sensible plan," Hassan quipped.

***

The smell of body odor in the Hummer was nauseating. Hana was screaming and crying—Canan could not calm her. Their captors seemed oblivious to the noise. The terrain was uneven. The car seat had been left behind in the van. Mother and child were brutally bounced around the back seat of the truck. Canan tried to remain calm. From time to time, she glanced out the window, hoping to see a landmark, something, anything, that might identify their approximate location. All she saw was moonlight and desert. She turned her head to look out the back window and observed what she thought was a faint cloud of dust, perhaps a half-mile back. Distances were hard to measure in the desert. Before she could turn back to the front, the butt end of a rifle struck her in the head, causing severe pain, ringing, dizziness, and, finally, total unconsciousness.

When she awoke, she was lying on the hard stone ground. Her hands were tied behind her back. Her body ached. Apparently, she was violently tossed to the hard ground. Her head pounded from the rifle butt, and she was immediately overcome with nausea. She managed to rise to her knees but became so dizzy she almost passed out. Overwhelming nausea induced intense vomit. She crawled away from the spot and noticed it contained a mixture of vomit and blood. *Mine?*

Where is Hana? What have they done with her? Her maternal instincts suddenly overcame pain, fear, dizziness, and omnipresent nausea. "Hana?" she cried. "Hana!"

"Sleeping beauty has awakened," a voice mocked from a distance. It was almost pitch black. Canan turned in the direction of the voice but could see nothing.

"Where is my daughter? Bring her to me immediately," she demanded.

Her invisible captor began to laugh, a chuckle at first, then a loud, obnoxious, taunting guffaw, torturing Canan, somehow knowing that Hana was the most important person in the world. Her captor decided to let her off the hook.

"She is safe, asleep nearby. If you behave, you will see her soon. We need to get you cleaned up. It stinks in here. Take off your clothes."

"I am handcuffed. I can't do anything."

"I forgot."

Canan heard a faint grunt as the man rose from a reclining position. Slowly, he emerged, first a large shadow, and then the features of a man came into focus, the man who stood at the driver's side window and demanded they all exit the van.

"What do you want from us?" She insisted.

"What I said earlier—money. If your men come through, you will both be released, unharmed."

"And I said earlier that it is impossible. We are poor people. We have no money."

"The United States government has lots of money. When they discover a citizen is being held hostage, they will offer assistance."

"The United States does not negotiate with terrorists."

"Terrorists? *We* are the terrorists?" he mocked. "That is naïve, pretty one. The U.S. *always* negotiates with terrorists if the photo opportunity at the end is worth the money. In this case, saving an American woman and child will be worth a fortune."

"Where is my daughter?" Canan changed the subject.

"I told you, she is sleeping. Behave and you'll see her soon. Do you wish to clean up a bit, change clothes, perhaps?" Canan found it amusing that this smelly, foul man believed she needed to freshen up, but he was correct—she needed a bath and a fresh outfit.

"Yes, but these handcuffs? And I am not removing my clothing in front of you." She wanted to add "swine" at the end but held her tongue.

"If you behave, you will soon see your child. If you don't . . ." He floated the ominous threat.

"Please remove the handcuffs, sir. A wash rag, soap, and warm water, a fresh *abaya* and *hijab* would be nice."

"Let me see what I can do. I will be back." He pulled back the flap of what she now knew was a tent and exited through the opening. He did not return for almost an hour, making Canan quite anxious in his absence. She hated him, to be sure, but, at that moment, he was the only link between her and her precious Hana. Besides, he warned her that misbehavior would result in prolonged separation from her daughter. That threat alone was enough to assure her compliance.

Finally, the flap opened. A woman entered, fully covered, holding a basin of water and some bandages, an *abaya* and *hijab* over her arm. Silently, she removed the handcuffs, helped Canan undress and wash, cleaned and dressed her wounds, and helped her into the fresh traditional garb. After her mission was completed, the woman reapplied Canan's handcuffs. Still, the captive woman felt much better.

"My daughter? Have you seen my daughter?" Canan pleaded. Only the woman's eyes were visible through her *burka*. She glared at Canan with soft eyes and shook her head up and down. She turned, pulled back the flap, and surveyed their surroundings. Satisfied they were alone, she lowered the flap and turned back to Canan.

"The little one is fine," she promised. "I am charged with her care."

"Where is she? Can you bring her to me?" Canan pleaded.

"I cannot. I must follow commands. If and when I am permitted to do so, I will bring her to you. I will do all I can to assure her safety. I'm sorry this is happening to you, but I fear for my safety and my life, as well."

"I understand. Please tell Hana you saw me and that I love her."

"I will do what I am permitted to do, nothing more, nothing less." With a grim expression, she turned and exited the tent.

After the woman's departure, Canan walked to the entrance and pressed her ear to the opening. She could hear heavy footsteps stomping around the complex. In the distance, she could barely make out men speaking Arabic, indecipherable voices engaged in conversation. And she heard their loud, haunting, chilling laughter. *What is so damned funny?*

Chapter Eight

Angry looking men in combat gear stormed the school. They surrounded the first adult they encountered and demanded directions to the school office. The terrified hall monitor pointed them to the office. In a scene reminiscent of a *Star Wars* episode, ten 'storm troopers' strutted over to the school office and barged inside. Stunned administrators and clerical workers dove for cover, contemplating how they might protect children currently in classrooms, terrified this was some type of school shooting or hostage-taking event.

"Who's in charge here?" One of the storm troopers demanded.

George Curley bravely emerged from his office and confronted the men.

"I am Principal Curley. Who the hell are you? What are you doing here? What is the meaning of this? You are scaring my staff, which, I presume, is your intent. Can we please turn down the temperature?" Curley stood, eye-to-eye, toe-to-toe, with the man.

The commander looked down at a piece of paper and read from it. "We are looking for Emma and Emilio Gonzalez."

"For God's sake! They are elementary school *children*. What do you want with them?"

"That's none of your business, sir. By authority of the United States government, Immigration and Customs Enforcement, I demand you take me to them."

"I will do no such thing." Curley turned, walked into his office, and picked up the phone to call Marshall Mann.

The commander trained an assault rifle on Curley. "Put down the phone, sir."

Curley ignored him and began pushing telephone buttons. "I'm calling our lawyer. We have a right to discuss this with counsel, do we not?"

"Later, perhaps. Right now, I am commanding you to put down the phone and take us to Emma and Emilio Gonzalez. If you do not obey this lawful command, I will have no choice but to place you into custody."

Curley completed dialing and waited for the phone to connect.

"Law Offices of Zachary Blake, may I help you?" Before Curley could respond, the commander rushed over to him, grabbed the receiver, and slammed it down in disgust.

"Jensen!" He addressed a young subordinate.

"Sir, yes sir?"

"Arrest this man!"

"Sir?" Jensen was stunned.

"Did I stutter, Jensen? Arrest this man."

"Yes sir." Jensen walked over to Curley and fumbled with a pair of handcuffs.

"Seriously?" Curley exclaimed. "Is this really necessary? I demand to see a warrant or any other paperwork that identifies you as *ICE or* authorizes you to storm into this peaceful place of learning and treat United States citizens in this manner!"

"We are authorized to conduct raids and arrest any, and all, foreign illegals. We may also arrest anyone who obstructs our efforts to do so. You, sir, are obstructing those efforts," the commander blustered.

"I'm not questioning your authority; I am questioning your methods and your intent. You did not need to storm in here and scare the living daylights out of everyone. You only needed to walk in and make a legal request. For your information, sir, the Gonzalez children are not 'foreign illegals,' as you call them. They are American citizens. Now, for everyone's sake, especially the Gonzalez children, please let me call our lawyer. I'm sure he can straighten this out."

Nine officers turned to the commander, thinking this suggestion made perfect sense. However, they weren't in charge.

"I'm going to give you one more chance, Mr. . . . ." He glanced at the principal's desk and nameplate . . . "Curley. Either show me to the classrooms of Emma and Emilio Gonzalez, or I will place you under arrest and have one of these other fine people show me the way." He turned to Curley's administrative staff. "I'm sure you do not wish to be arrested, correct?"

One of the senior staff members nodded. The others stayed completely still.

"What's it going to be, Curley? You can call the lawyer after we leave."

"You can count on that, sir. And I will also be talking with your boss."

"Have at it. We are here on his orders. Now take me to these children. I am losing my patience."

"This way." Curley pointed out the door. As the ten men turned to leave, Curley motioned to an assistant, put two fingers to his ear as if they were a telephone, and mouthed 'Call Blake.'

The men followed Curley down the hallway toward the classrooms. Curley stopped at Mr. Haskel's room and ventured in. The young elementary students were excited. One cried. "It's Mr. Curley! Mr. Curley came to visit!"

When the other kids turned toward the door, they were stunned at the sight of ten armed men tailing behind Curley.

"What the . . ." Haskel began.

"Emma or Emilio Gonzalez!" The commander roared, frightening the children. No one spoke. No one moved.

"Emma or Emilio Gonzalez!" The commander repeated.

"What is the meaning of this?" Haskel demanded. Tall and extremely thin, Haskel towered over the commander but was outweighed by at least fifty pounds of muscle.

The commander ignored him. "Emma or Emilio . . ."

"Here, sir," Emma stood.

"Come with me, young lady."

"Don't move, Emma," Haskel ordered. Emma stopped in her tracks.

"Now, see here, officer . . ." Curley began.

"Silence!" The commander snapped. "Emma Gonzalez, come with me now."

Emma began to cry. The commander walked over to her and lifted her up, intending to carry her out of the room. Emma screamed and began to punch the officer with her fists. The commander shifted Emma and wrapped his arms around hers, completely restraining the child. She continued to scream and cry hysterically. The commander walked out into the hall, followed by Curley, Haskel, and the other officers. Haskel was yelling at the top of his voice as Emma continued to scream. Classroom doors opened. Teachers entered the hallway to investigate the source of the commotion.

"Emilio Gonzalez!" the commander roared.

"Emma!" A child came running out of a neighboring room and up to the commander. "Let go of my sister!" he screamed, pounding his fists on the commander's legs.

"Will someone please secure this child?" the commander requested, exasperated, facing his soldiers.

"Sir, yes sir," replied an officer, coming forward and scooping up Emilio, much the same way his commander scooped up Emma.

"Let's go, men," the commander ordered.

"Where are you taking these children?" Emilio's teacher demanded. "You have no right . . ."

"We have the full weight and authority of the United States Government, ma'am. Take it up with your elected officials. To answer your question, we are taking them to the Detroit Detention Center. Inquiries may be made there."

"Where is that?" Curley demanded.

"Downtown Detroit, on East Jefferson. Now, if you'll excuse me. Thank you for your cooperation," he sneered.

Ten men and two screaming children scurried down the hall, past the school office, stunned teachers and administrators, and exited the building. They entered official-looking *SUV*s and drove off. Curley wrote down each license plate and ran back to his office to call Blake and Mann.

"Law Offices of Zachary Blake, how may I direct your call?" Kristin had been the office receptionist for years.

"Emergency call for Zachary Blake or Marshall Mann! This is George Curley speaking."

"May I reference a client, Mr. Curley?" Kristin remained calm. "Mr. Mann is in; Mr. Blake is not. Will that be okay?"

"Yes, please hurry. This is an emergency. The clients are Emma and Emilio Gonzalez."

Kristin was not familiar with these names and would ordinarily have pushed back. Curley sounded so distraught, though, she decided to alert Marshall Mann.

"Marshall? I have a Mr. Curley on the line. He says it's an emergency. He referenced Emma and Emilio Gonzalez."

"Patch him through, Kristin. Thank you," Mann replied.

"Marshall Mann here. George? What's wrong?"

"Oh, Mr. Mann! *ICE* agents just stormed into our school and walked off with the Gonzalez children! Help us, please!" He implored.

"Calm down, George. Tell me what happened. Where are the children?"

"They took them, Marshall! The guy in charge said something about the Detroit Detention Center on East Jefferson."

"Okay, George, that's very helpful. Did they say anything else?"

"Not really. They said that they were here by authority of the United States Government. They behaved like Nazi storm troopers. Scared the living daylights out of everyone at the school."

"I'll get on this right away, George. Thank you for calling. By the way, Mary Carmen and Miguel were released today. I will let them know what has happened. Perhaps we can get Senator Stabler or your district's Congressman involved. Do you know who it is?"

"Deidre Drummond."

"I will try to get her involved, too. You might want to call her yourself."

"You've got it, Marshall. Please, sir, help these poor people! They've done nothing wrong!"

"I'm on it, George. Thanks for the alert."

"Wait! Marshall? Are you still there?"

"Still here, George. What is it?"

"I copied the license plates of every vehicle they were driving."

"Excellent. I'm going to hire you as an investigator. Let's have the license plate numbers."

George read them off the sticky note in his hand.

"Thanks, George. We'll be in touch."

"Thank *you*, Marshall."

Marshall Mann hung up and immediately called Zachary Blake's cell phone.

"What's up, Marsh?" Zack answered.

"We've got a big problem, Zack. Where are you?"

"Just leaving the City-County Building, why? What's wrong?"

"*ICE* just picked up the Gonzalez children."

"Wha . . .what do you mean, 'picked up'? Can they do that?"

"These kids are American citizens, Zack. Of course they can't do that. I am guessing this is a case of *ICE* assuming these kids are undocumented because their parents are. I'm sure this is just a bureaucratic snafu. According to the school principal, the kids were taken to the Detroit Detention Center over on Jefferson, about a mile east of where you are. Do you have time to run over and straighten these creeps out? I'll get ahold of Mary Carmen or Miguel and get the kids' birth certificates. *ICE* can't detain or deport American citizens for crying out loud."

"If they have cell phones with a camera, any camera, have them take photos of the birth certificates and text them to me so I can show them to the detention center people."

"Will do. Good luck. Keep me posted."

"No problem, Marsh."

***

One half-hour later, Zachary Blake parked his car in a pothole-filled parking lot of the Detroit Detention Center. The place looked like an abandoned building, the kind the media displays in documentaries tracking Detroit's demise and decay. While there is absolutely urban blight in Blake's favorite city, he despised the focus of these documentaries.

There were less than ten cars in the parking lot and one large black van with no official markings. Zack approached the van, cupped his hand, and pressed his hand and face against the side window, hoping to see inside. Tinted glass prevented him from seeing anything.

"Excuse me, sir," a gruff male voice caused him to jump backward. "Please step away from the vehicle."

"Is this the Detroit Detention Center?" Zack questioned the middle-aged mustachioed man with a potbelly and a non-descript uniform.

"Who's asking?" The man grumbled.

"My name is Blake, Zachary Blake. Yours?" Zack challenged.

"Billings, Captain Gordon Billings. State your business, Blake, or get the hell out of here. You're trespassing."

"I'm a citizen, Billings. This *is* a government facility, is it not?"

"It is, but it is not open to the general public, by order of the president himself," Billings blustered. "Now, are you going to tell me what you're doing here, or do I have to have you escorted off these premises?" Without taking an eye off Zack, Billings unhooked a walkie-talkie from a shoulder strap and pressed the device to his mouth.

"Okay, Billings. Let's lower the temperature a bit. I'm an attorney, and I have been advised that my clients were taken to this facility. They are small children, probably frightened to death. I'm sure you'll agree this is no place for a child."

"Well, Blake, we do agree on something, but you have been misinformed. There are no children here."

"I have it on good information there are," Zack insisted.

"Your information is inaccurate, sir," Billings softened. "There are no children here. I'm not supposed to do this, but I will let you see for yourself if you promise to behave."

Zack raised two fingers in the air and smirked. "Scouts honor, chief."

"I'm *Captain* Billings, not chief."

"Aye-aye, Captain," Zack saluted.

"I'm changing my mind . . ." Billings turned away and pressed the button on his walkie-talkie. Someone on the other end responded, "Yes, Captain?"

Zack capitulated. "I'll be good. I promise."

They walked into the building. Much like the center in Riverview, the sights and smells were astonishing. It was hot, humid, and smelled of human feces. Zack gagged and pulled out a handkerchief to cover his nose. His eyes watered. This center was larger than Riverview, and hundreds, if not thousands of Latino adults were crowded into makeshift cages, crying, coughing, and screaming in Spanish. Snack food wrappings and empty water bottles were scattered all over the floor. There were no temperature controls or windows.

"See, Blake, no kids." Billings scanned the room in a casual manner. The sights and smells of the place did not seem to bother him.

"What is it with you people, Billings? These are human beings! This is just like the center I visited in Riverview. You jam people into cages without showers, sanitation, or change of clothing. What did these folks do to deserve this deplorable treatment in the United States of America?" Zack ranted.

"They're illegal. They have no civil rights," Billings argued.

"Bullshit, Billings. *Flores* mandates safe and sanitary . . . *God Dammit!* That's the national standard!" Zack roared.

Billings ignored him and placed his hand on Zachary's back, gently pushing him toward the door. "Not my pay grade, counselor. Take it up with Homeland. No kids here."

"Take your hand off my back. I know the way. I'll be back with a court order shutting this place down, you son-of-a-bitch."

Billings removed his hand as Zack headed for the door. Zack's cellphone buzzed. Marshall Mann was texting the children's birth certificates.

"Knock yourself out, counselor. We'll be here when you get back," Billings blustered. "This shit has been tested before and these centers are still here. They serve a vital purpose."

"What purpose is that?" Zack cackled over his shoulder. "Total dehumanization of Latinos?"

"*Undocumented* Latinos; *non-citizens* with no civil rights in our country," Billings corrected.

"We'll see about that, asshole."

"One more word of disrespect out of you and I'll have you arrested and detained for disorderly conduct and disobeying a federal officer."

Zack stopped in his tracks and turned back to study Billings. "Go for it, Captain. You have no idea who you're dealing with," Zack threatened.

"One more arrogant lawyer is the way I see it. You have two choices, Blake. Turn your ass around and get the hell out of here, or I will have my men arrest and detain you." He retrieved his walkie-talkie and held it to his mouth.

Part of Zachary Blake wanted to be arrested and detained. It would make a terrific news story and focus attention on the deplorable conditions he witnessed at two separate *INS* detention facilities. He wanted to file a massive and very public wrongful arrest and imprisonment lawsuit against the *INS* and Homeland Security. *Prominent attorney Zachary Blake illegally detained at INS detention center—files multi-million dollar lawsuit against the Feds for civil rights violations—details at eleven.* However, the practical side of Blake overrode his emotions. *I can't do my clients any good locked up in these filthy and disgusting cages.*

With great restraint and without another word, Zachary Blake turned and walked toward the exit. When he reached the door, without turning back, he raised his right hand, extended his middle finger, and offered Captain Gordon Billings the respect the man deserved.

Chapter Nine

Canan paced around the tent. It seemed like hours since her last encounter with the woman who attended to her cuts and abrasions. *Is Hana okay? Will they let me see her? Be with her? She must be terrified! What are they doing to her? Is the woman protecting her?* In many ways, her mental torture was worse than captivity. Fear for her daughter's safety prevented worry over her own physical and mental welfare. She was frantic.

The slit in the tent opened, and a large dark-skinned man in a *dishdasha* robe and headscarf entered the tent. The woman who cleaned and dressed Canan's wounds followed closely behind, head lowered, staring at the dirt floor. Canan was excited to see someone, *anyone*.

"Where is my daughter?" Canan demanded.

The man raised his arm and backhanded Canan across the face, knocking her across the room. The stunned woman lay on the hard dirt floor whimpering in pain.

"I ask the questions, understood?" The man roared.

"Yes," Canan managed a whisper. "But my daughter . . ."

The man raised his arm a second time, but the woman interrupted. "I told you; she is fine. I am taking care of her."

The huge beast glared angrily from one woman to the other. Suddenly, his mood softened. "Where are you from, woman?" he asked Canan.

"U-United States," Canan muttered, still on the floor. She rubbed the left side of her face, dazed, in obvious pain.

"I know you are from the demon country. Where?"

"Michigan."

"You are a long way from home. What are you doing here?"

"I came to visit my mother. She's never met her granddaughter," Canan whispered, recovering her wits.

"Where does your mother live?"

"Kobani."

"Kobani no longer exists," the man growled.

"But . . ."

"Silence, woman! Enough!" the man roared. His eyes blazed with fury as he started toward Canan with a raised hand. Canan, still on the floor, cowered in fear. The woman stepped between Canan and the man. The brute stopped short, shocked at her intervention.

"Leave her be, Qassim. She's terrified. She cannot hurt you, and you have her child. She will obey. Besides, is it wise to abuse a woman you are attempting to ransom?"

Surprisingly, the man yielded. He seemed to consider the potential wisdom of her observation.

"Abuse equals fear, Rima! They will pay more when they see cuts and bruises. Out of my way, woman!"

"No, Qassim. She will behave. I will take responsibility. If she does not obey, you may beat *me*."

"I need no permission to beat *you*," he roared. He raised his arm to strike the woman, expecting her to retreat. She stood her ground and glared at him, not moving, not flinching. Qassim paused, huffed, turned, and left the tent.

"Thank you," a shocked Canan gasped, rising from the floor.

"You must not antagonize this man," Rima warned. "He is a brutal, inhuman bully."

"Who has my daughter," Canan reminded her.

"You do not believe he would hurt a child?"

"I'm certain he would. I am not naïve. I want him to focus on me. Hana is all that matters. Where is she? Can you take me to her?"

"Be patient. She is safe for now."

"For now?" Canan quivered.

"I meant nothing by this. She is safe. No one will hurt her. She is too valuable as a hostage."

"I pray you are correct."

***

Hassan and Avi followed the Hummer at a safe distance and stopped about a quarter-mile from the camp, as close as they could get without being spotted by the terrorists. Avi scanned the area through a pair of binoculars and spoke to Hassan as he considered their surroundings.

"There are ten, maybe twelve of them—at least one is a woman. There's this huge, dark man who appears to be their leader."

"Let me take a look," Hassan motioned for Avi to hand him the binoculars. Hassan fiddled with the focus and looked through the binoculars. A few seconds later, he gasped.

"What is it, Hassan?" Avi inquired.

"I'm almost positive the big guy is Qassim Al-Baklavi, number two at *ISIS*. He's a very bad dude. This is way above our pay grade."

"What does that mean? We have been well paid. We have an obligation to Karim and Canan. They are family friends," Avi argued.

"We have an obligation to live through this ordeal, Avi. We have no obligation to *die*. Besides, I do not suggest we abandon your friends. However, we need reinforcements and a plan. These men do not know we followed them and that is to our advantage. We need money and men."

"Money?"

"We must buy the men we need; the best men money can buy, especially if our target is Al-Baklavi. The best thing we can do now is to get out of here before we are spotted."

Hassan motioned Avi to the Mercedes and ventured toward the van. Avi paused, weighing his options. He quickly determined there were no good alternatives. He obeyed Hassan.

As they climbed into the van, Avi pulled out his cellphone and began to dial. Hassan started the van and took off in the direction they came from. Hassan glanced at Avi.

"Who are you calling?" Hassan inquired.

"Canan's husband, Karim Izady."

"Does he have money?"

"I do not know his finances. I have let him down. His wife and daughter were my responsibility. Why should he trust me? I have failed him."

"We need money, Avi. What other choice does he have?"

The phone rang. A man answered.

"Hello?"

"Karim?"

"Avi? Is that you?"

"Yes, Karim."

"Are Canan and Hana with you? Please, let me talk to them."

"They are not with me, Karim. Please, let me explain."

"Explain?" Karim was confused.

"Listen to me, Karim. I am sorry to report that your worst fears have been realized. Canan and Hana have been taken hostage."

Karim reacted with total silence.

"Karim? Are you there?"

"What do you mean, 'taken hostage'? Where? By whom?"

"In Syria, Karim. We believe they were taken by *ISIS*."

"*ISIS*? No! What would *ISIS* want with a young woman and a child?"

"Money, Karim. They want money."

"But I am not a wealthy man, Avi. Surely you know this!"

"We will need money for ransom or men for a rescue. I do not know what else to say."

"I thought these terrorists were no longer a threat. How could you let this happen? I *trusted* you! You let me down. Canan and Hana are my *life*!"

"I'm so sorry, Karim. There was little we could do. Men blocked the road, stopped our van, and took them. We followed them . . . we know where they are keeping them. But we need men, lots of men."

"You know your country better than I. *You* obtain these men you need."

"I do not have access to these types of men. We need *specialists*. I don't have the kind of money we need to buy this level of talent."

"My precious family . . . what am I going to do? How much time do I have?"

"They want money more than they want to kill your family. They will give us some time to raise money. A few days, perhaps a week, we must act quickly. Is there anyone you can call?"

"I have to think. I can reach you at this number?"

"Yes, Karim. I am so, so sorry, my friend."

"I know you are," Karim softened. "I am sure you did everything you could." Karim was quite angry, but *what value is anger?* "I will make phone calls."

***

Karim Izady terminated the call and quickly dialed Imam Ghaffari. Ghaffari answered on the first ring.

"*Salaam Alaikum*, Karim. How is your family?" Ghaffari recognized the number.

"Imam Ghaffari. All praise to *Allah.* I need help."

"What's wrong?"

"My wife and daughter have been taken hostage in Syria. The guide we hired thinks it is *ISIS.*"

"Syria? What are they doing in Syria?"

"Canan wanted to take Hana to meet her mother. I did not want her to go, but a grandmother has a right to meet her grandchild, yes?"

"Yes, Karim. Of course."

"I need to raise money."

"Ransom?"

"Yes, Imam Ghaffari. We need to raise the ransom, or we need to hire a team of professionals to rescue them."

"Is this possible?"

"Avi says it is."

"Who is this Avi?"

"The guide in Syria who lost them."

"How do you know this Avi is not pulling a scam to get your money?"

This thought never occurred to Karim. He considered the idea for a moment.

"Avi is a family friend. He would not do this. This is real, Imam, a hostage crisis."

"Very well, Karim. Allow me to make a phone call. I will get back to you as soon as I can."

"Thank you, Imam. Thank you from the bottom of my heart."

"I haven't done anything. Let me make a call."

***

Baquir Ghaffari hung up the phone and immediately dialed the Dearborn Police. He asked for one of his congregational members, a police lieutenant named Shaheed Ali. Ali was part of an elite anti-terrorist task force for the Dearborn P.D. and second in command to Captain Jack Dylan. A few years ago, a couple of white supremacist groups bombed the mosque and plotted to release Sarin gas on the Dearborn Muslim community. Dylan, Shaheed, their task force, and Zachary Blake foiled the plot and brought the terrorists to justice.

In the middle of it all, a young Muslim woman named Arya Khan was accused of murdering one of the terrorists. Arya, represented by attorney Blake, was exonerated at trial. In an act of revenge, she was taken hostage. After Arya was rescued, Blake, Dylan, Ali, and the Dearborn task force became permanent heroes in the Dearborn Muslim community.

"Lieutenant Ali speaking. How may I assist you?" Shaheed answered the phone.

"*Salaam Alaikum*, Shaheed—Imam Ghaffari here."

"Imam Ghaffari! So nice to hear from you. How can I help you?"

"One of our members has a serious problem. Do you know Canan and Karim Izady?"

"I do not believe so. No matter, what's the problem?"

"Karim's wife and daughter, Canan and Hana, have disappeared in Syria. We believe *ISIS* has taken them hostage for ransom."

"Syria? Why are they in Syria?"

"Canan's mother still lives in Kobani and has been unable to leave because of the conflict. Canan apparently decided to take her daughter to see her grandmother."

"Syria is dangerous enough. There is war at the border with Turkey. She took a child into a war zone?"

"It is done, Shaheed—no use dwelling on why."

Leave it to Imam Ghaffari to put things in proper perspective. "How can I help you Imam? I have no jurisdiction overseas." Shaheed grew impatient.

"I don't know who else to call, Shaheed. Hana and Canan were taken at a highway checkpoint. They were traveling with a guide and bodyguard. When they were taken, the guard and the guide followed the getaway vehicle. They know where they are being held. They need money, a rescue team, and perhaps a hostage negotiator. Karim and Canan are wonderful people and citizens of the United States. Zachary Blake's firm did the immigration work."

"Zack knows these people?" Shaheed inquired. *The connection might be promising.*

"I'm not sure. Zachary's firm has an immigration lawyer, Marshall Mann. He handled the case."

"Marshall is a great lawyer, too. How about this? I'll talk to Jack, tell him what's going on, and see if he has any thoughts about the situation. Maybe he or Zack will know someone that can help. Do you know what I mean?"

"Yes, Shaheed. I appreciate it. I know the Izady family will be very grateful. So will I."

"I'll do what I can. Let me see if Jack's in. I'll call you back."

The two men ended the call. Shaheed made a beeline for Jack Dylan's office. Dylan was on speakerphone with Chief Acker. He pointed to a side chair and signaled for Shaheed to have a seat.

"I understand, Chief. But why is he coming to Dearborn of all places? No one likes him here," Jack grumbled into the speaker.

"Like him or not, we are honored to have a sitting president come to our city. The Secret Service will take the lead on security. They want you and the task force to provide back-up and local expertise," the chief responded.

"Because I have always played so nice with the feds? Aye-aye, Chief," Dylan quipped.

"Seriously, Jack? Take this seriously, please?"

"So long as it isn't Ronald John. I'd be inclined to assist in any attempt to harm that bastard!" Jack did not like the former president, who would soon be the first in history to reside in federal prison.

"Hush, Dylan. Comments like that might land *you* in prison for treason."

"He's no longer president, and he'll be an inmate to boot. Treason won't apply to a convicted criminal private citizen in the federal pen." Jack glanced and winked at Shaheed.

"Perhaps not, but play nice with President Golding."

"When is this supposed to happen again?"

"No firm date has been set. I'll keep you posted."

"Anything else?"

"That's it for now."

As Acker was about to sign off, Jack terminated the call without saying goodbye.

"Why do you deliberately antagonize the boss?" Shaheed shook his head, slightly bewildered.

"Because it's fun. Besides, you know how I feel about the chain of command."

"It ends with you?"

"Did I say that? What brings you here this fine morning?"

"One of our citizens has a situation."

"Situation? What kind of *situation*?"

"I just got off the phone with Baquir Ghaffari. One of our mosque's members called him for help. Apparently, this guy's wife and daughter went to Syria to visit the wife's mother. En route, their van was stopped at a checkpoint. It turned out to be *ISIS* and all hell broke loose. The wife and kid have been kidnapped for ransom."

"That's what they get for going to Syria. This is a matter for Homeland or the *CIA*. What's it got to do with us?"

"I believe Karim Izady would like to handle this privately without involving the feds. He's afraid their anti-negotiation policy will hamper efforts to get his wife and daughter home safely."

"He's not wrong, especially since remnants of the John administration are still in charge in Washington. But again, what's it got to do with us?"

"Karim wants to privately put together a team to either handle the ransom and recovery or to rescue his family."

"Oh, that's all?" Jack grunted. "You still haven't told me. What's . . ?"

"I know, I know, what's this got to do with us? Karim and his wife are naturalized citizens. Blake's firm handled the immigration work. I was thinking. Between the task force, Zack's legal and financial connections, and Micah Love and his team, maybe we could put something together. What do you think?"

"These people are that important to you?"

"No, but Imam Ghaffari *is* that important, and he asked me, personally, for help."

"Can't argue with that. The Imam is an important man in this town, especially in East Dearborn. Want me to call Zack?"

"Would you mind?"

"Not at all. Anything else? I've got a lot of work to do." Jack rose, dismissing Shaheed. The lieutenant did not move. "Shaheed? Oh, I get it. You want me to call Zack right this minute?"

"Would you, boss? That would be great!" Shaheed smiled.

Jack grumbled and rolled his eyes. He picked up the telephone and punched in Blake's number.

"Law Offices of Zachary Blake, how may I direct your call?" Kristin answered the phone on the first ring.

"Hey, Kristin. Jack Dylan here. How the hell how you? Long time—no talk."

"Captain Dylan! How nice to hear from you. Staying out of trouble?"

Jack was very familiar with the Blake firm. He had been a client after being accused of murder in a small northern Michigan town. Zack came to his rescue and got him fully exonerated at trial. While cops and criminal defense lawyers do not usually get along, *this* cop and *this* lawyer were good friends, with great respect for each other.

"I'm behaving these days. I'm calling for a citizen. Is Zack in?"

"He's not. May I give him a message?"

"How about Marshall Mann?"

"Let me check for you."

"Thanks, Kristin."

Jack listened to music on hold until the line clicked.

"Marshall Mann. May I help you?"

"Hey, Marshall. Jack Dylan here."

"Jack—nice to hear from you. Everything okay?"

"Yes, but one of your clients has a problem." Jack filled Marshall in on the Izady situation.

"That's awful, Jack! You may not know these people, but I know them very well. They are great people. How can I help?"

"I'm not sure yet. Do you know where Zack is?"

"I do. He's on his way back from an *ICE* detention center. Have you seen any of these places?"

"Can't say that I have. I have *heard* a few things. Not our country's finest work."

"Understatement of the year. Animals in shelters are treated better. What's the plan?"

"Karim Izady wants to put together a rescue or hostage negotiation team. I thought with our task force and Zack and Micah's connections, maybe we could put our heads together and come up with a plan."

"Karim and Canan are the best. They deserve our best. I'll talk to Zack as soon as he returns. He's due any minute."

"Thanks, Marshall. You'll call me after you talk to Zack?"

"You bet, Jack. Thanks for letting me know. How do we know Canan and her daughter are safe?"

"We don't."

"Love your positivity. Glass half empty person?"

"I'm a realist. No sense sugar-coating the truth. We have no idea what's going on halfway around the world. All I can say is these guys want money. They know they won't get it without proof of life—I would have to assume they are safe . . . for now."

"Makes sense. I'll get back to you.

"Thanks, Marshall."

Jack's cellphone chirped about fifteen minutes later. He glanced at the screen and connected with Zack Blake.

"Zack?" Jack usurped the call.

"Yeah, Jack. Marsh filled me in. How can we help?"

"We need money, men, and a plan, in that order."

"Is that all?" Zack chuckled. "I love your no-bullshit approach to these things. Marsh says these people are clients and great people. That's all I need to know. Money is no object. Micah once mentioned a private security firm he uses from time to time. They specialize in Middle East ops. Mind if I bring Micah into this?"

"Not at all. I was hoping you'd get him involved. I figured he'd know someone."

"I'll talk to him. If he can help, we'll set up a meeting."

"We need to do this *yesterday*, Zack. I don't know how long the lady and her daughter will be safe."

"I read you, Jack. I'll talk to Micah and call you back."

The following day, Jack, Shaheed, Karim Izady, Zack, Marshall, Micah, and a huge muscle-bound tough guy, dressed in black, sat in the main conference room of the Blake law office. The room was huge. A twenty-foot coffee and cream-colored marble table stood in the middle with plush executive chairs on all sides. Table and chairs sat on a stunning oriental rug, surrounded by mahogany bookcases full of law books on all four walls. A large screen television hung in the middle of cabinets on one side. A large projector screen hung on the opposite side.

An ornate platter sat in the center of the table. Two servers stood on opposite sides of the table, prepared to serve the attendees coffee, fresh-squeezed orange and grapefruit juice, and a buffet of breakfast items.

Micah—of course—ignored the servers and began to help himself. He grabbed the orange juice pitcher, poured himself a full glass, drank the whole thing down, and finished with a loud "ahh." He wiped his mouth with his sleeve, picked up and inspected a firm-logoed mug, and filled it with more cream than coffee. He took a swig, put the cup down on a logoed coaster, and grabbed two plates. He piled eggs, bacon, sausage, and hash browns on one plate and a variety of pastries on the other. Finally, he picked up a cloth napkin wrapped place setting and three extra paper napkins as he studied the entire buffet a second time. Temporarily satisfied, he sat down, unrolled the cloth napkin, retrieved a fork, and began shoving food in his mouth.

Suddenly, he glanced up and noticed everyone was staring at him.

"What?" he mumbled with his mouth full, spitting food on the table in front of him.

"Wow, Micah . . . this is not an ocean cruise buffet!" Zack zinged, cracking everyone up.

Micah stood his ground. He would not be shamed or intimidated. "Why put the food out if you don't want people to eat it?" he whined.

Zack glanced at Micah's two five thousand calorie plates. "The food is for *everyone*, Micah. I'm sure others would like a turn. Besides, I thought you were on a diet."

"I'm on the see-food diet. I see food—I eat it." He cleared his throat, pounded on the table, changed the subject, and grumbled: "I hereby call this meeting to order. I presume we are not assembled here today to discuss my eating habits?"

"That's correct, Micah. Nice to see you," Shaheed laughed.

"Likewise. Thank you all for coming. Be sure to eat lots of Zack's food. By the way, people, allow me to introduce my colleague and good friend Wayne Parsons. Wayne owns *PISS*—that's Parsons International Surveillance and Security, a private security firm made up mostly of former Seals, operators from US Military Special Operations, and other select US agencies. *PISS* operatives possess elite skill sets and experience required for complex, high-risk operations. The firm specializes in Middle Eastern situations. Wayne?"

"Jesus, Micah. I've asked you a thousand times! Stop calling my company *PISS*. Nice to meet all of you." Wayne sighed.

"P-I-S-S, huh? I presume you didn't consider people like Micah when you named the company. Am I right? I also presume you never thought you'd deal with anyone so immature," Zack observed. "I'm Zack Blake, by the way."

"Nice to meet you, Zack. Micah's told me a lot about you. I'd like to think my firm is to private security and surveillance what the Blake firm is to law. And you're correct—I didn't consider the possible acronym or the warped mind of someone like Micah."

Everyone laughed, including Micah, who again spit food everywhere. The meeting commenced, and the servers began to politely serve food and drink as business was being conducted. Avi and Hassan appeared by speakerphone and provided an update on ground conditions in Syria. Karim displayed an electronic map of the area and approximated the location of the camp.

There were clear negatives and positives with the location. There was minimal cover, other than darkness. So, the rescue attempt would have to be launched in the evening. However, if Wayne's operatives were able to surround the camp and surprise the terrorists, there appeared to be nowhere for the bad guys to run or hide. The group spent long hours, though a catered lunch and dinner—much to Micah's delight—planning and plotting until a cogent operation began to develop.

Parsons was indeed a pro. He displayed a PowerPoint slide describing a hostage-taking or hostage crisis as a three-phase event. The first phase had already happened—Canan and Hana were taken. Parsons officially called this the Initial Phase. In this phase, the hostages might be roughed up, injured, even killed. The Initial Phase begins with the abduction and subduing of the prey and ends with a ransom or other demand, perhaps a hostage exchange. Because Avi and Hassan indicated that Canan and Hana were taken without incident or injury, Parsons opined, the group should consider itself fortunate.

The next phase occurs when a law enforcement negotiator or private mediator arrives and acknowledges the hostage takers' demands. Parsons called this the Negotiation Phase. If the team decided negotiations were feasible, this phase would likely last hours, days, weeks, or even months. Parsons opined that specialists in the field often referred to this phase as the Standoff Phase. Nothing much seems to happen—hence the term standoff—but numerous things actually *do* happen during the Negotiation Phase. Practical and emotional relationships are developed between all involved. The negotiator tries to establish some measure of trust with the hostage-takers or otherwise manipulate the relationship toward a peaceful end to the situation.

Parsons referred to the third phase as the Termination Phase. One possible result is peaceful—the hostage-takers' demands are met and both sides escape the event unharmed. Other possibilities are often violent. Negotiations fail to prompt a resolution, and rescue is attempted. One scenario might be an arrest or peaceful surrender without injury. Another might be an assault by the team, resulting in possible injury or death to the hostage-takers or hostages.

Parsons wondered aloud about the aim of the operation. Did they want an Initial Phase and a Negotiation Phase, or was this a Termination Phase mission only? They did not have to make that decision, but the retainer and ultimate cost of the operation depended on its scope and complexity. Given the logistics of the situation, Parsons opined that they might want to ignore the initial two phases and go straight to the rescue or Termination Phase.

In addition to helping to plan and implement the negotiation and rescue, Parsons' company would also handle security and training for all personnel. Each of his operatives had twenty-plus years of experience providing armed protection in some of the most dangerous environments on the planet. His team would make a threat assessment, develop a plan. They would then engage in operational intelligence, submit the plan for approval, and, upon approval, implement it.

Dylan and Ali wanted to be part of the operation. Micah wanted to assemble a backup team and participate. Zack had a busy schedule, but he was intrigued by the operation and wanted to tag along. Each participant would also be provided with or taught to use an emergency communications link, so phone and cyber communications would remain private and could not be intercepted. Since Blake was the principal source of funding for the operation, he could not be denied a seat at the table or a place in the operation. Parsons' service included a fully equipped private jet with white-glove executive service, an armed security detail, and access to his best and brightest operatives. There would even be a short training session in self-protection. Zack was excited—*maybe I can finally learn to shoot!*

Chapter Ten

The entire team at the Law Offices of Zachary Blake met each week to discuss the firm's caseload, specific problem cases, and to share opinions or propose a strategy. The meeting usually lasted a couple of hours and always featured a catered breakfast much like the one Micah Love enjoyed at what the investigator referred to as the '*PISS* on Izady' meeting.

This particular meeting went overtime. After a lengthy discussion over the firm's caseload, the lawyers were anxious to discuss and offer opinions on Zack's venture into a terrorist hostage negotiation crisis.

Zack permitted an open discussion, but it soon became clear that he'd made up his mind to proceed with Parsons and defer to the company's expertise. As such, there wasn't much to talk about, so most of the lawyers returned to their respective practices. Those that remained were Zack, Marshall, Marshall's top associate, Amy Fletcher, and the firm's long-time managing partner, Sandy Manning.

"Zack, be reasonable. This is going to cost a fortune. Are you sure this is something we want to take on?"

"Aside from the obvious humanitarian aspects of this situation, Imam Ghaffari, Jack Dylan, and the Dearborn Muslim community are important sources of business for this firm. We've been through a lot together. I want to help.

"Sandy, I respect your position as the firm's watchdog. If you prefer I do this with private capital and manpower, I will. I expect you to look at these things from a dollars and cents perspective—that's your job. One way or the other, I'm going to do this."

"I'm sure you know that the East Dearborn Muslim community represents over one-third of the immigration department's cases. Sandy, that's almost one-half of the department's revenue," Amy added.

"I understand how you guys feel—there is a role for the firm to play. Zack hit the nail on the head. It is my job to mind the store and ensure these things make economic sense. However, it is also my job to determine whether they will bring about a positive result for a client or good PR for the firm. I am warming to the possibility that this operation could have a net positive revenue-generating effect in the long term. If the operation is successful and the right public relations campaign follows, it could be even better. I'm on board. How can I help?"

"Your job will be to handle the money and the logistics. We must make sure the operation is funded at all stages. Parsons' bills and expenses will be paid in a timely manner. Marshall, Amy, and team will handle the international law aspects of the situation and any litigation, diplomatic, bureaucratic, legislative, or executive branch snafus that occur. Parsons and I will try to limit the immigration division's role. The longer we keep the operation private, the better off we'll be. If things go wrong and Marshall or Amy must call in the feds, we'll just have to adjust on the fly. Our immigration division has superior expertise— they will deal with the blowback and get us the support if, and when, we need it." Marshall and Amy nodded their appreciation and understanding of their role.

"Sandy, the most important person in this room is you. The money must be there and must flow as needed."

"I have your backs, guys. You can count on the firm and me."

The conversation continued into the lunchtime hours. Sandy Manning gagged when he heard the initial sum Zack needed to commence the operation. Wisely, Sandy kept his opinion to himself. Blake made Manning rich beyond his wildest imagination. Sandy owed him everything. The operation would proceed, and the money would be there.

After Sandy left the room, Marshall, Zack, and Amy sat in contemplative silence for a few minutes, and then Zack raised the Gonzalez case.

"Anything new on Gonzalez, Marsh? What a nightmare having these two cases at the same time. Have we located the kids?"

"Amy?" Marshall turned to his chief associate.

"No," she retorted. "We have been unable to locate anyone at Homeland or *ICE* who knows where they are."

"How cruel and incompetent can these people be?" Zack wondered.

"Under RonJohn's zero-tolerance immigration policy, thousands are in the same boat as the Gonzalez family. That makes finding them much harder—a needle in a haystack situation," Amy grumbled.

"President Golding, to his credit, rescinded John's draconian orders, but the damage was already done. As this case demonstrates, there are communications issues between the administration and *ICE*. This incident would not have shocked anyone when RonJohn was president, but under Golding's new guidelines, this seems to have taken everyone by surprise," Marshall added.

"Marshall, Amy, I am sorry to say this, but I think you guys are going to have to sit out the Izady operation and handle the Gonzalez case. We have to find these kids. Like Izady, spare no expense—find them!" Zack bristled.

"I appreciate what you're saying, Zack. My department is a new one here, and some of our lawyers are too inexperienced for either situation. I assure you, though, that Amy and I can handle both. If we need help, we have plenty of resources to tap into. The largest hurdle will be untangling inter-department government bureaucracy. There is no coordinated tracking system between the Office of Refugee Resettlement, Health and Human Services, and Homeland. These pricks separated families without any established protocol."

"This was a new low, even for someone as corrupt and unfeeling as RonJohn," Zack growled

"The idea was to deter migrant families from coming to the United States. Sounds good on paper, but the administration failed to consider how bad things were in these migrants' home countries. Extensive violence and extreme poverty are a way of life in Central America. People felt it necessary to take a chance on the land of the free," Marshall suggested.

"The plan was to *prosecute* those who entered the country undocumented. As it played out, however, the policy resulted in thousands of migrant parents spending months in cages. Parents were unable to communicate with their kids, and in many cases, like Gonzalez, they don't even know where they are," Amy retorted.

"Isn't the *ACLU* involved? Can they help us?" Zachary wondered.

"The short answer is yes; the ACLU *is* involved. They filed a lawsuit and persuaded a federal judge to stop the separations and reunite families. However, as we have seen here, small numbers of separations continue. *HHS* means well, but the sheer volume of families makes kids hard to find and reunions almost impossible. We're talking about *thousands* of kids," Amy groused.

"Holy shit!" Zack exclaimed.

"It gets worse. According to *HHS* officials, it would normally be quite easy to track the kids and return them to their parents. Unfortunately, records were automatically deleted because the computer system was not properly modified to account for separations. Each step in the process is vulnerable to human error, which increases the risk that children will be lost in the system. Perhaps the Gonzalez kids were taken so late in the debacle that corrections have been made and they'll be easier to find," Amy continued.

"Please stay on it, guys—spare no expense."

"We will, Zack. I promise. Now go rescue the Izady family. We'll hold down the fort," Marshall assured.

Chapter Eleven

"As you exit the plane, you will follow Sergeant Matthews."

An *ICE* operative was unloading thirty scared, hungry, filthy children from a government plane. This was a first-time plane ride for almost all of the children, and they were relieved to land safely at what looked to be a small military airbase. A large yellow bus sat running alongside the plane.

Many of the children were screaming and shouting for their parents. The operatives and soldiers did not understand Spanish and were oblivious to their cries. They were unloading the kids regardless of the commotion they made.

Emilio and Emma hung close to one another, holding hands. Emma was determined to resist any attempt to separate her from her brother. Emilio was so young—they had taken him from his parents. *Would they now take him from his sister?*

Fortunately, as they descended the plane, they were permitted to stay together, holding hands, comforting one another. The siblings followed the guy named Matthews, who pointed to a line-up of kids standing in front of the unmarked yellow bus, the size and shape of a school bus. When the plane was finally empty and all kids stood whimpering in line, Matthews ordered them to march onto the bus and find a seat, loading from back to front.

The kids now understood the routine. One of the men would shout out orders and the kids were required to obey. They climbed up the bus steps and found seats without incident. Matthews waited at the door, a grim look on his face, making sure everyone got on the bus, motioning kids forward with a wave of his arm. When all were on board, the bus took off. Emilio jerked forward and almost fell to the floor. His face scrunched up, the beginnings of a cry, but Emma grabbed him, pulled him back in his seat, and put her finger to her lips.

"Don't cry, Emilio. I've got you. I won't let them hurt you," she comforted. Emilio took a deep breath in and calmed. He put his finger to his lips, imitating his sister.

Thirty minutes later, they arrived at their destination—another abandoned warehouse that might have been a Costco or Sam's Club. Three female attendants exited the building and walked up to the bus. They lined up parallel with the bus, hands folded in front of them. Matthews stood at the door and hand-gestured the kids off the bus, much the same way he ushered them on.

As they exited, the kids were again told to line up. They did as they were ordered, making a long 'T' top, standing in front of the three attendants. Matthews walked up and down the line and stood eye-to-eye with each child.

"Do all of you speak English?" He demanded. "Raise your hand."

Thirty hands shot up into the air. These kids were not captured at the border and separated from their parents. Whether or not their parents were citizens, *these* children were born and raised in *America.* They were American citizens, a fact lost on Matthews and his subordinates.

"Good. *Bueno.* I am sure the diplomats are working on reuniting you with your parents as soon as possible." The kids looked back and forth at each other. *What's a diplomat?*

Matthews continued. "This is a *military* operation and military rules will apply. *Los militares, comprendo?*"

The children nodded their heads. Emma wondered why he repeated things in Spanish when all thirty children indicated they spoke English.

"We will tolerate no misbehavior of any kind. There are beds inside. A chair sits next to each bed. There will be no sitting on the floor, *comprendo?*"

The children remained silent.

"You will receive food and water three times per day. Do not share food or water with others. We have all of your names. You are to call each other your given names. No codes or nicknames."

Emma grunted. *What?*

"Is there a problem?"

Emma realized Matthews was addressing her.

"No, no problem," she replied to the floor.

"Lights out at 9:00 PM—no noise will be tolerated after lights out. If you need to use the bathroom, turn on your bedside nightlight and someone will assist you. Do not get out of bed until dawn and lights on. You rise at dawn. Make up your beds in accordance with step-by-step instructions you will find posted on a nearby wall. After that, you will wash and mop the bathroom, scrub the sinks and toilets. Cleanliness is next to godliness in this facility, *comprendo?*"

Everyone shook their head.

"On the way over here, we permitted you to hold hands or put arms around each other—no more of that. Touching is a no-no and will not be tolerated. Do not touch another child, even if that child is your brother or sister or has fallen or is hurt."

Emma and Emilio glanced at each other. Everyone needed a reassuring hug now and then, especially in these austere, almost bucolic surroundings and circumstances.

"You will all go to school together, every day, no exceptions. You will learn about America, her history, her laws, and what makes this the greatest country in the world.

"You will finish all your classwork and homework and do all your chores. If you've behaved, you might be granted free time or recess. Does everyone know what recess is?"

"Yes, sir," the children responded in unison.

Emma already decided that she would use her free time to write letters to her parents. *When will I see you again?* She wanted them to know how much she missed them and how she longed to be with them. *How could this happen in America?*

Her worst nightmare, one she could never share with Emilio, was that they might never see their parents again. She decided to maintain hope, write, and hide her letters after she finished chores and homework. She didn't know whether letters were permitted and did not wish to run afoul of the rules. There was no mail delivery service at the camp. Someday, somehow, when it was safe, she'd get them to her parents. She had already written and hid one letter to her mother. She knew their address—all she needed was a postage stamp.

Dear Mommy: I hope you and Daddy are okay. I miss you so much. Where are you? Where are we? Why did they take us

*away? Do you know? Please find us and take us home. I love
you, your daughter, Emma.*

Mary Carmen Gonzalez prepared her daughter for this
moment. Emma promised her mother she would obey orders, be
brave, and always take care of her little brother. She proudly
reflected upon the fact that she followed every single one of her
mother's commands. When they first put her and Emilio on the
airplane, Emma believed they were taking her to meet her
parents. Instead, the children ended up in this place. Her biggest
job in *this* place was to act as a role model to her brother.

Matthews completed his speech, and the assistants escorted
the children to their assigned beds. Emma was pleased and
mildly surprised when they brought Emilio to the bed opposite
hers. She was concerned that boys and girls might be separated.
A large plastic bag sat on each bed. They contained what the
children would soon refer to as their uniforms. Each bag
contained two unisex shirts, shorts, a sweatsuit, and three pairs of
underwear. Each child was also issued a comb, plastic cup,
toothbrush, tube of toothpaste, and bar of soap.

After a traumatic first night, the days became remarkably
similar. As they settled into a routine, the kids began to realize
that they would not be reunited with their parents any time soon.
Most became friends. They went to class and played sports
together. The camp had a 'buddy' system of sorts—the older
children could earn 'big brother' or 'big sister' status by setting a
good example for the little ones. Excellent behavior and a
positive example would earn points and a chance for free play.

However, the children were still forbidden to touch each
other. They woke at dawn every morning to staff members
banging on metal objects until every child was out of bed. They
were required to scrub bathrooms, remove trash bags full of dirty
toilet paper, and clean toilets. Every child, regardless of age, took
turns doing these chores.

They ate together. Meals consisted of rice and beans,
processed deli 'beef,' vegetables, or pizza (if the children were
good). On very special occasions, they might earn ice cream or
cake.

When a child was naughty, he or she might have to perform extra chores or be denied dessert. If a kid exhibited chronic misbehavior, he or she had to visit the doctor for a shot. Emma would later say these shots caused kids to fall asleep in the middle of class. These shots were reserved for children who threw tantrums, hurt other children, or broke things.

The most common emotions were fear and hope. The children feared punishment and hoped to be reunited with their families. Wherever they were, they knew this was not Michigan. In this place, it was always hot outside. Emma continued to wonder where they were but was too afraid to ask. Attendants assured the children that these conditions were temporary. People called lawyers were working to reunite them with their parents. Emma remained positive and optimistic.

Birthdays were causes for celebration in the camp. The children would be told it was someone's birthday. They knew this meant cake and ice cream. Everyone gathered around and sang Happy Birthday to the birthday boy or girl. The birthday child was excused from chores for the day and got to enjoy a day of leisure and an extra helping of cake and ice cream.

The most promising events occurred when someone was permitted to leave to be reunited with his or her parents. These events gave everyone hope. Children would make going away presents for the lucky traveler. They were forbidden to kiss or hug the person goodbye.

The children were sometimes permitted to be just that, children. The building was spacious and sounds reverberated and echoed throughout. Kids would make animal or farting noises, giggle, and point to each other as the guilty party. Everyone, including the attendants, would begin to laugh. Some would try to 'solve the crime' by guessing who the guilty party was. With fake (or real) fart sounds, the children usually decided that 'he who smelt it dealt it.' In other words, the first person to point out a perpetrator was usually the guilty party. When the guilty party was identified, everyone would crack up. Bedtime and lights out were promptly at nine in the evening. As things quieted and children began to drift off to sleep, some mischievous child

would let out a howl, moo, or another fart sound and the revelry
would begin again.

***

   Twenty days passed since Mary Carmen and Miguel
Gonzalez returned home to a call from Principal Curley that *ICE*
agents stormed the elementary school and took their precious
Emma and Emilio. Mr. Blake and Mr. Mann tried to find out
what happened to them, but no one seemed to know where they
were. A private investigator named 'Love' was trying to find out
who authorized the raid, who carried it out, and where these
people might have taken the children. So far, no one could
provide the couple with any positive news. It was as if Emma
and Emilio vanished into thin air. Twenty days after their
imprisonment and separation, there was still no news of their
children. Their kids were gone, and they were devastated.
   Miguel and Mary Carmen prayed every day that their
children were safe, healthy, and would soon be returned to them.
They trusted Marshall Mann and knew he was working hard on
their behalf. But where were the children? Every day they were
apart felt like a month.
   Marshall would also have to deal with Miguel and Mary
Carmen's status. They were undocumented; their children were
not. Even if, by some miracle, the family was reunited, they
might easily be separated again. One thing was certain—no
matter what a judge decided, the Gonzalez couple would not
expose their American children to the oppressive conditions in
Venezuela, even if doing so meant not being together.
   The most traumatic aspect of the ordeal, aside from the initial
arrest and separation, was the waiting. They tried to be strong for
each other, continue working, and stay busy; anything to-take
their minds off their kids. But the days passed slowly, drip, drip,
drip, like water torture.
   People would visit, offer kind words of hope, and bring
meals. Every Sunday, they attended church service, where the
pastor and the congregation prayed and offered words of
encouragement. One day, to the couple's great surprise, they

were presented with a check for over two thousand dollars. The congregation hosted a fundraiser to help pay attorney fees. Someone created a 'GoFundMe' page and raised three thousand dollars more.

The couple had much to be thankful for. They escaped oppression in Venezuela and enjoyed a good life in America. They had good friends, great neighbors, good jobs, and wonderful kids. Wonderful kids . . . the inescapable obsession that always brought their world to a grinding halt—where were their children?

The telephone rang in their modest Lincoln Park home. Mary Carmen answered.

"Hello?"

"Mary Carmen? This is Amy Fletcher. I work with Marshall Mann. We finally have some news. Judge Lieberman has scheduled your case for court."

"Thank you for calling, Miss Fletcher. Is this important? Does the judge know where the children are?"

"Call me Amy, please. The short answer is no. The judge does not know. But I'm hopeful she can order those responsible for their disappearance to produce names and ranks of the people who took them, records of the operation, and where they might have been taken. There is a lot of red tape to unravel, after all. We are dealing with the federal government, but I am hopeful. This is a positive first step."

Mary Carmen smiled. *These lawyers are godsends.* "Thank you, so much, Amy. We appreciate everything you are doing. We will see our children soon?"

"I honestly don't know, Mary Carmen. This is a case of first impression. Until Ronald John became president, our government has never been this aggressive. They have never deliberately separated families or conducted raids like the ones at the plant and the school. With a court order, *ICE*, *HHS*, and Homeland will have to provide information."

"Keep us posted, *por favor*?"

"I will. Hang in there. I speak for Marshall, Zack, and everyone at our firm when I say, we will not rest until we locate your children."

"Thank you, Amy. God bless you."

Mary Carmen Gonzalez hung up their living room telephone, turned to her husband, and told him the news. The couple looked into each other's eyes, embraced, and nodded. They walked arm in arm to a small desk in the corner of the room. A bible sat on the desk. A crucifix hung on the wall, directly above. Miguel and Mary Carmen got down on their knees in front of the desk, made signs of the cross, bowed their heads, and began to pray.

On the other side of the call, Amy Fletcher reflected on her conversation with Mary Carmen Gonzalez. Amy graduated, Phi Beta Kappa, from the University of Michigan, majoring in International Relations and World Politics. She was fluent in Arabic, French, and Spanish. While most students were partying or dating, Amy was studying. She was an attractive woman and could have had her choice of men on campus. But she wasn't interested in men—her career was what mattered.

She completed her four-year undergraduate program in only three years and was accepted to Michigan's law school before she graduated. She excelled at the graduate level, achieving valedictorian status upon graduation, and was recruited by the finest law firms in the country. Her proud family, faculty advisors, and counselors expected her to choose one of these silk-stocking law firms. She surprised everyone by choosing the Blake firm.

Amy Fletcher was proud of her accomplishments, proud of the fact that she achieved her life-long dream of becoming a lawyer. She was honored to receive such generous and prestigious offers. The law was a calling for her, but her passion was helping people. She could never settle on a career that made wealthy corporations wealthier. She couldn't represent insurance companies or corporate interests that put profits over people. She applied with Zachary Blake's firm in Bloomfield Hills. Blake did not typically recruit the best of the best. He preferred to train exceptional people, his way, and *make* them the best. He preferred to mold new lawyers in his own image.

Zack Blake knew that Amy Fletcher was an exceptional young woman, exhibiting qualities Zack seldom observed in new applicants or even in seasoned attorneys. He recognized Amy's innate desire to make a difference in people's lives, one client at a time. He knew she would make a terrific trial lawyer, dominating a legal specialty once populated exclusively by white men. Zack liked trail-blazing and saw an opportunity to mentor a talented female trial lawyer. The male dominated defense bar wouldn't know what hit them.

But there was an opening in Marshall Mann's new immigration division. Immigration was a new area of the law for the Blake firm. From the minute Zack added Marshall and established the division, it became a huge success. The government's unconscionable treatment of immigrants became a rallying cry for the left, and lawyers and politicians did not hesitate to refer business from all over the Midwest. Amy's undergraduate degree was well-suited to an international practice, and she spoke several languages. Both aspects made her a perfect fit for Marshall's division.

Zack gave Amy a choice—work with him in the trial division or work with Marshall in the immigration division. Amy replied with two questions. They weren't the questions Zack expected; they made him realize, instantly, that his recruitment of Amy Fletcher was a wise decision. Zack assumed she would ask which division paid the most money. But Amy Fletcher asked: "Where can I help the most people and what people need the most help?"

Her questions sent chills down Zack's spine. He knew, at that moment, that he could not let Amy Fletcher walk out the door without accepting an offer from Zachary Blake. He told her that immigration was the hottest legal issue in America, that the division was new and exciting, and was the firm's biggest growth specialty. Furthermore, immigration was the clear answer to her questions. She could help the most people, as well as those who needed the most help. It was a match made in heaven. The only issue was that immigration was Marshall Mann's division and Marshall had full autonomy to hire and fire his own legal staff.

Zack arranged a meeting between the two lawyers and Marshall immediately saw in Amy everything Zack promised, an accomplished law school graduate with tremendous legal acumen, a head for business, and the compassion and kindness of the finest underpaid social worker. Marshall had no doubt Amy would, one day, head the division.

Amy happily accepted Marshall's offer. Once on board, she achieved instant success, becoming Marshall's second in command in less than two years. Less than two years out of law school, Amy Fletcher was an accomplished immigration specialist, uniquely qualified to assist Marshall in all phases of the Gonzalez case.

Gonzalez was a dream come true. This family desperately needed quality representation. *How does the United States government rip children from the arms of their parents, place them in detention centers, and lose them? Worse, these kids are American citizens! Not on my watch. No way. No how.* She meant what she said to Mary Carmen Gonzalez: She would not rest until the Gonzalez family was reunited.

***

As Parsons Security, the Dearborn law enforcement officers, and Zachary Blake prepared to leave for Syria, Marshall Mann, Amy Fletcher, and Micah Love sat in an Immigration Courtroom in the McNamara Federal Building in Downtown Detroit. Micah was not happy to be excluded from the Syrian operation, but he understood the importance of this case.

The case was part of a legal cattle call of lawyers and clients awaiting the arrival of Judge Marsha Lieberman. All cases on the docket were scheduled for 9:00 AM sharp and all those with business before the court were required to be present at that time. Unless yours was the first case called, it might be heard at any time after nine and until the court adjourned for the day—hence, the well-known reference in the legal business, 'hurry up and wait'.

The good news, if one could call it that, was that cases involving lawyers were called first. Some lawyers have matters in multiple courtrooms on the same day at the same time. But Lieberman's docket was clogged with cases involving lawyers, so this was hardly an advantage. Judge Lieberman took the bench at 9:20 AM and the mundane business of the court began.

Most of the oral arguments were routine, taking five minutes or less. The number of cases and people in the courtroom began to dwindle. Government lawyers sat at a table to Marshall and Amy's left, and attorneys took turns handling the government side of the various cases.

Micah was fidgety. He was happy he didn't do this for a living. He was a man of action—*how do lawyers like Amy and Marsh put up with this bull? There must be a better way. What a waste of time!*

In the Matter of Mary Carmen and Miguel Gonzalez was finally called at 10:45 AM. Amy rose and approached the counsel table to the right of the government lawyers.

"Appearances of counsel for the record?" Judge Lieberman commanded.

"Amy Fletcher and Marshall Mann, for the petitioner, Your Honor."

"Which of you will argue the case, Ms. Fletcher?"

"I will," Amy replied, turning to Marshall, who nodded his assent.

"And for the government?" Judge Lieberman requested.

"Daniel Dickson, Your Honor."

"Ms. Fletcher? This is your rodeo. What seems to be the problem?" Judge Lieberman smiled. Fletcher knew Lieberman well and was pleased with the draw. *She's going to be quite pissed!*

"May it please the court—this case can only be described as government-sponsored child abduction. Miguel and Mary Carmen Gonzalez are aliens. They seek asylum in this country. While there are conflicting points of view regarding their immigration status, I would argue their status is totally irrelevant to these proceedings. The subjects of *these* proceedings are their *children*. Emma and Emilio Gonzalez were born in this country and are citizens of the United States.

"In an act of unbelievable callousness, while Mary Carmen and Miguel were being released from a detention center in Riverview, *ICE* agents raided an elementary school. Agents demanded that school officials produce Emma and Emilio. When officials complied, agents seized the children and took them to an unknown location.

"This occurred almost a month ago, Your Honor. As we stand before you today, thousands of children are in the exact same boat as Emma and Emilio. Parents are trying to find their children, children are trying to find their parents, and the government claims they don't know where these kids were taken. We have been in contact with multiple detention facilities in Southeastern Lower Michigan. The Gonzalez children are not interred at any of them. Micah Love, a private investigator from Love Investigations, is present today. Mr. Love is prepared to testify that he has scoured Michigan looking for the children and they are not here. The question of the day is: Where are Emma and Emilio Gonzalez?

"It is almost one month after their illegal abduction. This is the correct and only term for the government's behavior, Your Honor. We cannot locate these kids in *any ICE* detention center. Furthermore, according to my conversations with *HHS* and Homeland officials, there is no process for reuniting these families. No one at *ICE* or *HHS* has a location, phone number, file, records, or *anything* to help us locate the shelter that houses these kids.

"Zero-tolerance may be a great political sound bite for the John and Golding administrations. But their immigration policies have major legal and constitutional issues. The federal government was woefully unprepared for these actions. There are inadequate tracking systems and substandard facilities to handle the flow. This is *America!* We are now the country that abducts and places children in cages. What kind of nation does that? What have we become?

"Our petition seeks all records relating to this operation, including the names of the decision-makers and soldiers who carried out their orders, a list of every child detention facility in the United States, and any records that would permit us to track these specific children to their current location. Thank you, Your Honor." Amy glanced at Marshall, who flashed thumbs up and a smile.

"Mr. Dickson, Ms. Fletcher's request seems compelling and reasonable to me," Judge Lieberman began. "What exactly is going on out there? Are *ICE* agents abducting children, American citizens, no less, and placing them in cages in parts unknown?"

"Your Honor, in the past several months, undocumented immigration at the southern border has exceeded 50,000 people each month. Furthermore, there has been an almost 500% increase in family units entering the country without proper documentation or status.

"As long as undocumented entry into the United States remains a criminal offense, *ICE* and *HHS* can no longer look the other way. We are a nation of immigrants who entered this country legally and paid the price to do so. A just nation must also have a system of laws and law enforcement. We must enforce the law. It is unfair to all law-abiding citizens to look the other way in these cases."

Amy Fletcher exploded in rebuttal, her voice echoing in the courtroom, almost beyond the scope of appropriate courtroom demeanor, surprising even her mentor, Marshall Mann, who turned and suppressed a grin.

"Undocumented entry *is* a crime, Your Honor, but it is a low-level offense, rarely enforced against asylum seekers, especially families. At least, that was true before the John administration's so-called zero-tolerance policy. When the administration decides to suddenly make undocumented entry a serious offense, officials have a duty to create an infrastructure to track people in the system and not arrest and illegally incarcerate American citizens.

"This administration has decided that hurting families and children is a viable method of achieving its general immigration policy goals. The government's policies and actions related to these family separations are an enforcement tool. This should shock the conscience of anyone involved in constitutional law or law enforcement. The scale of harm to these families is grossly disproportionate to the government's stated policy aims. This is an unconstitutional abomination, Your Honor!" Amy pounded the table.

"These histrionics are . . ." Dickson began to respond.

"I've heard enough, Mr. Dickson," Judge Lieberman interrupted. "I have been on the federal bench for many years. Most attorneys consider me to be a tough but fair judge. I enforce the law and require citizens and aliens to adhere to our system of justice. These draconian policies and their enforcement against American children are a bridge too far. I hereby declare and rule these so-called family separations unconstitutional. I order you to locate all records related to these abductions and turn them over to Ms. Fletcher, Mr. Mann, and their firm forthwith. The family separation program shall be immediately terminated. I order all families separated under this policy reunited, forthwith. Aggrieved parties may petition this court for damages. I will consider separation compensation at an appropriate future date. Have I made myself clear, Mr. Dickson?"

"But Your Honor . . ."

"Have I made myself *clear*, Mr. Dickson?" Judge Lieberman snarled.

"Yes, Your Honor." Dickson conceded.

"Wonderful!" The judge smiled. "Ms. Fletcher, I'll sign an order."

"We just happen to have one handy, Your Honor." Marshall Mann spoke for the first time, stood, and handed a document to Amy who, in turn, handed it to Dickson. Dickson shrugged and assented with a head nod. Amy approached the bench and handed the document to the judge. She signed and handed the document to the court clerk who entered it and handed copies back to Amy.

The Law Offices of Zachary Blake now had the full legal authority to locate and facilitate the return of Emma and Emilio Gonzalez. The firm would now have to interview hundreds of agents and engage in a mad scramble to obtain and review hundreds of thousands of records. Would they be able to determine who went where and who went with whom? Worse, Marshall and Amy discovered that agents had accidentally deleted identification numbers from the system that could have

been used to locate the children. *Only in America*, Amy sighed—
only in Ronald John's America.

Chapter Twelve

Wayne Parsons didn't build a solid, nine-figure security business by being careless. Before the group of fifteen men, including Zachary Blake, jetted off to Damascus, the rescue plan was unveiled and discussed in detail. A ransom demand was communicated to Karim, and as instructed, he advised the terrorists it would take some time to raise the required capital.

Blake was to lead a three-man negotiating team into the lions' den. Zack's firm transferred the required funds to a newly created account at the Bank of Syria and awaited further instructions from the boss, who, in turn, awaited further instructions from the hostage-takers.

Parsons opposed the inexperienced Blake taking a lead role in the negotiations but had to concede that Zack was a superlative negotiator. Parsons' concern was that litigation and terrorist hostage negotiations were two completely different animals. Zack had no experience dealing with terrorists and illegal transactional negotiations. He wouldn't be permitted to file a motion, consult with a judge, point out rule violations, employ common sense, or expect cooler heads to prevail. One wrong move and the hostages would be in grave peril.

Parsons conceded one other rather important point. Zachary Blake was the boss. The mission was financed, one hundred percent, with Zack's money. In the security business, like most others, money talked; bullshit walked. Zack could call the shots because he paid the bills.

Parsons was grateful that Zack, while cocky and arrogant, was also a pragmatist. Zack had no interest in calling the shots on matters in which he had no expertise. Hostage rescue was one such area, and he was very pleased to leave the logistics to those with expertise.

The long plane ride was divided into two distinct groups of raid participants, a hostage negotiating team and a hostage rescue team. The negotiating team had only one strategic function: Negotiate for delay. The team was to suggest numbers and terms that might entice the terrorists, keep them at the negotiating table, but delay and ultimately prevent an ultimate settlement.

While these negotiations were ongoing, the ten-man rescue team would sneak up to the terrorists' camp, implement the plan, and snatch back the hostages.

Parsons was a by-the-book and chain of command type individual. His business success was achieved via his military success. His Washington D.C. reputation and connections were earned on merit, not on any personal or family ties to movers or shakers. He'd conducted numerous hostage rescue attempts and had an outstanding record of success. Experience told him that a successful rescue operation required five basic elements: surprise, intelligence, an experienced and skilled leader, precision, and deception. Parsons firmly believed that if any one element was missing in any operation, it was doomed to fail.

While timing is also an important element, it is also one of the most troubling. Oftentimes, the rescue team does not have the power to choose the timing of the rescue. It is dictated by events in real-time. Ideally, the best time to execute a rescue operation is late in the game. The team has time to prepare, learn its opponents' objectives, strengths, and weaknesses. Later execution also provides a better opportunity to plan for the most effective window of opportunity. A lot would depend on Zachary Blake and his negotiation skills and strategy. When Blake finally 'failed' to resolve the crisis as planned, the team had to be at its highest state of readiness. At this point, Al-Baklavi will have gone from a driven negotiator to a reluctant executioner. His psychological stress might make him more vulnerable.

Parsons opted for a direct action or commando-style operation. The fundamentals of commando-style are speed, surprise, precision, planning, and on-the-fly flexibility if something fails to go as planned. In this case, Parsons was concerned about the terrorists' motivation. He still wasn't sure whether this was a kidnapping for ransom or a terrorist hostage situation. The former seeks money—the latter money, power, and, perhaps, other demands.

Parsons did not mention this to Karim when they spoke, but Parsons was concerned about Al-Baklavi's history of brutality. A kidnapper's success depends upon the safety and well-being of his victims. A hostage-taker, by contrast, is far more willing to torture or kill for purposes of political shock or maintaining his terrorist aura.

Logistics and intelligence gathering were of vital importance and that concerned Parsons. While the operation was well planned, it was conceived at great distance from the strike site. The team had blueprints, chosen breach points, and diagrams of the terrorist base. However, these were no more than educated guesses from reconnaissance photos. Parsons was hopeful he could send in an advance team to determine whether intelligence gathering was accurate. He especially desired to establish the exact location of mother and child.

Parsons was acutely aware that sniper-observer teams were excellent sources of intelligence, reconnaissance, and surveillance of the target area. He considered his snipers to be essential to the surprise and precision elements of the operation. A few seconds could mean the difference between success and failure. Parsons wanted to eliminate any opportunity for Al-Baklavi or his men to shoot the woman and child or, worse, detonate an explosive device. Absolute precision was critical to success. Rescuers would rely heavily on those two elements to gain relative superiority.

Parsons' second in command was Peter Graham, another former *SEAL* who also happened to be a master sniper. He made a name for himself during the Iraq War when he single-handedly rescued a high-level American diplomat and killed all four hostage-takers at long range, one shot for each terrorist. *This* operation involved Qassim Al-Baklavi, and no one expected it to be resolved by one long-range sniper. If, however, Graham was able to put Al-Baklavi in the crosshairs, the terrorist's reign was over.

Al-Baklavi was shrewd. He earned number-two status by being effective and elusive. He successfully completed numerous missions, always managing to escape, often times miraculously. He was equally skilled in sophisticated explosives and automatic weaponry, as well as unsophisticated, hand-to-hand combat, like a knife fight or beheading. No member of the rescue team would underestimate him.

Specialist Jarrod Lane was the team's hand-to-hand snatch expert. The plan was for Graham and the other shooters to coordinate and employ a sniper attack from three sides. At the same time, Lane and his snatch team would secure and escape with the hostages from behind a tent Avi and Hassan identified as the hostage location. Lane silently prayed for the opportunity to come face-to-face with Al-Baklavi.

The most important part of the operation was, of course, the act of saving the hostages. Parsons' team had an excellent reputation and record of success. Jack Dylan and Shaheed Ali were two extra hands, if needed, part of the team at Zack's insistence. Parsons knew these men were also highly trained, with an excellent track record against white supremacist elements. Parsons was uncomfortable because he'd never worked with them, and white supremacists were not as unpredictable as Islamic Fundamentalists. There was no margin for error. An errant shot or explosive charge miscalculation could lead to disaster. Every team member had to have the ability to kill a terrorist upon first engagement, a double-tap to the chest and, for good measure, one to the head. A miss would provide a terrorist with the opportunity to shoot back or, worse, kill a hostage. Ali and Dylan were good men—Parsons could see that. Blake was paying the bill, and Parsons would have to adapt and put these men to good use.

Parsons and his team wore company uniforms, black with grey trim and a grey company logo on the chest. Each wore a company beret bearing the same logo at the front of the headgear. They were a multi-national fighting force—the uniforms would prevent confusion if fighting broke out. They were ready—their presence of mind was such that the impossible was possible; they were unbeatable and indestructible. When the assault began, they would show no fear, dominate the opposition, work as one, and get the job done.

All equipment was state of the art. Each man was provided with Kevlar body armor and would wear headsets with microphones for continuous communication. Each would carry enough firepower, ammo, and weapons to kill or disable an army of terrorists, let alone a small group of hostage-takers. However, if the operation went according to plan, none of this would be necessary. The artillery ramp-up was needed only for the unlikely event that all hell broke loose.

The plane touched down, without incident, at an American military base in Damascus. An Army CH-47 Chinook helicopter stood nearby waiting to take the team to their next destination. Everyone involved, except perhaps, Zachary Blake, knew exactly what to do. It was crunch time—the mission was a go.

The Chinook rose into the air and took off at a high rate of speed. The men and equipment were tossed around inside the copter; Zack found the entire experience exhilarating. He glanced out his window and noticed the base and nearby city had quickly disappeared. All he could see was desert, a few huts, and some dilapidated stone buildings that had obviously experienced a war or two.

Surveillance experts, using weapons' scopes and binoculars, carefully scanned the area below, keeping a sharp eye out for possible spotters, snipers, or rising smoke and flame, a sure sign of a terrorist with a shoulder-launched missile device.

Their journey was uneventful. The Chinook touched down at a pre-planned location; a bombed-out, abandoned building about two miles from the target site. A Mercedes sport utility vehicle was waiting for them as expected. As the helicopter began its' descent, Avi and Hassan exited the Mercedes and waved at the approaching team members. At touchdown, Avi and Hassan were introduced to the team members. After the equipment was unloaded, communications specialists began the process of assembling and testing their equipment. The mission would not be successful without comms operating at one hundred percent efficiency.

Team leaders were confident yet cautious about Al-Baklavi's base of operations. Parsons was surprised that the shrewd terrorist chose such a flat, approachable desert location. On the other hand, assuming the terrorists possessed night vision capabilities, there was very little cover available and no easy means of escape if the rescue team was spotted before it could commence the operation.

One positive development was that Hassan knew the area exceptionally well, and he and Avi knew the precise location of Al-Baklavi's base of operations. One of the operatives arrogantly suggested Al-Baklavi expected negotiators, not an extraction team, which created very favorable conditions for the mission's likely success. Graham dressed the soldier down. He warned the team not to underestimate this man and to assume Al-Baklavi expected the assault and was prepared for it. The operative hung his head in shame.

After longer-than-expected time to set up communications, the equipment was tested and ready to go. The sun set, resting comfortably on the desert sand, before disappearing. As darkness began to envelop the building, the men tested their night vision goggles. The air cooled to a delightful temperature, and reality began to set in. The beginning of the negotiations phase of Operation Mother-Daughter was only moments away.

Chapter Thirteen

ICE does not always place or keep undocumented aliens in lock-up facilities. In this case, a mistake was made about the status of the Gonzalez children. Some high-ranking official believed the kids were undocumented brought to the United States by their undocumented immigrant parents. That these kids were born in the USA would be a huge subject of tremendous embarrassment to *ICE* and the Golding administration.

Once an undocumented immigrant is arrested, a deportation officer is supposed to make an initial determination as to appropriate charges, and whether to place the person into removal proceedings. The usual charge is unlawful entry. The normal process is for the officer to serve a notice and demand to appear in immigration court. In fact, if *ICE* detains a person, the law requires this notice to be served within seventy-two hours of detention. The law was completely ignored in the cases of Emilio and Emma Gonzalez.

The kids had a right to see an immigration judge, someone who has no ties to *ICE*, for a completely impartial review and ruling. If *ICE* commandoes had done this correctly, the children would have made a quick appearance in court, everyone would have discovered a mistake had been made, and Emilio and Emma would be back with their parents.

Another right not provided to Emma and Emilio was the right to make a free telephone call. Was it overlooked or a purposeful act? This legally required call, a simple act of kindness, might have prevented weeks of separation and anxiety for the Gonzalez family. *ICE* is not required to detain undocumented immigrants locally, and there were no facilities for children in the Midwest, which is why Emma and Emilio ended up in another state.

Micah Love was Zachary Blake's primary investigator. Micah was a short, slovenly, porn-obsessed, late forties Jewish guy with very little hair on top. Zack frequently kibitzed with him about his comb-over. On a windy day, strands of hair would blow from one side to the other, completely exposing his bald dome, hair hanging down his neck on the opposite side. Micah was also the best private investigator in Detroit. He and Zack were the best of friends.

The two men gained wealth and fame together, cracking a church conspiracy to cover up the crimes of a pedophile priest. Zack's lawsuit and Micah's investigation resulted in a nine-figure jury verdict in what became known in Detroit area legal circles as the civil case of the century. Zack's client, Jennifer Tracey, later became Zack's wife, and her abused children became his adopted sons.

In *this* case, Micah wanted to get the Gonzalez kids released on immigration bond, clear up their citizenship, and get them released for good. After all, they were American citizens. When he began his investigation, the first thing he did was to obtain their birth certificates, both of which proclaimed for *ICE* and anyone else who would have bothered to check that Emma and Emilio Gonzalez were born in the U. S. of A.

However, to facilitate their release, he had to find out where they were being held. Because of the sheer volume of people arrested by the John and Golding administrations, the commando-style raids, haphazard arrests, and worse, the horrible record-keeping and post-arrest tracking, many of those detained simply 'disappeared' into the system without a trace. Unfortunately, two of those people were Emma and Emilio Gonzalez.

Micah decided to begin his investigation online. His cyber specialist, a computer nerd named Reed Spencer, once served time for cyber fraud, having stolen wealthy people's identities. He was only caught because of his own stupid arrogance—he created a password containing his dog's name and hacked into AmEx's black card system, stealing thousands from high-net-worth individuals. Cyber investigators tracked him down and arrested him. A deal was cut on a ten-year sentence, and Reed served seven. Reed Spencer did not exactly learn his lesson. He refused to grow up, was still a nerd, and disrespected the police. He enjoyed working for Micah because Micah liked to stick it to the police from time to time. He hoped the investigation would totally embarrass the already highly criticized Immigration and Customs Enforcement Agency.

Reed began his investigation by logging onto the *ICE* website. He immediately located something called the ICE Online Detainee Locator System. *This is promising*, he thought. *Wrong*, he concluded. To conduct a search, he needed an 'A-Number,' a nine-digit Alien Number assigned to the detainee, usually found on the person's green card or work permit. The obvious problem here was that these were *American* children. They had no work permit, no green card, and no A-Number. The other search method was by the immigrant's home country. This was also a dead end because the home country was the United States of America in this case. Reed did try 'Venezuela' to see what would happen. Thousands of 'Gonzalez' entries popped up, but no 'Emma' or 'Emilio.'

He tried their first and last name, family country of origin, and dates of birth but had no luck narrowing the search. After numerous trials and errors, he discovered a small print warning: 'Our Locator System may only be used to search for detainees over the age of 18'. *Now you tell me!*

Reed's next step was to call in a favor. Someone at the child welfare office owed him a favor. It was quite possible that when *ICE* rounded up the kids, agents placed them in state or local social services facilities. He contacted his friend, gave her all of the information he had, and came up empty. No Emma, no Emilio, no Gonzalez.

He decided to talk to Micah about a more aggressive approach. Direct confrontation, not cyber, was the way to go. He walked to Micah's office and found the boss on the telephone with Jessica Klein, his longtime girlfriend. Micah saw Reed at his door, motioned him to come in, and pointed to a seat on one of his office side chairs.

"Jessica, you are insatiable," Micah grunted into the receiver. "I cannot keep up with you. You're going to give me a heart attack . . . What? No! We can't! I have a business to run and a reputation to consider. What if someone follows me? Uh-huh . . . I like the sound of *that*. Yes, we can absolutely start with dinner. Right, money is no object. Somewhere near the hotel and *very* expensive is fine . . . Sounds good . . . sounds *wonderful* . . . looking forward to the weekend . . . Yes, dear . . . whatever you say, dear. I'll be there—I *promise.* Love you too, sweetheart. Bye."

The investigator hung up the phone, folded his hands on his desktop, and glared at Reed, giving the cyber-specialist his full attention.

"What the hell was that?" Reed wondered.

"*That* was Jessica and *none* of your business."

"Come on, Micah . . . what is it . . . a little weekend rendezvous?"

"My lips are sealed. I plead the fifth. What the hell do you want?"

"How *is* the lovely Ms. Klein?"

"Same as ever, as you might have gathered from listening to the telephone call."

"But I only heard one side of the call. What was *she* saying?"

Micah put two fingers on one side of his mouth and brought them across to the other side, symbolically 'zipping' his mouth shut.

"What's up, Reed?" Micah changed the subject.

"We're not going to locate these kids using cyber or any type of remote or online tools. The government's tracking system sucks. There are all kinds of cracks. For instance, they have a numbering system for undocumented people, but you can't give American citizens numbers. Did anyone think to ask these kids where they were born? That should have been the end of this nightmare.

"These kids were snatched without due process, without anyone caring about due process, all because John and Golding wanted to punish or put pressure on undocumented parents to self-deport. The administration's so-called 'zero-tolerance' policy put thousands of kids in the same boat. And get this. There is no requirement for *ICE* to keep these kids in *local* detention centers. These kids could be *anywhere.* We are literally looking for a needle in a haystack."

"What do you suggest?"

"A two-step process—one, Zack goes back to court and gets an order compelling all records relating to the raid, the name, rank, serial number, and current location of all participants, especially those in charge. Zack takes their depositions under oath and gets the information we need."

"We are up against the clock here, Reed, and that might take some time. What's the second step?" Micah queried.

"Good old-fashioned leg work. You and every one of our investigators go to these *ICE* command offices, one by one, and demand to speak to the people in charge. Otherwise, we sneak in, under color of authority, and get a peek at some records. There has to be a record or two about the plant raid and the school raid. Maybe we can find out where the kids were taken."

"If they screwed up and took two American citizens to a detention center in who-knows-where, why wouldn't they just admit they screwed up and help us find them?" Micah grumbled.

"Zero-tolerance? Embarrassment—unwillingness to admit a screw-up? This is the John-Golding administration, Micah! You expect competency and reasonableness from *these guys*?" Reed waved his arms in the air.

"Let's assume for the moment I agree with you. What's your play?"

"Try to quickly identify the right place to search. Send a couple of our ex-military guys in there. Full uniform, phony credentials, the works . . . and . . . simply *demand* to see the records." Reed sat back and smiled, folding his hands behind his head.

Micah glared at him, stupefied. "That's it? *That's* your plan? Are you nuts? That's illegal! We could end up in federal prison!"

"These guys are worse than the cops. Look what they've done. They hijacked two American *citizens* for crying out loud! One hand doesn't know what the other one is doing, and many of them don't care, one way or the other. This must be the dumbest, most haphazard government operation in the history of dumb, haphazard government operations. With the right uniforms and proper forged documents, *my* department, and the right guys in your department, we can absolutely pull this off. They won't know what hit them! Better yet, they won't report the fuck-up for fear they'll look like the idiots they are."

"Do you have anyone in mind for the operation?"

"As a matter of fact, I do . . ."

The conversation continued for over two hours. Reed thought of everything. The more Micah heard, the more comfortable he became. *This could actually work!*

Chapter Fourteen

Zachary Blake and the communications teams awaited contact and instructions from Al-Baklavi's terrorist network. The call finally came, and Parsons' principal hostage negotiator engaged in a brief conversation, uttering only three words: "understood," "understood," and "understood."

The call was recorded. After the caller terminated the connection, a tape of the call was played for all operatives.

"We demand ten million US dollars, in fifty-dollar bills, with non-consecutive serial numbers, in unmarked, older currency. We have tested this, and the money will fit into five large duffle bags. If we discover a marked bill or a tracking device of any kind, the woman and child will be executed. We also demand the release of the follow five *ISIS* prisoners of war, currently residing in Guantanamo Bay."

The caller provided the names of five terrorists currently imprisoned in Cuba and told the operative that he had seventy-two hours to comply or the hostages would be executed. Parsons shuddered. If Al-Baklavi was serious about the Guantanamo releases, this made him more dangerous—he became a terrorist hostage-taker rather than a kidnapper. Money would not be his sole motivation. Since Parsons Security was a private team—the government was unaware of its efforts and negotiations—it had no power to release or even try to arrange for the release of Al-Baklavi's comrades. This was an off-book, unsanctioned negotiation. If the government knew Parsons was in Syria, negotiating with a member of *ISIS,* the government would shut them down. The United States does not officially negotiate with terrorists.

Blake or the Parsons negotiator would have to have further discussions with the kidnappers. Someone had to talk them out of the Guantanamo release demands because these negotiators lacked the ability to meet their demands. Zachary Blake worked up a strategy and presented it to Parsons, who was so surprised at its plausibility and Blake's audacity, he granted Blake permission to deliver the message.

Twenty-four hours later, Blake took the terrorist's follow-up call.

"You have forty-eight hours left. Do you have progress to report?"

"I am sorry to report that I do not. We have problems on both fronts," Zack began.

"Continue."

"Our negotiating team is made up of high net worth friends of the Izady family. We do not represent the government. The government did not sanction our visit and is not aware of our presence in Syria. As such, we have no power to release hostages currently imprisoned by the United States government.

"As you know, the United States' official position is that it does not negotiate with terrorists. If you force us to contact the government to ask them to release the prisoners, they will recall our negotiators and take over the operation. This will turn the situation into a dangerous hostage rescue, rather than a peaceful financial transaction, which I am more than willing to complete if given more time."

"More time?"

"Ten million dollars is a great deal of money. Converting such a high dollar amount into fifty-dollar bills takes time. Furthermore, I am having trouble raising the whole ten million. Would you entertain less money?"

The caller paused. "How much less?" he inquired.

Yes! The amount is random, and the abduction was not planned.

"We can provide two point five million in twenty-four hours."

"Unacceptable!" The caller roared. "You keep our brothers and pay us a quarter of the amount we demanded? I will terminate the woman and child on national television!"

"Wait," Zack urged, wondering if he'd carried the ruse too far. "I can get you more money; I just need more time."

"How much more money and how much more time?"

"Five million in seventy-two hours?"

"Time may be negotiable—price is not. Ten million dollars in seventy-two hours."

"I believe in complete honesty," Zack lied. "I'm not sure we can meet your demands."

The caller paused again. Someone was yelling in the background. "Time or money?"

"Time for certain. Money is possible, but it is difficult to obtain that amount in fifty-dollar bills here in Syria. I may need either more time or less money. And one more thing I must tell you."

"What is it?"

"The child has a medical condition and needs her medication." Zack glanced at Parsons and smiled.

"I thought you believed in complete honesty."

"I do. That is why I am telling you this. If the child does not get her medicine and dies, the father will not pay the ransom."

"Then we kill the mother, too."

"Neither parent will care. Without their precious daughter, both are dead anyway."

"I will call tomorrow for progress. We can discuss medicine, but I warn you. Patience is running thin."

"I will do my best—that's all I can do, okay?"

No answer.

"Are you there?"

No answer.

"He's gone." Zack hung up the telephone.

"Nice job, Blake. You bought us an extra twenty-four hours and a whole lot of internal strife on their side. That is crucial."

"I sense desperation. I believe there is room for further negotiation if we can demonstrate progress on the money."

"What do you have in mind?"

"When he calls tomorrow, I will express frustration—maybe I can't raise enough money. Maybe I can't obtain enough fifties. I'm not sure. I want to frustrate him, perhaps make him even more desperate."

"But not desperate enough to kill the woman and child," Graham warned.

"Of course not," Zack sighed. "I floated five million and seventy-two hours. Do you honestly think he would kill them and pass on that kind of money in three days?"

"True, I suppose, but you are assuming rational thought from irrational savages."

"No, I am assuming these guys took these hostages for a reason. And the reason is m-o-n-e-y. No way they are leaving these negotiations with this kind of money on the table."

"I'm inclined to agree with Mr. Blake," Parsons acknowledged. "Let's hope there is more progress tomorrow. In the meantime, we can fine-tune the rescue operation. Precision and practice, gentlemen, are the words of the day."

***

The tent entrance opened, and the woman called Rima eased in. To the delight of both mother and daughter, Hana was in Rima's arms. Rima held Hana out to Canan, and the jubilant mother completely forgot her captive status. She took and hugged the child, holding on for dear life and savoring the reunion. As things calmed, Canan sat on the dirt floor with Hana on her lap. She faced the woman.

"From the bottom of my heart, thank you for bringing me my daughter. When I met that huge, evil man, I didn't know what to think. I am positive you had a hand in protecting her, and I am very grateful."

"All praise is due *Allah*. I did nothing. They are trying to collect a ransom for you. I persuaded them they could negotiate whether you were separate or together."

"You talked sense into the senseless. That is an accomplishment. Thank you so much!"

"Listen to me. A woman has very little power here. Kidnapping a woman and her small child . . . " she faltered. "This should not be who we are, but I have no say. Do you understand?" She walked to the tent's entrance and stuck her head out the slit for a moment.

"What is it?" Canan wondered.

"Nothing." Rima brought her head back into the tent and turned to Canan. "I don't want anyone to hear me or mistake my intentions. I cannot help you."

"But if you don't agree . . ."

"I cannot act. These men will kill me if they believe I'm an infidel. I cannot risk this."

"I understand."

"Be patient. A negotiating team is here. They are negotiating."

"Negotiating team? Who?"

"I don't know. All I know is they are American."

"Is my husband with them?"

"I do not think so."

"Good. He would trade himself for us or do something stupid."

"Because he loves you."

"Because he loves us. He cannot be involved. Who is handling the negotiation? Who is offering money? How much?" Canan wondered. *Where is this money coming from?*

"I don't know anything, pretty one. This is dangerous. I must leave. Please do nothing to anger these men. They will take the child."

"I will behave."

"By the grace of *Allah*." The woman turned and exited the tent.

Chapter Fifteen

While Zachary waited for the telephone to ring, Parsons and his team continued to plan and rehearse the rescue operation. The plan required surgical execution. Parsons knew the approach and assault phase of the operation were the most volatile parts of the attempt—the team needed to remain undetected up to the time of breach, so they could maintain the element of surprise. Once the assault commenced, neutralization of the threat and control of the hostages would become the priority.

The team also rehearsed multiple contingency plans, including an emergency plan of action in the event anyone became compromised. One such plan included explosives, and team members practiced controlling the flow of force into the target area in such a way to avoid injury or death to team members or hostages.

They also practiced protecting the hostages after the assault commenced. They knew that breach, possible explosives, and rifle fire would shock the female hostages. Hostages are not prepared for this type of firepower. Their reactions are unpredictable. An assault from an unknown force might cause a hostage to turn to her captor for help. A braver or more aggressive hostage might even try to neutralize a guard. Whatever a hostage might or might not do, it was important to rehearse all possible scenarios. Everyone inside the breached crisis site had to be considered armed and dangerous until the rescue attempt identified all participants.

While many of the practiced scenarios were 'here's what to do when something goes wrong' type drills, one practice scenario dealt with a completely successful mission. When everything goes well, the rescue force might react with euphoria and overconfidence. The team practiced discipline in this scenario, focusing on complete self-control and hostage safety. The men studied maps of the compound and practiced securing the target area from outside intervention until the commander sounded an 'all-clear.' Comms were vital at this stage. The 'all-clear' message had to be delivered to all outer rim snipers to prevent any chance of fratricide.

Parsons delivered recent photographs of Canan and Hana to all team members. It was vital for all hostages to be carefully identified and accounted for in the operation. The men also practiced exfiltration of healthy *and* wounded hostages or team members who required attention. This included verifying and photographing the remains of anyone killed in the assault.

Securitization of the target area, the final step in the operation was practiced ad infinitum. The site would eventually be handed over to forensics experts and legal personnel—it was imperative to treat it as a crime scene. Keeping busybodies, curious onlookers, or reporters out of the target area would become a priority at this stage.

Success of the mission required unity of command, and no one questioned or doubted that Wayne Parsons was in command of the operation. While he ceded the negotiations phase to Zachary Blake, he supervised, communicated with, and directed Blake at all phases of negotiations. The team was quite familiar with failed hostage rescues in the past, and every failure featured a decentralization of command. In other words, one hand did not know what the other was doing. Thus, Parsons was firmly in control of each element of the plan, with complete control of every sub-element. Every operative would wear the Parsons uniform. Each would receive orders and commands from a centralized tactical operations and command center. This assured a coordination of all elements of the campaign, optimum communications at all phases, contingency planning on the fly, and a non-chaotic atmosphere. Decentralization led to a failed rescue operation. Parsons' favorite target in emphasizing this was the 1980 failed Iran Hostage Rescue.

Four telephones rang at a table that served as Zachary Blake and the negotiating team's operations station. Zack, Parsons, and two other commanders studied each other and counted to three on their fingers. They picked up receivers simultaneously—Zack would do the talking while the others listened in.

"Blake," Zack answered.

"Progress?" The voice demanded.

"A little." Zack fabricated.

"Define 'a little'." The caller insisted.

"Al-Baklavi?" Zack dropped a bombshell.

"So you know of me? Then you know this woman and her child mean nothing to me except as a tool to raise capital. If I do not get what I want, they will soon be with *Allah*."

Zack accomplished his goal of confirming that the captor was Al-Baklavi. "I have more money, but not what you asked for." Zack delivered the phony news.

"How much and when?"

"$3.5 million in thirty-six hours. The time issue is the bank, not us. They need time to convert the cash into fifty dollar bills."

"$3.5 million will not be enough to save their lives."

"Then, execute them and leave all that money on the table," Zack blustered. The three commanders heaved at the comment.

"Not a problem, goodbye." Zack heard an audible clicking sound. Al-Baklavi had hung up the phone.

"Nice work, Blake. The woman and child are dead, and we came all this way for nothing," Graham snapped. The others, except for Parsons, nodded in agreement. Parsons rubbed his chin, studying Zachary Blake

"Patience, gentlemen." Zack countered, with less bravado than normal. He, too, second-guessed his approach. "This man will not leave three and a half mil on the table. He'll call back."

"Well, Mr. Blake," Parsons chimed in. "He'd better because we aren't among his circle of friends. We don't have *his* number, now, do we?" he grumbled.

"He'll call back," Zack assured.

The men sat back and waited. No one spoke. The assault team ceased practice maneuvers and joined the others, getting a quick briefing from Parsons and Graham. Everyone in the room focused on the bank of telephones.

The telephones suddenly rang, startling the men, causing all trained operatives to jump.

"Blake."

"Mr. Blake? I will give you one last chance. I am a reasonable man. You have your thirty-six hours, but I require $5 million. If I do not get what I want, I will execute one of the hostages and the price for the other will rise to $7.5 million. Do you understand and agree?"

Zack glanced over at Parsons, who shook his head in the affirmative.

"I'll see what I can do," Zack retorted, ever the negotiator. "What about the child's medicine? According to her father, she could become quite ill." He held his breath awaiting a response. Parsons wanted to grab an assault rifle and shoot him.

"The child seems fine to me. She has no symptoms. Her medication must wait until we complete our business. Get me what I need as soon as possible. Act as if the life of the child depends on it because it does. I will call for confirmation at this time tomorrow. When I call, you will have twelve hours to come up with the money and have it ready for delivery. I will provide further instructions at that time."

"If anything happens to that child, all bets are off. The child is this couple's number one priority." Zack poured it on. Parsons scowled.

"How do you say in America? We cross that bridge when it comes upon us," Al-Baklavi reasoned.

"Her safety is your responsibility. If you want the ransom money, she must remain healthy and safe. We'll talk tomorrow, okay? Okay? Hello?" Al-Baklavi was gone. Zack was speaking to a dead line. Everyone breathed a sigh of relief.

"Zack, I know you're financing this operation, but you cannot go all cowboy on us like that. There is a chain of command, and you breached it. We have tons of experience; we know what we're doing. Stay with the program. Follow orders or keep your money. Find someone else and we'll be on our way. This only works if we are all on the same page, understood?" Parsons ranted.

"You're right, commander. I apologize. It's the lawyer in me. I can't resist maximizing a negotiation. It won't happen again," Zack pledged.

Silence enveloped the room. The mood became solemn as each man now knew engagement for Operation Mother-Daughter was only hours away.

***

Canan was enjoying precious moments alone with Hana, unaware that only a few miles away a precision covert team would soon execute a rescue operation. Mother and daughter were bonding and reacquainting from their time away. They sang songs and played games to help maintain Hana's suddenly happy mood. They played 'Itsy-Bitsy Spider,' 'Patty-cake,' 'Peek-a-Boo,' 'Wheels on the Bus,' 'Open Shut Them,' 'Funny Face,' and 'Simon Says.'

As most parents know, children love to play the same games over and over again. They are wired to practice until they get the game or song right, almost to the point of obsession. Under normal circumstances, the repetition of the same songs and activities, to the point of exhaustion, would have caused Canan to cut Hana off. In captivity, however, a happy, laughing toddler was priceless. Canan was more than happy to endure the repetitive activity.

Canan almost welcomed the interruption when Al-Baklavi and Rima entered the tent.

"We have good news. Your husband has agreed to our terms," Al-Baklavi boasted.

"So, you will let us go?" Canan brightened.

"I haven't decided," the terrorist mocked. "Maybe I will let *you* go, keep the child, and train her in our ways."

"I would *die* before I would let that happen," Canan blurted with unintended truculence. Al-Baklavi made her pay for it, smacking her across the face, knocking her to the floor.

"Your death can be arranged," the terrorist snarled.

"Mommy!" Hana screamed, crawling toward her mother.

"Mommy is fine, sweetheart," Canan whispered, opening her arms to the child.

"He's a mean man!" Hana scolded, glaring at Al-Baklavi.

"Ha-ha-ha-ha-ha-ha!" Al-Baklavi laughed maniacally. "She has, what do they call it in America? Spunk? She's got spunk. She will make a great warrior."

Canan wisely held her tongue.

"I expect we will know more in the next twenty-four hours. Perhaps I should have Rima take the child until you learn some manners," Al-Baklavi taunted.

"Please, no. Please, sir," Canan pleaded. Squeezing Hana tightly. Rima bowed her head and shook it from side to side.

Al-Baklavi paused, tugged on his beard, and studied mother and daughter. He purposefully made a game of deciding whether to take or leave the child, taunting Canan. The young mother was terrified. "If you behave until then, the child may remain with you," he finally determined.

"Thank you!" Canan cried. "Thank you so much."

"Rima will get you and the child cleaned up and ready. Behave!" he ordered. "Both of you!" He glared at Canan, then at Hana, and back again to Canan. "Have I made myself clear?"

Canan nodded silently. Hana buried her face in her mother's shoulder. Al-Baklavi turned and stormed out of the tent.

"What did I tell you, pretty one? You mustn't antagonize this man!" Rima warned.

"I know, but he is an infuriating bast . . ." Canan stopped mid-sentence with a glance toward Hana.

"I understand. This is exactly why I caution you."

"I'm sorry," she conceded. After a few moments of silence, Canan considered Rima and wondered aloud, "Do you think this man will release us if the ransom is paid?"

"Only *Allah* knows for sure."

"But you know this Al-Baklavi. Does he keep his word?"

"To those he knows, loves, and trusts, yes. But he is capable of raining down terrible evil and terror on any sworn enemy. In his mind, anyone from America is an infidel from the west."

"So, if he is paid—will he keep his word?"

"Time will tell. Let's get you two cleaned up."

***

The woman known as Rima finished her cleaning tasks and
returned to her tent. She reclined on the sand floor, alone, silent,
reflecting on the past. *What could I have done differently?*

She was born in Palestine, but her family migrated to Syria
for reasons unknown to her. She attended high school and even
studied sacred knowledge at the University of Damascus. Rima
wanted to be a teacher.

Before the Syrian Civil War began in 2011, woman had more
freedom and access to education. Women's issues in Syria were
gaining attention, and Rima intended to be on the front lines of
change. As the war dragged on and *ISIS* rose to prominence,
women's issues were shunted to the side.

Women were relegated to stereotypical female roles of
childcare and housework. Husbands could prohibit wives from
working outside the home. In two short years, the percentage of
women working outside the home decreased by over twenty
percent.

Despite being unable to complete her education and find
work in her chosen field, Rima saw opportunity where other
women saw only despair and degradation. The violent war
caused large numbers of men, husbands, sons, fathers, and
brothers, to be disabled, killed, or go missing. A shortage of men
resulted in a mini rise to power for women, an unusual
circumstance that suddenly made women heads of households.

Rima used this temporary situation to self-educate, learn self-
defense techniques, and plot her eventual escape from Syria. She
founded an underground women's rights group, mobilizing
women to educate themselves, engage in political activism, and
learn skills that would make them more productive members of
society.

But war eventually causes displacement, and Rima found
herself in a camp where women and children needed leadership.
The shortage of men meant that strong women like Rima would
become the main source of income to feed less accomplished
women and children. With community support, Rima set up a
soap-making business, founded a factory, employed other
women, and found success. Her customers thought her business

was run by a man, her brother, who happily accepted credit in exchange for doing nothing.

Rima and some friends became involved in an underground group that reported on the war. She eventually created a small communications company that included an underground radio station where she and her colleagues interviewed freedom fighters. In her reporter role, she interviewed a young idealist named Qassim Al-Baklavi. At the time, Qassim was open to female empowerment, education, non-traditional employment, and even women in the military. Things began to go from bad to worse, however, and police officers and security personnel began to demand sexual favors in return for safety. Women were required to comply and stay silent, threatened with death or public humiliation.

Al-Baklavi was sickened by this behavior, and promised to rescue Rima from such a fate, offering her cheap passage to safety. Rima was responsible for the care of many and determined that a strong man might change the dynamic, protect her and others, and help them escape tyranny, the prospect of domestic violence, and poverty.

For a time, Al-Baklavi was a gentleman, true to his word. He provided protection and safe passage, as promised, and Rima continued her journey of self-improvement, studying the English language and mathematics. But Al-Baklavi began to meet with other men, violent men, and slowly began engaging in disturbing behavior.

He restricted her activities, denied her access to books, and, worse, began to show signs of becoming radicalized. As time passed, Rima rued the day she met Al-Baklavi, who rose to number two status at *ISIS*. Rima was, once again, relegated to second class citizenship. She longed for freedom, the day she could rejoin the fight for literacy and work skills for women. *How can a woman who loses her husband obtain the skills necessary to support her family?* Unknown to Rima, she was about to learn this lesson the hard way.

Chapter Sixteen

Emma and Emilio Gonzalez struggled to remember their parents. Days became weeks—weeks became a month and then two. And not once in all that time did any *ICE* official think to question the two children about their country of origin or current citizenship status. That's how sure these immigration professionals were that they were doing good work for the government, rounding up and eventually deporting people, regardless of the tragic consequences to their families. If just one government employee had asked, "hey kids—where are you from?" these two children would be at home with their parents. Alas, no one thought to ask Emma, Emilio, or anyone else.

El Paso city residents were unhappy about the camp and perceived conditions there. As a result, they constantly called out and complained to their elected officials. El Paso County votes decidedly 'blue' in 'red' Texas. The public and its elected officials were consistently pushing back against the feds.

The *El Paso Times* wrote scathing op-eds about immigration policy, first targeting former president Ronald John. The press was relentless, especially when it became clear that President Golding would continue President John's outrageous and unconstitutional immigration policies. High-profile celebrities and political leaders from all over the country descended upon El Paso. They held rallies, denouncing the 'humanitarian crisis at the border,' demanding the release of the children.

"The Golding administration dehumanizes young immigrants, locks them in cages, and ignores their status as asylum-seekers. Seeking asylum is *not* illegal. We are seeing chilling reports of inhumane conditions at these detention centers," a local official argued.

"The words 'America' and 'detention center' should never be uttered in the same sentence, yet here we are." A protestor shouted from a makeshift podium at one rally. "We want all our citizens to know what is happening here. Kids from all over the country and the world are being brought here by the thousands.

They are imprisoned in detention camps thousands of miles from home. They're alone, in make-shift tent cities or abandoned warehouses. We are better than this. I ask my fellow citizens across this great country: Do we want to be a country of prison camps for children and walls at our borders or the land of the free, building bridges to citizenship? America is a nation of immigrants. Their story our story? This isn't a red or blue issue—it is a uniquely *American* issue!" The crowd erupted in cheers and shouts of "free the children."

Micah Love and Reed Spencer watched the protests on television.

"That is despicable, Reed. You expect this in a third-world country, not in America," Micah wailed.

"True that, Micah. If you recall, when we first started looking into this, someone said that these kids were being transported all over the country. You don't think there's any chance they would have sent the Gonzalez kids as far away as *Texas*, do you?"

"Not under normal circumstances. But if they were sent that far away, I've got two better questions for you: How many camps are there and where is the nearest one? That's where I'd start my search. Meanwhile, I've talked to a couple of local actors. They're willing to help us implement your plan. Let's try both tactics. We'll go with whatever bears fruit first," Micah decided.

As Micah and Reed were finalizing strategy, Emma and Emilio were cleaning toilets in the very same El Paso immigration camp that was the subject of the televised protests. They'd been at it since 6:30 AM, when the staff made the usual loud banging noises to alert the kids it was time to rise.

Before breakfast, Emma and Emilio were ordered to the bathrooms and made to scrub them spotless. This was their day to empty all waste, trashcans, and bags full of dirty toilet paper. Everyone took turns doing it. When the children finally finished, without little opportunity to wash, they were fed breakfast, eggs the consistency of a sponge, some mysterious and unrecognizable breakfast meat, and a glass of sour milk. The kids always followed orders and always behaved because they were taught to obey adults. They also believed good behavior would one day be rewarded with a reunion with their parents.

They learned which staff members were "good guys," which were not, and to stay away from the "bad guys." If they encountered one or the other, they determined to be on their best behavior. One of their friends, a young boy from Haiti, was injected with drugs to deal with his 'agitation.'

The condition manifested itself in fits of rage where he would pitch a fit, throw things, run from staff members, and damage or destroy things. After his 'shot,' the boy would calm, fall asleep, and staff members would carry him to bed. Emma warned Emilio that this could easily happen to one of them if they behaved as the boy from Haiti did. Emilio managed to toe the line, always trying to please his big sister.

Their saddest and happiest days were always 'goodbye days.' Once in a while, a judge would find a camper's parent and order the family reunited. Each time this happened, campers and staff members gathered to say *buena suerte, hasta luego*, good luck, see you later. These occasions were always bittersweet for Emma and Emilio. They were happy for the departing child but sad that they weren't chosen. Still, these events kept them going and gave them hope.

***

Back in Michigan, two uniformed officers in an official-looking vehicle, with federal government plates, pulled into the parking lot of the infamous Detroit Detention Center. The officers exited the vehicle and walked toward the entrance to the building. Their uniforms identified them as two-star generals.

The generals entered the building and approached the front desk. The male receptionist immediately stood at attention and saluted. The two generals glanced at each other and saluted back.

"As you were, soldier," one general ordered.

"Sir, yes sir!" The receptionist barked.

"Be seated, soldier," the other general ordered, suppressing a grin. The soldier sat down.

"We're here to see your commanding officer, Cap . . ." The general looked down at a piece of paper in his hand, reading the name off the paper. "Captain Gordon Billings." The tone was more 'order' than 'request.'

"I'll see if he's in, sir. Who shall I say is calling?"

"General Moreland and General Philpot. We're from Washington."

"Right away, sir." The nervous desk clerk pointed to a row of seats. "Would you like to have a seat? Can I get you anything, coffee, tea, water?"

"You can get me Billings! What's your name son?" The general squinted to read the name off the desk clerk's badge.

"Burkes, sir. Private first-class Jeremy Burkes."

The other general cut Burkes some slack. "Burkes—we'd like to see Captain Billings. Sooner rather than later because we are on a tight schedule."

"Yes, sir!" He picked up the telephone and punched some numbers. Someone picked up on the other side of the call. "Captain Billings? Generals Moreland and Philpot from Washington are here to see you, sir. Stat!"

"I'll be right out, Burkes. Offer them some refreshments."

"Way ahead of you, Captain. They are on a tight schedule, sir."

"I'm coming."

In less than a minute, Captain Gordon Billings appeared at the door leading from the reception area into the detention center.

"Generals, I'm Captain Gordon Billings. Welcome to the Detroit Detention Center. How may I assist you?" Billings was deferential in posture and tone. Private Burkes suppressed a grin.

"Something to eat or drink?"

"Burkes was very kind, Captain. He offered but we declined. We have very little time."

"Duly noted. Come on in." Billings looked exactly as Blake described, with the stick up the ass and everything. They walked a short way down a narrow hallway and stopped at a small office. Billings motioned the two senior officers into the office and hand-motioned them to occupy two seats in front of his desk.

General Philpot ignored him and sat in Billings' executive chair. He motioned for Billings to have a seat next to Moreland, on the opposite side of the desk. Billings did as he was ordered.

"We are looking for someone," Philpot revealed. "Actually, we're looking for two kids. Supposedly, they were brought here. I doubt they're still here, the way we move these people around, but this was their initial stop. We need to find them and stop the bleeding."

"The bleeding, sir?" Billings inquired.

"Two children were picked up in a raid on their school in . . ." Philpot again referred to the paper in his hand. "Lincoln Park," he appeared to read off the paper.

"I remember the raid, sir. What about these kids?"

"Did anyone bother to inquire as to their citizenship?" General Moreland demanded.

"No, sir. The orders to raid the school came directly from Washington. Why would we question orders?"

"I'm not asking if you questioned orders, soldier! I'm asking if you questioned citizenship!" Philpot snapped. "Aren't all detainees interrogated?"

"These were children. If I recall correctly, they were the children of a couple of undocumented workers from the raid on the Riverview filler plant. Most of those were from Venezuela. We don't usually interrogate children."

"Did it occur to you or anyone in your charge that these kids might have been born in the U.S.A., Captain?" Philpot dropped the hammer.

"Sir? How is that possible?"

"That's what we want to know, Billings. How is it possible that you and your staff could be so incompetent as to arrest and imprison two completely innocent *American citizens*?"

The color drained from Billings' face. "Sir, as I indicated, the orders to conduct the raid on the school followed the raid on the filler plant. We were ordered to locate and detain these two children . . . uh . . . I forget their names, 'Rodriguez,' 'Lopez,' 'Hernandez,' or some other Mexican name of some sort," Billings stammered.

"All those names sound alike, do they, Billings? They all look alike too, right?"

"Sir, with all due respect, I was only following orders."

"Isn't that what the Nazis claimed, Billings?"

"Sir?"

"Forget it, Billings. Gonzalez – Emma and Emilio Gonzalez. Ring a bell?"

"Sir, yes sir!" Billings cried.

"Are they here, Billings?" General Philpot appeared anxious.

"Sir, no sir," Billings replied.

"Their parents were, indeed, part of the Riverview filler plant raid, Billings," Moreland advised. Billings relaxed a bit, expelling a short-lived sigh of relief. "But these two kids were born in the United States, you moron! They are American citizens! We have confirmed this. We must find them. *Homeland* and *ICE*'s tracking system is awful, to say the least."

"We agree on that, sir. Let me check and see if I have a file on the children. What are their names, again, sir?"

"Emma and Emilio Gonzalez."

"Permission to leave to go check the file, generals?" Billings rose.

"Ahem, permission granted!" Philpot cleared his throat, suppressing another grin. Billings exited the room. Moreland addressed Philpot immediately after Billings left the room. "You're laying it on way too thick. Take it down a notch. Micah won't be happy if we blow this."

"In a situation like this one, isn't this how a pissed off general *would* behave? These boobs have arrested, kidnapped, and imprisoned two American children for over two months! They separated them from their parents and sent them God knows where. How pissed should a genuine two-star general be? This Billings character needs to feel our wrath."

The door opened and Billings entered the room with a file in his hand. He sat down, opened the file, and began to read. "Emma and Emilio Gonzalez, Lincoln Park, Michigan—children of Mary Carmen and Miguel Gonzalez—undocumented immigrants arrested in the filler plant raid. They were first brought here, then flown to a detention camp in El Paso."

"Texas?" Philpot exploded. "Why the . . . why would they take Michigan children all the way to Texas?" Philpot fought to curb his outrage and language.

"Because we have no facilities for children here in the Midwest or anywhere in the northeastern sections of the country. All children's detention centers are located in the south, most near the Mexican border," Billings advised. "Surely you know this, General." For the first time since they walked through his door, Billings regarded Philpot with suspicion.

Philpot gathered himself. "Of course, I know this, Billings. I'm just angry as hell about this whole affair. How the hell does Washington order the arrests of American citizens? There will be hell to pay for whoever screwed the pooch on this one," Philpot raged. Billings recoiled back into his defensive cocoon.

"Be a good gent, Billings. Copy that file for us? We'll be on our way, hopefully, to correct this travesty and prevent the damned lawsuit that will surely be filed if we don't fix this." Moreland promised, playing good cop to Philpot's bad cop.

"Right away, sir." He rose and left the room.

"Good save," Moreland sighed. I really thought you were going to blow our cover with that 'what are they doing in Texas' shit."

"Couldn't have pulled it off without your 'good cop,' General Moreland." Philpot saluted. Billings walked back into the office.

"Generals, here's a full copy of the file and the report. I'm awfully sorry about this. Is there anything else I can do for you?"

"No, Billings, I think you've done quite enough, don't you?" Philpot snapped. He drew another glare from Moreland.

"Sir, again, I only followed the orders I received from *Homeland.* I have them in writing, in the file."

"We will note that in our report, Billings," Moreland 'good copped.'

"That would be greatly appreciated, General."

"In fact, Billings, we *could* keep your name out of the report entirely." Moreland floated the life-saving device.

"Sir?" Billings seemed to like the idea.

"Say nothing of our visit, your participation, or our receipt of the file. We weren't here and we never met. We obtained this information of our own devices. Sound good?" Moreland floated.

"Sounds *great*," Billings cried. "But how could you possibly obtain the information on your own?"

"Leave that to us. Do we have an agreement, and do I have your word?"

"Pleasure to be of service, General." Billings stood and saluted. The two men rose awkwardly and saluted back, banging elbows in the process. Billings looked confused.

Billings escorted the two generals to the lobby. The receptionist was gone. A yellow sticky note with the names Generals Philpot and Moreland sat on the desk. Moreland scooped up the notes and crumbled them in his right fist.

"A pleasure to meet you, Billings. Thanks for your assistance," Philpot blustered.

"We've never met, sir," Billings smiled and winked.

"You're a quick study, Billings. When this is all over, I am going to recommend you for a promotion," Moreland promised.

"Hard to do that for someone you never met and don't know, but thanks for the thought. Your secret is safe with me, gentlemen. I'm content with having no role in this entire affair."

"What affair, young man? What's your name?"

"Exactly, sir. Have a great day."

The two generals walked out into the parking lot, eyed each other, and breathed a sigh of relief.

"Wow, that bit worked beyond my wildest dreams. Wait until Micah and Reed get a look at this file. They'll be thrilled! Maybe we'll get a bonus," Moreland exclaimed.

"From Mr. Cheap, Micah Love? Dream on!"

"Well, bonus or no bonus, that was a great performance, best of your career."

"Back at you, man. What career?"

Chapter Seventeen

Waiting to execute is an advisable strategy in hostage negotiations. It allows the negotiations process to take hold, intelligence to be gathered, and the rescue team to practice and appropriately prepare to execute a skillful recovery plan. To this point in the crisis, negotiations had been effective on three fronts: 1. Al-Baklavi's demands had been considerably whittled down. 2. Ongoing talks and agreed-upon delays led to important reconnaissance missions and actionable intelligence about the location of the hostages and terrorists. 3. The rescue operatives were able to develop, repetitively practice, fine-tune, and effectively amend the rescue plan.

The time had come for what Parsons and Zack presumed would be the last telephonic ransom and hostage recovery negotiation. When Al-Baklavi and Blake last spoke, the terrorist reduced his demand to five million dollars within thirty-six hours. Twenty-four hours had passed, leaving the parties a million and a half apart with a maximum of twelve hours to reach an agreement.

When the call finally came, Zack's goal was to negotiate a twelve-hour increase in the timeline, which would move the exchange to the evening hours. The time difference was crucial because it would provide the rescue team cover of darkness to carry out its mission. The plan included assuring the safety of the negotiating team. By design, Jack Dylan and Shaheed Ali were made part of the negotiating team and placed in charge of Zack's personal security. The two veteran police officers took their work seriously and understood the importance of the assignment. Dylan, true to form, couldn't resist needling Blake about the two cops' role in the mission.

"Yeah," Jack stretched and yawned, feigning boredom. "I guess Parsons didn't consider you important enough to be guarded by the 'A' team, so he created a 'B' team to protect your ass," he chuckled. "A young mother is a much more important commodity than a scum-sucking lawyer, wouldn't you say,

Shaheed? Say, what's the difference between a lawyer and a catfish?"

"I don't know, Jack. What's the difference between a lawyer and a catfish?" Shaheed played along.

"One is a scum-sucking bottom-feeder and the other is a fish." Zack and Jack revealed, simultaneously, conflicting attitudes.

"Jinx!" Zack yelled, recalling a childhood game. The first to cry 'jinx' after two people spoke the same words, at the same time, had the power to prevent the other from speaking again until the jinx caller freed him to speak.

"Screw you, Blake. 'Jinx' is for kids," Jack muttered.

"So are lawyer jokes, asshole," Zack retorted.

"Especially when the lawyer you joke about is responsible for the freedom you currently enjoy," Shaheed playfully rebuked.

"Yeah, you ungrateful bastard, everyone hates lawyers until they need one," Zack blustered.

Jack became serious. "No one loves and appreciates you more than I do," he conceded. "You saved my ass in Manistee. It will be my pleasure to protect yours in Syria."

"I did my job. Just make sure you do yours," Zack challenged.

"You can count on me, Zack."

"Me, too," Shaheed added.

"I am lucky to count you two among my friends," Zack admitted.

"Us, too," Shaheed and Jack responded.

"Jinx!" Jack shouted.

***

A few minutes later, the telephone rang, and everyone became dead serious. Zack and the usual participants picked up their respective receivers. A call recorder was automatically activated.

"Do you have the money?" The caller demanded.

"Yes, but there is one little . . . uh . . . hitch."

"*Hitch?*" The caller gasped.

"The bank needs more time to convert the money to fifties. We can get the five million bucks in twenty-four hours, but not in twelve." This was a vital part of the plan—mission success probability was far greater under cover of darkness than in daylight hours. Would Al-Baklavi detect the ruse? The long period of silence on the other end of the line was deafening.

"Agreed," Al-Baklavi finally whispered.

"Wonderful, how shall we make the exchange?"

" I will contact you in twenty-two hours."

"Works for me," Zack acknowledged. "Hello? Hello?" Al-Baklavi was gone.

"The guy's a brilliant conversationalist," Zack quipped.

***

The operations strategy was to have two strike teams. A larger team would storm the compound where the hostages were being held. A smaller team, including Dylan and Ali, would protect negotiating personnel at the proposed exchange site. The plan was for the larger team to hit the target site forty-five minutes to an hour before the proposed exchange meeting, depending upon its proximity to the compound.

After the telephone call, drills began again in earnest. The negotiating team practiced various scenarios in anticipation of a strike occurring before, during, and after the meet. Would Al-Baklavi bring the hostages? Did he intend to appear in person? For obvious reasons, Zack, Jack, and Shaheed hoped that the rescue mission resolved the crisis well before the planned meeting time.

The rescue team continued to fine-tune operational techniques and strategy. Rescue drills were conducted, ad nauseam. Parsons decided to surround the compound in twenty to twenty-one hours and commence the rescue operation simultaneous with Al-Baklavi's call. The terrorist's guard would be down at that juncture, as he would be engaged in a discussion about how and where the exchange would be made. Instead, all hell would break loose. The deception and surprise elements of the operation would completely disorient the terrorists, giving the assault team precious time to dominate and eliminate any remaining threat to the hostages. Reconnaissance missions provided the team with more specific details such as the number of terrorists and their choice of weapons, the geography of the compound, location of the hostages, and number of guards assigned to them. Almost nothing was left to chance. Parsons felt good about the prospects for success. He called a halt to all mission maneuvers and ordered the men to get a good night's sleep.

***

The following morning, the men continued to practice operational maneuvers. Strategists discussed 'if this then that' scenarios, trying to cover all possible contingencies and outcomes. All scenarios placed hostage safety and recovery at the forefront. As they observed from the command table, Zack, Shaheed, and Jack marveled at the expertise and professionalism of the operatives.

"These guys should train local, state, and federal officers," Zack opined, expecting pushback from Shaheed and Jack.

"I must admit, they are unbelievably proficient," Jack agreed. "As we have learned, a team can practice as much as it wants. The key is to execute in the actual operation as well as it does in drills."

"Practice makes perfect," Shaheed noted.

"True, but practice is still practice. Hopefully, their execution in real-life situations is as flawless as their preparatory drills. How do they think and adjust on the fly to situations on the ground? What if things are not exactly as they seem? We had that experience dealing with Blaine and Breitner, remember?"

"All too well," Shaheed recalled.

'Blaine and Breitner' were white supremacists Jack and Shaheed went toe-to-toe with back in the day. Benjamin Blaine kidnapped Arya Khan, now Shaheed Ali's wife, after Zack Blake proved her innocent of another white supremacist's murder. Bart Breitner was a Blaine protégé who sought revenge against Dylan and Blake for Blaine's downfall. Breitner devised and attempted to implement a chemical weapons attack against the Dearborn Police. Jack and his team foiled the plot, chased down Breitner, caught up with him in Manistee, and found himself on trial for the terrorist's murder. Zack flew to Manistee to represent Jack, and, in the aftermath of the trial, the men became friends.

"As a devout pacifist, I hope they're as good as they appear to be. I'd prefer to skip negotiating with a psychopathic terrorist who wouldn't mind a rendezvous with seventy-two virgins in heaven," Zack cracked.

"Amen to that, counselor. A successful operation would make all of our jobs easier."

***

While Zack, Jack, and Shaheed were reminiscing about white supremacists, Canan and Hana were eating some type of breakfast mush that resembled cream of wheat but tasted like cardboard. Rima was assigned to get them prepared for the exchange.

Aside from the foul taste of the food, Canan had no appetite—she was too apprehensive. *Will money satisfy this brutish terrorist? Will he honor his word? Or are murder, mayhem, and terror the only language he understands? What would happen to Hana if something happened to me? Will they imprison her and turn her into one of them?* She shuddered at the thought and hugged herself.

"What is it, pretty one?" Rima noticed Canan's distress.

"Nothing. Just thinking. Is it almost time for the exchange? I worry Al-Baklavi won't keep his word. What will become of us?"

"He has done this a few times before and kept his word," Rima softened.

"With the United States on the other side?" Canan wondered.

"Well . . . no, never with the United States, with western countries aligned with the United States."

"This man would probably like nothing more than to embarrass the United States," Canan presumed.

"Probably true. But he *loves* himself and American dollars. I do not think he will break his promise."

"Have they actually reached a final agreement? We have no money. Where is this money coming from? Are you sure it was promised?"

"That is my understanding. I am a woman. In Syria, a woman does not have a role in these matters. My only job is to attend to you and your beautiful daughter."

"Thank you," Canan's eyes darted toward Hana, happily eating the dreadful breakfast concoction. "She is beautiful, isn't she? You won't let anything happen to her, will you?" Canan pleaded.

"No, my pretty one. I will do everything in my power to protect both of you."

Hana sensed the women were talking about her. She stopped eating and glanced at the two of them. She had mush all over her face. "Mama?" she mumbled, spitting out cereal as she spoke.

"Everything is fine, precious. Finish your breakfast." Canan smiled at Hana and turned to Rima, grim-faced. "I'm counting on you."

* * *

Approximately ten hours later, the telephones rang at the Parsons Security command center. As all participants practiced, each silently mouthed a three count and simultaneously picked up receivers. Once again, the call recorder automatically clicked on. Zachary Blake said nothing, waiting on the caller.

"Has all been arranged?" Al-Baklavi demanded.

"Yes," Zack lied.

"You have the money in fifties?"

"Yes."

"Excellent. We can set up the exchange."

"We want proof of life."

"Hold."

The phone went silent. Minutes and seconds seemed like hours.

"H-hello?" A timid female voice came on the line. "To whom am I speaking?"

"My name is Zachary Blake. Is this Canan Izady?"

"Yes."

"Ms. Izady, I am so sorry to meet you under these circumstances. Your husband has asked me to negotiate your safe return home. Just to confirm you are who you say you are, what is your husband's name, and where do you live?"

"My husband's name is Karim. We live in Dearborn."

"Very good. How are you and the child doing? Have you been harmed in any way? How is Hana doing without her heart medication?" Zack floated the ruse, hoping she'd catch it and play along.

"Med . . .? Oh . . . yes . . . she needs her medication. So far, though, she seems to be holding up. She's scared. We're both scared. We have not been seriously harmed, roughed up a bit."

Quick study—can think on her feet. "Thank you, Ms. Izady. Hang in there. We will do everything we can to get you out of there. Let me speak to . . ."

Al-Baklavi abruptly cut Zack off mid-sentence. "I am here. You are speaking to me. As you can see, the woman and child are fine."

"Roughed up a bit is not fine."

"These are rough conditions. That is all she is referring to. Confirm, please. Everything is in place?"

"It will be. The child must have her medication. Would you consider an early compassionate release of the child, so we can get her medical care and the medicine she needs? You keep the mother, and the numbers remain the same. How about it? This would make things much more cordial," Zack pleaded.

"The child is fine. No more negotiating. Do we have a deal or not?"

"When and where do we make the exchange?"

"So you can prepare an ambush? Stupid, I am not, Mr. Blake. I will make contact one half-hour before the time of exchange. And if I see any sign of Syrian military or U.S. operatives, I will execute the woman and child."

"Seven hours?"

"Maybe."

"We will need more than one half-hour to get to the exchange site. We don't know where we're going or what type of vehicles we need," Zack argued. Al-Baklavi did not respond.

"Hello?" Zack cried. "Son-of-a-bitch! He's gone! I hate this asshole!"

"We got what we needed. It appears the timetable is seven hours. Al-Baklavi may now be wondering about the health of the child, one more item to worry about. It will be dark well before the time set for the exchange, which will permit us to launch and execute the assault and rescue operation effectively and efficiently. We could not have asked for more optimum ground conditions. They'll never know what hit them. The deception and surprise elements of the operation are in place. All we need to do is execute with precision." Parsons rallied the troops.

"This may be Monday morning quarterbacking, but wouldn't it be better to stage the rescue at the exchange? Better yet, perhaps we just pay the ransom and finish the negotiation without resorting to violence." Jack suggested. "Let them bring the hostages to us, one way or the other, so to speak."

"That is what Al-Baklavi expects us to do. He's expecting a smooth exchange or some kind of heroics at that time. He has no idea a paramilitary operation is planned or that high-level operatives are in place. He has no idea we know where he is holding the hostages. He has no idea we have reconnoitered the site.

"Surprise is an important factor in these types of rescues. Past successful rescue operations have featured both deception and surprise. We have been able to obtain surprisingly detailed and solid intelligence. We know the layout and how many terrorists are in the compound. We also know where the hostages are located and how many people are assigned to that area. We've had excellent, almost pinpoint reconnaissance. The plan is solid—we're ready to implement. Trust me, Dylan, all we need to do now is execute. These guys are the best in the business." He turned to and proudly watched his men engaged in training exercises.

"I will defer to your expertise," Jack capitulated. He shrugged. His eyes shifted to Shaheed and Zack, seeking their silent opinions. Their expressions suggested assent to the plan, with deference to Parsons' careful planning, training, and experience.

"Everything will be fine, Jack. These guys are unbelievable!" Zack encouraged, wondering if he really believed it.

Chapter Eighteen

Generals Joshua Moreland and Frederick Philpot, aka actors Sam Roth and Liam Nelson, sat in the Love Investigations conference room, being debriefed by Micah Love and Reed Spencer. As Sam predicted, Micah and Reed were thrilled with the outcome of the mission. The four men now plotted their next move in anticipation of a go-ahead from Marshall and Zack. Micah was about to call Zack to give him the good news.

"The operation was exhilarating! I wasn't just playing the part of a general. I *was* a general! This Billings character never knew what hit him. 'Sir, yes sir' and all that shit!" Sam stood at attention and formally saluted the others.

"Zack will be very pleased," Micah smiled. "He didn't much care for that Billings character."

"Billings *is* kind of an asshole. Mr. Blake was right about that. The captain wasn't terribly concerned about the fact that he was part of a group of soldiers who have detained and imprisoned two American citizens for over two months. The prick just wanted his name kept out of the report." Liam reported.

"The ultimate asshole," Micah sighed. "So, gentlemen . . . I am thinking that now is not the time to retire your two-star uniforms," he floated.

"What do you have in mind?" Liam was intrigued, and . . . greedy.

"Have you guys ever been to El Paso?" Micah glanced at Reed.

"Can't say that we have. Long-distance travel is extra," Sam advised.

"Look, boys. I am notorious for being cheap. I admit it. I hire people to do a job and expect them to do it well for the fair price agreed upon upfront. You did your job; you will be paid. The good news is that you don't work for me. You work for Zachary Blake. And he's a very generous chap. Look around, gentlemen. His generosity paid for most of what you see."

The four men scanned their opulent surroundings. Micah's entire office was state-of-the-art. Renovations for this room alone cost mid-six figures. They sat at a marble conference table with ergonomic executive chairs all around, plush leather couches, a full kitchen, and mahogany bookshelves adorning all four walls. An eighty-inch television monitor was built into one wall—remote control devices operated the large screen television, built-in computers, monitors, cameras, and security equipment. Micah pressed a button, the table opened, and a phone appeared from its bowels. Micah's voice commanded the phone to call Zachary Blake. The large screen television came to life. A dial tone was instantly heard. After the number was automatically dialed, the phone began to ring. A clicking sound was heard. Zachary Blake's face suddenly appeared on the big screen.

"Blake here. Micah? Is that you?"

"It's me, Zack. Can you see and hear us okay? I know you're in a Syrian desert somewhere."

"I see you guys. The office looks great. What the hell? Do you refurbish every year?"

"We do have to stay on top of technology. Business success depends on it. *Capiche?*"

"Tish, you spoke French," Zack laughed, recalling *The Addams Family* television show.

"Italian, actually," Micah corrected.

"I knew that."

"Sure you did."

"So, what's up, Micah?" Zack noticed Reed and the other two gentlemen. "Hey Reed," he chirped. "All good? Who are these fine gentlemen?"

"These guys are Sam Roth and Liam Nelson. They are investigators who also happen to have acting experience."

"Liam Nelson, not Neeson? Some parent's wishful thinking?"

"Both gentlemen have worked as actors. That's where the similarity ends."

"That's not true," Liam protested. "I'm very talented, just waiting to be discovered. This investigating stuff is *temporary*."

"He *is* very talented, Zack. So is Sam over there."

"Nice to meet you, Sam—you too, Liam. We're kind of busy rescuing hostages here, Micah. Can we get to the point?" With Zack and Micah, the banter never stopped.

Sam and Liam glanced at each other. *Rescuing hostages? Who is this guy?*

"Sorry, Zack. I'll get right to the point. There is a reason Sam and Liam have visited today. In fact, you're *paying* them to be here."

"I am? I'm sure it was for a very good cause."

"It is, Zack. It most certainly is. Do you remember a military *ICE* dude named Gordon Billings? Captain Gordon Billings?"

"Asshole!" Zack retorted. The four men laughed out loud. Billings' assholiness was now unanimous.

"Everyone who meets this guy seems to feel the same way, Zack," Micah chuckled. "Anyway, about Captain Billings . . ."

"What about him?"

"We ran an undercover sting of sorts."

"Oh? What kind of sting?"

"We sent Sam and Liam into the detention center dressed as two-star generals. Zack, meet Generals Frederick Philpot and Joshua Moreland."

Zack grinned. "Nice to meet you, gentlemen. Thank you for your service."

"You're welcome," the two responded simultaneously.

"Jinx," Zack chirped.

"What?" Sam puzzled.

"Never mind," Zack laughed. "Back to the sting—what did you guys do?"

"These two brass-balled 'generals' walked into the Detroit Detention Center as two-stars Philpot and Moreland. They met with Billings and persuaded him to divulge the location of the Gonzalez children, ordered a full copy of the kids' *ICE* file, and, incredibly, walked out with the whole file. On top of it all, they convinced Billings that the whole operation was top secret! He won't utter a word to anyone. Everything is fine, Zack. We now know exactly where these kids are."

"Wow, Micah! That's the best news I've heard in weeks. Nice job, fellas. There will be a bonus waiting for you when I get back. Micah is such a cheap-ass! Am I right?"

"That's what I . . . " Liam began. Sam kicked him under the table. Sam understood who buttered the bread. "Ouch!" Liam groaned.

"They did their jobs and were well paid for it," Micah argued.

"Micah, pull the stick out of your ass. Give these guys an extra twenty-five hundred each. I'm good for it."

"Wow! Thanks, Mr. Blake!" Liam exclaimed.

"Yeah, thanks, Mr. Blake," Sam concurred.

"You're welcome. Thank *you* for your brilliant performances. Although, I can't say I'm surprised Billings went for it. He's kind of an idiot, right?"

"We met the man, remember?" Sam quipped. "Idiot is an understatement."

"So, what's next?"

"That's why I called. We have two choices—the straightforward, honest, and through the front door approach, or a less than honest, back door approach, using our two-star generals. What's your pleasure?" Micah wondered.

"How do *I* want to play it? What do you think they'll do when they discover that two of their captives are American citizens? They'll be looking at an eight or nine-figure false arrest and imprisonment claim. Shit, man! Could be even more when I file it and turn it into a multi-district class action that includes *all* of the kids they've done this to. Can anyone spell *cover-up*? I vote to put our two generals back in play. Just keep me out of this. I don't see how tricking the government into releasing American citizens from an immigrant detention camp can be illegal, but I don't want to be involved. I've got a reputation to uphold. Understood?"

Micah and Reed nodded. "We understand and agree, Zack." Micah turned to Sam and Liam. "Boys? You up for some travel and a repeat performance?"

"Can we discuss compensation with Mr. Blake?" Liam inquired.

"Zack? Zack? You're breaking up," Micah feigned. As Zack opened his mouth to reply, Micah pressed a button and terminated the call. He turned to the actors with a scowl on his face. "You guys work for me! Don't forget that! Zack's a good guy, as you now know. We don't take advantage. Are you in or not?"

"We're in," Sam agreed.

"I'm sure you'll be well taken care of," Micah glared at Liam.

"We're in, Micah. We're in!" Liam capitulated.

"Good! Let's get to work."

Chapter Nineteen

As the sun set in the Syrian Desert, darkness began to envelop the camp. The negotiations phase of Operation Mother-Daughter was over. Al-Baklavi telephoned twenty minutes earlier to demand a ransom/hostage exchange for twenty hundred hours. He refused to provide details until the exchange time drew closer, but Parsons didn't care. He had no intention of showing up at the arranged time or place. The operation would be over long before the scheduled exchange. Operatives were busy checking equipment, ammunition, backpacks, and other supplies. They would drive to within a mile of the camp and hike the rest of the way.

Jack and Shaheed wanted to be helpful. The veteran cops again offered their services to Parsons. He again declined; everything was in place. Those who trained for the mission were best equipped to execute and complete it. In stark contrast to Jack and Shaheed, Zack was quite pleased to be left behind.

"My Jewish mother does not approve of violence of any kind," he kibitzed.

When Parsons was satisfied with the conditions, he and the team left the camp. A few disgruntled team members drew short straws and were left behind to guard the camp, the attorney, and the two cops. When the operatives arrived at the designated mission launch site, they exited their vehicles, re-checked equipment and supplies, and proceeded on foot.

As the hostage compound came into view of their night vision goggles, a special support unit broke off from the larger group and belly crawled near the terrorist command center. These operatives planted technical surveillance equipment to monitor conversations and pinpoint the locations of certain terrorists. They also strategically placed explosives in front of several tents, a safe distance away from the target tent where they knew the hostages were being held.

The plan was to ignite the explosives at an allotted time, which would create a diversion while soldiers stormed the targeted tent. Between new surveillance and previous reconnaissance of the compound, there was virtually nothing the operatives did not know about the camp prior to strike time.

At exactly nineteen hundred hours, Parsons gave the signal to launch the attack on the terrorist base. The planted explosives were detonated; the commotion prompted the terrorists to emerge from tents. Snipers promptly acquired targets and put down those terrorists quickly and efficiently.

A second round of explosives was detonated as the designated hostage rescue team advanced on the hostage tent, occupied by a woman and a man. The second blast had an effect similar to the first. Terrorists panicked, scattered about, and were easily picked off by sniper fire. Others grabbed weapons, turned, kneeled, and opened fire toward the area where the sniper fire was coming from. Snipers fired back, killing more terrorists, prompting more panic, and causing the remaining terrorists to retreat. So far, the only wild card preventing this from being a flawless operation was that there was no sign of Al-Baklavi. Was their number one target in the hostage tent?

As the rescue team approached the hostage tent, a woman screamed. Shots rang out inside the tent, followed by an eerie silence. Men raced to the opening, guns at the ready, and ducked inside. A middle-aged Muslim woman stood, an anguished expression on her face, pointing an AR-15 rifle at the lifeless body of Qassim Al-Baklavi.

The woman turned, held up the rifle, and presented it to the rescuers. A young woman and small child lay in the corner of the tent, face down, the woman covering the child, almost to the point of smothering her. The woman's hands and feet were tied. A makeshift bomb sat on the ground nearby. Explosives experts quickly diffused the bomb. Rescue operatives retrieved and untied the terrified hostages' hands and feet.

Another operative secured the other woman and led her out of the tent. Snipers and back-up operatives descended on the site but quickly realized they were no longer needed. Thanks to a diminutive Muslim woman turning on their principal antagonist, Operation Mother-Daughter was a total success. Cleanup personnel were now the only specialists required.

***

Parsons, his rescue team, the uninjured former hostages, and a middle-aged female returned to the operations compound. The total success of the mission was already communicated to those who remained behind. Loud cheers erupted as the caravan approached the compound.

As Canan, Hana, and Rima were helped out of a custom Hummer, Canan turned to the handcuffed woman.

"From the bottom of my heart, thank you for saving our lives," she exclaimed.

"I had no choice," Rima cried. "I could not let him kill a young mother and a child, no matter what."

"Maybe so, but this was still an act of unbelievable courage. How does a nice woman like you hook up with terrorists?" Canan inquired.

"Qassim wasn't always a terrorist. We met and fell in love when he was a man of peace." Tears formed and ran down Rima's face.

"You mean . . ."

"Yes, my pretty one, Qassim Al-Baklavi was my husband."

"I'm so sorry for your loss," Canan offered, tears rolling down her cheek.

"From *Allah* we come, and back to *Allah* we shall go," Rima rationalized. "His death is his fault, my pretty one, not yours, not mine."

"Still . . ."

"I am at peace with my decisions today. May *Allah* forgive his sins and mine, and reward us with the highest heaven."

Canan turned to Parsons. "She treated us with tremendous kindness throughout this ordeal."

"It would seem you were a hero today, ma'am," Parsons turned to Rima. "I will do everything in my power to see you are treated with leniency."

"I do not deserve leniency. I deserve punishment. I submit myself to the will of *Allah*."

"Good," Canan steeled. "*Allah* loves and forgives you, despite the sins you committed. Man is harsh, judgmental, and critical—his laws can be unjust. But *Allah* loves you unconditionally. He created you. He tested you, and you passed with flying colors."

Canan turned back to Parsons. "What will happen to her, Mr. Parsons?"

"As I said, Ms. Izady, I will do everything I can to obtain leniency. Perhaps we can get Mr. Blake involved. I hear he's a pretty good lawyer."

"I have heard the same. I also understand I owe him our thanks, our freedom, and, perhaps, our very lives. When may I meet him?"

"How about we get all of you cleaned up and debriefed first. You'll meet him soon enough."

"I'm in your capable hands, my savior. Lead the way."

"Savior? I like the sound of that. I'm pleased it all worked out. If it wasn't for Ms. Al-Baklavi here, things might have been a lot different. I'm afraid we messed up. I have no excuse."

"You and your men risked your lives to save my daughter and me. You have nothing to apologize for. Let's get cleaned up. Do Hana and I get to wear army fatigues or one of your fancy uniforms?"

"Yes, ma'am, I'm afraid so. They're all we have. We'll have to cut them up as best we can to approximate size."

"Hana will love it."

***

Following a cold bath over a makeshift sink, Canan, Rima, and Hana dressed in oversized Parsons Security uniforms. Hana's had to be crudely cut and sewn in various places for her to be able to use her arms and legs. The three were brought to the operations center for dinner and debriefing. The trio was introduced to Zack, Jack, and Shaheed. Canan was already acquainted with Shaheed from the mosque. Zack's immigration division, led by Marshall Mann, handled her immigration to the United States. Thus, she was aware of Blake and knew he financed the operation and ransom. She was also pleased and surprised to discover that two Dearborn cops would fly all this way to save her and Hana. Attitudes were changing.

At the debriefing, Canan expressed her profound gratitude to Zack for his willingness to finance the operation and ransom. Parsons announced he had a surprise for Canan and Hana. He placed a monitor in the center of the dining table and dialed a number. Karim Izady's face appeared on the screen.

"Daddy!" Hana shrieked with delight.

"Sweetness!" Karim shouted with joy at the sight and sound of his freed and unharmed daughter. "Are you okay? Did those mean men hurt you?"

"No, Daddy," Hana squeaked.

"What are you wearing? Such a beautiful outfit," Karim joked.

"It's my form," she boasted. "Like them." The child pointed to others in uniform.

"Oh, your *uniform*. You are a soldier?"

Hana giggled. "No, Daddy—silly. I'm a little girl." Everyone laughed.

"Canan? How are you, my love?" Karim became serious.

"I'm fine. Look around this table. These are all the people we must thank for saving our lives. Glory be to *Allah* for sending them to us."

"All glory to *Allah*. Thank you all. Which one of you is Mr. Blake?"

Zack meekly raised his hand. He didn't seek praise or believe he deserved it.

"Thank you for all you did. None of this could have happened without you," Karim told Zack.

"You're welcome, Karim. But I only risked money. The men around this table deserve praise for risking their lives. They're terrific at what they do. They planned and executed a flawless rescue."

"Thank you, all of you, so much!" Karim exclaimed.

"What Mr. Blake says is not exactly true, Mr. Izady. I'd like you to meet and thank Rima Al-Baklavi." Parsons directed the telephone camera over to where Rima was seated.

"Al-Baklavi? Isn't he the terrorist who kidnapped my family?" Karim was confused.

"Yes, Karim. Rima is his wife. As Mr. Parsons will tell you, this woman was forced to kill her own husband to save Hana and me. Without her intervention, I am not certain the rescue team would have gotten to us in time. She is a hero. I will be forever grateful to her." The room quieted as Karim considered her response. All eyes were focused on the monitor.

"Mrs. Al-Baklavi, thank you for saving my family. Hana and Canan are everything to me. I am so sorry you lost your own loved one in the process of saving mine," Karim finally offered.

"Thank you. That is very kind of you. My husband put himself and me in this position, money and cause ahead of reason and goodwill. He would have killed a young woman and her child had I not stopped him . . ." The words caught in Rima's throat.

"Glory be to *Allah* for placing you there to protect my precious ladies."

Hana giggled at being called a 'precious lady.'

"Are you sure you're okay, my precious baby?" Karim asked Hana.

"Yes, Daddy. Mommy too. Bad man hit her."

"He did?" Karim grimaced.

"Knocked her down."

"Oh no, precious! But she got up?"

Hana giggled again. "Yes, Daddy. Told you so."

"The nice lady took care of me." Hana smiled at Rima. The embarrassed woman had tears in her eyes. She looked away.

"Thanks for taking care of my baby," Karim praised.

Rima burst out crying. She ran from the table, followed by a guard from Parsons' crew.

"What will happen to her?" Canan asked Parsons.

"I don't know, Ms. Izady. She is a Syrian citizen and a kidnapper. I'm rather certain the Syrian government will want to arrest her and put her on trial."

"But the government doesn't know she was involved, right?" Canan hinted.

"The government doesn't know anything about the kidnapping or the rescue operation," Parsons admitted.

"Can't we keep it that way?" Karim completed his wife's thought.

"Who would know the difference?" Zack added. "For all we know, Syria might enforce the death penalty for terrorism or kidnapping. We can't have that."

"She was involved in the kidnapping. What would you have me do, folks? Release her?"

"Take her with us. Her husband is dead. Can't she apply for asylum in the United States?" Canan suggested.

"Counselor?" Parsons punted the unwanted football to Blake.

"We don't even know if she'd be willing to come to the United States. We don't know anything about her. She did a brave thing and saved your lives, but she was still a part of Al-Baklavi's network. To answer your question, though, yes, she could apply for asylum. With the Golding administration still in the White House, it's an uphill climb. Let's just say it's *theoretically* possible," Zack explained.

"Good, then it is settled," Canan determined. "She will come with us and request asylum."

"*That's* your take-away from what I just said?" Zack groaned.

"We will work it out," Canan insisted. "There is nothing for her here but misery. She has no children."

"How do you know that?"

"She never spoke of them. All women speak of their children."

Zack rolled his eyes and glanced at Parsons, who shrugged. "Okay, Canan, okay, I guess there is no harm in talking to her," Zack relented.

"I have to cut this little reunion short, people. We have to break down this command center and get the hell out of Dodge before we are spotted by people who would not appreciate our visit." Parsons pushed out his chair and stood. Everyone at the table followed his lead.

"If all goes according to plan, Mr. Izady, you should see your family in a couple of days."

"Thank you again, all of you. Goodbye, my loves!" Karim blew kisses to his wife and child. The call was disconnected, and the monitor went blank.

"Are we going to see Nana, Mama?" Hana wondered.

Canan had completely forgotten the reason for their visit. She addressed Parsons, who immediately glanced at Blake. *Seriously?* A visit to Kobani was risky, time-consuming, and *very* expensive.

Zack's eyes wandered over to Hana and then to Canan. Suddenly, there was hope, even joy, in those eyes. What would he do? What else could he do?

Chapter Twenty

Marshall Mann, Micah Love, Reed Spencer, and the two 'generals' arrived at El Paso International Airport. The men rented an *SUV* from a local car rental agency and drove to the Hotel Paso Del Norte, a one-hundred-year-old gem located in the heart of the city. The hotel was famous for its opulent lobby, stained glass ceiling, fine dining rooms, and spacious guest rooms.

Micah booked three rooms. He and Reed would share a "Queen/Queen" room, as would Sam and Liam. Marshall would stay in his own "King" guest room. They did not plan to stay more than one night.

The detention center was on the outskirts of town, less than halfway between the airport and the hotel. They knew exactly where the center was located—in fact, they passed it on the way to the hotel. They decided to check into their rooms, freshen up, and enjoy a quick bite. They planned a reconnaissance visit for later in the evening. Operation Child Recovery would commence at 0900 the following morning.

Micah's preliminary investigation revealed that the detention center was once a Sam's Club warehouse store. While the others were napping or freshening up, Micah visited the city offices and bribed a very willing clerk to provide him with a blueprint of the building that housed the detention center. The prints depicted the building as a shopping warehouse, not a detention center. Micah, however, was focused on the size and location of the offices. He also wanted to calculate how many children the government could shoehorn into the place. He expected to be shocked at the deplorable conditions, made an inquiry to that effect, and even offered more money. But the clerk knew nothing about the center's operation. He didn't know how many guards or administrative personnel were on duty or how many kids were imprisoned there.

Micah returned to the hotel and found his three companions loitering around the lobby.

"Where've you been?" Reed wondered.

"I bribed a clerk for plans to the detention center."

"Anything interesting?" Marshall asked.

"Not really. The guy knew nothing about the operation, and the plans show the place as a Sam's Club. Size dimensions and the lay of the land are all I've got. Not sure whether it's going to be helpful or not."

"What's the plan? Same as Detroit?" Sam wondered.

"What exactly was the plan in Detroit?" Marshall asked. "I can't be involved or know anything about anything illegal. I've got a law license to worry about."

"That's why we haven't discussed Detroit or what we have in mind for El Paso. Plausible deniability, baby, plausible deniability."

"I don't like the sound of that."

"Zack didn't have any problem with it," Micah reasoned.

"Zack is in *Syria*, Micah! Did he help you plan the Detroit caper? Was he involved in the operation? Was he with you when you pulled it off? I'm an officer of the court! I can walk in there and tell these morons I'm the Gonzalez family lawyer. I show the *ICE* representative the children's birth certificates, and I walk out with the kids."

"We discussed the whole thing with Zack. He's concerned the kids might disappear if we play it straight. He strongly believes the Golding Administration, especially embarrassed *Homeland* and *ICE* officials, might try to cover up their involvement in the false arrest and imprisonment of these kids to protect the government from the eight-figure lawsuit he's going to file. He authorized us to move forward."

"I'm not sure I disagree. If the kids are not being incarcerated legally, how can subterfuge to obtain their release be illegal? I get it. But, like I said, Zack hasn't been directly involved in any of this, which begs the question: Why am I here? Sounds like you don't have any use for my legal services or opinions." Marshall opined.

"Well, if the 'caper,' as you call it, doesn't pan out, we will revert to 'plan B' and do this the legal way. You are our 'back-up plan,' so to speak," Micah advised.

"Ugh!" Marshall expelled.

"You don't want to see the place?" Micah wondered.

"I visited the centers in Detroit and Riverview. Keeping people in cages because of their immigration status is despicable and the conditions are inhumane. These are *kids*, dammit! No, I am not keen on seeing the place," Marshall grumbled.

"Then go to your room," Micah sounded like a parent scolding a child.

"Not on your life," Marshall argued.

"Huh?" Micah was confused.

"I said I wasn't *keen* on seeing the place. I didn't say I wouldn't go. What else do I have to do? I agree with Zack, though. I have a law license to protect. Keep me out of this when the time comes."

"Well, okay, counselor. Let's go."

Thirty minutes later, Micah pulled the rental car to the side of the road, an eighth of a mile away from the facility. The men could see an outline of the warehouse store letters where the sign used to be. There were no official markings on the building to identify it as an *ICE* detention camp.

A few official-looking *SUV*s were parked near the entrance; otherwise, the lot was virtually empty. Micah wondered if there were more security people in the daytime. The building was completely encircled by a tall fence with a layer of barbed wire at the top. A short road marked the entrance to the camp facility, leading to a wrought iron front gate, manned by two armed guards. A mechanical arm prevented vehicles from entering the premises without permission from the guards. This was *not* a warehouse market.

"The only difference between this place and Detroit is that Detroit *looks* like a detention center."

"We didn't have any problems getting into the other place with our phony credentials. I don't see why we'd have any problems with this one," Liam bragged.

"Who knows, Liam? These guys might be smarter? Might check with their superiors? We know for a fact that Billings wasn't the sharpest knife in the drawer," Micah cautioned.

"True, but with the right vehicle and those uniforms . . ." Sam began.

"Shit!" Micah cried. "The right vehicle . . . I forgot to obtain a government vehicle befitting two generals."

"Calm down, Micah. Let's think about this," Marshall considered. "How about a limousine? Might two generals travel in a chauffeur-driven limo?"

"I suppose, but we have to involve a limousine company and a driver. I don't want to have to trust them to keep quiet."

"For the right amount of money and assurance that we have a competent driver, a limo company will rent us a vehicle." Marshall studied Micah.

"Competent driver?" Micah asked.

Marshall continued to study Micah. "With a black suit, a chauffeur's cap, and the right undercover attitude, you'd be perfect." Marshall declared.

"I can't wear a suit. I have Dunlop's Disease," Micah argued.

"Huh?" Liam shrugged.

"My stomach done lops over my belt. I'm too fat to wear a chauffeur's outfit. You do it, Marsh."

Marshall and the two actors giggled at Micah's play on words. "I told you, Micah—I can't be involved. We'll just have to wake up a fine tailor and offer him or her appropriate incentive."

"A limo and a custom suit and cap? This operation is getting expensive," Micah groaned.

"Stop being so cheap, Micah," Liam wailed.

***

Two hours later, the four men sat in Micah's hotel room, awaiting the arrival of Gino Cavelli, owner of Cavelli's Custom Tailored Suits in the Glen Cove neighborhood of El Paso. After Micah handed him five one hundred dollar bills, the hotel concierge was extremely helpful in securing Mr. Cavelli's services. Micah cringed at the thought of what the suit might cost.

The room telephone rang. Marshall answered the phone and gave permission for the desk clerk to send Cavelli up to the room. Shortly thereafter, Liam opened the door to a short, slight, dark-haired man, holding two large garment bags and a bulky plastic shopping bag.

"*Ciao*," the man chirped.

"*Ciao*, baby," Micah retorted. Cavelli chuckled, deferentially, as if he didn't actually think Micah was funny.

"May I enter?" Cavelli requested.

"Oh, sorry. Yes, absolutely, come on in," Micah invited.

Cavelli entered and laid the garment bags on the couch. He turned and studied the four men, finally setting his sights on Micah.

"I take it *you* are my customer, sir?" he decided.

"How could you tell?" Micah kibitzed.

"Come, let's have a look at you," Cavelli rubbed his chin, studied Micah up and down, and pulled out a yellow tape measure. "Eighteen-inch neck, forty-two-inch waist, twenty-nine-inch pant legs?" he guesstimated. Micah shrugged.

Cavelli walked over to the couch. He opened the garment bag and pulled out several black suits. Next, he grabbed the shopping bag, pulled out a chauffeur's cap, and placed it on Micah's head. Micah's companions laughed out loud.

Three hours later, Micah Love stood in the center of the hotel room in a perfectly fitted chauffeur's outfit. He could not have looked more like a chauffeur than if he actually was one.

"Mr. Cavelli, you are the master," Marshall extolled.

"Wow," Liam exclaimed.

"Unbelievable transformation," Sam marveled.

"*Grazie*," Cavelli bowed.

"*Prego*," Marshall retorted.

"I feel like an idiot," Micah groaned. He pulled out twenty one-hundred-dollar bills and handed them to Cavelli.

The man's eyes lit up. "*Grazie mille*," he exclaimed. "A thousand thanks."

"You're welcome, two thousand times," Micah grumbled.

"He's really very grateful, Mr. Cavelli. We appreciate your coming here on such short notice," Marshall assured.

"No, *I* am very grateful. You have been most generous. Will there be anything else?"

Marshall looked around at his companions. "No, sir, I think we are all set."

"*Arrivederci*," Cavelli chirped. He picked up the garment bags and headed for the door.

"*Arrivederci*. Thanks again . . . uh . . . *grazie*," Micah prattled.

"*Prego*," Cavelli bowed several times as he moved toward and out the door.

"Where to, sirs?" Micah joked, turning to his men after Cavelli departed.

"Now?" Marshall yawned. "To my room, I'm exhausted. And you guys have a big day tomorrow."

"Come on, Marsh! Let me drive you somewhere!" Micah protested.

"We don't have the limo yet," Marshall reminded. "Tomorrow morning, bright and early, gentlemen. We will go limo shopping."

Chapter Twenty-One

After sending a squad of men to reconnoiter their route and destination, arrangements were made for travel to Kobani. A caravan of *SUV*s carrying a team of Parsons paramilitary professionals and all the weary travelers left the command center. They followed the same route Avi and Hassan had originally planned, without incident, and arrived, about two hours later, in what used to be known as Kobani, Syria.

Canan was apprehensive about the visit. Kobani had been at war for years, first with *ISIS* and later with Turkey. She and Karim fled Kobani during the war with *ISIS*. They personally witnessed many of the devastating blows suffered by the community. Nothing, however, prepared her for what she was now seeing from the safety of her transport vehicle.

Kobani residents were accustomed to war. Canan, Karim, and many others lost family members, friends, and treasured possessions in multiple military confrontations. Buildings, landmarks, and family homes were destroyed—citizens were slaughtered or maimed. The sights, sounds, and smells of war were everywhere. As the caravan drove down the main drag, people looked lost, full of dread, perhaps awaiting the next conflict. Canan was grateful for her life in America; happy her beloved Hana escaped the invisible psychological scars of war. Her *American* family happily avoided the fear and anxiety experienced while awaiting the next round of warplanes, artillery shells, explosions, and devastation, as well as the emptiness that followed survival.

As they drove through the rubble, homeless dogs roamed the streets. Curious faces of displaced families looked up, locking eyes with Canan as the caravan drove by. Canan began to feel terribly guilty for leaving her relatives behind, especially her mother, in the confusion and haste to evacuate. In the end, though, her mother made her own choice to stay. Canan was powerless to change her mind, no matter how hard she tried.

The Kurds famously helped defeat *ISIS* in the area. The People's Protection Units, known as the *YPG*, was a dominant force in an alliance with Syrian Democratic Forces. Part of a United States-led multinational coalition, they captured huge swaths of land in Northeastern Syria. In return for their success, the Kurds sought autonomy in the region. Turkey had other plans. The Turks opposed Kurdish autonomy in the region, even though the Turks benefited from the success of the military campaign.

The Turkish president decided to create what he called a 'safe zone' in the region and attacked the Kurds. The United States, instead of assisting its Kurdish allies, ordered its troops to pull back from the area. As a result, hundreds of civilians and *YDG* fighters were killed by the Turkish assault. The intense battle caused the displacement of almost two hundred thousand people, and critical civilian infrastructure was decimated. The Kurds were forced to make a deal with Syria, permitting the Turks to keep captured areas, with Russian and Syrian troops patrolling the area to keep the peace. Since the Kurds' only ally in the region, the United States, abandoned them, peace now depended on an alliance between Syria, Russia, and Turkey. Unfortunately, all were unfriendly to the Kurds. The alliance only increased Kurdish anxieties about endless war in the region.

For Canan, the piles of rubble paled in comparison to friends and family members lost forever in the region's various conflicts. The caravan continued through the ruins. As it headed northwest, conditions noticeably improved. People strolled down partially rebuilt streets. The urban center had shifted west, away from the conflict. Men and women chatted on street corners while kids played in a playground at a makeshift school, once a large home.

They drove past a bakery run by a family whose patriarch decided to remain in operation despite the siege. The owner famously provided free bread to all fighters and citizens who stayed behind during Kobani's many conflicts. Once destroyed by *ISIS* mortar shells and forced to close down, the reopened bakery stood tall, symbolic of victory and a vital source of food to the community. This portion of the city seemed almost vibrant, 'normal' was the word in Canan's thoughts.

The caravan continued and came upon a modest neighborhood, a fraction of which was spared from the conflict. Modest, well-kept homes dotted the landscape amidst others that were uninhabitable. A few boys kicked a soccer ball around a clear patch of land. The caravan stopped at one home, which was miraculously spared of serious damage. An old woman sat on the porch, sewing a child-sized garment. Canan began to weep, scaring Hana. The child also began to cry, prompting Canan to turn to her daughter.

"I'm so sorry, my sweet. I didn't mean to upset you. These are tears of joy. Look, over there." She pointed to the house, the porch, and an old woman. "That is your *Jadda*!"

The child squealed with delight and shouted, '*Jadda*!' through an open window. The old woman looked up and saw the caravan. Frightened, she rose and began to retreat into the house.

"Mama," Canan cried. "It's Canan!"

The old woman turned back to the caravan. "Canan?" she cried, straining to see her daughter. Canan emerged from the *SUV*. She unbuckled, gathered Hana from her seatbelt, and pulled the child from the vehicle.

"It's me, Mama, and this beautiful child is your granddaughter, Hana!"

"*Jadda!*" Hana cried.

Canan hurried to the porch. The three embraced, weeping with joy. Back at the caravan, some tough paramilitary soldiers, two guides, a couple of Dearborn cops, and a trial lawyer were in tears at the reunion they witnessed. After a short time, Canan's mother, Zoya, invited the entire caravan in for tea and coffee inside the modest home, a combination living room and two bedrooms, where Canan and her siblings were raised.

Parsons' group sat on the floor. The others sat on a large old microfiber couch and some bridge chairs. Zoya sat on an oversized easy chair with Hana in her lap. The child was joyfully attempting to teach *Jadda* how to play 'open-shut them.'

"Mama, how are you doing, *really*?" Canan challenged.

"I am fine, my precious. How are *you* doing after such a terrible ordeal?" The old woman had listened, in horror, to her daughter and granddaughter's experience in the Syrian Desert.

"We are well, Mama. But I must say, Kobani is still in far worse shape than I expected. How have you managed? How do you live like this? Please consider coming with us to America. There is nothing for you here. America is where your family lives."

Parsons and Blake shot Canan and each other a 'one more Syrian immigrant applying for asylum?' glare. *Can't help but admire her spunk!* Zack marveled.

"This is my home, the only one I have ever known. I was born in Kobani; I will die in Kobani. I am happy you have a nice life in America, but it is not for me."

"You would see Hana all the time," Canan cajoled.

The old woman held the child high in the air. Hana giggled with delight. Zoya smiled and retorted, "Ah, it is tempting. She is so beautiful." Her thoughts drifted. A tear rolled down her cheek. "I have missed you so, Canan."

"So, come to America, Mama," Canan pleaded.

"I cannot leave the people who need me behind. Some are old, sick—your *grandmother* in one of them. Please, Canan, leave it be," the old woman implored, hugging her granddaughter.

"If this is your final word, Mama, I will respect it. How is *Jadda*? Will we see her? Promise me you will come for a visit someday soon."

"Yes, my sweet. I promise. Your visit will soon cause me to yearn for more time with you and Hana. Your grandmother is fine, but too old to travel. We will probably not be able to visit with her. How is Karim, Canan? You married a fine man."

"Karim is fine. And, yes, he is a wonderful husband and father. We couldn't be happier."

"I am so pleased. Tell him that I hope to see him soon."

"I will, Mama. Please tell *Jadda* I love her and miss her."

Canan wanted to stay with her mother for a few days. Parsons and team determined the family was relatively safe for the time being but did not want to travel a long distance for lodging. Zack had to approve their stay since he was financing the mission. A sucker for family reunions, he readily supported the extended time.

Unfortunately, the team determined there were no hotel options nearby—the closest being in Aleppo or Harran, Turkey, both far away. Parsons had no desire to cross another border and wanted to stay somewhere close to Zoya's home. The group finally decided to find a location to set up camp similar to the operations command post they created in the desert. Parsons team was used to such accommodations. Zack, Jack, and Shaheed were less enthusiastic about the arrangements. They preferred a Hyatt or a Hilton, a shower, and a comfortable bed. All of them, however, understood the need for Canan, Hana, and Zoya to spend time together. No one needed to mention the obvious: *Would these three ever be together again?*

Zack urged Parsons to contact a local restaurant. The owner/chef, suffering in Kobani's post-war environment, was more than happy to deliver a feast of feasts to Zoya's western visitors. Zack offered the owner a sizeable financial incentive, more than any sale he'd made over the past four months. The entire group enjoyed a fantastic mid-eastern meal, courtesy of the Law Offices of Zachary Blake.

After their fabulous dinner, which included a fine assortment of Arabic desserts, the Parsons group, Rima Al-Baklavi, Zack, and the two cops bid the 'three ladies' farewell. Parsons gave Canan a cell phone and walkie-talkie to use in case of emergency. Parsons' numbers were pre-programmed into both the phone and walkie-talkie. All Canan had to do was push a button to directly connect to a Parsons' operative. After the caravan rolled out into the desert, Zoya, Canan, and Hana enjoyed a wonderful three-day reunion.

Too soon for 'the three ladies', the caravan returned. It was time to say goodbye. Hana now had a grandmother, a *jadda*, to pamper, spoil, and love her, as only a grandmother could love a grandchild. Canan experienced the joy and privilege of watching her mother and daughter bond, a sight she once never thought possible. Zoya was over the moon with the unexpected opportunity to meet her grandchild and see her daughter, perhaps for the last time.

The trio promised to keep in touch. Each promised, someday soon, to visit the other. However, somewhere, deep inside, they wondered if this was the final chapter. The 'three ladies' hugged each other tight, tears flowing, refusing to terminate their embrace. Parsons cleared his throat, and the threesome separated, wiping eyes and noses with tissues provided by *Jadda*, smiling, laughing, then crying once again.

The caravan began to drive away, and Zoya chased after it, waving frantically, mouthing 'see you soon, go with *Allah*.' Canan and Hana turned to the back window and waved back. Hana, in tears, screamed, "Bye-bye *Jadda*, we love you—come see us soon!"

As Zoya disappeared, Canan studied her euphoric daughter, and reflected on the past three days. At the same time, she recalled the days of pain and extreme peril leading up to them. *A mother does not put her child in danger. I was a fool to believe we could safely visit Kobani. Karim was right to push back. Thank you, Allah, for Karim and his stubbornness. We could have been killed. We must never return to Kobani. Maybe Mama will . . .*

Canan's thoughts and eyes drifted to Wayne Parsons, driving the *SUV*, and then to Zachary Blake, gazing out a half-open window, taking in the sights and sounds of the Syrian Desert. *Allah, in His infinite wisdom, sent you, Mr. Parsons, and you, Mr. Blake. I will never forget your generosity and bravery. My family is forever in your debt.*

Chapter Twenty-Two

The sun rose in the El Paso sky, announcing the dawn of a beautiful morning. Micah and the two actor-investigators were donning uniforms and rehearsing lines. Micah would have a limited 'speaking part.' His primary roles would be to drive these official-looking characters to and from the detention center via limousine and provide clandestine security for the two 'generals'. He fervently wished that anything more drastic would not be necessary.

Micah hoped to accompany the generals into the center. All three men wore hidden listening devices. Marshall Mann would hang back at the hotel and record the entire sting on his laptop computer. A transcript of the entire episode might one day be necessary to play for a future judge or jury deciding any espionage or other quasi-criminal case the government might bring against the trio.

Micah, a man who had conducted multiple sting operations in his storied career, was quite nervous. Were these two-bit actors up to the task? They had no military or police training. However, they quite easily fooled Billings and his Detroit Detention Center staff. Was their success attributable to skill or luck? When the Detroit caper was over, Micah listened to the entire recording. He came away with newfound respect for Sam and Liam's thespian capabilities.

A local car rental agency manager had a limousine gassed and ready to go at the entrance to the hotel. This once totally disinterested manager became keenly invested in the operation after Micah waved a boatload of pocket cash in his face. The limo cost the average dignitary about three hundred fifty dollars a day. Micah agreed to execute a contract for the retail cost *and* pay the greedy manager an additional one thousand dollars in exchange for a half-day rental and the manager's signature on a non-disclosure agreement. After the mutual signing ceremony, the investigator counted out ten one hundred dollar bills and smacked them into the gleeful manager's palm. Sam and Liam marveled at Micah's consistent ability to manufacture hundreds out of thin air.

The three men exited the hotel elevator in full uniform. They strolled through the elegant lobby, prompting stares and 'thank you for your service' comments from hotel guests. Sam and Liam soaked up the attention. They smiled and tipped their caps to everyone who acknowledged them. As they headed out the hotel's main exit, the hotel staff and guests broke into spontaneous and vigorous applause. Sam turned, doffed his cap, and bowed as if he were responding to a theatre curtain call. Micah tugged on his pant leg to pull him away from the adoring crowd.

A doorman opened the back door to the limo and gestured for them to enter.

"Wow!" Liam exclaimed. "I could get used to this!" The doorman shot him a curious glance but continued to perform his duty.

"I've never received a standing 'o' at the theatre, that's for sure," Sam agreed, after the doorman closed them into the spacious luxury vehicle.

"That's because the only theatre you've ever done is *community* theatre, moron," Liam cracked.

"Let's cut the crap before you guys start pounding on each other," Micah warned. "You are not two-bit actors—you are two-star generals. Get into character, please. Stop acting like spoiled kids and start acting like professional command soldiers. We will be at the detention center in a few minutes."

"He's correct, General Philpot," Sam addressed Liam officiously.

"I quite agree, General Moreland," Liam shot back. "Hey Sam, check out this vehicle! Holy shit!" They were traveling in a sixteen-passenger stretch limo, stocked to the rafters with booze and snacks. "I could get used to this!"

"That's better," Micah sighed. "Now, children, no more fighting or name-calling. Stay in character until we've driven off with the Gonzalez kids."

"Sir, yes sir," shouted Philpot. He shoved a cookie in his mouth and saluted to the rearview mirror.

The actors stuffed their faces and rehearsed their lines for the rest of the trip, fully embracing their characters. Micah studied them in the rearview. They were enjoying the rehearsal, playing the best roles of their failed careers. *They've been solid, loyal operatives who prefer these acting gigs. Maybe Zack can find them a lawyer who moonlights as a theatrical agent or something.*

The limo arrived at the detention center. Micah steered it to the front gate and lowered the window. The generals were brushing cookie crumbs off their uniforms.

"Generals Philpot and Moreland to see the center director," Micah announced. "What is his name, again?"

"Who?" The startled guard was confused.

"The center director, of course, young man," Micah admonished.

"That would be Lieutenant Moore, sir, Lieutenant Gale Moore."

"A female?" Micah gasped. Women possessed a much keener bullshit-meter than men.

"No, sir. Sorry. It is G-A-L-E, not G-A-I-L." The guard spelled out both names.

"I see," Micah relaxed. "Would you please tell Lieutenant Moore that Generals Philpot and Moreland request his presence," Micah repeated.

The guard snapped to attention at this second mention of two generals. "Right away, sirs!" He leaned out the guard window to see into the limo. "Sorry for the delay, sirs," he called into the limo. Micah wasn't sure the guard could see into the back seat.

"No worries," came an officious voice from the back seat. "However, we are on a serious mission with a specific time crunch. If you could speed things along." General Philpot leaned forward and continued. "We'd be extremely grateful, Private . . . Young." Philpot strained to read the nametag on the guard's chest. Young didn't notice; he was proud to have a two-star address him by name and rank.

"Sir, yes sir," Young shouted, saluting the limo. "I'll only be a second." Young picked up a telephone receiver, turned his back, and spoke into the phone. He finished the call and turned back to the limo.

"All clear, Generals—the lieutenant will see you straight away." He
leaned out of the guard shack and addressed Micah.

"You see the main entrance?"

"Yes." Micah stretched to study the entrance.

"Don't use it," Young instructed. "See the smaller door to the right of the entrance?"

Again, Micah stretched to look. "Yes, I see it."

"Lieutenant Moore will be waiting for you there. You can park the limousine alongside the service entrance."

Micah leaned forward a third time and glanced at the service entrance. A lanky uniformed officer propped open the door, his eyes trained on the guard shack. He nervously straightened his tie and brushed something off his shoulders. He tugged at the bottom of his uniform jacket. Micah surmised the lieutenant had never entertained a general, let alone *two* generals. Private Young interrupted Micah's thoughts by remotely opening the entrance gate. Micah began to slowly ease the limousine through the gate. *Showtime!*

Micah pulled the limo up, parallel to the service entrance. He turned off the ignition, exited the vehicle, and saluted Lieutenant Moore. Moore was confused. He'd never saluted a civilian.

"Sergeant Michael Clark," Micah shouted, making up the name and rank on the spot. "I am acting undercover, escorting and protecting the generals, sir." Micah saluted the lieutenant a second time. The lieutenant saluted back.

Micah turned his back on the lieutenant and opened the drivers' side back door. Generals Philpot and Moreland exited the vehicle and saluted the lieutenant. Moore stood at attention and saluted back.

"As you were, Moore," Philpot ordered. "We are here on a serious matter. We have very little time to correct a grievous error before we must return to Detroit."

"Detroit, sir?" The confused lieutenant replied.

"Yes, Moore. Detroit is where the grievous error occurred," Moreland declared.

"Error, sir?" Moore was now totally confused.

"Have you received orders about our visit?"

"Sir, no sir," Moore confessed.

"I am not pleased, Lieutenant. I have to be honest with you," Philpot grumbled. "Let's get inside, see what's what. We'll explain why we're here. You might want to take us to where we can set up a Zoom or WebEx conference. Do you have that capability here?" Philpot inquired.

"Yes, sir."

"Excellent, Moore. Have a staff member contact the Detroit Detention Center and get a Captain Gordon Billings on Zoom conference," Moreland ordered. "And take us to the room where the conference call will take place. We're on a tight schedule—need to catch a flight back to Detroit."

"Yes, sir," Moore stood at attention and saluted.

"Well, get going, dammit!" Philpot roared.

Moore took off down the hall, forgetting to take the generals to the conference room.

"Great," Micah muttered after they were left alone. "He was supposed to escort us to the conference room."

"All the better," Sam rationalized. "He'll realize he left us alone in the hall and he'll really be discombobulated."

"Whoa! That's a twenty-dollar word, *General*!" Liam quipped. "Let's hope you're right."

In less than two minutes, Lieutenant Gale Moore returned. He apologized for leaving the generals unattended and without escort to the conference room. The generals excused the oversight, repeated that time was of the essence, and demanded to be taken to a conference room.

As they headed down the hall, Micah inquired, "Is the call to Detroit being facilitated?"

"Yes, Sergeant. My administrative assistant is placing the call as we speak. Presuming Captain Billings is at the center. We should be talking to him shortly."

"Excellent, Moore. If anyone can straighten this out, it's Billings. He's the one who screwed this up in the first place," Philpot added.

"What's this all about, if I may ask, Generals?" Moore wondered.

"Detroit arrested and incarcerated two young American *citizens*. They dumped . . . eh . . . delivered them to you here in El Paso. At least, we have information to suggest they are here in El Paso," Moreland advised.

"That's absurd, Generals. With all due respect, that could not happen here."

"It didn't happen here, Lieutenant. It happened in Detroit," Micah corrected.

"But we check citizenship at the door when the kids first arrive."

"Citizenship of who, the kids or their parents? What if the kids have no citizenship papers?" Philpot charged.

"Well . . . uh . . . ." Moore stammered.

"Answer me, Lieutenant!" Philpot demanded.

They reached the conference room, and Moore showed them in. He was grateful for the short respite, which permitted him to gather his thoughts.

"To answer your question, sir, we would check the parents if the kids had no papers."

"And if the parents were undocumented, your people would automatically assume the kids were undocumented, correct? Regardless of what the kids say or where they are from?" Micah queried.

"I suppose that's true."

"What's true?" A voice chirped from a monitor on a conference table in the center of the room.

"Who is speaking?" Moore inquired.

"This is Captain Gordon Billings. Is this Lieutenant Moore? *You* called *me,* sir. What's this all about?"

"I have Generals Moreland and Philpot in my conference room."

"Hello, Billings! So nice to see you again," Philpot blustered at his computer screen. Billings became apprehensive and began to sweat.

"Billings! How are things in Detroit?" Moreland added.

"Um . . . uh . . . Generals? How are things? Did not expect to . . . uh . . . see or hear from you again, remember?"

"That *was* the plan, but, as you well know, plans frequently change based on circumstances on the ground," Philpot huffed. "We have located those two citizens we spoke about. They are here in El Paso. I need you to confirm for Lieutenant Moore that their arrest and incarceration may have been a mistake and that you provided us with their profile back in Detroit. We believe the mistake was caused by an assumption that if the parents are undocumented, the kids must be undocumented. I understand you have a file on the matter?"

"You know I do, General. You *saw* the file," Billings grumbled. He did not wish to admit he copied and handed the entire file to the generals.

"We did, indeed, Billings. Would you be a sport and grab that file for us?"

"Right away, sir." Billings aimed to please, especially if the generals were concealing the fact they possessed a copy. He vacated the video screen—the El Paso group could hear file drawers opening and closing, feet shuffling, and a chair grinding along the floor. Billings returned to the screen. "I have the file," he gasped.

"As I recall, there are two birth certificates in the file?" Philpot prompted.

"I don't remember . . . ah . . . two birth certificates . . ." Billings was confused. Birth certificates would have prevented the mishap in the first instance.

"Check the file, Billings. I believe we can clear this up rather quickly for Lieutenant Moore." Philpot glanced at Moore and smiled.

Billings opened the file and began to leaf through it on the screen. "I am not seeing . . . " His expression suddenly changed to confused horror. "Here they are . . . not filed correctly . . . wrong coding . . . I don't understand."

"Calm yourself, Billings. This is not on you. This error was made in the field. It wasn't made at your pay grade."

"Thank you for saying so, sir." Billings calmed a bit.

"Billings?" Mooreland inquired.

"Sir?"

"Would you please inform Lieutenant Moore that a mistake was made and that these two children may be immediately released into our custody? If you can do that, we see no reason why we can't maintain the discretion we suggested when we met back in Detroit. Get my drift?" Philpot floated.

"I'm not sure we can release them without running this up the chain of command. Perhaps we need a court order of some sort?" Moore pondered.

"Who in your chain of command here in El Paso or back in Detroit outranks General Philpot or me?" Moreland challenged.

"No one I know of, General, but perhaps we should discuss this with Homeland, *HHS* or *ICE*?"

"Moore? Let's put all cards on the table. We are trying to diffuse a ticking time bomb and prevent a massive government screw-up from becoming an international incident. By doing so, we may avoid a nine-figure legal shit-storm. What if the press gets wind of this?

"I'm sure these kids will be happy to get the hell out of here and back home to their parents. And I'd lay a substantial wager that this unfortunate family would rather thank than sue the public servants who made this family reunion possible. If we start involving political appointees and branches of government other than the military . . . well . . . that would move things out of our control."

"I will need a copy of those birth certificates. Perhaps an affidavit from you two Generals?" Moore suggested.

"The birth certificates will have to do, Moore. We are operating as cleaners, so-to-speak, in a *quasi*-official capacity. This is all rather hush-hush to avoid publicity and further embarrassment."

"I can fax the two copies I have in the file," Billings offered on the monitor.

"Thanks, Billings, but that won't be necessary. We have the originals right here," Philpot revealed. The general turned to Micah. "May I have the file, please?" Micah handed him the red folder from the Detroit meeting.

Philpot opened the file and retrieved the two birth certificates.

Billings glared into the screen, trying to catch a glimpse of the documents. *Those weren't in the file I gave those guys!*

"They seem to be in order," Moore agreed. "I will have to at least contact my immediate superior officer."

"Is he or she a general?" Philpot inquired.

"No, sir. This is routine procedure. Captain Lynch has to sign off."

"Then, get to it, Moore. Make sure he knows we generals are here, waiting on his signature. In the meantime, why not summon the children? We'd like to meet and debrief these kids."

"Sir, yes sir!" Moore stood and saluted.

"Am I still needed?" The monitor chirped.

"Yes, Billings. If you don't mind, scan and email those copies with a memo or affidavit. Because of a bureaucratic mix-up of some sort, these kids might be right here in El Paso; get my drift? Blame the logistics supply chain or some damn thing. We have to paper the file." Moreland recommended.

"Sounds like a plan, sir. Thanks for your continued support."

"No problem, Billings. You're a good soldier who had a unique problem dumped in his lap. We are sympathetic." Moreland turned to Micah and shoved two gag fingers in his mouth. Philpot disconnected the conference call and Billings disappeared.

Ten minutes later, Moore returned with two kids in tow. They were slightly unkempt and undernourished, perhaps, but otherwise healthy and normal. Moore also carried two copies of a written memo from Captain Lynch ordering the release of Emilio and Emma Gonzalez into the custody of Generals Moreland and Philpot. He handed one copy to Philpot. Moore smiled and placed his arm around Emilio, now his best pal. "These guys are released into your custody. They can go home to their family. One stumbling block going forward, though, which I am certain you generals have considered."

"What might that be, Lieutenant?" Moreland demanded.

"What happened to these kids happened because their parents are undocumented. If the parents are deported, what happens to the children?"

"Excellent question, Moore. Obviously, your sharp mind is why you have a command position. One problem at a time, young man—we will have to cross that particular bridge if, and when, we come to it. Do these kids have a travel bag? Any belongings?"

"Right here, sir." Moore handed over two small backpacks. The generals handed them to Micah, who scowled. *When ICE agents grab helpless kids from their classrooms, how much in the way of 'belongings' could they possibly have?*

Micah and the generals rose. "That will do it, Moore. Nice job wrapping this up. Thank you for your service in difficult times."

"Just doing my job, sir, like all enlisted men."

"Indeed, Moore. Our country and these children are lucky to have men like you." Moreland puffed. Micah wanted to shove two fingers down *his* throat.

"Thank you, sir."

Philpot turned to the children. "Ready to go, kids?" the general inquired.

"Go where?" Emma wondered.

"Home to your parents."

"Really?" Emilio brightened.

"Really!" Moreland exclaimed, tears forming.

"Can we say goodbye to our friends? Everyone who leaves gets to say goodbye."

Moreland and Philpot considered Emilio's request, shrugged, and turned to Micah. The investigator tried to ignore the gesture and signal that 'the generals' were in command in this situation. Philpot caught on before Moore could notice the indiscretion.

"Absolutely! We can't have you guys leaving without saying goodbye!" Philpot exclaimed. Micah wasn't pleased with this new wrinkle. He wanted to get the hell out of Dodge. However, these kids were in the camp with other kids for almost two months. Relationships were developed—bonds were forged.

Lieutenant Moore led the group into the bowels of the warehouse where Emma and Emilio had spent most of the past several months. The place was bustling with activity, a far brighter atmosphere than the center in Detroit. This facility was built for and populated by *children*. Children were more resilient and adapted to their surroundings better than adults. The center had the feel of a rustic overnight camp facility.

Word had spread around the camp that Emma and Emilio were being sent home. When the kids walked in with Micah and the three servicemen, spontaneous applause erupted. Groups of kids ran to the Gonzalez children, tears flowing, hugging them, patting their backs. Many gave Emma and Emilio original drawings or trinkets as mementos. When it was time for a final farewell, everyone, including every adult in the large room, was crying.

Moore led the visitors and the two kids to the service door. Emma and Emilio turned to the warehouse one last time. Cheers erupted again—everyone was yelling and singing. Emma and Emilio Gonzalez threw kisses to all and walked out of the El Paso Detention Center for the last time. Their prayers were answered. Their dreams had come true—they were going home.

Chapter Twenty-Three

Parsons' private jet made a flawless landing at the Oakland/Troy Airport in Troy, a northeastern Detroit suburb. Canan had never flown private before and was overwhelmed. She and Hana were treated like VIPs, pampered and fed like no commercial flight she'd even flown. After landing, the plane didn't stop at a terminal requiring passengers to walk a long way to baggage claim. The Parsons Security private jet taxied right up to the main building. Canan and Hana saw Karim through the glass, anxiously awaiting their arrival.

The plane stopped moving, a bell sounded, and lights were illuminated. Canan rapidly unbuckled the seatbelt from her all-leather plush executive seat. She kneeled in front of Hana and unbuckled her daughter's built-in child's seat. Canan hoisted Hana into her arms and dashed off the plane.

"Karim!" She shouted and waved as she scaled the airplane stairs.

Karim saw and heard his wife, pushed open the terminal door, and ran toward the plane. The three met somewhere between plane and terminal and embraced, alternately laughing, crying, and hugging.

"I'm so happy to see you, my sweet ladies. Let's have a look at you!" Karim gently placed Canan and Hana squarely in front of him and rubbed his chin studying his family.

"Daddy!"

"Still the most beautiful ladies in the whole wide world," Karim gasped, bursting with joy. "And all mine!"

"Always," Canan smiled. "I'm so sorry I didn't heed your warnings, Karim. Can you ever forgive me?"

"For wishing to visit your mother? Who can criticize?" he conceded. He looked down at Hana. "How is my little princess? Did you take good care of Mama like you promised?" It was an innocent question. He did not intend to be critical, but Hana didn't see it that way. She began to cry. "No, Daddy! The bad man hurt Mama! I'm sorry!" She bawled.

"No, sweetheart, Daddy is sorry. I didn't mean it that way. You brought Mama home to me. I'm so happy and so, so proud of you!"

Hana dried her eyes, sniffed, and smiled. "Yes, I did," she boasted. "There she is." She turned and presented her mother to her father.

"And who are all these fine people? We have not met." Karim addressed the other travelers. Introductions were made. Karim thanked all for their bravery and sacrifice. He requested a moment to speak privately to Wayne Parsons and Zachary Blake.

He thanked Parsons for his heroism and strategic planning. He thanked Blake for his incredible generosity. He pledged to pay back every dime, even if it took him the rest of his life.

"It's not necessary, Karim. I am a very fortunate man. I enjoy sharing my good fortune with deserving people. You and your beautiful family are most deserving," Zack maintained. "You don't owe me a thing. Well, I take that back. One favor, if you don't mind?"

"Anything! You name it."

"Don't let your wife make any travel plans for a while?"

Everyone laughed. Even Canan, initially embarrassed, laughed long and hard. Hana didn't quite understand, but she laughed because everyone else was laughing.

A porter walked up to the Izady family and asked where they would like the luggage. Karim pointed to his Camry and hit a button on a key fob, which caused the trunk to pop open. The porter dropped the bags into the trunk and clicked it shut. Karim handed him a generous tip. The Izady family waved goodbye to their travel companions and started toward the car. At that moment, a Parsons operative exited the plane with Rima Al-Baklavi in handcuffs in front of him.

"Oh, Karim, wait," Canan stopped. "I want you to meet someone." She scooped up Hana, grabbed Karim by the hand, and walked back toward the plane. They met the woman as she descended from the last step.

"Karim—this is Rima Al-Baklavi. She saved our lives. She is as much responsible for our survival as everyone here in front of us." An embarrassed Rima hung her head in shame.

"Mrs. Al-Baklavi, thank you! From the bottom of my heart, thank you for keeping my family safe from harm. Canan told me of your incredible sacrifice. I am so sorry for your loss. Is there anything we can do to repay you?"

Rima could not look at the man. More than anyone on the tarmac, she knew how close his family came to being slaughtered and what her role was in the terrorists' actions. She was in agony and undeserving of praise.

"I am owed nothing," she finally muttered. "I put your family in danger. *I* did that. No one else standing here can say this. I do not deserve your gratitude. The United States may do what they will with me. *That* is what I deserve."

"Nonsense, Rima! How could you have known?" She turned to Karim. "She had no power, Karim. Mr. Blake will assist her. Right, Mr. Blake?" She turned to Zack, who stood off by the terminal building.

"We are all glad you and Hana made it through this ordeal. I will help in any way I can, Canan. Call me 'Zack' please? 'Mr. Blake' is my father or grandfather."

"You will help? She needs your help."

"I will help, Canan. I promise."

"Perfect. Thank you. Karim? We can go now. We shall have all of these fine people to dinner one day soon."

"Yes, dear," Karim capitulated.

"Smart man," Zack smiled.

As the Camry drove off, Wayne Parsons approached Zack. "Talk to you for a minute?"

"Sure, Wayne. What's up?"

Parsons nodded toward Rima. "We have not yet reported her arrival. This is your rodeo. She has no papers. What do you want me to do?"

"If you can spare the handcuffs, leave Rima and the key with me. I'll take it up with my partner, the immigration guy, when he returns from El Paso. I'll take the heat if there's fallout from this decision."

"Are you sure? This is some serious shit. She's a terrorist sympathizer, at the very least. We can't smuggle her into the country. We must notify the feds. It would be treason not to report her arrival."

"I have no intention of smuggling her anywhere. I just want to confer with my immigration guy before we take any action. He'll know what to do. Trust me."

"A lawyer? Are you kidding?"

"Et tu, Brute? More lawyer jokes?"

"Counselor, I will leave her in your capable hands." Parsons chuckled.

"Thanks, Wayne. And thanks for the incredible job you did out there. You guys are the best of the best," Zack praised.

"High praise from the King of Justice," Parson retorted. "And back at you. Nice job extending the negotiations the way you did. I wasn't sure about you as a lead negotiator, but you came through. We were much better prepared because of the time you bought us. This was truly a team effort. And I hope to work with you again."

"I sure hope not!" Zack gasped. "The courtroom and the boardroom are tough enough places to negotiate and navigate— but in the desert with a terrorist? No thanks! I'll pass on a second go-around."

Parsons laughed. "I completely understand. This international security stuff is not for everyone."

"Someone has to keep us safe, even when we put ourselves in harms' way. You do it better than anyone."

"What's that?" Jack Dylan walked up with Shaheed Ali.

"Doing what you guys do—keeping us safe," Zack advised.

Jack sighed and deadpanned. "All in a day's work, Zack. All in a day's work."

***

Shortly after the Parsons private jet landed in Troy, a Southwest Airlines commercial flight landed at the Blue Terminal at Detroit Metropolitan Airport. Among the passengers on board were two actors, a private investigator, a lawyer, and two young Latino citizens of the United States.

Before departing from El Paso to Detroit, Marshall Mann telephoned Mary Carmen and Miguel Gonzalez with the fabulous news.

"We've located your children! They're here with me, now! We're getting on a flight to Detroit. Your children are coming home!"

"Oh my God, Mr. Mann! I cannot believe this! Miguel, do you hear? The children are coming home! They are safe!"

"Thank you, Jesus!" A euphoric Miguel exclaimed.

"We have a 5:00 PM flight. That's 6:00, Detroit time. We should be landing at around 8:45 PM. He gave the couple the flight details and terminal location. Because of post 9-11 heightened security, waiting family members could no longer meet arriving family members at the terminal gate. Marshall advised Miguel and Mary Carmen to meet the kids at baggage claim.

The plane landed on time. The two actors entertained and played games with the children throughout the almost three-hour flight. The kids' somber mood brightened considerably. After the landing, the group deplaned and headed down the tarmac toward the terminal. Emma and Emilio were excited to see their parents. They ran ahead, expecting to greet them at the gate—and were disappointed to discover that no one was there. A despondent Emma turned to Marshall. "Where are our parents, Mr. Mann?"

"Emma, Emilio, they are here. We can't meet them at the gate," Marshall tried to explain. "They are downstairs. Come. I'll show you." Marshall picked up Emilio and extended a hand to Emma. She grabbed his hand, and the entire group headed through the terminal, past several gates, and onto an escalator. They rode down the escalator to the baggage area.

As they came down the escalator, someone shouted. "There they are!" In a moment of sheer joy, Emma and Emilio Gonzalez spotted their parents and forgot their months-long ordeal. They were home—there were their parents!

The children ran into their parents' arms. Tears of pure joy began to flow all around the baggage claim area. While a large contingent of family and friends had accompanied Miguel and

Mary Carmen to the airport, perfect strangers joined in the celebration as the story became known.

Someone must have called in a tip to local news stations because reporters, photographers, and cameramen from all the local TV stations were at the terminal. Reporters and cameramen from the Free Press and News also shouted questions and took photographs. The family reunion was a major feel-good story in a time of confusion and despair for the Latino community of Detroit.

Reporters interrupted the euphoria and struck microphones in Mary Carmen's face, seeking comment. Mary Carmen glanced at Marshall Mann, seeking permission to speak. Marshall nodded his head.

"How do you feel at this moment, Mrs. Gonzalez?" A reporter shouted.

"We feel wonderful, over the moon!" She laughed and cried at the same time, tears rolling down her cheeks.

"What have these past few months been like for you?" Another reporter queried.

"We were desperately concerned for our children. We had no idea where they were. The government took them and didn't say a word to us. Officials claimed they didn't know where they were. My children were born here in America! They are American citizens! We came here for a better life. We lived in fear in Venezuela every day. How can America take American children from their parents?"

"Mr. Gonzalez? Do you have anything to say?"

"I wish to say *muchas gracias* to our attorneys, Marshall Mann, Amy Fletcher, and Zachary Blake. They have made this day possible," Miguel exclaimed.

"May we speak to the children?" Another reporter wondered.

Mary Carmen looked down at a determined Emma. "If they are willing," Mary Carmen consented.

"Emma? How do you feel at this moment?" The reporter wondered.

"We are happy. But, we are sad, too," Emma murmured.

"Sad? For heaven's sake, why?"

"We left so many friends behind at the camp," she cried. "I wish for them to know, if they are watching— you will soon be home with your parents, too."

Marshall could not have scripted a better response. Judges would watch the news on television or read the newspaper in print or online.

'So many friends,' innocent children, some American citizens, were left behind in a quasi-prison, separated from their parents. There wasn't a dry eye in the place. Marshall motioned to a reporter who grabbed a cameraman and ventured over.

"Sir? Do you have a comment?"

"Yes, I'm Marshall Mann. I practice Immigration with Zack Blake's firm. I've got an alert for the local and national press about two important issues: One: These folks have been through a terrible ordeal. Please respect their privacy until they get reacquainted. Two: Emma and Emilio Gonzalez are American citizens! Shout this from the rooftops. I don't care about party or your political position on immigration. These kids were locked up because no one from our government bothered to check their birth certificates. They could easily have confirmed that Emma and Emilio Gonzalez are American citizens. Print *that*! Show *that* on television!

"We will petition the court for asylum for their parents and for the right to sue *ICE*, *HHS*, and Homeland.

"This reunion is a joyous, wonderful story, and I am pleased to be a part of it. But as Emma just told you, the more important story is that children are being ripped from their parents' arms and locked up in prison camps. The real story is that 'so many' of Emma's friends are still separated from their parents. Some of these parents have been deported or can't be found. What will happen to *those* children? How does this happen in *America*?

"'Zero Tolerance' is an effective political sound bite for someone running for office or seeking to remain in power, but this is an unconscionable situation. It must be remedied. Bureaucratic hurdles that prevent family reunification must be torn down. This cannot be who we are—we are locked in a battle for the very soul of our nation.

"Children and parents are frantically traveling the country looking for each other. In some situations, when they find each other, justice is delayed or denied. Some legal technicality is used to keep them apart. Fingerprint or DNA analysis is inconclusive. Government malfeasance will no longer be tolerated. We will be filing an asylum claim as soon as the court can set a date. Thank you."

After reporters and cameramen packed up and left the airport, the celebration continued. Relatives, friends, and classmates took turns embracing the children and welcoming them home. As other planes arrived, passengers entering the baggage area wondered if important dignitaries were visiting the city. Slowly, the area began to clear. People headed for home.

The five people principally responsible for the joyous reunion stood off to the side and watched the celebration. Liam and Josh reveled in their roles in securing the freedom of two innocent kids. Micah, usually stoic in the success of his investigative missions, was moved to tears at the sight of the Gonzalez family reunion. Marshall was happy for the family and extremely grateful for the publicity. Significant public pressure would be brought to bear on any federal judge who sought to separate this young family a second time.

Marshall thought back to his partners-in-crime's visit to the El Paso Detention Center that morning. *Was that really this morning?* The delay at the gate, the engagement with Lieutenant Moore, the Zoom call to Billings, and, finally, the release of the kids. The entire caper went off without a hitch. Marshall was skeptical when Micah suggested the plan. He was glad he didn't actively participate, curious whether any laws were broken, but extremely satisfied that this family was finally reunited.

The battle would now be fought in his domain—federal court. The battle could be fierce. The Golding Administration might fight like hell and dirty as hell.

Marshall Mann knew how to fight dirty. He had quite a few legal tricks up his sleeve, developed from years of experience. Amy and Zack also knew how to fight—the courtroom was *their* stage. In court, *law*, not political gamesmanship, should win the day. But Marshall wasn't naïve—he knew this wasn't always true. The judicial assignment for the Gonzalez case would be a huge determining factor in its success or failure. Judges were assigned by random draw.

The celebration was ending. Micah Love and the two actors were summoning Marshall to the parking lot for the ride home. The legal battle was tomorrow's challenge. Today? *Wow! What a fabulous day!*

Chapter Twenty-Four

The following day, Zachary Blake, Marshall Mann, Amy Fletcher, and Micah Love met in the Blake office conference room. To Micah's delight, Zack furnished the usual buffet-style breakfast. Wayne Parsons, Jack Dylan, and Shaheed Ali attended by Zoom. A split-screen monitor was set up in the center of the elegant conference table.

The purpose of the meeting was to discuss the multi-faceted agenda going forward. The Gonzalez family had been reunited, but was their status temporary? What was the strategy for preventing the parents' deportation?

Zack wanted to file a multi-million dollar lawsuit for the wrongful arrest and imprisonment of Emma and Emilio Gonzalez. Perhaps the government would reconsider their parents' deportation. The very real prospect of a nine-figure payout to the kids should have a chilling effect on deportation proceedings—did Marshall agree? Did Amy? Rima Al-Baklavi was a fugitive from Syria. Her entry into the United States was undocumented. The men had to turn her over to the authorities, but how and to whom? Perhaps Dylan and Ali could assist.

Zack commenced the meeting.

"Thank you all for coming. It has been an interesting week. Wayne? Jack? Shaheed? Are you guys there? Can you hear me?"

"Loud and clear," Parsons retorted.

"Ten-four, good buddy," Jack chirped. "Hey, is that breakfast? Why wasn't I invited in person?"

"Didn't want to make you drive all the way from Dearborn. I'll owe you a breakfast, okay?" Zack rolled his eyes.

"Okay. You all heard him. I have witnesses, Blake."

"Understood," Zack chuckled.

"Don't worry about it, Dylan. I'll eat your share." Micah spoke with his mouth full again, with the same result. Bits of food sprayed the table in front of him. A server came over and wiped off the table.

"I'd like to discuss three important issues going forward. Two of them are more in Marshall's or Amy's wheelhouse than mine, but all of us will be involved in one way or another. I want to make sure we have all our ducks in a row.

"For starters, we have the Gonzalez deportation case. This is Marsh's and Amy's baby. I'd like Micah to do a deep dive into their background. What's life like in Venezuela? What kind of citizens have Miguel and Mary Carmen been since they arrived in America? How do their lives here compare to their lives in South America? Can you do that, Micah?"

"It'll cost you." Micah spit out more food.

"What a surprise. But it's something you can do?"

"Sure," Micah promised.

"Marsh? Amy? I'm no immigration guru, but I presume we need to get these people asylum status. What are our strategies going forward?"

"As of now, they're out on bond. We're waiting for a notice to appear. The court, and *ICE* for that matter, will look at whether these parents pose any danger to the community. Do they have any kind of criminal record? We know they do not, but Micah's investigation and subsequent report will be a great piece of evidence for the court. We also must deal with their current undocumented status. Some judges believe this alone satisfies the test for criminality," Amy replied.

"What are their chances? They've lived here undocumented all this time. Doesn't that work against them?" Shaheed asked.

"It could. That's why we're defending their removal with a green card application. We're seeking an adjustment of status to permanent residency. This will be a family-based petition predicated on the fact that their kids are American citizens. This is also where the kids' arrest, imprisonment, and Zack's potential lawsuit will help," Marshall explained.

"Sounds reasonable. Piece of cake?" Zack smirked.

"It would have been easier if they hadn't overstayed their welcome in the first place. The judge will ask, and rightly so, why they didn't petition for permanent residency when conditional residency first expired," Marshall opined.

"And our response?" Zack inquired.

"The failure to timely file the I-751 petition to remove the condition is a problem, but the I-751 petition can be *renewed* as a defense to removal before a judge. Success depends on the situation and the judge," Amy warned. "In this case, if the judge allows all the facts to be heard, Marsh and I are confident we can get the I-751 renewed."

"That sounds promising," Micah opined.

"It is promising, but we must consider the politics in play and the judge's ability to preserve the cause of justice through all the political noise. We've filed petitions for waivers for 'bad acts,' such as lying about status or overstaying visas to stay in the country. Some judges require these waivers before they will consider an I-751 renewal," Amy continued.

"Why not just petition for asylum? Conditions suck in Venezuela. Micah's deep dive will demonstrate how tough it is down there." Zack suggested.

"We filed an asylum petition. These filings are not mutually exclusive. You can file them all—you don't have to pick and choose. If the immigrant petitioners have suffered past harm or fear they will suffer harm if they return to their home country, they are eligible for asylum. It's not automatic, but they *are* eligible. Under the Convention Against Torture, applicants must show that the harm they've suffered—or may suffer—rises to the level of *persecution,* based on race, religion, nationality, social or political status," Marshall explained.

"How well do you know the players in the system?" Zack wondered.

"Very well. In fact, we have written a request for prosecutorial discretion, requesting that the assigned prosecutor terminate removal proceeding on humanitarian grounds. These are hard to get under the Golding Administration, but we have an election coming up. If the good guys prevail, we might have a shot at a compassionate dismissal," Amy suggested.

"As Jennifer would say, perhaps we should pray for a miracle." Zack smiled at his own mention of the love of his life. "As my Jewish grandmother always said, it's like chicken soup—it wouldn't hurt."

Parsons spoke up for the first time. "What about . . . I'm not sure what they call it . . . temporary status? You know, where unrest in a country renders it unsafe. Would that buy you some time?"

"That's called *TPS* or 'Temporary Protected Status.' Yes, it could be used as a temporary measure, similar to the argument about persecution, but in Venezuela, the long-term persecution argument is a better alternative. Good thought, though." Marshall acknowledged Parsons with the tip of the finger.

"We have also filed an EOIR-42B petition. A person must be physically present in the United States for at least ten years prior to when the proceedings began and show good moral character during that time. If, and this is on point, the person has a United States citizen or legal permanent resident child, spouse, or parent, and that person will suffer extreme and exceptionally unusual hardship if petitioner is not permitted to remain in the country, petitioner can qualify for permanent resident status and have the deportation proceeding canceled. With two citizen children and what happened to them in El Paso, we think we've got a great shot at this status with the right judge," Amy predicted.

"That sounds very promising. It is almost as if the provision was *written* for our situation. It's quite compatible with the lawsuit, with kids being arrested and jailed. Talk about extreme and exceptionally unusual hardship! I like that a lot, guys."

"We aim to please, boss." Marshall turned and winked at Amy.

"I don't know much about the situation, but I do know something about persecution in one's home country. That's a real thing. Can we shift gears a second? What are we going to do about Rima Al-Baklavi?" Shaheed voiced concern on the monitor. "We were hoping Marshall or Amy could give us some guidance."

"Actually, the same kinds of things we just discussed apply to Rima as well. No criminal past, humanitarian relief and gratitude for saving a mother and her kids, fear of persecution in her home country, and dragged here by private plane by a couple of hooligans." Marsh quipped.

"Hey, I resemble that remark!" Parsons cracked on the monitor.

"Speak for yourself, Wayne. I like the whole 'lawyer saves woman who saved mother and daughter' idea." Zack concurred.

"We need to get her into federal custody sooner than later. We need to square our stories about who she is, what she did in Syria, and why she should be granted asylum rather than being thrown in prison." Jack suggested. "Want Shaheed and me to handle this? After all, we're the only law enforcement officials at this meeting."

"That would be great, Jack, but we need to find friendlies. I'd want it set up so she can turn herself in, tell her story, and avoid charges if possible. If it's not possible, then I'd like her arraigned, bonded, and released in our custody in one fell swoop. Will that be doable?" Zack wondered. "Either way, Marsh would take it from there on the immigration side, and I would jump in on the criminal side."

"Sounds like a plan, fellas," Jack retorted. "Wish I was there. The food looks great."

Chapter Twenty-Five

Micah returned to the office with food stains all over his silk shirt. He checked his messages and summoned Reed Spencer into his office.

"Hey, boss," Reed greeted Micah as he walked in. "Enjoy breakfast?" he chuckled and pointed to the stains on Micah's shirt.

"Yes, as a matter of fact, I did enjoy breakfast, smartass," Micah growled. "Sit down for a minute. I've got a research project for you."

"Do I need to take notes?"

"I don't think so. Zack wants a deep dive into Venezuelan politics and the plight of its citizens."

"I can handle that, I guess."

"But?"

"I didn't know there was a crisis in Venezuela."

"That's because you, me, and every other American only worry about ourselves. Who cares about the plight of people in third world countries?" Micah scolded.

"Okay, that's pretty harsh. Besides, I admit I don't know much, but I don't believe Venezuela is a third world country. Don't they have a shitload of oil over there?"

"They may have a ton of oil, but, apparently, they also have massive corruption, incompetence, and mismanagement of resources."

"I will investigate and report back. Anything else?"

"That's it for now."

Reed returned to his office and entered 'Crisis in Venezuela' in his search bar. Multiple articles appeared on the screen. He studied them, one by one. Micah was spot on about the corruption and mismanagement. The country was dealing with a spike in malnutrition, especially in children, where almost twenty thousand had died in the previous two years. Severely malnourished children were being admitted to hospitals in record numbers. He read about one child who was suffering from *marasmus*, a type of malnutrition caused by a general lack of nutrients. Others suffered from *kwashiorkor*, a potentially deadly type of malnutrition that causes swelling in the legs and face, resulting from a lack of protein. Doctors claim incidents of this condition were skyrocketing because impoverished families could not afford infant formula and were instead feeding babies rice cream, cornmeal, wheat flour, and even spaghetti. According to various news reports, large families were living on wages equivalent to five to seven dollars a month. Reed was astounded. *Who wouldn't flee such a country?*

People were dying in record numbers amid crushing sanctions imposed by the United States. Hyperinflation reduced the purchasing power of the country's ten dollars per month minimum wage to almost nothing. The economic crisis turned into a humanitarian crisis and forced the migration of over five million Venezuelan citizens.

The country was also locked in a power struggle as an opposition leader declared himself 'acting president,' even though the country had a sitting president. The country's armed forces and highest court remained loyal to the current socialist party, even though the economy has been in free fall since the 2013 election. As the two sides dug in, the United States imposed sweeping sanctions in an attempt to drive the current president from office. Socialist policies were supposed to reduce inequality, but the strategies backfired. Price controls were aimed at making goods more affordable, but inadequate profits for merchants caused them to cut production, resulting in shortages of needed goods and services.

A lack of infrastructure investment and U.S. sanctions crippled the country's vital oil industry, which provided almost all the government's revenue. All of this resulted in a mass migration of Venezuelan citizens like Mary Carmen and Miguel Gonzalez, who, thankfully, left the country before conditions had reached crisis levels. Reed read stories of immigrants hiking through the mountains, all their belongings stuffed in backpacks, traveling thousands of miles on foot, with less than ten dollars to their name.

United Nations investigators stepped in and accused the Venezuelan government of committing crimes against humanity. The United Nations Human Rights Council made this determination after a detailed fact-finding investigation of killings, torture, violence, and disappearances. The UN team accused the country's security services of engaging in a pattern of systematic violence aimed at suppressing political opposition and keeping citizens in check by acts of terror. A typical operation involved the government planting weapons in a community loyal to the opposition. Security services would then enter the community, shoot people at point-blank range, detain them, torture them, or otherwise kill them for possessing the weapons. By the end of its investigation, the United Nations had corroborated what it called 'patterns of violations and crimes.'

Reed spent a few more hours reading about a country in serious crisis. He was a key player on Micah's team of investigators handling the Gonzalez case for Zachary Blake and Marshall Mann. Mary Carmen and Miguel Gonzalez were smart to leave Venezuela when they did, but they overstayed their visa and did nothing to secure citizenship. Perhaps they couldn't afford a lawyer? The bottom line, however, was that while their children were citizens, they were not. Separating parents and children was a bridge too far for Reed Spencer. He intended to use his research to prove that conditions were terrible in Venezuela and even worse for people who escaped and were forced to return.

Reed's report would combine the humanitarian crisis in Venezuela with the current "President Golding" crisis at the southern border. Political cries to "send them back" and the government's practice of placing undocumented people in cages and separating families would also be part of his report. In this case, two under-aged American *citizens* were caged and separated from their parents. Multiple press accounts and video footage would buttress his presentation.

Still, Reed could not overcome their status. The Gonzalez parents were not criminals in a traditional sense. They hadn't hurt or killed anyone. They didn't steal from or rob anyone. Mary Carmen and Miguel had never even gotten a traffic ticket.

They worked hard, sent their kids to school, went to church every Sunday, and were well-liked in their community. Still, they were 'undocumented,' and only a judge could change that fact.

Reed was angry. He spent much of his adult life investigating bad actors, criminals, and criminality. Reed Spencer had to prepare the report of his life. Mary Carmen and Miguel Gonzalez could not be sent back, not on Reed Spencer's watch.

***

Armed with Reed's preliminary findings on the crisis in Venezuela, Marshall Mann and Amy Fletcher made their first court appearance *In the Matter of Mary Carmen and Miguel Gonzalez.* The two lawyers were pleased to discover that the judge assigned was the Honorable Leo J. Farhat, the same judge who once tore former President Ronald John a new one in the Khan deportation case back in the day. That case resulted in Marshall moving over to the Blake law firm.

In that case, Zack represented Arya Khan, a young woman who was falsely accused of murdering the white supremacist who bombed a local mosque. President John attempted to use the woman's parents as a poster child for his 'Muslim ban.' The president wanted the couple deported, even though both were American citizens and had done anything wrong.

Farhat wrote a blistering opinion, a historic repudiation of the president's immigration policies. The judge read his written statement into the record and quoted the movie *The American President,* referring to then-President John as the 'President of Fantasyland.'

Thanks in part to Zack's superlative legal work, the infamous former president was close to serving time in a federal penitentiary, accused of multiple crimes while in office. His successor refused to grant a pardon for the former president's crimes. In Marshall's mind, that was the only positive move Steven Golding made as president.

The first court date in the Gonzalez case was called a master calendar hearing, a fancy term for a method to bring the parties together to set dates and submit documents for future court appearances. Miguel and Mary Carmen were required to attend. Marshall wanted them present to become comfortable with the surroundings and meet the judge and opposing counsel. The couple furnished drivers' licenses to establish identities, as well as expired immigration papers from their original entry into the country.

Marshall advised them that oral arguments would take anywhere from five to twenty minutes. At the same time, he warned that they might be tied up for an hour or two because of the 'cattle call' nature of court administration. In this scenario, several cases on the docket are scheduled on the same day, at the same time. Attorneys and clients are required to attend. The cases are called, one by one, until all are administered. Typically, those who arrive first are called first, but 'arrive first' requires all parties be present at check-in. People who are represented by counsel receive priority, but all participants must be in attendance, including the attorneys, for the case to be placed in line.

Marshall didn't want the case called first. He wanted Mary Carmen and Miguel to observe proceedings for a time to see that there was nothing to worry about. A half-hour after their arrival, the clerk called the case. He shouted out the couple's Alien Registration Numbers. Marshall turned to the couple, smiled, motioned them to rise, and move toward the bench. James Theurer, the attorney representing the government, joined them in front of Judge Farhat.

The judge asked for appearances for the record, and the two attorneys identified themselves. The judge next required Mary Carmen and Miguel to state their names and addresses for the record. He asked if they spoke English or needed an interpreter. Marshall indicated that their English was sufficient to communicate and understand the proceedings.

The judge reviewed the list of charges for the record. He put forth reasons why the government sought to deport the couple. To their benefit, Miguel and Mary Carmen entered the country legally. They did not use false travel documents or sneak across the border. Fraud was not an issue in this case.

Without making any admissions against his clients' interest, Marshall carefully explained that they were accused of overstaying a visa. They were requesting asylum, withholding of removal, or a status adjustment. He sought protection for them under something called the United Nations Convention Against Torture, which sounded quite ominous to everyone in the courtroom.

The judge suggested various dates. An arduous process of synchronizing lawyer and judicial calendars began—the initial five dates suggested by the court were not compatible with all schedules. A second preliminary hearing was set first, subject to cancellation if deemed unnecessary.

Because this was an asylum case, the judge asked Mary Carmen and Miguel to designate their home country. Miguel, misunderstanding the question, politely answered, "The United States of America." Marshall was silently pleased with Miguel's response. If a client is afraid to return to a country, his attorney does not want to hear the client call that country "home." Marshall corrected Miguel, for the record, indicating that the couple did not wish to designate a country of removal and that the pair was afraid to return to Venezuela for fear of torture or retribution.

"Conditions are terrible there, Your Honor," Marshall reported.

"Duly noted," the judge grunted without looking up. "The record will reflect that the Gonzalez's country of removal is Venezuela."

"May we have an expedited date, Your Honor?" Mann requested.

"Mr. Theurer?"

"No objection, Your Honor."

The three men repeated the calendar synchronization process. They attempted to agree on a date for the Individual Merits Hearing and finally came to an agreement on a date five months away. The period was sufficient for Marshall and Amy to prepare and present a detailed asylum application and strong supporting documents of the extreme conditions facing anyone who returned to Venezuela. Acceptance of an expedited hearing was required for Mary Carmen and Miguel to continue to work in the United States. Marshall knew that Reed Spencer was researching and preparing a comprehensive report on conditions in Venezuela, lining up witnesses and official documents, especially as it pertained to returning dissident citizens. Marshall and Amy were confident that they could demonstrate a legitimate fear of persecution in Venezuela if their clients were returned.

After the hearing was over, Marshall sought and located a small conference room to explain things to Mary Carmen and Miguel. Amy persuaded Marshall to delay mention of Emma and Emilio's recent abduction and incarceration. They would surprise Theurer at the Individual Merits Hearing, and place the issue, front and center, in Leo Farhat's lap.

Prior to any hearing on the merits of the petition, Marshall and Amy also intended to use Zack's soon-to-be-filed lawsuit against the federal government as a tool to persuade the government to grant asylum without a judicial order. The family would happily swap money for citizenship and freedom. Humanitarian issues at the southern border and the Gestapo- like treatment of American children were not something James Theurer would wish to discuss at the Individual Merits Hearing. The strategy was to ramp up pressure on Theurer and the government to voluntarily grant the Gonzalez's asylum petition.

"He won't know what hit him," Amy laughed.

Miguel and Mary Carmen studied each other, not understanding what Amy thought was so funny. She noticed their discomfort.

"Do you trust us?" she asked.

"Yes, I do.

"Marshall and I don't believe Mr. Theurer will not want the court to know what happened to your children. We know Judge Farhat. He will be *appalled* by the government's behavior. We're hoping to leverage Emma's and Emilio's abductions and incarcerations into a settlement."

"What kind of settlement?" Mary Carmen wondered.

"One that makes your whole family citizens of the United States. How does that sound?" Marshall floated.

"We like that kind of settlement." Mary Carmen laughed.

Marshall smiled. They talked about the next few months and what to expect in the future. They would have plenty of time to discuss the details before the court date. Both Farhat and Theurer were good draws, easy-going, fair, and amenable to negotiation and settlement. For the time being, the family was safer than it was before the raid. No one would harass or arrest anyone. The family could enjoy an unprecedented five months of freedom in the United States of America. But would their status be permanent?

Chapter Twenty-Six

Marshall and Amy had another looming immigration case to consider. Rima Al-Baklavi surrendered to *ICE*. As Marshall prompted her to do, Rima told immigration officials she came to the United States by private charter to escape a terrorist network. Following the death of her husband, she was threatened by terrorists. She knew that those who assumed power in Syria would execute her if she returned.

The legal process for Rima to remain in the United States was similar to that of Mary Carmen and Miguel Gonzalez, with one significant difference. The premise of Rima's application, while truthfully averred, contained elements of deception. It was undoubtedly true that Rima faced death in Syria. However, *she,* not some terrorist network, killed her husband.

Rima traveled to the United States to avoid a *revenge* killing at the hands of her husband's terrorist network, a network she once prominently and loyally served. Marshall planned to handle the oral argument with Amy as second chair. His difficult legal challenge was to argue the positive aspects of Rima's application for asylum without revealing the negatives. He couldn't permit her to lie under oath because he'd be suborning perjury, a felony punishable by up to five years in prison.

Attorneys also have a special duty as officers of the court. Not only was Marshall barred from trying to influence Rima to lie under oath; he was also not permitted to call her as a witness to testify if he knew she would lie under oath. Marshall's obligations under the law had to be carefully explained to Rima. Under no circumstances could she answer a question dishonestly.

Marshall's duties as an officer of the court also extended to his own arguments before the court. If he knowingly made false statements or deliberately misled the court, he could be disbarred for misconduct, or worse, be guilty of a crime. So, the challenge for Marshall and Rima, the needle Marshall had to thread, so to speak, was to direct the testimony toward facts and situations that would compel the judge to grant asylum, without Rima ever being asked a question which, if answered, might tend to incriminate her.

Three short weeks after they appeared in front of Judge Farhat on the Gonzalez matter, Marshall and Amy were back in court on the Al-Baklavi case. This time, the immigration judge was Irving Tucker, a veteran jurist appointed years earlier by George W. Bush. Tucker was far more conservative than Farhat, but his many years on the bench resulted in a moderation of his previous conservative leanings. Amy had never appeared before Tucker. Marshall was pleased with the draw. By sheer coincidence, James Theurer again represented the government.

Tucker (and most immigration court judges) utilized the same cattle-call type approach to his docket as Farhat. The courtroom was packed with attorneys and clients waiting their turns for justice. Cases were called in order of appearance time, with attorney-represented cases and clients being called before the cases of those who had no lawyer. About forty-five minutes after they checked in, the clerk called: *In the Matter of Rima Al-Baklavi.*

Rima heard her name and looked over to Marshall in a panic. Marshall smiled and raised his hand to his waist, palm up, signaling for her to rise.

Judge Tucker introduced himself to Rima, had the attorneys identify themselves for the record, and asked Rima to state her name and address for the record. Rima quietly muttered her name and turned to Marshall in desperation. She was in federal custody at a detention center and had no formal 'address' in the United States.

"Your Honor, my client is currently a guest of the federal government, a resident of one of its fine detention centers."

"We'll ignore the sarcasm for now, Mr. Mann. Which detention center, please?" Judge Tucker grunted.

"Detroit, Your Honor. The East Jefferson facility," Marshall replied.

"Circumstances, Mr. Mann?"

"Yes, Your Honor. My client has escaped from Syria. Two American citizens were being held hostage in northern Syria by *ISIS*. My partner traveled to Syria and attempted to negotiate the release of the hostages. His security and negotiating teams encountered, shall we say, armed resistance. Ms. Al-Baklavi provided intelligence and assistance to the negotiating team, which resulted in the safe recovery and return of the hostages. Her assistance made it dangerous, no . . . *life-threatening*, for her to remain in Syria, so the team brought her to the United States and turned her over to immigration authorities. At that time, I filed an asylum petition, Your Honor. She has been in custody ever since. We seek *ROR* pending a decision on the merits of her petition."

"So, she entered the country without following appropriate protocols?" Judge Tucker presumed.

"Technically true, Your Honor. She does not have a passport but surrendered herself to authorities upon arrival. Her return to Syria would be a death sentence, judge."

"Understood. How's her English? Does she understand the nature and purpose of these proceedings?"

"She speaks some English, Your Honor. An interpreter would be appropriate in the future. For the purpose of *this* hearing, I will accept the responsibility of explaining what happens."

"Very well, counselor. What's your pleasure?"

"Your Honor, petitioner seeks protection under the United Nations Convention Against Torture and an immediate release into our custody until your final ruling on her petition. She barely escaped Syria alive, surrendered herself immediately upon arrival, and submitted herself to U.S. jurisdiction, our laws, and this honorable court. We seek visitor status, petition for asylum, and a withholding of removal proceedings until her status can be determined."

Proceedings droned on, very similar to Gonzalez. Future dates were proposed, calendars compared, and new dates were scheduled. The judge asked Rima to designate her home country. She again turned to Marshall, confused.

"My client has escaped from Syria, Your Honor. She is confused by the term 'home country.' She no longer regards Syria as her home," Marshall pontificated. "She is terrified to return to Syria, Your Honor."

Marshall then reiterated his requests.

"Understood, counselor. The record shall reflect that the petitioner's country of removal is Syria. I hereby order *ICE* to review our various no-fly lists and appropriate databases as they may relate to the petitioner herein. The United States, post 9-11, has an extensive visa security program, and I hereby order all security program protocols be implemented. I am instructing *ICE* to treat Ms. Al-Baklavi as if she was seeking a visa to come to the United States on a non-emergency basis. Would she qualify to get a plane ticket to America if she wished to visit? I invite the attorneys to work out petitioner's current lodging status. Do we require a bond? Does she need to stay in detention? Does the petitioner have relatives in the area? Rather than clog the record, I'd like you to find a conference room. Work out these details, considering the safety of our citizens, the safety of the petitioner, and the likelihood that she will appear at her next scheduled court date. Are we clear, gentlemen?"

"I believe we can work these things out, Your Honor." Theurer spoke for the first time since announcing his appearance.

"I agree," Mann assented.

"Then get to it. Officer Jackson, find these attorneys a room, please?"

"On it, Your Honor."

"Call the next case."

Officer Jackson led the attorneys into a conference room. Rima was taken to 'holding,' a *guarded* conference room.

"Good to see you again, James," Marshall began.

"You, too, Marsh. We're becoming such good friends."

"I'm counting on it, good buddy," Marshall grinned.

"Amy? How's it going? Learning a lot?" Theurer quipped.

"Learning superior advocacy skills from Marshall, and deplorable government conduct from your client," Amy snapped.

"Hey, I just work here, guys. I don't have much latitude in these types of situations, especially with Syrian rebels."

"She's *not* a Syrian rebel, James. Come on now, both of you, can we curb the hostile rhetoric?" Marshall suggested. Amy nodded her assent.

"What's your pleasure?" Theurer changed the subject.

They discussed a somewhat factual version of Rima's harrowing escape from Syria, with Marshall carefully steering away from disclosing her marital and criminal status in the eyes of Syrian law. The ultimate question was securing her attendance for the next court date. Amy suggested a release into Marshall's custody, indicating that she or Marshall would readily agree to accept full responsibility for her appearance. Theurer wanted her to remain at the detention center, in custody, until a final determination was made on the merits of her petition.

The law permitted either of these extremes, as well as a middle ground. Eventually, the attorneys got around to discussing bond. *ICE* has the discretion to grant bond to someone in immigration custody—both lawyers were acutely aware of the law in that regard. A bond would allow a petitioner to post, be released from custody, and return home while proceedings are pending. However, not all immigrants are eligible for a bond. Rima Al-Baklavi had three hurdles to overcome to make James Theurer feel comfortable agreeing to-bond: She had no 'U.S. home.' Could Marshall and Amy truly guarantee her multiple court appearances? Would her release create a danger to the community? While she had no criminal record, she hadn't been in the country long enough to have one. Her short-term status in the United States, on paper, all but rendered her ineligible to post bond. Bond is discretionary with the judge, though, and Marshall reminded Theurer that it was the judge who mandated this meeting. He offered to stipulate to and post a high bond. He also agreed, as an officer of the court, that Rima would appear for all scheduled court dates that required her appearance. When the discussions became contentious, Mann stood up and demanded to see the judge. He knew that bond refusals and amounts are reviewable by the presiding judge and was testing his adversary. Theurer caved, ultimately agreeing to a $25,000 bond. Marshall also had to agree to find Rima mutually acceptable lodging within three days.

When an agreement was reached, the attorneys returned to the courtroom and placed it on the record in front of Judge Tucker.

"Glad you could work it out," the judge lauded. "See you soon."

Marshall and Amy exited the courthouse, accompanied by their bewildered but jubilant client. Both wondered what flags the name 'Al-Baklavi' might raise for *ICE*. After all, Rima's country of removal was Syria, the principal sponsor of *ISIS* and Mid East terror. The judge was correct to be cautious—his ruling was sensible. Marshall, with Amy's help, made the best deal he could under the circumstances.

Contrary to his strategy in Gonzalez, Marshall did not request an expedited hearing. Barring any affirmative presentation of evidence that Rima was connected to terrorists, Marshall and Amy were confident they could obtain asylum. Judges do not like to sentence women to death. If Rima was permitted to stay in the United States and stayed out of trouble, time was her friend. The two lawyers would happily agree to time delays and adjournments to put significant time distance between the events of the hostage escape and Judge Tucker's final ruling on her application.

If the judge granted asylum, the time element would make no difference to the outcome. However, if Tucker decided to deport Rima, and his ruling was rendered a year or two post-incident, the terrorist threat might be diminished. Rebels seeking her death might be defeated or otherwise neutralized. This was Rima's best hope, short of asylum.

Reed Spencer would be spending additional time researching the extreme conditions that existed on the Syrian-Turkish border and the legitimate threat to the life and safety of Rima Al-Baklavi. An asylum hearing loomed, at present, six months from now. Could Reed develop compelling evidence that a return to Syria would mean death for Rima Al-Baklavi? Time would tell.

Chapter Twenty-Seven

"How did things go in court?" Zachary Blake sat at a huge desk in his home office, talking to Marshall Mann on his iPhone.

"As expected. With some negotiation and compromise, we obtained her release on bond. We have people watching and working with her on her story and, especially, her English. She's staying at the Doubletree on Woodward, out by the office. Amy was a big help."

"That's good news, Marsh. Great work by both of you. Good location for our purposes."

"We thought so."

"What are her chances?" Zack tensed, awaiting the response.

"Pretty good as long as the full circumstances of her escape from her husband don't derail things."

"Chances of that?"

"We've got some tricks up my sleeve."

"Care to share?"

"I'm exhausted. Can we discuss it in the morning?"

"Sure, breakfast?"

"You buying?"

"I pay either way."

"True, invite Amy?"

"Your choice. As far as I'm concerned, Amy's always welcome. She keeps me on my toes. Is anyone smarter than Amy?"

"Not sure. Certainly not me."

"It's been a tough couple of weeks. She's been a big help."

"More than you know, boss. She's a Godsend."

"Hiring her was one of my better moves."

"As I recall, I hired her, not you."

"True, but I sent her your way."

"I'll concede the point, if it makes you feel better."

"It does. See you in the morning."

"You got it, boss. My love to the family."

As if on cue, Jennifer, Jake, and Kenny strolled into Zack's office.

"Hard day, Dad?" Kenny wondered.

"For Marshall, Amy, and our recently acquired immigration clients, yes—for me, not so much. Delegation is one of the best perks of being the boss. How's everyone doing today?"

"Everything's good on the home front, Dad," Jake advised.

"How's school going?"

"Doing well, Pop. Doing well," Kenny replied.

"All A's and B's this semester," Jake boasted.

"We're very proud of you guys, you know," Jennifer beamed. "We know it's been a tough ride."

"We're fine, Mom," Jake grunted. He and his brother were tired of dredging up the past and living in the aftermath of two tragic events. They were happy Zack came into their lives and anxious to move forward. With professional counseling and parental devotion and love, they were doing remarkably well. Kenny was pre-law in college. Jake would soon follow in his footsteps.

"Tell us about these cases, Dad. Zachary Blake on his white horse, riding into battle, righting wrongs, and fighting injustice, as usual?" Kenny cracked.

"Something like that, only Marshall Mann is the hero right now."

"The Syria thing?" Jake wondered. The boys were happy Zack returned from Syria with nary a scratch.

"The Syria thing, as you call it—a southern border thing, too. We've got a twofer on our hands."

"Care to share?" Jennifer was curious. Zack could be introspective at times. His wife liked to make sure he talked things out. Attorney-client privilege sometimes made that impossible.

"Sure. What do you want to know?"

"Whatever you're willing to tell us." Jennifer nodded at the boys and motioned for Zack to continue.

"As you know, we have this humanitarian crisis at the southern border. Our clients, a family of four, were caught up in it. *ICE* raided the parent's workplace. Agents arrested the parents because they overstayed their visas. That makes them undocumented. The parents got sent to this disgusting detention center in Detroit. Marshall and I got them released, only to find out that *ICE* rounded up their children and sent them to an unknown location. We shifted our focus to locating the kids. It took quite a while, but we were finally able to locate them at a detention center in Texas. Temporarily, at least, the family is reunited."

"Temporarily?" Kenny inquired.

"They're still undocumented, Kenny. We've got to convince a judge to grant them a path to citizenship. Otherwise, they will get deported, and the choices become impossible."

"Impossible?" Jennifer asked.

"If they're deported, they have two choices. Leave their American-born kids behind or take them to the dangerous country they fled. See? Impossible."

"What's wrong with Venezuela? Lots of oil there, no?"

"Too much tyranny and government corruption. There is a virtual civil war going on down there over the oil and other resources. The riches do not flow to the citizens."

"Is that what's troubling you, Zack?" Jennifer looked concerned. She always knew when Zack was struggling with a case. She possessed a wife's 'sixth sense.'

"You should see these detention centers, guys. I wouldn't house stray dogs in these places. I'd love to find a way to provide legal help for every single person caught up in this terrible system we have in place. And the government is doing almost nothing to help. The frigging ghost of Ronald John strikes again."

"We've been studying this in our political science class. Weren't these detention centers conceived and built by Obama?" Kenny debated.

"Yes!" Zack exploded. "But who cares which party started this mess? I want it to be over!"

"Whoa! Sorry, Dad, I didn't mean to piss you off." Kenny retreated.

Zack softened. "No, Kenny. I'm the one who's sorry. I didn't mean to go off on you like that. This is an extremely frustrating situation. It shouldn't be a political issue; it should be a *humanitarian* issue. This is *America*—we can do so much better. It all connects with white supremacy, white America feeling that immigrants are coming to take jobs away from so-called *real* Americans. Of course, this is code for people of color taking jobs from white people, right?"

"So, what's the plan?" Jennifer changed the subject.

"The plan is to handle their deportation case, prove that Venezuela is an unsafe venue for their return, obtain asylum and citizenship for the parents. The kids were born here, so they are citizens."

"They locked up *citizens* in a cage in Texas?" Jake was stunned.

"See why I'm so agitated? Sounds like something out of World War II, doesn't it?"

Zack's grandfather was a Holocaust survivor. The family knew the story and wisely did not challenge Zack on the comparison.

"I'm sure it will all work out, honey," Jennifer chirped, always the optimist.

"What about the other case, Dad, the one from Syria?"

"Attorney-client privilege," Zack retorted.

"What?" Kenny challenged. "Come on, Dad. What happens in the Tracey-Blake family stays in the Tracey-Blake family."

"So say you all?" Zack smiled.

"So say us all," Jennifer nodded and prodded the boys to nod their assent.

"We now represent a woman who was dragged here by our own security force. She killed her husband to save the hostages we went to Syria to rescue. Her husband was the head guy, the terrorist who kidnapped our client's wife and child. She was a rather unwilling participant in the kidnapping plot. It will be tough to argue for asylum while, at the same time, keep out evidence of her involvement."

"Wow, Dad! That sounds like something out of a Daniel Silva novel!" Jake exclaimed.

"I never thought about it that way, Jake, but I see the comparison." Zack drifted off in thought.

"There's more, darling?" Jennifer sensed additional consternation.

"I'm glad you can't be on my jury, Jen. You read me like a book."

"Spill it, Dad," Kenny demanded.

"It's not my expertise. I'm not used to taking a back seat. Marshall and Amy are both terrific. I know they'll get the job done. Still, I feel a need to be in there fighting for my clients—it's frustrating here on the sidelines. I can't do much on the civil side until Marshall and Amy do their thing on the immigration side."

"It could be worse, sweetheart. You could be the clients." Jennifer had an annoying knack for putting things in perspective.

Zack glanced around the room and out the large French door of his office. The family lived in what anyone would call a mansion.

"This is hardly a cage," he conceded. "And I will never allow anyone to separate me from you guys."

"Come on, Dad," Jake chided. "That's some sappy shit."

"Deal with it. I love you guys. I'm proud to say it out loud. Besides, as your mom always says, I am the luckiest man in the world."

"So go save it, Dad," Kenny encouraged.

"What?"

"The world, Zack. Go save it! Duh-uh . . ." Jennifer laughed.

***

The following morning, Zack met Marshall for breakfast at the Little Daddy's location near the office. Zack was anxious to hear how Marsh and Amy intended to keep Rima from being deported and executed in Syria.

"Where's Amy? I thought she was coming." Zack was disappointed.

"She's already working with Reed on our next presentation in court. She's something else."

"Tell me something I don't know."

The two men exchanged small talk, ordered omelets from Norma, their favorite server, and got down to business.

"I didn't get much sleep last night, Marsh. Worried about these clients and their situations. What's the scoop? How do we help them?"

Marshall smirked and shook his head. "You just can't stand not being *the guy*, can you?"

"What do you mean?" Zack knew exactly what he meant. Marshall had him pegged.

"Don't play coy with me, hotshot—you can't stand that this case is playing out in immigration court, my world, Amy's world, rather than civil court, *your* world. Isn't that the size of things? At least have the balls to admit how you feel."

Zack laughed. "I readily admit it, man. This is very frustrating for me. I feel helpless. You got me—now, talk me down, please? I need reassurance."

"We talked about most of this at our conference call the other day. The law recognizes only two types of credible fear. We plan to prove they were present in *both* cases. We're going to demonstrate that the Gonzalez parents and Rima Al-Baklavi have credible fears of persecution and torture as defined by law."

"That's pretty broad, Marsh. What law?"

"Under Title 8 of the Code of Federal Regulations, our clients must demonstrate in court what's called a significant possibility—evidence that tends to show they've already experienced persecution in their home countries.

"Second, and Amy's briefing this, they must demonstrate that, if returned to the home country, they have a well-founded fear of persecution or harm, based upon their race, religion, nationality, membership in a particular social group, or political opinion. Those are the magic grounds for asylum."

"Sounds achievable in both cases, anything else?"

"A similar standard applies to torture. An alien must demonstrate a significant possibility that he or she is eligible for withholding removal or deferring removal under the Convention Against Torture in Title 8. To dumb this down, will they be tortured, or are they likely to be tortured if they're sent back?"

"It sure seems like we can meet those thresholds in both cases, no?"

"We're confident we can meet the criteria. Amy and Reed Spencer are working to obtain the evidence we need. The Federal Rules of Evidence don't apply in immigration proceedings. We can get all kinds of hearsay stuff into evidence. Facebook posts, newspaper articles, and witness affidavits; stuff like that—it all comes in. There is plenty of material in both Syria and Venezuela. I've been reviewing it, and it's compelling."

"You seem stressed, though. What's the problem?"

"We have to demonstrate a nexus between our evidence and our client's situations. Are *they* being persecuted? Do *they* have a reasonable fear of persecution? We have to personalize both situations and present them from the clients' perspectives. That's a more difficult burden."

"Understood. And Reed is working on that, too?"

"Reed, Amy, and everyone else in Micah's office."

"Good. We can count on them. How much time do we have?"

"A couple of months for Gonzalez—a bit more for Al-Baklavi. The clients will be required to testify. They must present direct evidence of prior experience and current fear of persecution and torture. Remember Zack; these are not sophisticated people. Still, they've got to know our evidence cold, be able to regurgitate sections of it on the witness stand, look judges and the prosecutors in the eyes, and convince these judges that they face torture, persecution, or both, if they're sent back.

"We will have our work cut out for us—Micah's people, Amy Fletcher, and her team are already working with the clients as we speak. I think we'll be okay. The Al-Baklavi case presentation will be a bit more difficult."

"Because you somehow have to present evidence and her testimony without disclosing that she killed her husband?"

"Correct. Her testimony is the tricky part, especially on cross, but we've got some ideas about that."

"Care to share?"

"Nah. Just formulating some ideas for now—I'll keep you posted."

At that moment, Norma brought their omelets and all discussions about the cases ceased. For the first time in a long time, the two partners simply enjoyed each other's company, exchanging legal war stories, firm successes, Detroit sports, family, and other relationships. For a moment, all was right with the world.

Chapter Twenty-Eight

Teams from Love Investigations and the Blake firm continued developing the evidence, working with the clients, and preparing the documents and presentation for Marshall's oral argument. As Reed, Amy, and the briefing team developed formal statements of fact in both cases, these statements were edited by the clients. Despite their limited education and zero legal experience, the clients rose to the occasion, understood the serious stakes, and provided valuable assistance.

They studied and re-studied their asylum applications and statement of facts. They read them, ad nauseam, until they knew them by heart. Their 'coaches' understood that even someone telling the truth in court might succumb to nervousness, have a memory lapse, and, perhaps, fail to keep dates or other particulars straight. They also reminded the clients that demeanor in court is vitally important and observed. The judges, in particular, would be observing client demeanor and taking it into account.

"Look the government's attorney in the eye when you answer his questions. If the judge asks a question, or it is otherwise appropriate to directly address him, look *him* in the eyes. Direct eye contact is considered a sign of honesty to many law enforcement and legal officials. Staring at the floor, up in the air, down at one's hands is considered a sign of dishonesty."

Reed and his team collected an impressive array of human rights reports, government documents, news clippings, Facebook and blog posts, Google Earth snapshots of on-the-ground unrest, and multiple additional social media documentation. In addition, investigators contacted family members in Syria and Venezuela. They readily supplied sworn affidavits about conditions, now and when the clients fled their respective countries. Investigators also used backchannel connections to communicate with opposition leaders and families of political prisoners. All eagerly provided detailed statements of human rights violations, injuries, deaths, torture, intimidation, and other forms of cruelty and suppression of speech in opposition to oppressive regimes.

The evidence was neatly assembled, indexed, and annotated in a folder of exhibits. The documents were paginated consecutively and alphabetically tabbed. Due to the sheer volume of the presentation, country condition documents were annotated with the most critical parts of those documents in the index.

Amy reasoned that a judge would not likely read all the evidence. However, she was reasonably confident that the judge would at least go through the index and, perhaps, seek out the most important aspects of the cases. For example, Amy felt that extreme country conditions would be very important to an immigration judge. In fact, Marshall told her that some judges literally read these types of documents into the record—to support a ruling granting asylum—pieces directly from the firm's annotated index. Judges often cited corroborating pieces of evidence and country condition documents, reading verbatim from the index itself. Marshall implored Reed and Amy to be detailed because detailed records of support for these cases would rule the day.

In most branches of the federal court system, the Federal Rules of Evidence applied to the inadmissibility of testimony and documents. This is not true in immigration court, where the sole test for admission of evidence was whether it is probative and fundamentally fair. Amy knew evidence that complied with the rules was more probative or persuasive—judges might give the evidence more weight—she also knew non-compliance did not make the evidence inadmissible.

Because of his command of these lax rules, she instructed Reed and the others obtain sworn affidavits and corroborate them using social media tools. Every single communication with a witness was carefully indexed and annotated with some form of social media corroboration. All audio or video evidence was converted to stills and transcribed in print, as technology is *not* admissible. Foreign documents were translated in English, and a certificate of translation was included, indexed, and annotated each time. Amy and Reed left no stone unturned in fine-tuning Marshall's presentations to Judges Farhat and Tucker.

All exhibits and annotations were assembled with detailed statements of facts. Amy knew the presentations required strong written records and experienced oral advocacy. What emerged in both cases was a compelling and persuasive argument to grant asylum. It was time for Marshall, Amy, and the briefing team to write legal briefs on the law and apply the law to the facts of each case.

The 14th Amendment confers all the rights, privileges, and protection of citizenship to anyone born in the United States. The Civil Rights Act of 1866 declared that all individuals born in the US, regardless of race, were US citizens. This act overturned the infamous Dred Scott decision, in which the Supreme Court ruled that anyone who was a descendant of a slave, free or not, was not a citizen nor eligible to become one. To prevent amendment or repeal of the Act, Congress ratified the 14th Amendment to the Constitution. Citizens are entitled to life, liberty, and the pursuit of happiness. The children of parent citizens are automatically citizens, but not the other way around. Thus, in Gonzalez, Marshall would argue that these kids were being denied their constitutional rights by being subjected to a divided family and the possible loss—deportation—of their parents through no fault of their own.

Next, Amy focused the firm's briefs on the so-called 'two fears' of persecution and torture. With Venezuela, Reed's report detailed a country in turmoil, with starvation wages, malnutrition, illness, and death. Was this enough? Amy wasn't certain. Marshall didn't think so, even though most citizens fled the country because of this humanitarian crisis.

Doctors claim incidents of this condition were skyrocketing because impoverished families could not afford infant formula and were feeding babies rice cream, cornmeal, wheat flour, and even spaghetti. Marshall and Amy decided to focus on Miguel Gonzalez's support of the opposition leader instead of the sitting president, who was supported by the country's armed forces and Supreme Court. As Miguel and his family fled the country, the United Nations Human Rights Council was charging that the

Venezuelan government committed crimes against humanity after a detailed fact-finding investigation of killings, torture, violence, and disappearances. The two lawyers included portions of the UN report, which contained evidence of violence and acts of terror aimed at opposition leaders and followers. People were tortured or shot, point-blank, in what the United Nations called 'patterns of violations and crimes.'

The UN report was compelling evidence in the Gonzalez case, and Miguel's active support for the opposition created the necessary nexus Marshall needed to connect the law to the facts. If Miguel and Mary Carmen were sent back, they would be imprisoned and permanently separated from their children. Marshall would argue that this would be cruel and unusual punishment for the simple crime of overstaying a visa. The threat of torture and persecution should be enough to grant asylum to these visitors, people who had never been in trouble with the law in the U.S., worked hard, were parents of U.S. citizens, and pillars of their community.

The facts and law in Rima Al-Baklavi's case were equally compelling. Ronald John and his successor, Steven Golding, were outspoken proponents of border walls and Muslim Bans. The Iran Hostage Crisis, 9-11, and other terrorist incidents resulted in the designation of certain Middle Eastern countries as terrorist sponsors. America and Americans were hated in these banned Muslim countries. Two American citizens, a mother and her infant daughter, were detained and held hostage by *ISIS*. Rima Al-Baklavi rendered aid and comfort to the enemy, helped them escape, and a bounty was now offered to anyone who successfully located and executed the infidel.

All of this was bound up in a neat little binder of evidence, indexed, annotated, and tabbed with corroborating evidence of potential torture, persecution, and certain death. The firm's exhibit package, fact statement, and legal brief laid out the stark and detailed case that told the judge: "If you send Rima back, you are sentencing her to death."

The two briefs were completed and delivered by courier to James Theurer, Judge Farhat, and Judge Tucker, one month prior to the court date set for the Gonzalez case. The government's response briefs would be due two weeks before each scheduled court date. It was literally all over but the shouting. It would soon be time for Marshall to argue both cases in a court of law.

Chapter Twenty-Nine

Petitioners' friends and family members, lawyers, law students, reporters, and other media types packed a large immigration courtroom for the asylum hearing of Miguel and Mary Carmen Gonzalez. Emma and Emilio sat directly behind the counsel table, dressed in their Sunday best. A couple of family members, Zack Blake, and an army of paralegals and investigators sat to their left. Miguel, Mary Carmen, Reed Spencer, and Amy Fletcher sat with Marshall Mann at the counsel table.

James Theurer, supported by a contingent of government lawyers and paraprofessionals, occupied the counsel table on the opposite side of the courtroom. The lawyers and assistants on each side were mumbling to each other, shuffling papers back and forth. All awaited the arrival of the Honorable Leo J. Farhat.

"All rise!" The court officer stood and shouted. The murmuring stopped almost immediately. Everyone rose as a door behind the bench opened, and the honorable one ventured into the courtroom.

"Be seated," Farhat ordered. Everyone in the gallery and at counsel tables noisily sat down. "Calling: *In the Matter of Mary Carmen and Miguel Gonzalez*," Farhat barked. "Appearances for the record, please?"

"Marshall Mann for the petitioners, Your Honor."

"James Theurer, for the government, Your Honor."

"Thank you for that, counselors. Any preliminary matters?"

"May we approach, Your Honor?" Theurer requested.

"By all means," the judge replied, motioning them forward. A long, animated conversation developed, in camera, out of earshot of the others in the courtroom. When the confab was terminated, each attorney returned to his respective counsel table to brief their co-counsel and administrative staff.

"Mr. Mann, are you ready to proceed with your opening statement?" The judge inquired after waiting a minute or two for the conversations to end.

"Yes, Your Honor." Mann stood and addressed the court.

"Proceed," invited Judge Farhat.

"May it please the court? Our country has a long tradition of taking in immigrants from other countries who become loyal and prosperous Americans and whose children and grandchildren now make America the country it is today. However, despite that proud tradition, with time, the American success of certain minority citizens turns into resentment, even hate, along with accusations like 'they're bringing crime;' 'they're bringing drugs,' and similar epithets.

"With this long tradition of taking in immigrants comes a long tradition of anti-immigrant prejudice and hatred. In the late 1800's it was the Chinese, the Chinese Exclusion Act of 1882, and the so-called 'yellow peril.' During World War II, it was the Japanese. More recently, following 9-11, it was Muslims and a so-called 'Muslim ban.' Today, it's people of Hispanic origin. Our president and his immediate predecessor have openly referred to immigrants of Latin descent as lacking education, drug traffickers, and socio-economically inferior . . ."

Marshall continued his opening statement, offering what he intended to prove. He focused first on the Gonzalez citizen-children, pointing them out to the judge and asking them to stand. He emphasized what removal or deportation of their parents would mean to these young citizens of the United States. He painted a portrait of this mixed-status family.

"What forces motivated the parents to make the treacherous journey to the U.S. and a better place and life for their family? Why would they break the law and stay here without proper documentation, knowing their actions might affect their children for years to come?"

Marshall promised to introduce testimony from a clinical psychologist. He referred Farhat to the doctor's report, by exhibit number, page number, and tab contained in the brief. In the report, the doctor shed light on the social and psychological experience of children born US citizens-to undocumented parents. What impact does their parents' undocumented status have on them? How do they see the world? What is criminal and what is not? What effect has guarding their parents' secrets had on them? The doctor referred to such children as a 'special class of orphan.' When parents are taken, children lose their daily physical presence, love, and affection. While they may still be alive, they are not accessible—hence the word 'orphan.' They might as well be dead. Above all, Marshall effectively *humanized* their situation.

"These children were brought into the world without knowledge or choice about deportation. They did not expect to discover that their parents might someday, any day, be sent back to the country they came from. These kids grow up in constant fear, psychologically damaged by perpetual worry. They are 'collateral damage' in a political war to enact laws, policies, and immigration enforcement practices."

Marshall looked directly into Farhat's eyes. "Do *their* rights merit your attention, Your Honor? They are U.S.-born *citizens*, innocent of any wrongdoing. Their situations seldom rise to the critical attention of legislators, policymakers, or law enforcement officers.

"These brave people who decide to come to America— arrive on foot, smuggled in car trunks, or smoldering hot trailers of eighteen-wheelers. They encounter disease, hunger, even *death* to get to this country. And, *surprise*, they are greeted with public scorn and humiliation, criticism from our leaders, punishment and possible arrest, detention, and, finally, deportation in an increasingly harsh legal system.

"Your Honor, these cruel acts are contrary to the American Convention on Human Rights signed by the U.S. in 1969. Article 17 states: 'the family is the natural and fundamental group unit of society and is entitled to protection by society and the state.' Article 19 states: 'Every minor child has the right to the measures of protection required by his condition as a minor on the part of his family, society, and the state.'

"These are not statistics, Your Honor. They are *people*. Their immigration status does not alter their intrinsic humanness. They seek protection for their children and have goals and aspirations like all parents. Here, at this moment in time, however, they may be torn apart by deportation and separation."

Judge Farhat was sharply focused on Marshall throughout the presentation, following the exhibits and accompanying corroborative evidence. The judge was obviously impressed with both the oral and written presentation.

Marshall continued, discussing the 'two fears' - torture and persecution. He did not discuss Miguel's political advocacy in Venezuela, only the fact that he stood *accused* of political advocacy. The accusation placed a target on his back in his home country. He did not *choose* to leave Venezuela—he was *compelled* to go, based on circumstances on the ground. Marshall referred the judge to numerous exhibits in the brief package to corroborate his statements and observed Farhat consistently referring to sections in the folder as Marshall argued. Marshall also noticed, with a wry smile, that James Theurer was doing the same.

Social media posts, Google Maps printouts, and eye-witness affidavits, chronologically presented by a master litigator, painted a compelling portrait of a corrupt country in turmoil and the torture and persecution of anyone who dared to criticize those in power. Marshall promised to present live testimony, written documentation, witness statements, and affidavits of family members and friends left behind as evidence to support his claim.

He knew the evidentiary standards were loose, but he endeavored to present most of it in compliance with evidentiary rules. He also knew the judge would afford it more weight. Perhaps the rules weren't important, but the power and quality of the evidence was.

In the end, Marshall argued that Miguel and Mary Carmen had nowhere else to go. Miguel's 'protected grounds' for asylum were his participation in a particular social group and for persecution and potential torture for speaking up about it, expressing a contrary political opinion to that of the Venezuelan government. This caused the local and national police to view Miguel as an enemy combatant, someone who was considered 'against the government,' a protected ground, a legitimate reason for an alien to seek asylum in the United States of America.

James Theurer's opening statement was considerably shorter than Marshall's. His presentation brief and folder were boilerplate yet still impressive. Theurer and his team hit on all the necessary points of contention, focusing on Miguel's opportunity to seek asylum before he became undocumented and Miguel and Mary Carmen's "utter failure to even attempt to seek permanent status." This, as Amy Fletcher noted, was the weakest part of Marshall's case. Despite a dynamic opening, Marshall, Miguel, and Mary Carmen had their work cut out for them.

As the trial droned on, it became apparent to all in attendance that Marshall's advocacy, passion, organization, and preparedness were winning the day. Theurer and his team were doing their best to weather the onslaught, but a combination of Marshall's superior oratory skills, Zack Blake's money, and the power of the Blake firm machine were wearing them down. When Theurer and team would raise a solid point, Marshall and team would counter it with dozens contrary facts, along with tabbed and paginated exhibits offered as corroborating evidence.

"Mr. Gonzalez did nothing to attempt to solve his issues with local authorities. He never directly involved the police and made zero effort to stay and fight for better conditions—he just suddenly decided to flee and never go back," Theurer argued.

"That's not true, Your Honor," Marshall interjected. He looked to Amy, who handed him a section of the brief. "I refer you to our brief, tab 3, page 74, where you will find multiple affidavits and other documentation of retaliation against witnesses who report incidents to the police, documentation of corruption, and infiltration of law enforcement by the criminal element, gang, and cartel members. That's the reason it was unreasonable to expect my client to rely on local authorities, then and now. The evidence of persecution is overwhelming, Your Honor."

The hearing droned on. Zack, recalling Farhat's ruling in the Khan case a few years ago, began to feel confident about the outcome. He marveled at Marshall's advocacy and trial preparation and was honored to have him as a partner. Zack couldn't be more pleased that he created the firm's immigration department, with Marshall running the show.

The only evidence standing in the way of victory for Marshall, Amy, and their clients was their failure to seek permanent status while still in legal status. To his credit, Theurer made this a consistent theme in argument, evidence presentation, and testimony. Not one piece of evidence could refute the truth of this averment. While Marshall could not directly rebut the evidence, he could certainly explain it. As usual, he approached this burden with a sledgehammer rather than a gavel. He hammered the official record with detailed facts, corroborating evidence, and relevant law.

Easily located—if one knows where to look— but buried in obscure sections of Marshall's briefing documents, was an argument demanding that Miguel and Mary Carmen's removal proceedings be dismissed without prejudice. Again, Amy efficiently located the section and handed the documents to Marshall. The pair was a well-oiled courtroom machine. In this section, Marshall argued, with solid, supportive case law, that *ICE* lacked authority to institute the plant raid, carry out pre-planned mass detentions, interrogate, and make arrests at the plant. Where was the requisite probable cause or individualized reasonable suspicion that *Miguel* and *Mary Carmen* were undocumented?

While the search warrant for the plant's employment records was executed, Miguel and Mary Carmen were detained, interrogated, and, ultimately, arrested for immigration violations, along with multiple co-workers. Based on statements made by the couple while in detention, *ICE* agents prepared a Form-213. A 213 is a form used on an apprehended undocumented foreign national. It describes the alien's history of apprehension and detention, the manner which the person allegedly entered our country, any history of prior contact with authorities, or crimes committed. In the Gonzalez case, the 213 alleged that Miguel and Mary Carmen came to this country legally and overstayed their visas. Somewhere along the line, the government obtained copies of the couple's birth certificates.

Marshall now argued that this evidence should be suppressed, with charges dismissed on Fourth Amendment grounds. The government was arguing that its search warrant for records that the plant routinely hired undocumented people permitted them to detain, interrogate, and arrest many individuals without any specific evidence or reasonable suspicion as to the guilt or innocence of any one individual.

Marshall argued the opposite; that the government's warrant did *not* permit agents to retain or interrogate anyone who was not a target—under reasonable suspicion—in the underlying objective of the raid. He argued that the purpose behind the agents' raid was relevant because the agents had no pre-existing suspicion that Miguel or Mary Carmen was undocumented. A pre-stated valid purpose to detain and interrogate the Gonzalez couple was required.

Referring to the warrant as 'administrative,' Marshall argued that the search was invalid due to an inadmissible purpose and whether the agents would have detained Miguel and Mary Carmen but for that purpose. To buttress his argument, Marshall subpoenaed the government's planning documents and maintained that the Gonzalez couple satisfied this burden because the planning documents clearly demonstrated that the central purpose of the raid was not to find documents but to arrest undocumented workers.

"Your Honor, under section 287 of the C.F.R. (Code of Federal Regulations), a person cannot be detained or questioned unless an *ICE* agent has reasonable suspicion, based upon specific facts, that the person is in the country without proper documentation. Since the agents in this case had no pre-existing suspicion, any evidence of status obtained from detention or interrogation of this couple must be suppressed. If you suppress the evidence, there *is* none to support their deportation and the case must be dismissed. Once you make that determination, and we are convinced that you will, all that is left for you to consider is our clients' petition for asylum. But, *not* under threat of deportation."

Marshall was proud of Amy and her briefing team. Having read their carefully prepared legal memoranda on these issues, Marshall was convinced that this argument conclusively prevented deportation on Fourth Amendment grounds. The government's plan to target for detention hundreds of workers at multiple Detroit area plants, turned on obtaining and executing search warrants for employment records. But the real purpose of the *Riverview* warrant was to detain, interrogate, and ultimately *arrest* workers.

To do any of those things, especially as to Miguel and Mary Carmen, agents had to have reasonable suspicion that they were undocumented. Since *ICE* agents did *not* have the requisite suspicion, any evidence obtained was inadmissible as the so-called *fruit of the poisonous tree*. If the warrant is tainted, so is all the evidence obtained after its execution. Marshall was almost giddy as he made these arguments, confident that they would win the day.

Chapter Thirty

The reunited, trial-weary Gonzalez family sat down to Sunday dinner, truly grateful to God for delivering Zachary Blake, Marshall Mann, and Amy Fletcher in their time of need. Marshall and Amy seemed excited about the outcome of the trial, and their excitement was infectious. Miguel and Mary Carmen continued to be terrified, tormented by the possibility of permanent separation from their children, but buoyed by Marshall and Amy's exuberance and confidence that victory was inevitable. Emma was invited to say the grace before the meal.

"God is great, and God is good. Let us thank him for our food. By His blessings, we are fed. Give us Lord, our daily bread," she recited from her Sunday school class.

"*Maravillosa, mi amor!*" Mary Carmen gushed.

The family settled in to enjoy their traditional Sunday feast, something none of them thought possible a short time ago. Their arrests and separation still shook the family, but a positive and hopeful trial experience, counseling arranged by the Blake firm, and a return to semi-normal in their community, made current life a bit easier.

"Mama?" Emma mumbled, food dribbling down her chin.

"Don't talk with your mouth full, *Chiquita,*" Mary Carmen laughed, leaning over, wiping her daughter's chin. "What is it?"

"Why did they take us away, Mama? Why did they lock us in cages? I know you had the secret, but why does it matter? Did you and Papa do something wrong?"

"That is a hard question to answer, my darling. You and Emilio were in cages for no reason. You deserve to know the truth. Let me try to explain." Mary Carmen looked to Miguel. He shrugged and motioned for her to continue.

"Many years ago, things were terrible in Venezuela. The government treated the citizens poorly, much worse than here in America. We were very poor and had very little money, even for food. Some people were trying to make things better. They went into the streets and to the Capitol and protested."

"What does it mean to protest, Mama?" Emilio wanted to know.

"You get mad when I take your video game and tell you it is time for bed. What do you do?"

"I yell and cry," Emilio giggled.

"*That* is a protest, *hijo*," Mary Carmen smiled. "*Comprende?*"

"*Si*, Mama."

"These protests involved lots of people. The government did not like the protests or the people. They starved and beat some of us—many people were locked in cages."

"Like we were, Mama?" Emma wondered.

"Worse, my sweet. There was no playground. People could not leave their cages and had very little to eat. Many people starved; some even died. Papa and I could no longer stay in Venezuela, do you understand?"

"Yes, Mama. So what did you do?" Emma implored her to continue. She felt like a big girl, as this was a grown-up story. Emilio was mesmerized.

"We told our families we were leaving and begged them to come with us. Our parents, your grandparents, were too old. Your aunts and uncles wanted to stay and fight. But they understood why we needed to leave. They promised to help us escape.

"We packed up our belongings; we didn't have much. We snuck out of the city in the middle of the night. We walked all night and all the next day. We camped out in the forest or at bus stations. We could not afford to take the bus, but in one town, a very nice man took pity on us and bought us bus tickets to Mexico. We had relatives there. We didn't think our papers would be enough, but no one ever told us we couldn't continue our journey.

"When we got to Mexico, I called my cousin on the telephone. He was very happy to hear from us; happy we made it to his little town. He picked us up at the bus station and took us to his house. The house was very small. We lived there for a few months, but Papa could not find work. Everyone told us we could find work in America. We had relatives here in America. You know, Aunt Consuela and Uncle Carlos."

"They came here before you?" Emma was surprised.

"Yes, and they lived here in Lincoln Park. They invited us to come to America for a visit. My cousin helped us get a passport and a visa. He drove us to the border and spoke to the border patrol. We didn't speak much English back then, so I don't know what he said, but we were allowed to cross into America. Papa and I looked at each other—we were so happy, and I was going to have a baby . . ."

"Me?" Emma shrieked.

"Yes, my sweet, you!" Mary Carmen laughed, reaching across the table and cradling Emma's cheek.

"Me, too?" Emilio cried, upset to be left out.

"No, Emilio. You were not born yet. But we loved the idea of having you soon." Mary Carmen smiled and blew the child a kiss.

"Go on, Mama. Finish the story." Emilio encouraged.

"*Si*, Mama—finish the story," echoed Emma.

"Well, once we got across the border between Mexico and the United States, we took a train across the country, all the way to Michigan. For a while, we stayed with Uncle Carlos and Aunt Consuela. Uncle Carlos got Papa a job at the plant. Soon I got one, too. Later, we were able to afford our own home. We have lived here ever since."

"So, why are they mad at you, Mama? What did you do wrong?" Emma was confused.

"When you are not citizens, the government wants you to check in with them from time to time, try to become citizens, have your papers looked at and approved. We decided not to do that."

"Why?" Emma wondered.

"Because we were afraid."

"Afraid of what, Mama?" Emilio inquired.

"Because you both were born in the United States, you were *citizens*. You could stay here forever. But Papa and I were not citizens. We could not stay without permission, without the government *making* us citizens. We were afraid the government wouldn't make us citizens—afraid we would have to leave the country and leave you here with Carlos and Consuela. So, we never went back to get permission."

"And that's why they're mad at you?" Emma was still confused.

"Yes, my sweet, that is why they are mad at us." Mary Carmen groaned.

"That's silly. Don't they know how wonderful you are? You take such good care of us. Do they know you're our Mama and Papa? How can they do this?"

"I don't know, honey. These things do not matter to them. What matters is that we stayed here too long and are now undocumented. If Mr. Marshall doesn't win the case, we will be sent back to Venezuela. It is too dangerous there for you; we would have to leave you here."

"No!' Emilio screamed.

"Never!" Emma cried.

"Don't worry. Mr. Marshall and Miss Amy will win the case, and we will be allowed to stay."

"For sure, Mama?" Emilio demanded.

"No, sweetheart, not for sure, but things look much better."

"Should we pray again, Mama?" Emilio suggested.

"Why not, my sweet boy? It certainly can't hurt."

The family joined hands, bowed their heads, and prayed.

Chapter Thirty-One

Less than a month after Gonzalez, the Rima Al-Baklavi hearing was scheduled to begin. Marshall, Amy, and their team were burning the midnight oil, putting the finishing touches on their second masterpiece presentation. The brief, like the one filed in the Gonzalez case, was filed days earlier. Marshall's immigration briefs were something for which he was now famous, thanks primarily to Amy Fletcher.

The Gonzalez brief documents, attachments, and annotations were released to the press, which was calling the case a slam-dunk for Marshall. Marshall's briefing, handling of the trial, and closing arguments, were social media and legal circles legends. Postings said Marshal beat down James Theurer. Lawyers were contacting the Blake firm to refer immigration cases long before a final decision in the case was made. State and local bar associations inquired whether Marshall, Amy, or both might be available to chair legal 'how-to' seminars on 'Effectively Briefing and Arguing an Asylum Case.'

Amid this 'notoriety nonsense,' as Marshall referred to it, he and Amy had another important case to argue. Their method and success in hunting down documents, exhibits, relevant material, and witnesses in the Gonzalez case were immeasurable in helping to assemble similar evidence in the Al-Baklavi case. However, there was one important caveat – Syria was on the terrorist watch list, and evidence was much harder to come by.

Flexing financial muscle and a relentless pursuit of justice were becoming hallmarks of the Blake firm. In recent years, Zack, his partners, associates, and support staff, had taken on the Church, the President of the United States, the Manistee Police, White Supremacy, the City of Cedar Ridge, the Bloomfield School District, the *NRA*, a powerful gun manufacturer, and, most recently, the Republican Party and its rich and powerful candidate for the United States Supreme Court. Every case resulted in victory for the 'little guy.' The press referred to Blake's legal conquests as 'David beats Goliath' achievements. In truth, though, at this stage of his career, Zack's wealth and power had leveled the playing field. These cases had become "Goliath vs. Goliath" battles.

Government efforts to vilify and deport Rima Al-Baklavi were similar to their efforts in the Gonzalez case. Government documents identified the petitioner as the wife of slain *ISIS* leader, Qassim Al-Baklavi. James Theurer argued that Rima belonged on the terrorist watch list, not on *any* list of people seeking asylum and citizenship in the United States. However, the government lacked proof of terrorist activities engaged in by Rima. Perhaps she consorted with terrorists. She was married to one. Rima was present when terrorists acted or were arrested, but the government could not prove that Rima Al-Baklavi ever committed a terrorist act. At best, Amy noted, the government decided she was guilty by mere association.

Marshall still had a tough hill to climb. The Al-Baklavi name sent chills down the spines of government officials and agencies whose jobs were to keep American citizens safe. Anti-terrorist watch groups weighed in with *Amicus* briefs, arguing that one woman's precarious situation must be considered in light of the devastating potential harm to a large number of American citizens. If in the Al-Baklavi case, the judge erred on the side of a possible terrorist and got it wrong, the consequences could be catastrophic. One clever attorney even quoted Mr. Spock of *Star Trek* fame. *"The needs of the many outweigh the needs of the few . . . or the one."*

Judges are professionals, but they are also human. While they are required to listen only to the facts of the case and apply the law to those facts, it was virtually impossible to ignore the public outcry and media nonsense generated by the Al-Baklavi case. After all, this was not a couple of immigrant parents, separated from their American-born children, and deported for overstaying a visa—Rima was a potential terrorist, asking for shelter in one of the countries her 'comrades' vowed to wipe off the face of the earth.

Rima Al-Baklavi spent most of her days in her hotel room, a virtual prisoner, as she waited for her court date. Security personnel retained by Parsons and paid by Blake brought meals to her room. She sought no entertainment and rarely ventured outside her suite. When she did, she never left the hotel lobby. Marshall and Zack knew her comings and goings because Parsons had someone watching her and anyone who came near her, twenty-four/seven.

Finally, the time had come. On the morning of the hearing, Marshall picked Rima up at the hotel. She was waiting for him in the lobby and waved as he approached. A Parsons security officer sprang into action, rushed to the front door, but backed off when he saw that Rima was greeting Marshall Mann. *A simple memo would have been nice.*

Marshall thanked the guy for his service and turned to leave. As the automatic doors opened, the security guy stepped in front of Marshall and Rima.

"Where do you think you're going?" he demanded.

"We have court this morning," Marshall advised.

"Why wasn't I informed?"

"That is a question for Wayne Parsons, not me. Please step aside. We can't be late."

"I can't do that without authority."

"My firm hired you. Isn't that enough?"

"I take my marching orders from Wayne Parsons."

"Well, sir, get ahold of him now because we're leaving. You're welcome to tag along for protection," Marshall suggested. Rima suppressed a giggle.

The bewildered security guy frantically looked around, hoping to see Parsons or his number one. As Marshall and Rima began to push by him, the man again stepped in front of them.

"Hold the phone, Mr. Mann. I'm going with you."

"Suit yourself. What's your name?"

"Branson, sir. David Branson."

"Well, David Branson, it's nice to meet you. We appreciate the company. The protection will come in handy when we get to the courthouse. We will probably be mobbed by reporters."

"Good thing I'm coming along," Branson asserted.

"Indeed. Let's go."

The three climbed into Marshall's Land Rover and headed south on Woodward Avenue toward Detroit. The thirty-plus mile trip was uneventful, made in complete silence. Branson had no attorney-client privilege. Marshall parked the car in a lot on Fort Street and headed toward the courthouse.

Detroit Police had the courthouse entrance roped off in advance of what they knew would be a high-profile case. Reporters were required to stand east or west of the entrance, or across Fort Street, in an area at least one hundred feet from the entrance. Marshall surveyed his surroundings, observed the crowd and commotion, and crossed the street from south to north, a block east of the courthouse. He stopped halfway and led David and Rima down the middle of Fort Street. Most reporters didn't notice them until it was too late. Others, unable to cross the rope line, were helpless to do anything. They didn't speak up because they were likely to hand their competitors a scoop.

As the trio approached the entrance, reporters identified them and began to scream rapid-fire questions. Photographers snapped photos while cameramen shot and captured video. All Marshall and Rima saw and heard was a cacophony of human noises, reporters screaming questions in rapid succession, flashes, and lights, all completely obscuring any particular inquiry. Police rushed the threesome into the building. Sudden quiet ensued as the entry doors closed on the mob.

Marshall led a shell-shocked Rima through security, where one-by-one they passed through a body scanner. After an uneventful screening process, they headed toward a bank of elevators. They rode the elevator to the third floor. It was a tad crowded outside Judge Irving Tucker's courtroom, but nothing compared to the mob they just encountered or would encounter once reporters gained access to the premises.

Marshall led his companions to the courtroom. Once inside, he directed Branson to the gallery seats and pushed Rima forward to the counsel table where Amy Fletcher was already seated, organizing briefing papers. James Theurer greeted Marshall as he breezed by to check in with the court clerk. On this day, given the intense scrutiny and publicity afforded the case, the familiar cattle call approach was nixed, and Al-Baklavi was the only matter on Tucker's morning docket.

Just as the clerk told Marshall to be seated at the counsel table, the courtroom doors opened, and reporters streamed in, shouting questions. The court officer cried for order, but the unruly crowd pressed forward. The clerk grabbed the judge's gavel, slammed it, and shouted, "Sit down and shut up, or I swear to God, I will call in the cavalry and have this courtroom cleared." Fear of being evicted and replaced by alternate reporters was enough to restore order. Finally, after everyone had settled and quieted, a buzzer sounded.

"All rise!" cried the clerk.

Judge Irving Tucker stormed into the courtroom, rushed to his seat on high, and slammed his gavel.

"Be seated," he ordered, clearing his throat.

Tucker was a small, elderly man, maybe 5' 3" with lifts in his shoes. His too-tight black robe failed to obscure his rotund stomach and large tush—he resembled a penguin. Lawyers famously referred to him as the familiar character from the Batman comic books and movies. However, whether or not attendees and lawyers thought he was odd-looking, this was *Tucker's* courtroom, and he was not pleased with what he heard from his chambers.

"Before I call the case, I wish to address the pandemonium that erupted in my courtroom as I prepared to take the bench. While I understand this case has garnered significant publicity, the parties seek justice, a fair hearing, and a decision on the merits of their respective cases. I will not tolerate disrespect for them, this proceeding, me, my court officer, or other staff members. Anyone causing a disturbance, no matter how tiny . . ." Tucker squinted and pinched his thumb and forefinger together, simultaneous to saying 'tiny' . . . "will be asked to vacate these premises. When I ask whether this warning is clear, you will respond, 'crystal.' Is that clear?"

"Crystal," the gallery shouted.

"Excellent!" The judge snapped. "No more damned outbursts!" He slammed the gavel for additional impact, glanced over to the counsel tables, and immediately changed his expression and tone. "Nice to see you again, Mr. Mann, Ms. Fletcher, Mr. Theurer," he crooned with a smile, syrupy sweet. "The clerk will call the case."

"*In the Matter of Rima Al-Baklavi*," the clerk announced.

"Appearances for the record, gentlemen?"

"Marshall Mann, for the petitioner, Your Honor."

"James Theurer, for the government, Your Honor."

"Any preliminary matters before we proceed, gentlemen?"

"No, Your Honor, we have worked most of our procedural differences out. May we approach?"

"By all means."

The two attorneys walked up to the bench. An animated conversation developed, with Judge Tucker engaging in various odd gyrations and reactions to the arguments. Rima and the reporters wondered what was going on.

"Step back." The judge finally ordered the attorneys away from the bench with a wave of his hand.

"Proceed, Mr. Mann," the judge commanded.

Marshall leaned toward Rima and whispered something into her ear. He stood and walked to the podium.

Opening statements were routine—Marshall promised to demonstrate that Rima Al-Baklavi was never in trouble with the law in Syria and only fled the country after her husband's failed kidnap and ransom plot against two American citizens. Marshall promised the evidence would demonstrate that Rima was not a co-conspirator but was, however, instrumental in assuring hostage safety and rescue. He promised to call multiple witnesses, including operatives from the Parsons firm and private investigators from Micah Love's office. Marshall's basic premise was that Rima did not seek to come to the United States. Rather, she was dragged here by private security forces after helping to foil the hostage plot.

"As things turned out, these security force witnesses will testify that Rima Al-Baklavi was a principal reason the security force and the hostages escaped Syria with minimal casualties."

Theurer's argument was exactly what Marshall expected.

"The evidence will show that petitioner was part of the terrorist circle, played an intricate role in the planning and implementation of the kidnapping plot, had a deep hatred of the United States, and represents a clear and present danger to the citizens of this great country. If she is granted asylum and citizenship in the United States, every citizen of this country will be in great danger."

After opening statements, Judge Tucker invited Marshall to call his first witness. He called Rima Al-Baklavi. As Rima approached the witness stand to be sworn in, Judge Tucker interrupted and addressed Marshall.

"Before you begin, Mr. Mann, do you mind if I ask the witness a few questions?"

"Not at all, Judge," Marshall responded. He glanced at Amy, wondering where this was going. Amy was fluent in Arabic and would handle any communications issues.

"Ms. Al-Baklavi, may I call you Rima? It's much easier." He smiled

"Yes, sir."

"Good. Rima, are you familiar with the evidence contained in your application for asylum and the brief and attachments filed by your attorney?" The judge held up the briefing notebook. Rima looked to Amy, who immediately translated the judge's question. This procedure continued throughout her questioning.

"Yes, Your Honor. My attorney has shown me these documents."

"In your application, you say that you will be in trouble if you are sent back to Syria. How do you know this?"

"Well, Your Honor, I know because I have multiple family members still in Syria. Their statements are in those documents." She pointed to the briefing notebook.

"Page 18, et seq., Your Honor," Amy directed, speaking for the first time.

"Thank you, Ms. Fletcher. I found it. For the record, I'm looking at these statements now. Your relatives signed affidavits indicating that they've had to go into hiding following the death of your husband. Why is that?"

Judge Tucker was dangerously close to requiring her to testify about her own criminal act. Instead, she responded as she'd been intensely coached.

"Because my husband's family unjustly blames my family for my husband's death and the hostage escapes, without payment of ransom."

"Do you know why?"

Amy interrupted again. "It is all in our brief, Your Honor, page 22, beginning at line 7. We also have letters and affidavits from family members specifically on point. We might have gotten even more. However, it became too dangerous for these people to emerge from hiding from the terrorists. After all, it is Syria, Your Honor."

"Again, I have found and read the reference. Still, I would like to hear it straight from the horse's mouth. Ms. Al-Baklavi?"

"I have no idea why they would blame my *family*, sir. They have done nothing wrong."

Rima held up well through the judge's questions, Marshall's direct examination, and Theurer's cross. Miraculously, she escaped having to answer the question about whether *she* did anything wrong. Concerned about terrorist activities rather than the details of her husband's death, both judge and government lawyer missed the opportunity to inquire whether Rima was involved in her husband's death. Instead, both focused on the possibility that she aided and assisted in her husband's organization. She could honestly answer, under oath, that all she did was cook food and tend to the injured.

Theurer questioned Rima's allegation that she assisted the hostages. He suggested, instead, that she offered aid or comfort to terrorist groups. She specifically denied this, and Marshall interjected that he had plenty of witnesses, Wayne Parsons' entire rescue team, who would testify that Rima was a primary factor in the safe retrieval of the hostages. Marshall presented multiple affidavits of Parsons, other security officials, and some civilians present on the scene. The entire rescue team testified one way or the other.

Experts in the field of international Islamic terrorism testified that Al-Baklavi's death, coupled with Rima's escape, made her public enemy number one in Syria, a target in her own country. Rima and the others read witness statements and affidavits into the record, a very effective tool of persuasion. Evidence delivered from a live witness permitted the judge to evaluate the credibility of the witnesses *and* the sum and substance of the evidence. Rima was so well-coached by Amy's trial prep team; she had no trouble testifying to the content of these documents.

Theurer objected throughout the presentation, claiming that Marshall was presenting hearsay documents and testimony, presenting, essentially, a weak house of cards. Marshall pushed back.

"Every lawyer and judge in this courtroom knows that hearsay rules are loosely applied in immigration court, Your Honor. Please read my materials and, with all due respect, study the witness statements—take judicial notice of their consistency. These witnesses are being presented in this manner for expediency only. I can produce many of these witnesses in person if you so desire, but the test, as counsel well knows, is not that hearsay can't be admitted, but whether it is fundamentally fair for this evidence to be admitted, hearsay or not.

"As Your Honor and brother counsel well know, the evidence does *not* need to pass all Federal Rules of Evidence requirements. Origin of the documents goes to the *weight* of the evidence, not to the *admissibility* of the evidence. Even if you *were* to accept counsel's arguments relative to the origin of the docs, origin is *not* suspect here. Read our presentation, Your Honor. We have authenticated every document and statement presented today. In fact, every piece of evidence, regardless of character, has been checked and rechecked, verified and re-verified, and corroborated by multiple sources. In other words, Your Honor, every single piece of evidence presented has been absolutely authenticated."

Marshall's final witness entered the courtroom. As Canan Izady walked through the double doors at the rear of the courtroom, there was quite a buzz. Marshall summoned her forward, pushed open the gate to the witness stand, and held it open for her to pass through. He guided her to the witness stand, where the court officer awaited her to administer the oath.

"Do you solemnly swear that your testimony will be the truth, the whole truth, and nothing but the truth, so help you God?" The officer inquired.

"I do," Canan swore.

"Please be seated and state your name for the record, please."

"Canan Izady."

"Proceed, Mr. Mann," the judge prompted.

"Ms. Izady, may I call you Canan?" Marshall smiled.

"You may." Canan cleared her throat. Marshall took her through personal information, such as her upbringing, marital status, children, religious beliefs, etc., and then got down to business.

"Are you acquainted with the petitioner, Rima Al-Baklavi?"

"Yes."

"How did you first meet?"

"Her husband took my daughter and me hostage in Syria. She was brought into our tent to tend to our needs and clean us up."

"Did she harm you in any way?"

"No. On the contrary, she was very kind and caring. She tried to comfort Hana and me and helped us out throughout the rather horrible ordeal. I don't know that we would have made it through without her."

"Did she work for the terrorists?"

"I did not know this when we first met, but I later discovered that she was married to the guy in command. In my opinion, however, she did not agree with his taking us hostage."

"Objection, Your Honor!" Theurer shouted from his seat at the counsel table. "Calls for speculation!"

"Sustained. Move on, Mr. Mann. I get the idea." Trying a case to a judge rather than a jury is an entirely different animal.

"Certainly, Your Honor. Canan, are you speculating when you say she didn't agree, or do you have reason to know she didn't agree?"

"I *know* she disagreed. She intervened every time someone tried to hurt us. She shielded us from her husband and protected us from his temper and his wrath. She literally saved our lives and helped us escape."

Marshall could not ask how she did this. Canan would have to admit that Rima killed her own husband to assist the hostage escape.

"How do you know this?"

"Because I didn't know she was the man's wife until after we were rescued. She confided in us that she did not condone the taking of hostages and could not stand aside and let her husband execute a young mother and child, no matter the cause."

Marshall was treading on thin ice. "Do you know what, if anything, she did about it?"

"No. I have no personal knowledge, but I know, in my heart, she was opposed to this violence. That much was obvious. I asked her how a nice woman like her could hook up with terrorists."

"What did she tell you?"

"She fell in love with her husband when he was a man of peace. He became a terrorist after they met and fell in love. She was in agony, crying. She did not agree with his transformation to evil. In that culture, there is little a woman can do about these things. Rima Al-Baklavi is a woman of remarkable courage, a *hero* in my eyes."

"Your Honor . . ." Theurer rose to object.

"Overruled," Judge Tucker ordered. "She is testifying from her own memory. You may continue Mr. Mann."

"Thank you, Your Honor."

"How did you leave it with her after it was all over?"

"I told her: 'From the bottom of my heart, thank you for saving our lives.'"

"Thank you, Canan. That's all I have."

"Your witness, Mr. Theurer."

Theurer cross-examined and was rather harsh in his treatment. Judge Tucker did not appear to appreciate the approach, and Theurer risked alienating the judge. Worse, Theurer could not shake Canan's resolve that Rima was a victim of circumstance rather than a willing participant in acts of terror. And the miracle continued—James Theurer never asked Canan if she had personal knowledge of the circumstances of Qassim Al-Baklavi's death. Theurer and Judge Tucker were apparently content that Al-Baklavi somehow was killed in the assault on the campsite.

Canan was excused after cross-examination. As she walked by Rima, she gave her a smile and a thumbs-up sign. Rima was terrified to react to the gesture and remained stone-faced. Marshall called several members of Parsons' strike force; all testified that they found Al-Baklavi riddled with bullets after the assault. Not a single operative could testify that he or she killed the terrorist. Each testified that he or she personally witnessed Rima Al-Baklavi providing comfort and shelter to Canan and Hana. Rima was handcuffed, as a precaution, brought to the United States, interrogated, and offered an opportunity to seek asylum. Not a single operative could identify Rima as a terrorist or participant in the hostage-taking.

Marshall rested his case. Theurer had no direct witnesses to tie Rima to the terrorists. Other than emphasizing Rima's marriage to Qassim, Theurer could do little to dispel the notion that Rima was opposed to terror and hostage-taking. He could not prove, by any means, that Rima participated in the plot to kidnap, the actual kidnapping, or the imprisonment of Canan and Hana. Instead, he focused on her husband, known associates and family members, her family members, and their common associates and comrades.

In Marshall's opinion, Theurer didn't come close to puncturing Rima's claims of innocence. Amy was astounded that Rima's role in Qassim's death never became an issue at the trial. Everyone involved seemed satisfied that Qassim was killed in the raid on the camp.

On rebuttal, Marshall returned to the theme of the two fears. His brief and attachments artfully portrayed a woman whose courage and actions supporting the two hostages made it impossible to return to Syria. She would be imprisoned, tortured, and finally, killed. Marshall had the proof, witnesses, records, and reports that supported these theories. He also tried to reduce the societal concern that Rima would be a threat to American citizens. No one witnessed her doing anything illegal. There was no evidence linking her to terrorist activities. The issue that seemed to be of the most concern to Homeland officials and Theurer was what Marshall referred to—very effectively—as guilt by association. She might be guilty because she married the bad guy before he became a bad guy.

In his closing argument, Marshall claimed that guilty in the eye of public opinion was not a legal standard. Theurer was required to prove her guilt in a court of law. He failed to meet this burden. Theurer continued to stress the danger to innocent Americans and demanded that Tucker weigh the good of society, even if he was wrong, against the civil rights of one non-citizen. Marshall believed the argument was weak and borderline pathetic. Finally, the record was closed. Rima's bond was continued pending a ruling, which Judge Tucker promised within sixty days. *In the Matter of Rima Al-Baklavi* was almost over.

***

Marshall and Amy met Zack at the Moose Preserve Bar & Grill in Bloomfield Hills. Zack had other civil matters scheduled and could not attend the hearing. He wanted a blow-by-blow description of the proceedings.

"To tell you the truth . . ." Marshall began.

"No, *lie* to me! I hate that expression," Zack snapped.

"Huh?" Marshall was stunned at the retort. "What did I say?"

"To tell you the truth —" Zack grumbled.

"Geez, Zack. It's just an expression." Amy defended her direct supervisor.

"Sorry, bad day." Zack was genuinely apologetic.

"Have a drink and stop being an asshole," Marshall snickered. "This was a great day for Rima Al-Baklavi. At least, we think it was. No telling what Tucker will do, but the case is there for him. All he has to do is ignore all the press and public circus and do the right thing."

"Hard for a judge, sometimes."

"True, I guess. Anyway, I could not have asked for a better day. The testimony went better than expected—almost perfect. Amy's briefing was incredible. Everything that supported Rima's kindness and bravery came in, and never, *not once,* did Tucker or Theurer assume that anyone other than Parsons Security forces took out Qassim. It's the shock of my career. I never thought we'd pull it off."

"Unbelievable! What a break! What a story! Too bad we can't tell anyone."

"Too bad? Why too bad?" Marshall wondered.

"Rima could make a fortune on the novel or movie rights."

"Oh. Yeah, I guess she could. But freedom here in America and a new lease on life will be enough reward for her—want the blow by blow?"

"Absolutely."

Zack ordered another round. Marshall and Amy spent the next hour telling what would, one day, be their most famous legal war story.

"Remarkable," Zack concluded. "One for the record books."

Chapter Thirty-Two

Miguel Gonzalez's cellphone rang. The caller ID screen read 'Law Offices of Zachary Blake.' Miguel quickly answered the call.

"This is Miguel. How may I help you?"

"Miguel? Glad I caught you. This is Amy Fletcher."

"Hi, Amy. How are you doing? Any news?"

"That's why I'm calling, Miguel. We have heard from the judge. He wants us in court on Friday. He's going to publish his decision from the bench."

"His decision? What bench?" Miguel was confused.

"I'm sorry. Let me put this in layman's terms. The judge is ready to announce whether you win or lose your case. He's going to announce his verdict on Friday and wants us to appear in his courtroom."

"This is a good thing, no?"

"If we win, yes, it's a good thing. I believe we are going to win, but you never know."

"What time do we have to be in court?"

"10:00 AM sharp."

"Okay, we will see you there . . . uh . . . and . . . Amy?"

"Yes, Miguel?"

"From the bottom of our hearts, thank you for all you have done for my family. Please tell Marshall and Zack. I can never repay your kindness."

"You're welcome, Miguel. Representing you, Mary Carmen, and your beautiful children has been our pleasure. And don't forget, we aren't finished yet. Zack Blake is filing a civil suit against *ICE* and the feds for damages relating to your family being held in detentions. If I know Zack, I think we are all going to share a very nice payday."

"That would be wonderful, Amy. My main concern is keeping my family together here in the United States."

"But the money will help, Miguel," Amy opined. "I'll see you Friday. Don't be late."

Miguel couldn't argue with that. "We will be there. Thank you very much. Goodbye."

"Bye, Miguel."

***

Three days later, Miguel and Mary Carmen met Marshall Mann, Amy Fletcher, and Zachary Blake in front of the courthouse. Word leaked that Judge Farhat would be issuing his opinion, causing the front of the courthouse to be packed with news crews from local and national television and radio stations. Blake never met a camera or a microphone he didn't love, but neither Marshall nor Amy Mann wanted to give a statement to the press ahead of the decision. They were afraid Judge Farhat might be watching. Marshall implored Zack and the clients to say 'no comment' to anyone seeking comment. As they approached the entrance, a reporter shouted: "Hey, there's Blake and Mann!" The mob turned and rushed the four of them.

"Marshall! Zack! How do you feel going into court this morning?" A reporter stuck a microphone in Zack's face, and a cameraman began to film the encounter. Multiple reporters stuck their microphones in the vicinity of the original.

"We're confident Judge Farhat will do the right thing," Zack announced, earning a scowl from Marshall, who mouthed 'No comment.'

"What makes you so cocky about this case, Zack? Your clients *are* undocumented, right?" A reporter inquired.

"No comment," Zack muttered, putting his head down and charging through the crowd.

"Mr. Mann, care to comment?"

"No comment."

"Ms. Fletcher?"

"No, we just want to get inside and hear Judge Farhat's ruling. I'm sure Marshall will have a prepared statement for you after the judge publishes his decision." She knew it was true; she prepared the statement. Marshall began his own bull rush into the crowd, blocking for Miguel and Mary Carmen.

"Mr. and Mrs. Gonzalez, anything you wish to say?"

As Miguel opened his mouth to comment, Zack, Marshall, and Amy all turned back to their clients, put their fingers to their lips, and pulled them up the stairs.

"No comment!" Amy and Zack snapped.

"Jinx," Zack chortled. Amy glared at him like he was nuts.

They dragged Miguel and Mary Carmen up the stairway and through the entry doors of the courthouse. Once inside, they were free of the press because Judge Farhat refused to permit the press into the courthouse when the decision was read, except for a few lucky journalists who won a Farhat-ordered lottery to secure a seat in the courtroom.

The group glided through security and ventured up to a bank of elevators. Marshall pressed the 'up' button, and the elevator doors directly in front of them opened.

The elevator stopped on the third floor. Judge Farhat's courtroom was to the left. As they entered, Zack motioned for Miguel and Mary Carmen to be seated at the counsel table. At that moment, James Theurer entered the courtroom. He walked up to the trio of lawyers.

"Good luck today, guys. You've done a terrific job for your clients," acknowledged Theurer.

"High praise coming from you, James," Marshall replied.

Theurer turned to Miguel and Mary Carmen. "Good luck, folks. You have three terrific lawyers here."

"Thank you, sir." A bewildered Miguel mumbled. *Good luck? From the guy who wants to send me back to Venezuela?*

At that moment, the courtroom doors opened, and several press invitees entered. They knew better than to repeat their Al-Baklavi behavior in Judge Tucker's court. They filed in, found seats, and quietly awaited the judge.

After court personnel entered and took assigned seats, a court officer shouted the traditional "all rise," and everyone rose to their feet. A buzzer sounded, followed by a door opening. Judge Leo Farhat barreled in. He kept his head down, refused to lock eyes with Amy or Marshall, and sat down at the bench in the center of the room. Zack didn't know what to make of Farhat's sudden bullrush and refusal to acknowledge waiting counsel. Marshall told him to relax.

"Be seated," Judge Farhat suddenly stated, as if he had forgotten to say this earlier. "I have reached a decision in the Gonzalez matter. I am prepared, this day, to publish that decision. Do any of the lawyers wish to make a statement at this time?"

"No, Your Honor," Marshall advised.

"Not at this time, Your Honor," Theurer indicated, eyes on the judge.

"Very well, then, let's get on with it. The clerk will call the case."

"Calling *In the Matter of Mary Carmen and Miguel Gonzalez*," the clerk shouted.

"This is the day and time we allotted to announce my decision. This has been a high-profile case, with lots of publicity and speculation, even reports from members of the press who claim to have information as the result of high-placed leaks from my administrative and legal staff. I wish to assure the public and these attorneys and litigants that there have been no such leaks. No one has received an advanced copy of my opinion or any advanced word of any kind from my chambers.

"Everyone present here today knows that this decision, one way or the other, will have a serious impact on these petitioners. A decision against them today will effectively separate this family for the foreseeable future. If that is the appropriate penalty under the law, so be it. My job is to listen to the facts and apply the law. In my view, this is not a case where a judge may exercise judicial discretion. The law is our roadmap today. Do the facts result in a conclusion that permits Mr. and Mrs. Gonzalez to remain in the United States with a pathway to citizenship? Or does the law compel me to deport these parents, even though their children are American citizens and may choose to stay here in America if their parents are deported?

"How did we get here? Miguel and Mary Carmen Gonzalez fled their home country, Venezuela, when Miguel was accused of political espionage. It is not relevant to my decision whether Miguel actually did what he is accused of doing. My sole determination must be whether he and his wife can safely return home without fear of reprisal.

"In addition to that determination and somewhat in conflict with it, however, I have to determine whether Miguel and Mary Carmen's decision to overstay their visa is fatal to their petition for asylum. As a matter of law, a petitioner for asylum must be a good citizen, obey our laws, and not be guilty of any crime. While it is true that Mr. and Mrs. Gonzalez have been model citizens, without even a traffic violation to their name, the incontrovertible fact is that they overstayed their visa in violation of the law.

"So, where does this leave us? I turn to the merits of the case. On its face, this is an illegal detention and interrogation claim, and the government asks this court to authorize Miguel and Mary Carmen Gonzalez's detention under the *Summers* decision, cited and captioned in my written decision. I cannot do so. The Fourth Amendment protects the right of people to be secure in their persons, homes, papers, and effects against unreasonable searches and seizures. That is bedrock constitutional law.

"While the Fourth Amendment's exclusionary rule does not typically apply to immigration proceedings, there are two longstanding exceptions: 1. When the agency violates a regulation promulgated for the benefit of petitioners and that violation prejudices the petitioner's protected interests, and 2. When the agency egregiously violates a petitioner's Fourth Amendment rights.

"Mr. and Mrs. Gonzalez argue that I must suppress the evidence obtained in the raid on their place of employment because their interrogation and detention constituted either a violation of an *ICE* regulation or an egregious violation of the Fourth Amendment. Thus, I must first decide whether their detention violated any regulation or the Fourth Amendment.

"The government does not dispute that Miguel and Mary Carmen Gonzalez were seized and detained in their workplace, frisked and handcuffed, or that the *ICE* agents did so without individualized reasonable suspicion. The record confirms that agents detained petitioners and their coworkers at the outset of the raid, blocking all exits and prohibiting them from leaving. *ICE* agents' suspicions that the employer was employing undocumented workers did not provide reasonable doubt that

petitioners were undocumented. Under the Fourth Amendment of
our Constitution, a search or seizure of any person must be
supported by probable cause particularized with respect to that
person. In this case, in other words, there was no probable cause
to search either Mary Carmen or Miguel Gonzalez.

"Next, we must determine whether there was reasonable
suspicion. The government maintains that *Michigan v. Summers*
permits agents to detain Mr. and Mrs. Gonzalez without
suspicion because they had the right to execute their search
warrant. As a result, they could not have violated the Fourth
Amendment or §287 of the Immigration and Nationality Act,
which grants agents broad authority to interrogate people who
the government suspects are undocumented.

"There is one critical and *determinative* difference between
the *Summers* line of cases and this case. Mary Carmen and
Miguel Gonzalez have presented uncontroverted evidence that
the search authorized by the warrant was not even a principal
reason for the raid by *ICE*. Indeed, the agents' principal goal was
to detain, interrogate, and arrest a large number of individuals
who worked at the plant. The agents sought to initiate removal
proceedings against all detainees. All documents of record
indicate that this was the sole motive for the agents' activity—
they were there to arrest undocumented workers. Search warrants
based on probable cause cover the place being searched, not the
seizure of individuals.

"The case law cited in my written opinion does not authorize
this detention. Simply stated, the law does not approve detention
without any individualized suspicion where the officers' primary
purpose is *not* conducting a safe and efficient search pursuant to
a warrant. On the evidence before me, that was precisely the case
here—the agents' focus was *not* on conducting a safe search but
on engaging in a preplanned investigation and detention of a
large number of individuals present at the premises where the
search was authorized. I, therefore, so hold: Authority to detain
incident to the execution of a search warrant does not extend to a
preexisting plan whose central purpose is to detain, interrogate,
and arrest a large number of individuals without individualized
reasonable suspicion.

"In reaching this conclusion, I have reviewed various *ICE* planning documents contained in petitioners' briefing materials. These documents, provided by petitioners, not the government, unmistakably demonstrate that the agents were focused on detaining and interrogating any and all workers located at the plant to determine whether they were undocumented. One document, for example, states that *ICE* was targeting 150–200 undocumented workers at several plants in the area. This represents clear and convincing evidence that arresting those workers and not obtaining the documents mentioned in the warrant was the focus of the operation. In fact, the so-called search was not even mentioned in the documents. Only that *ICE* would be using the pretense of the warrant to detain and process all arrested individuals.

"In light of the foregoing, the decision of this court is that the raid, detention, interrogation, and incarceration of the petitioners, in this case, violated the Fourth Amendment to the United States Constitution and §287 of the Immigration and Nationality Act. All evidence obtained from *ICE* activities during the raid is hereby deemed inadmissible as fruit of the poisonous tree. The deportation proceedings against Mr. and Mrs. Gonzalez are dismissed due to these egregious violations of their constitutional rights . . ."

Spectators in the gallery interrupted the judge's statement with a loud cheer. Marshall sat between Miguel and Mary Carmen. The three had been listening intently to Judge Farhat's words. At this final statement, Marshall pumped his fist and whispered a loud "yes!" He grabbed his clients' hands and shook them, smiling broadly. Behind him, Zack patted him on the back and whispered, "Mazel Tov." Amy fist-bumped his arm. Marshall's exuberance was contagious—Mary Carmen and Miguel were smiling, tears rolled down their cheeks. However, Judge Farhat stood to the side of his bench, pounding his gavel, calling for order. His Honor had not completed his statements or his ruling.

"Order in the court!" He shouted, an angry expression on his face. "Order in the court! I will have the court officer clear this courtroom if we cannot come to order, now!" The gallery quieted, and the judge resumed the bench and his ruling.

"My ruling does not affect the immigration status of Miguel and Mary Carmen Gonzalez. They are, as they were when they were detained and arrested, undocumented. They deliberately overstayed their visas, defied authorities, and failed to work within the system to become legal citizens of these United States . . ."

The gallery reacted as if the air had been let out of a hot air balloon. Boos cascaded down from the gallery. The judge was, again, forced to stand and pound his gavel, shouting for order. He instructed the court officer to begin clearing the courtroom. The officer spoke into a communications device clipped to his shoulder. Within thirty seconds, four additional court officers entered the courtroom. The stunned gallery quieted almost immediately.

"I have been extremely patient, ladies and gentlemen . . ." the angry judge began. "I will not tolerate unruly behavior in my courtroom. The petitioners have waited a long time for this day and deserve to hear the judgment of this court. Court officers are instructed to remove the next person who misbehaves in any way, shape, or form. Does everyone understand? Nod your heads in the affirmative."

Everyone, including the litigants and the attorneys, was nodding.

"Very well, I shall continue. As I indicated before things became unruly, the petitioners are still undocumented, subject to deportation from the United States to Venezuela. They have requested asylum for important reasons, fear of persecution, fear of torture, fear of imprisonment, even fear of death in Venezuela. But are their fears legitimate?

"Let's examine the record . . ." Marshall and Amy were astounded to see Judge Farhat pull out petitioners' now-famous briefing notebook. The judge began to read 'the record' directly from Amy's carefully prepared documents and exhibits.

"The record is overwhelmingly clear that Miguel Gonzalez, for whatever reason irrelevant to this inquiry, stood accused of political advocacy against the government of Venezuela. He suddenly had a target on his back. As such, he did not leave Venezuela voluntarily. He was forced to leave because conditions in the country were extremely volatile and dangerous to someone who had voiced opposition to those conditions . . ."

The judge leafed through the notebook, pointing out and incorporating by reference in his decision the many exhibits that corroborated these dangers.

"Furthermore . . ." the judge continued. "We must examine deportation in the context of petitioners' American-born children. We can all agree, I presume, that our goal as compassionate human beings is to do what is reasonable to keep families together. We have reached a crisis level in this country, with children and parents coming across the border together, separated, and placed in detention facilities. In *this* case, the circumstances were worse. The parents were rounded up, detained, and incarcerated in violation of their constitutional rights. Their children, both *American citizens*, were likewise rounded up, flown to Texas of all places, and placed in a detention facility. Even *ICE* agents will admit that these border control facilities were not built to care for children, but Congress has been unable to fund *HHS* to do better.

"I digress. The point here is that part of my analysis of petitioners' asylum claims must consider the Gonzalez citizen-children, Emma and Emilio Gonzalez. What impact would their parents' deportation have on these innocent children? Why would these parents break the law, overstay their visas, knowing their actions might cause blowback for their children? Motive in this case seems quite important. Are we dealing with hard-core criminals who deliberately flaunt the system, or are we dealing with unsophisticated and uneducated parents, already abused in their home country, fearing similar abuse if they willingly permit the United States government to determine their destiny?

"I submit we are dealing with the latter. The children and an expert clinical psychologist have all testified that the parents' so-called 'secret' profoundly impacted these kids. Were their parents criminals? Do these children see themselves as 'criminals' as well?" Again, the judge pulled out the notebook and referred to the doctor's report by exhibit, page, and tab numbers.

"These children have become innocent pawns in a political game of chess. Their so-called crime was being born to people whose immigration status was in question. They had no idea that their parents might, someday, be deported. According to our expert, when they learned the truth of their parents' situation, they were forced to grow up in fear of our government and its immigration enforcement practices. To answer Mr. Mann's direct question of me, yes, Mr. Mann, their rights *do* merit my attention. As Mr. Mann correctly points out, they *are* United States-born *citizens*, innocent of any wrongdoing. As children of undocumented immigrants, they face public scorn in their own country and the possibility of having to leave with their parents to face punishment in a foreign land. Why do legislators, policymakers, or law enforcement officers ignore *their* circumstances? Is this justice? Mr. Mann correctly points out that the American Convention on Human Rights states that every minor child has the right to the measures of protection required by his or her condition as a minor on the part of a family, society, and the state. They do not deserve to have their parents ripped away from them because of this country's flawed immigration policies.

"Miguel and Mary Carmen Gonzalez may have once, technically, broken the law. My prior ruling, however, expunges their records. They are no longer branded 'undocumented' or subject to immediate deportation. Furthermore, their records are devoid of any other criminal charges, even minor traffic tickets.

"Miguel and Mary Carmen Gonzalez have nowhere else to go. The evidence conclusively demonstrates that local and national police in their home country have branded them as enemy combatants. Their protected grounds for asylum are their participation in a political group who dared to criticize government oppression and misconduct and for persecution and potential torture for speaking up about it. Miguel Gonzalez, especially, is considered 'against the government' in Venezuela, a protected ground, and legitimate reason for any alien to seek asylum in the United States of America."

Marshall grabbed Miguel and Mary Carmen's hands again, in anticipation of the final victory. He was literally holding his breath as Farhat delivered his final decree. Zack grabbed Amy's hand and squeezed it so hard, she let out an audible gasp.

"It is, therefore, the decision of this court that Miguel and Mary Carmen Gonzalez's petition for asylum is granted. The government is directed to take all steps necessary to institute processes toward making the petitioners lawful citizens of these United States. Mr. Mann?"

"Yes, Your Honor?" Marshall let go of his clients' hands and stood at attention.

"If you present an order consistent with my ruling here today, I will sign it. Your advocacy on behalf of your clients in this matter has been brilliant. Mr. and Mrs. Gonzalez . . ." Marshall signaled to Miguel and Mary Carmen to rise, and they did as he requested.

"The court apologizes for your ordeal on behalf of the United States government. Welcome to the United States of America."

A loud cheer was emitted from the gallery. Pandemonium erupted. Judge Farhat slammed his gavel, winked at his court officer, and abruptly exited the courtroom. The press descended upon Zack, Marshall, Amy, and their clients and began peppering them with questions. Miguel and Mary Carmen ignored it all, looking for family members who were 'babysitting' the children. Suddenly, through the crowd, Emma and Emilio appeared, tears rolling down their cheeks, broad smiles on their faces.

"Mama! Papa! We won!" Emma cried, wrapping her arms around her jubilant parents. Zack and Marshall turned away from reporters and high-fived Emilio while he waited his turn to embrace his folks. Miguel suddenly picked up his son and spun him around like an airplane, causing reporters to scatter to avoid being kicked in the face by a flying kid. Their long nightmare was almost over. Miguel and Mary Carmen Gonzalez would soon be citizens of the United States of America.

Chapter Thirty-Three

With the risk of government blowback erased, Zachary Blake put the finishing touches on his civil complaint against the Department of Homeland Security, Immigration and Customs Enforcement Agency, Department of Health and Human Services, various officers of these government agencies, multiple senior officials in the Golding Administration, and various other departments and department heads. The multi-count complaint, filed in Federal District Court, sought unspecified damages on behalf of Emma and Emilio Gonzalez and their parents for 'cruelly and inhumanely' separating them in Michigan, false arrest, false imprisonment, negligent application and enforcement of existing laws, intentional and negligent infliction of emotional distress, and conspiracy to commit all of those acts.

The complaint sought class-action status and invited the *ACLU* and thousands of similarly situated families to join the litigation. The complaint accused the Golding Administration, defendant agencies and officials, of 'tearing children from their parents' arms' without explaining and tracking their whereabouts. Many families have been separated indefinitely, with no prospect of discovering their respective locations.

The complaint contained detailed facts about Emma and Emilio's ordeal, citing key statistics differentiating the Golding Administration from previous presidential administrations, both Republican and Democratic. Prior to the John and Golding Administrations, family separations anywhere were exceedingly rare and only based upon a parent being declared a danger to the child or a parent's medical emergency. Zack and his team alleged that all of this changed when Ronald John took office five years ago. At all levels of government, the accused defendants conspired together to violate the law and the United States Constitution by ordering forcible family separations and arresting innocent people in violation of the Fourth Amendment and the Immigration and Nationality Act. The complaint further accused the various defendants of planning these widespread

family separations and incarcerations unlawfully, for no
legitimate reason, and notwithstanding that family separation
does irreparable psychological and physical damage to both
children and parents.

Zack and his team accused all defendants of deliberately or
negligently inflicting pain, suffering, and extreme emotional
distress against these plaintiffs, to deter them from seeking
asylum or other appropriate immigration relief in the United
States. According to the complaint, the children and parents were
held in punitive, separate conditions, which included being
provided no means of communication with their parents for
months. Parents had no idea where their children were or
whether they were alive. If alive, were they being properly cared
for? The complaint further alleged that Emma and Emilio were
not provided treatment for separation anxiety to address the fear,
isolation, abandonment, and other lasting effects of their
separation and confinement.

In addition, Zack accused all defendants of failing to take
proper steps to protect the children, keep tracking records of
whereabouts of family members and family units, or mitigate
plaintiffs' suffering while in government custody. Parents and
children now suffer from, among other things, fear, anxiety,
trouble sleeping, nightmares, headaches, increased risk of mental
health disorders and conditions, and other forms of extreme and
lasting trauma.

The complaint also took the extraordinary step of using the
government's reporting systems against the various defendants.
A recent report of the Health and Human Services Office of the
Inspector General issued a report—attached to the complaint as
an exhibit—that "intense trauma was common in incarcerated
family members who had been unexpectedly separated."

Quoting directly from the report, Zack alleged that separated
family members, especially children, exhibited more fear,
feelings of abandonment, post-traumatic stress, and feelings of
anxiety than did children who were not separated. In particular,
Emma and Emilio suffered from 'acute grief, causing them to cry
suddenly, inexplicably, and inconsolably' out of concern that this

might happen again or that they did something to cause these traumatic events.

The complaint sought damages for Fourth Amendment Violations—unreasonable seizure of parents and children, Fifth Amendment Due Process Violations—right to hearing before incarceration or separation and the fundamental right to family integrity, Fourteenth Amendment Equal Protection Violations—preventing discrimination based on ethnicity or national origin, and other violations of plaintiffs' civil rights.

The complaint finally alleged that these plaintiffs could never fully be made whole, but justice and fairness require that they receive redress for their pain and suffering. The complaint sought compensatory and punitive damages, costs, and attorney fees.

The self-proclaimed 'master of the media' issued a press release indicating the precise day and time he intended to file the complaint. He also promised a press briefing immediately after filing the complaint. After doing exactly what he promised, Zachary Blake stood at a podium, flanked on both sides by the Gonzalez family, Marshall Mann, and Amy Fletcher, who was getting a lesson in publicity, Zachary Blake style. Zack tapped on the microphone in front of him, leaned forward, and asked for quiet. The raucous crowd of local and national reporters slowly gave him their attention.

"Ladies and gentlemen of the press, thank you for coming. I am Zachary Blake, a local Detroit area attorney, for those of you who don't know me. These are my clients, Miguel, Mary Carmen, Emma, and Emilio Gonzalez. That handsome old guy to my far left is Marshall Mann, and the young lady to his left is Amy Fletcher. These are the brilliant attorneys who handled this family's recent asylum claim.

"Today, sadly, I was compelled to file a ten-figure federal lawsuit against the Golding Administration, various agencies in charge of the immigration system in our country, and numerous government officials who conspired to deprive my clients of various constitutional rights. Copies of the rather detailed complaint have been made available to you members of the press. I won't waste time telling you what you can read or what you already know.

"This family was literally torn apart by our government, despite the fact that two of its members are American citizens. The push to divide us, citizen against non-citizen, Caucasian against a person of color, rich against poor, is threatening our democracy and the very foundation of our society. This lawsuit represents an attempt to shine the light of justice on these efforts. We seek to assure that violations of our civil rights, especially by our own elected officials, do not go unpunished and, indeed, come at a high cost. What cost, you ask? I strongly believe that the price must be high enough to prevent this behavior from ever being repeated in our great country.

"I have invited other attorneys and citizens to join our litigation. I am uncertain whether they will or how many, but the aim of this litigation is "never again." Never again should parents be separated from their kids. Never again should children be flown across the country and locked in a cage, not knowing whether they will ever be reunited with their parents. Never again should a government agency issue and exercise a warrant for one stated purpose when its true purpose is something else entirely. Never again should an American citizen, especially a child, be imprisoned without due process. Attorneys for the government have already reached out to me in conciliation. They seek private mediation of our grievances. They have pledged to take our complaint seriously, redress our clients' serious damages, and address the behaviors that caused those damages."

Zack smirked. "As most of you know, I am very shy and retiring. I like to pursue my cases in private. I'm very hesitant to seek out publicity and prefer to stay out of the limelight," he deadpanned. Laughter filled the room—Zack stood at the podium and patiently waited until things quieted.

"I plan to take the government up on their offer. My goal is to seek just compensation for my client and others who choose to join our crusade without long-term harm to our country, its government, and our system of justice. I am cautiously optimistic we can accomplish these goals. The government knows me, knows I mean business, and knows I fight for my clients.

"If we cannot agree on a just resolution, know this: I will take this case to trial, fight tooth and nail for my clients, and emerge victorious. I have taken on the government before. They know they have a huge fight on their hands. I take cases to trial—I only settle cases if offers are consistent with the results I expect at trial. If the government takes conciliation, mediation, and settlement seriously, they will find a willing partner in Zachary Blake. If they do not . . . we will fight for our clients' rights all the way to the United States Supreme Court, if necessary. I am happy to answer questions . . ."

The press peppered him with questions. Zack and his clients stood on the makeshift platform until the last question was asked. The conference was vintage Blake. Public opinion was sharply in favor of Zack's clients and crusade. Almost everyone in America was aware of the crisis and constitutional violations. As usual, Zachary Blake had created a climate conducive to outstanding results.

Chapter Thirty-Four

"What the fuck?" President Stephen Golding was beside himself. "This is how he creates an atmosphere of conciliation?"

"It's Blake, sir. What did you expect?" Golding's chief of staff, Colin Gerges, inquired.

"I understand, Gerges, but this puts me between a rock and a hard place. If I'm gracious, I look like a wimp. If I take a hard line, I look like a bully!" The president was fuming.

"Blake is the master, sir. He knows all the legal, political, and publicity buttons to push. He knows how to win."

"He's an annoying twit, a thorn in my side. Look what he did to President John and Judge Wilkinson."

"With all due respect, sir, President John and Judge Wilkinson deserved everything they got."

"Wilkinson's *dead*, Gerges. *Jesus* . . ."

"*Everything* they got, sir," Gerges interrupted.

"Fine, whatever, but what does all this have to do with me? I'm no RonJohn or Wilkinson, not even close. I could have pardoned my predecessor, and Wilkinson came highly recommended by every bigwig in the Party. His appointment was not *my* idea."

"You *are* the president, sir. Everyone knows you could have issued a pardon, and thanks you for your restraint, sir. As for Wilkinson . . ."

"Enough, dammit. Don't patronize me, Gerges—it pisses me off."

"That was not my intent, sir. It is a fact, though, that you have continued many of President John's most disturbing policies."

"Such as?"

"*ICE* raids. Separating immigrant parents from their children. Locking immigrant children in cages. Our citizens are squarely opposed to those policies. And they tend to piss guys like Blake off."

"*I* didn't order the damn raid! I didn't lock kids up or separate them from their families. Shit!"

"With all due respect, sir, the government did those things, and you are the Commander in Chief."

"Yeah, yeah, yeah, blah, blah, blah. So what do we do?" The president roared.

"Legally or politically?"

"Is there a difference?"

"*Seriously,* sir? There is a *huge* difference," Gerges counseled.

"Well, spit it out, man! Stop beating around the bush!"

"Legally, the right thing to do is to instruct the U.S. Attorney for the Eastern District of Michigan to arrange a meeting with Blake. Together, hopefully, they can lay the groundwork for mediation and settlement of this case before things get out of hand. Politically . . ."

"Too late for that, don't you think?" Golding snapped.

"Maybe, but the part that scares me is Blake's invitation to other potential victims. This thing could escalate in a hurry. Maybe some diplomacy could nip things in the bud?" Gerges floated.

"Diplomacy? Zachary Blake? You've got to be kidding me!" The president exploded again.

"Blake has clients to represent and, as we both know, he will represent them with zeal. However, he has shown a willingness to mediate and settle important cases in our communities. He did so with Cedar Ridge and the traffic stop shooting and the same with the Bloomfield school shooting." Gerges recalled. "I believe an early reach out is the wisest course. As to looking like a pussy, we can reach out discreetly, agree to his terms for mediation, demand confidentiality, and see where it goes," Gerges recommended.

"That doesn't sound half bad, Gerges. Okay, talk to our guy in the Eastern District and set it up. Not much to lose—I'm not going to be re-elected anyway. As I said, I'm a realist," President Golding rationalized.

"I'll do it now, sir."

"Thanks, Gerges. Sorry, I lost my temper."

"Not surprising, given the circumstances, sir. Might I suggest something else that may ease things a bit, sir?"

"What's that, Gerges?" The president was genuinely curious.

"I would call a cabinet meeting, go around the room, and ask each cabinet secretary to discuss their most controversial policy or activity. Order each one to cease and desist from implementing any of those policies or activities until the new president is sworn in. You don't need any more of this crap."

"Great idea, Gerges. Take care of both, would you please?"

"Immediately, sir."

***

The phone rang at the Bloomfield Hills Law Offices of Zachary Blake. The caller was Daniel Wolfe, the United States Attorney for the Eastern District of Michigan. Zack and Wolfe had crossed paths in the past. Wolfe was part of a group of people who helped neutralize a couple of white supremacists involved in Zack's Arya Khan and Jack Dylan cases back in the day. The two lawyers had a great deal of respect for each other.

"Dan Wolfe! How the hell are you?" Zack exclaimed.

Wolfe chuckled. "I'm fine, Zack. How have you been?"

"Doing well, despite a whole bunch of stuff being dumped on me from every which way. What can I do for you this fine morning, Dan?" Zack looked out his window. A beautiful day was dawning in suburban Detroit.

"I suppose you can guess why I'm calling."

"I don't have a clue, Dan—to catch up? To invite me to speak at the next U.S. Attorneys' convention?" Zack quipped.

"Facilitation on the Gonzalez case?"

"Shit! I'm an idiot. A federal case against the government in the Eastern District, U.S. Attorney—I didn't even make the connection. So, buddy, it's you versus me in the biggest case since the Bloomfield school shooting case?"

"Unless you count bringing down a Supreme Court nominee." Wolfe retorted.

"Yeah, that was a big one, too, I guess."

"Be he ever so humble."

"Yeah, that's me, Mr. Humble." Zack laughed.

"So, Zack, facilitation? President Golding's Chief of Staff, Colin Gerges, reached out to me personally and asked me to make this inquiry."

"I'm the one who floated the idea at the press conference. I'm glad it's you, Dan. Pleased to have a friendly adversary in the government for a change."

"Don't expect me to roll over for you, bud."

"I expect you to be fair and honest, as you've always been. No baloney. The stakes are too high on both sides of these issues. Can we agree on that?"

"Wholeheartedly, my friend. Any ideas on a Facilitator?"

"I've always used Stuart Frazier. Solid credentials. Does a good job."

"Stu's a good guy and an excellent choice. Is this in his wheelhouse?"

"Is this in anyone's wheelhouse, Dan?"

"I guess not. We can discuss other choices if Stu's not available. Perhaps someone with federal or immigration experience?"

"How about Marshall Mann?" Zack kibitzed.

"You're a funny guy, Blake. That's why I like you. I suppose you could ask Marshall to recommend someone," Wolfe suggested.

"I'll ask him, but I'm comfortable with Stu if you are."

"If he's available, I'm game."

"I'll reach out to him and ask Marshall for another name. Hey, I've got an idea. Would you prefer to use both? A litigator and an immigration guy?"

"That might be a good way to go—cover both bases."

"I'll see who Marshall suggests, and I'll contact Stu."

"Sounds like a plan. Going to be downtown any time soon?"

"Day after tomorrow. Motion in front of Lockjaw."

"Oy, Judge Putnam? I'm glad I'm federal. What a putz!"

"And the way he talks with his mouth closed, teeth clenched tight. He looks angry 24/7. No one can understand a word he says. It's annoying."

"Such is life. Call me when you're done with Lockjaw. We'll have lunch."

"It's a date. Hopefully, I'll have news to report from Stu and Marsh."

"Sounds like a plan. Talk soon. Bye."

Zack placed the phone on the receiver and sighed. "Dan Wolfe . . ." He whispered aloud. *Is this good news or bad? Do I want an enemy or a friend, a 'frenemy' so to speak? Probably the latter; time will tell. Dan's as good a draw as I could hope for under these difficult circumstances. He sure didn't seem intimidated by the case, the situation, or me, that's for sure.*

Chapter Thirty-Five

Zack finished an early morning contentious motion and argument with a defense lawyer and Judge 'Lockjaw,' who Zack determined was in bed with the entire defense bar. He hurried to meet Dan Wolfe for a late breakfast at the Dime Store, a wonderful breakfast-brunch restaurant in the Chrysler House on Griswold, a short walk from the courthouse.

The grand old office-retail building was built in 1912. For most of its existence, it was known as the Dime Building. The restaurant pays homage to its heritage in the early days. As part of the recent post-bankruptcy resurgence of downtown Detroit, a local billionaire purchased the building, renovated it, tapped Chrysler as an anchor tenant, and changed the building's name. *Money talks and bullshit walks*, Zack mused.

Zack trotted through the building's beautiful lobby and barged into the tiny but crowded restaurant, scanning patrons for Wolfe. He spotted Wolfe waving from the counter, which had the feel of those old soda fountain counters he used to frequent with his grandfather.

As the two men exchanged greetings, Wolfe handed Zack a menu.

"Haven't been here in a while. Great place, great choice," Zack noted.

"The French toast is to die for," Wolfe salivated.

"Probably fifteen hundred calories."

"You only live once."

Zack laughed. "I'm looking at the omelets."

"Those are great, too."

A server brought two glasses of ice water and offered coffee, which both men accepted. Zack ordered the vegetarian omelet with house fries and multi-grain toast. Wolfe ordered the French toast. While they waited, Zack caught Dan up on the search for a facilitator/mediator.

"I talked to Stu. He's interested but a bit on the fence."

"Oh? Why?" Dan was surprised.

"He thinks the case is going to require a tremendous time commitment, and he's been super busy."

"What did you tell him?"

"I told him we could schedule blocks of time around his schedule and that he would also have an immigration specialist/co-mediator to assist."

"How did he react to that?"

"He was fine with it. I even think he preferred it."

"Great, do we have anyone in mind for the immigration side?"

"I offered the job to Harry Rosen."

"Wow, other than perhaps Marshall Mann and his up-and-coming associate, Amy Fletcher, Harry might be the best in the city. What did he say?"

"He doesn't do mediations. There isn't much call for them in the immigration field, but this case is so important, he promised to consider it."

"He'll do it. Who could pass up on an opportunity to mediate the biggest case of the year? Besides, he gets to work with the one and only Zachary Blake."

"And the legendary Daniel Wolfe." Zack smiled and winked.

"Ha! Probably a deal-breaker!"

The food arrived—everything was as wonderful as Zack remembered. He offered Dan a sample of his omelet, hoping Dan would offer a piece of French toast in return. In Blake's family lore, Zack was infamous for ordering healthy meals and then ogling the food of others until they broke down and gave him a taste. Dan declined the omelet but offered Zack a healthy portion of his large French toast order—Blake was a happy man.

They discussed Zack's morning in front of 'Lockjaw.' Zack caused onlookers to stare and gasp by doing a loud but perfect impression of the eccentric judge. Dan burst out laughing. The restaurant was packed with lawyers who heard the impression, recognized the subject, and politely applauded Zack's performance. Zack jumped off the counter stool and bowed deeply, creating a riotous scene of laughter and more vigorous applause.

When the commotion died down and lawyers returned to their breakfast conversations, Blake and Wolfe began to chat about the case. The case was a surefire win in any attorney's hands. In Blake's, the sky was the limit and both men knew it. The discussion centered on making the Gonzalez family whole without increasing the already serious political divide or causing serious damage to the country.

"With all due respect, Dan, that's not my job. I represent the Gonzalez family," Zack admonished.

"But you're an American citizen, Zack. I'm not telling you to back off. I'm urging you to pursue the case without the usual Blake histrionics."

"I offered mediation, didn't I?"

"You did, and I appreciate the good start."

"Good start? What does that mean?"

"I'd like you to pursue this case on the down-low, without publicly defecating all over the United States government in the process."

"Boy, you don't pull any punches. You think I'm a publicity hound. Is that it?"

Wolfe laughed out loud. "Your record speaks for itself, my friend. How about that low-key press conference you held when you filed the case?"

"It got your client to the table."

"Indeed. All I am asking is that you save the nonsense until after we mediate. If we can't settle the case, all bets are off."

"You mean that?" Zack was surprised. *This sounds like a government mandate to settle the case.*

"Full disclosure—don't abuse my confidence. I have been provided with an almost blank check and a mandate to resolve this quickly and quietly. I'm willing if you're willing." Wolfe repeated almost verbatim what Zack was thinking.

"What happens if others take me up on my class-action offer?"

"If the numbers are fair and reasonable, we'll resolve those too."

"Wow."

"Rumor has it that Golding does not want kids in cages and separated families to be his legacy even if he wasn't the president who implemented those policies."

"I understand his concern. He's the last man standing, the one in the hot seat with this litigation. Memories of who first separated families and locked kids in cages will fade. The last guy, the one who got his ass handed to him in court, will go down in history as responsible for the whole stinking mess and the costly cleanup."

"That's his concern. He's going to go down in history, much the same as Gerald Ford, as an ineffectual short-term president— a nice guy who followed a terrible, crooked president, and who found the clean-up process a bit too much to handle. The big difference is that Golding refused the pardon."

"God bless him for that."

"Amen. So, you'll try it my way, pretty please?"

"I'll give it a go."

Chapter Thirty-Six

Marshall Mann, Amy Fletcher, Zachary Blake, and Rima Al-Baklavi sat together at the petitioner's counsel table, awaiting the arrival of Judge Irving Tucker. Two days earlier, while Zack was waging war with Lockjaw, Judge Tucker announced he had reached a decision in the Al-Baklavi asylum case. Legal experts and talking heads were all over the local and national news, assuring everyone that Tucker would grant asylum, especially after the euphoria and public praise heaped upon Judge Leo Farhat for his decision in Gonzalez.

Rima exhibited no signs of nervousness. Marshall guessed she was on the nervous side of calm. Given what she'd been through in Syria, he understood why all of this seemed rather anti-climactic. Rima sat quietly and patiently, watching press observers, attorneys, and government workers slowly file into the courtroom. Of the three participants, the nervous one was Zachary Blake. He was proud of his team, proud of the work they did in Syria, and quite concerned that the government would err on the side of the many and punish the one. He hoped he was wrong, but that is what he expected. He sat for a while, stood up, walked to the back, and began pacing the back of the room, like an expectant father awaiting the birth of his first child.

James Theurer walked into the courtroom and greeted Rima and her legal team. Rima was expectedly cold in response. Despite her honest reaction, Theurer wished her good luck. The door behind Judge Tucker's bench opened, and the court clerk, reporter, and second officer came through, taking their seats. The first officer was already standing in front of the bench, waiting to announce the appearance of the judge. A buzzer sounded and a second door opened. The diminutive Irving Tucker dashed in.

"All rise!" The first officer shouted as Tucker raced to his seat. "Please be seated," Tucker cackled. He assumed the bench and pounded his gavel. Tucker welcomed the attorneys and parties and told the members of the gallery that they were guests in his house. He was aware of the noise and interruption that plagued the recent Gonzalez hearing, and he would evict anyone who violated proper courtroom etiquette. In fact, he threatened to hold all disruptors in contempt of court. He repeated a few housekeeping rules before reading his opinion for *In the Matter of Rima Al-Baklavi*.

"This had been an interesting case, one that has garnered extensive press coverage. However, justice is blind. My job requires me to shut down or filter out the noise of publicity and focus on the mandates of my oath. Regardless of the deluge of publicity, it is my job, in every case that comes before me, to listen to the facts, apply the law, and render a fair and just determination based upon fact and law. This Rima Al-Baklavi case is no different.

"Mrs. Al-Baklavi, as you know, I am Irving Tucker, Immigration and Naturalization Judge. We are here today to announce my ruling on your petition for asylum in this country. I have listened carefully to the arguments of attorneys on both sides of the case, and I compliment both on their advocacy and preparedness. Your clients, gentlemen, have been well represented. I have reviewed the briefs and attachments from both attorneys, listened to and reviewed testimony, and studied the many exhibits presented in corroboration of the evidence.

"After this rather exhaustive review, it is abundantly clear that Rima Al-Baklavi qualifies for and is entitled to asylum in the United States . . ."

As it did in the Gonzalez case, the gallery erupted in a mixture of cheers and boos. The court officer shouted for quiet. The judge banged his gavel and demanded order, threatening to have the courtroom cleared. The gallery quieted at the threat.

"One more outburst and I will find all of you in contempt," the irate judge snarled. "Every one of you will spend the rest of the day in lockup. How does that sound?" He scowled at the gallery. One could hear a pin drop.

"Very well, then; let's continue." Marshall turned to a stunned Rima and smiled.

"With respect, I will refer to Rima Al-Baklavi as 'Rima' to avoid confusing her name with that of her late husband. Okay, Mr. Mann?"

"Fine by me, Your Honor," Marshall grinned, glancing again at his stunned client.

"There is overwhelming evidence that Syria is a dangerous country, one that harbors and provides aid and comfort to Islamic terrorists. The evidence is far less clear that Rima was, at any time, a willing participant or sponsor of terrorist activity. It seems the only evidence of her possible involvement is the fact that she happened to marry a man *well before* he began to engage in terrorist activity. In addition to the government's failure to demonstrate Rima's direct or indirect involvement in terror, we have heard compelling testimony from hostage rescuers and the *hostage* that Rima provided comfort and care to the two hostages and, further, that she assisted in their rescue.

"The evidence also demonstrates that Rima's brave actions have been communicated to terrorist networks in Syria. She is now a woman with a target on her back, someone whose courage and actions make it impossible to return to her home country. If I deny her petition and deport her, she would, undoubtedly, be tortured, imprisoned, killed, or all three. Records and reports produced by petitioner, not rebutted by the government, corroborate these theories. Furthermore, there has not been a shred of evidence produced to even *suggest* that Rima poses any threat to American citizens. No one witnessed Rima being engaged in any illegal or terrorist activity. Of most concern to Homeland is her marital status, or, in other words, her guilt by association." Marshall was, again, amazed to have his words read back to him, almost verbatim, in a judge's ruling.

"I could ramble on, like some of my brother and sister jurists, but specific findings of fact, supporting case law, and persuasive exhibits are discussed in my written opinion." *A clear swipe at Judge Farhat's tendency to issue long-winded, politically charged opinions. Is Tucker a Republican?* Marshall wondered.

"For our purposes today, my ruling is that Rima Al-Baklavi has met the criteria, and I hereby grant her asylum status. Mr. Mann? Ms. Fletcher? You may present an order for my signature. Mr. Theurer? The *INS* is instructed to act in haste to implement the mandates of my order. Is that understood?"

"Understood, Your Honor."

"Excellent. We are adjourned." The judge slammed his gavel and quickly exited. The gallery erupted in mixed response. Cheers overwhelmed boos and other negative responses.

Marshall, respectful of Rima's Muslim heritage, did not embrace her. He politely smiled, put his right hand on his heart, and bowed slightly. Rima burst into tears of joy. Zack and Amy approached to the rear of Marshall and offered their hearty congratulations, imitating Marshall's respectful hand-on-heart gesture.

"Oh, Mr. Mann, Mr. Blake, Ms. Fletcher, from the bottom of my heart, thank you so much. I never thought this would be possible."

"You are very welcome, Rima. Good luck to you. Have you made arrangements here in the states?"

"Yes, I can now check out of the hotel?"

"Yes, but you must be careful. There are people here who disagree with Judge Tucker's decision and may seek to cause you harm. Mr. Parsons' men will continue to watch over you. Where do you intend to go?"

"I have relatives in Dearborn. I will be staying with them."

"I recommend you connect with Imam Ghaffari and Lieutenant Shaheed Ali of the Dearborn Police. I also have a wonderful client, Arya Khan, who can help you navigate the community. I have their telephone numbers if you want them," Zack offered.

"You are such a gift from *Allah*, Mr. Blake. Thank you," she gushed.

"You're welcome. I'm so glad that things worked out. Mr. Parsons' man will take you back to the hotel to check out and get your belongings. Then, he will take you to your relatives' place."

"Thank you, again."

As they exited the courtroom together, a horde of reporters descended upon them for the usual reactions to the ruling. Almost an hour after they began to leave, attorneys, security personnel, and one very happy client exited Irving Tucker's courtroom.

Chapter Thirty-Seven

Orders were drafted, presented, and executed by the judges in both cases. James Theurer advised, by formal letter, that the United States government would not appeal either ruling. Thus, Rima Al-Baklavi and Miguel and Mary Carmen Gonzalez would soon become citizens of the United States of America. With the deportation concerns behind his courtroom weary clients, Zachary Blake could now charge, full-tilt, into his quest for civil justice for the Gonzalez family.

Stu Frazier and Harry Rosen came on board, and the four lawyers agreed to meet to establish mediation protocol. The meeting was held at the U.S. Attorney's office downtown. The combatants and mediators decided to conduct the mediation in a quasi-trial format. The Law Offices of Zachary Blake featured a small courtroom, which the firm used for training and mock trials. Zachary offered unlimited use of the courtroom for the mediators to examine witnesses, hear evidence, and conduct negotiations.

Frazier and Rosen set up shop in the mini-courtroom and went to work. Negotiations commenced immediately, and it became clear that Dan Wolfe was true to his word. The Gonzalez family was brought in to tell the mediators their heartbreaking story. Government representatives were grilled on policy, implementation, and what went wrong. Micah Love, Reed Spencer, and the two actor/investigator 'generals' were questioned. The directors of the various detention centers were also interviewed via Zoom conference to provide a government perspective on the need for these centers. El Paso city officials, editors, and reporters from the *El Paso Times*, as well as high profile protestors and celebrities were also interviewed by Zoom, to educate the mediators on conditions at the El Paso Detention Center. Emma and Emilio described what it was like to live and work at the Center for months. The witnesses did not paint a pretty picture, and the value of the case increased with each one's testimony.

The lawsuit's progress was reported in the national press. Zach began to hear from attorneys representing families and children all over the country who wanted to join the lawsuit. Zack went before the federal court judge assigned the case, Leonard Mendoza, and asked for multi-district status. Mendoza readily granted Zack's request, making Miguel, Mary Carmen, Emma, and Emilio lead plaintiffs in a multi-state, multi-district court action. Over the weeks and months of a lengthy mediation process, the litigation's scope reached over forty states.

Evidence began pouring into the little mini-courtroom where Stu Frazier and Harry Rosen conducted the evidentiary portion of the mediation process. The stories were remarkably similar, raids on places of employment, kids ripped from the arms of their parents, children piled into planes, trains, and buses and whisked away to detention centers. Some of these children had still not been reunited with their parents.

Stu and Harry decided to create a damages grid, placing children and parents into categories based on their experiences. The harsher the experience, the higher tier the grid placement was for parents and children. In the end, Stu Frazier, Harry Rosen, Zack Blake, Dan Wolfe, and other prominent trial attorneys with multiple clients negotiated ten levels of potentially awardable damages. After the grid was constructed, attorneys were advised to determine their clients' appropriate grid and be prepared to make an offer of proof that they chose correctly. Zack, for instance, appropriately placed the Gonzalez family in the higher tiers. All of this was done under the supervision of Judge Mendoza and his subordinate team of judges.

Once all plaintiffs were placed in their appropriate place on the grid, the mediators and attorneys now faced the difficult task of assigning the amount of money damages to the particular category. Obviously, ten would be the highest damage category and one the lowest. If a plaintiff didn't like their negotiated place on the grid or damages level assigned, they could opt out of the multi-district litigation and go it alone. That plaintiff might get more or less than the assigned grid amount, and it could take years and multiple appeals to resolve the case. Only a small handful of plaintiffs decided to go it alone, which pleased Dan

Wolfe. His main goal in encouraging the mediation and multi-district process was to achieve specificity of damages and immediate closure, something these negotiated grids and damages assignments made a reality.

After all of the grid categories and damages award amounts were settled upon by the lawyers and the mediators, CPAs, and financial planners were brought to calculate the gross amount necessary to compensate all the victims. Adult victims could choose between a present value cash award or an annuity/structured settlement that paid less money now, but larger, aggregate amounts over time. Judge Mendoza mandated, by court order, that children under the age of eighteen be compensated via structured settlement to protect the children from possible predatory parents or guardians. In the end, the global settlement fund was ten billion dollars.

With most civil litigation, plaintiff attorneys charge a contingency fee, most often one-third of the recovery. Zack and the others wanted fees in this case to be paid by the defendants, not by their clients. Another contentious negotiating battle was waged over three point three billion dollars in attorney fees. Wolfe and his team pushed back, arguing that every plaintiff case since the origins of the contingency fee had required plaintiffs to pay their own fees unless otherwise ordered by the judge.

Zachary threatened to go to Mendoza and seek an order for attorney fees, which, he argued, might be higher than the current asking price. In the end, a compromise was reached. The defendants would pay the mediators' bills and expenses and kick in another two billion for attorney fees. The attorneys could take their appropriate share as payment in full or bill their clients for the difference. As lead attorney for the litigation, Zack's full cost outlay would be reimbursed. Further, all subordinate attorneys unanimously voted to increase Zack's clients' compensation and his respective fees to level eight. The 'bump' was provided in reward for filing and strategizing the virgin civil lawsuit, securing the mediators and multi-district status, providing premises for the mediators to conduct negotiations, and bringing the original immigration case that set standards for membership in the litigation.

When the dust settled, after almost fifteen months of arduous mediation and numerous court appearances, the Gonzalez family and all members of the class were fairly compensated. Zack recovered his expenses and attorney fees. Miguel and Mary Carmen were simple people. They wisely chose structured settlement option the court mandated for their children. Zack arranged for a financial planner he often used to assist them with their money. Stu and Harry did a yeoman's job in getting this resolved without contentious litigation and appeals that would have taken years to resolve.

Mary Carmen and Miguel insisted upon creating and operating a community foundation to assist immigrants, whether documented or undocumented. The funds would help with retaining counsel and any other fees associated with the process of obtaining citizenship status in the U.S. Zack loved the idea and graciously donated a portion of his fee to the Gonzalez Family Community Foundation.

***

A month after the final resolution of the case, Zack sat in his office, studying the deposition notes of his next high-profile case. His receiver buzzed. He picked up, and Kristin informed him that Miguel Gonzalez was on the phone. Zack picked up immediately.

"Miguel?"

"Hello, Mr. Blake."

"I've told you a thousand times: Call me Zack."

"I have a question. I wanted to ask you before I ask the financial guys."

"What is it, Miguel? Sounds serious."

"Not really, just a question."

"Let's hear it."

"Do I have to use my community foundation money only in Lincoln Park and only for the Hispanic community?"

"No, Miguel, I'm quite certain you can use the funds in any community and to assist any immigrant or any immigrant community. Why?"

"Because I have been following the story of your client, Rima Al-Baklavi, and I understand she is having a hard time assimilating, keeping a job, adjusting to life here in America, and fighting off anti-Muslim bias."

"I have been following this, too, Miguel. I am afraid it is true. Since she's my client, I can't help her out financially, and she doesn't have the skills necessary for me to give her a job."

"I want to pledge foundation money to support her and others in her community. I also want to give her a job establishing a branch of our foundation in Dearborn. Would that be okay?"

"Okay, Miguel? It would be wonderful!"

"As you well know . . . uh . . .Zack . . ." He was still uncomfortable using Blake's first name. "There is plenty of money, more than I will ever need. I would like to . . . how you say in America . . . spread the wealth?"

"Very well, Miguel. Would you like me to reach out to Rima?"

"Yes, please. I'm sure she is a proud woman. Make her say yes, and then perhaps we can set up a telephone call or a meeting? Would that be okay?"

"Absolutely, Miguel. Are you sure this is what you want to do? What about Mary Carmen and the kids?"

"This was Mary Carmen's idea. The kids have a fund of their own. They are well taken care of by your financial guys. We can trust them, right?"

"Yes, Miguel. They are the best."

"Wonderful! You will take care of this for us? It will make us very happy."

"I'll take care of it, Miguel. What a wonderful gesture of brotherhood. From the bottom of my heart, thank you!"

"Everything I have, I owe to you, sir. It is *I* who thanks *you*. None of this is possible without you, Mr. Mann, and Ms. Fletcher."

"Marshall and Amy."

"Huh?"

"No last names. We're all good friends and business associates."

"Right, thanks Mr. … uh … Zack."

"You're welcome, Miguel. I'll call Rima. Bye."

"Goodbye, Zack."

Zachary Blake hung up the receiver, wiped a tear from his eye, and buzzed Kristin.

"Yes, boss?"

"You know I hate when you call me that."

"What do you need, Zack? The phone is ringing off the hook."

"I need a telephone number for Rima Al-Baklavi."

"I'll buzz you back."

"No hurry, Kristin. Take care of business." He did not want to make her angry. She was a terrific, loyal member of the team.

A couple of minutes later, Kristin buzzed back with the telephone number. Zack thanked and disconnected Kristin, pressed a button for an outside line, and punched in the numbers.

"Hello?"

"Rima?"

"Speaking."

"This is Zachary Blake."

"Oh, Mr. Blake, it is so nice to hear from you."

"It's nice to hear your voice. How are things going?"

"I'm doing okay," she sighed.

"You don't sound like you're doing okay. What's the matter?"

"My cousins' place is fine, a bit crowded, but fine. I feel like I'm imposing. The worst part is that I can't contribute. I have no money, and I can't find a job."

"Funny you should mention a job. That's why I'm calling."

"Oh?"

"Do you remember Miguel Gonzalez? We were handling his family's asylum case at the same time as yours."

"I remember. I met him once when we were both at your office. Why do you mention him?"

"Miguel and his family have used some of their lawsuit settlement to start a community fund to help other immigrants, and he's looking to expand the reach of this fund."

"Expand? Expand how? What's this got to do with me?" Rima was confused.

"He wants to create a branch in Dearborn and assist displaced Muslim immigrants. He wants to hire you to help run the place. How does that sound?"

Rima was speechless.

"Rima?"

"I-I'm h-here," she stammered.

"What do you think?"

"Mr. Gonzalez doesn't even *know* me. Why would he do this?"

"Because he feels very fortunate, and he wants to pay it forward."

"Pay it forward? What does this mean?" Rima queried.

"People helped him out when he needed a hand. He wants to help others the same way."

"He said that?"

"In so many words."

"It is done out of pity. Charity."

"It is *not* charity, Rima. He wants to help the community. You are a member of the community; you need a job. He needs someone to help run the place. It is just good timing. Please let me tell him you will take the job."

"I am not qualified."

"You will be trained. You will learn on the job. I know you can do this. Now, say you will at least talk to Miguel about this. He is counting on you."

"All praise is due to *Allah*; I am willing to learn. I will talk to Miguel!" She burst into tears.

"Why are you crying, Rima?"

"Tears of joy, Mr. Blake! You are a blessing. How can I ever repay you and Miguel?"

"By doing a good job and helping out your community. Pay it forward."

"I will, Mr. Blake."

"Zachary."

"Pardon?"

"Call me Zachary, or Zack."

"Thank you . . . Zack." She smiled.

"Let me connect you to my secretary. She will get you Miguel's number."

Epilogue

The *Oath of Allegiance* has been used to swear in new citizens for over two hundred twenty years. The requirements and language of the oath have changed a bit over the years, and they once differed from courtroom to courtroom. In fact, at one point in time, because there was no precise text for the oath, there were as many as five thousand courts with naturalization jurisdiction, and each one could develop its own procedures and words.

In 1905, a Presidential Commission on Naturalization decided that U.S. naturalization courts lacked uniformity. The Commission recommended the creation of a federal agency to oversee naturalization procedures, re-codification of the law, and standard forms, one of which was a uniform oath of allegiance.

In 1906, Congress passed the *Basic Naturalization Act*, which implemented many of the Commission's recommendations, but did not mandate a uniform oath. It wasn't until 1929 that an official standard text for the *Oath of Allegiance* appeared in the Act's regulations. From that point forward, all new citizens have been required to take the exact same oath and repeat the exact same language.

Some minor additions and deletions were made over the years. The *Immigration and Nationality Act of 1952* added a section about performing work of national importance under civilian direction. This amendment stands as the last major addition to our nation's *Oath of Allegiance* as it appears today.

On this day, a large crowd gathered in Judge Leo Farhat's courtroom. Marshall Mann, Amy Fletcher, and Zachary Blake arranged the ceremony to honor three new citizens of the United States of America. Governor Whitman, Senator Stabler, Dan Wolfe, James Theurer, and several mayors attended at Zack's invitation. Local celebrities, attorneys, judges, reporters, television, and radio personalities were also in attendance. Two bright and beaming children were present to cheer on their parents. A young Muslim family also attended to honor the woman who saved two of its members.

Judge Leo Farhat stepped up to the podium and tapped the microphone. The boisterous crowd quieted immediately.

"Ladies and gentlemen, my name is Leo Farhat. I am an Immigration and Naturalization Judge here in Detroit. Welcome to my courtroom. Thank you for being here on this momentous occasion. First and foremost, I'd like to thank attorneys from Zachary Blake's office for granting me the privilege of swearing in our special guests. Marshall Mann, Amy Fletcher, and Zack Blake were instrumental in procuring justice for our soon-to-be citizens. It is not an overstatement to say that citizenship would not have been possible for our honorees but for the efforts of these fine lawyers.

"Throughout our nation's history, foreign-born men and women have come to the United States, taken the *Oath of Allegiance* to become naturalized citizens, and contributed greatly to their new communities and country. I have no doubt the same will be true for the three people who take the Oath today. These fine people have already honored our judicial faith by creating and managing Community Foundations for immigrants in the Latino community Downriver, and in the Muslim community in Dearborn. These foundations are doing important work all over the city, indeed, all over the country. I am proud to have played a small part in their path to citizenship. Rima Al-Baklavi, Mary Carmen Gonzalez, Miguel Gonzalez, please step forward, raise your right hand, and repeat after me:

"I hereby declare, on oath, that I absolutely and entirely renounce and abjure all allegiance and fidelity to any foreign prince, potentate, state, or sovereignty, of whom or which I have heretofore been a subject or citizen; that I will support and defend the Constitution and laws of the United States of America against all enemies, foreign and domestic; that I will bear true faith and allegiance to the same; that I will bear arms on behalf of the United States when required by the law; that I will perform noncombatant service in the Armed Forces of the United States when required by the law; that I will perform work of national importance under civilian direction when required by the law;

and that I take this obligation freely, without any mental reservation or purpose of evasion; so help me God (*Allah*)."

Miguel, Mary Carmen, and Rima each repeated these historic words and were declared American citizens. They weren't born into freedom—they *earned* freedom the hard way. Because of their addition to our citizenry and their service to the less fortunate, America became a better country.

THE END

Author's Notes

I hope you enjoyed *Betrayal at the Border,* my seventh Zachary Blake Legal Thriller series novel. The novel depicts the social justice struggles of two distinct immigrant populations who escape tyranny to seek a better life in a divided America.

In 2001, the *DREAM Act* was introduced for the first time. Its goal was to prevent undocumented children from being punished for the acts of their parents. The bill passed the House and was defeated in the Senate. In 2005, Senators Ted Kennedy and John McCain sponsored the *Secure America and Orderly Immigration Act.* The same two senators sponsored the *Comprehensive Immigration Reform Act* of 2006 and the *Secure Borders, Economic Opportunity, and Immigration Reform Act* of 2007. All three bills died in committee.

These failures have emboldened state sponsored anti-immigration efforts, most of which have been previously declared unconstitutional. President Obama's *DACA* law, the pathway to citizenship, and the *Immigration Modernization Act* of 2013 all passed the Senate but failed in the House. A Texas judge recently issued a decision that casts doubt on the future viability of *DACA.* Hundreds of immigrants now await a future ruling from the United States Supreme Court or hang on to scant hope that a divided Congress will pass a bill.

America is a nation of immigrants. Many of us are the children or grandchildren of immigrants who have realized the American dream. Isn't it time we put aside our fears, biases, and prejudices and welcome others who wish to realize that same dream?

President Biden believes we are in a battle for the soul of our nation. Have we given in to our worse tendencies? Have we become a country that has *already* lost its soul? We can do better; we can *be* better. Only *together* can we become one nation, with liberty and justice for all. Will you be part of the problem or part of the solution?

Thank you for reading, and I sincerely hope you enjoyed *Betrayal at the Border*. As an independently published author, I rely on you, the reader, to spread the word. So, if you enjoyed this book, please tell your friends and family, and I would appreciate a brief review. Thanks again.

Mark

Other Books in the Series

L'DOR V'DOR – From Generation to Generation
(A Novella)

Betrayal of Faith (Book 1)
Betrayal of Justice (Book 2)
Betrayal in Blue (Book 3)
Betrayal in Black (Book 4)
Betrayal High (Book 5)
Supreme Betrayal (Book 6)

The ***Zachary Blake Legal Thriller Series*** is also available in audiobook format, brilliantly narrated by Detroit's own legendary radio and television personality ***Lee Alan.***

About the Author

Mark M. Bello is an attorney and award-winning legal thriller author. After handling high-profile legal cases for over 42 years, Mark now treats readers to a front-row seat in the courtroom. His ripped from the headlines Zachary Blake Legal Thrillers are inspired by actual cases or Bello's take on current legal or sociopolitical issues. Mark lives in Michigan with his wife, Tobye. They have four children and 8 grandchildren.

Connect with Mark

Website: https://www.markmbello.com
Email: info@markmbello.com
Facebook: MarkMBelloBooks
Twitter: @MarkMBelloBooks
YouTube: Mark Bello
Goodreads: Mark M. Bello

Subscribe to our mailing list and receive notices of book giveaways and other surprises.

To request a speaking engagement, interview, or appearance, please email info@markmbello.com